Something metallic cracked against his teeth, pried his
jaws apart. He tried to clear his vision, to see who was
doing this to him, but the world was a smear of shifting,
boiling colors. His nose was punched shut, and a burning,
choking liquid was poured into his mouth. Reflexively, he
swallowed, and when his stomach tried to reject the stuff,
his mouth was held shut until it was accepted. Twice more
he went through the same process, and by then even his
drugged brain identified the whiskey for what it was.

Then he was being dragged by the heels, head bumping
over the juncture between the back door and the deck. The
chlorine smell of the water and Deb's lingering perfume
were overwhelming. Whoever pulled him to the deck
undressed him. He tried to shout for help as he felt himself
being rolled into the spa. He heard a faint, sickly noise and
wondered if it was himself. . . .

LIAR'S
DICE

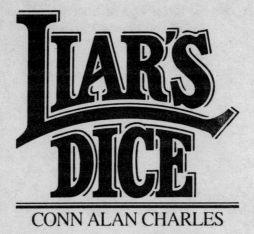

LIAR'S DICE

CONN ALAN CHARLES

A TOM DOHERTY ASSOCIATES BOOK

To the B and M Society:
Dean and Gerda Koontz
Friends

LIAR'S DICE

Copyright © 1985 by Tor Books

First printing: May 1985

A TOR Book

Published by Tom Doherty Associates
8-10 West 36 Street
New York, N.Y. 10018

ISBN: 0-812-50128-4
CAN. ED.: 0-812-50129-2

Printed in the United States of America

Chapter 1

Every major city has its Command Post bar. Maybe it's
called the Silver Dollar, the Bomb Shelter, or the Wagon-
wheel. No matter. They all look alike—scarred tables,
broken chairs nailed and screwed together with enough
iron to sink them. Worn shuffleboards and pinging elec-
tronic toys vie for space. Most of the light comes from
beer advertisements, wild splotches of color in a vaguely
threatening darkness.

At three o'clock on a Wednesday afternoon the crowd is
very small, very quiet. It's the right time and the right
place to look for a hungry man. Not the hunger that wants
a meal, but the inner hunger that needs to prove there's
still a man wrapped around it.

The majority of strangers step into a place like that and
nervousness coats them with sudden sweat.

It was different with the man who stepped from the
blazing San Diego sunshine into the cool gloom on this
particular Wednesday. He set himself to one side of the
entry and waited for his eyes to adjust. Tall, heavy, there
was an arrogant patience in the way he squinted curiously

at the old recruiting posters, and the fading photographs of men in uniform, athletes, ships, tanks, baseball teams—the cluttering souvenirs of a workingman's hangout.

Deliberately, he shifted his attention to the four men clustered at the bar, the only other customers. His examination was rude, a bored white-glove inspection.

Four pairs of shoulders tightened. A thin tension pushed its way through the smells of smoke and beer. Apparently unaware, the newcomer made his way to the unoccupied end of the bar. He swept the stool cushion before sitting on it and carefully checked the wooden counter before resting his elbows. The action seemed less a matter of concern for his expensive clothes than a comment on his surroundings. He told the gum-chewing bartender, "A draft," laying out a dollar. When his change came, he covered it with a closed hand. A bill stuck out from between the fingers. The bartender glanced at it, then did a wild double take.

The customer said, "You probably don't see many of those in here." The bartender's tongue slid across lips shocked to immobility.

"I thought not," the man went on easily. He let the bill fall free. It was torn in half. Downing half the beer, he said, "My name's Bullard. I'm looking for Ralph Curtin. You'll call him Buck." The bartender continued to stare at the thing on the counter. Silence trembled in the room as though a wrong word would collapse it, bring it down as a destructive force. The man added, "Curtin was Force Recon in the Marines, worked for the CIA at least once, a deal in the Caribbean. Got married, got out, got divorced, lost his construction company some time ago, and he's six months short on his alimony. That's so you know I'm talking about the right man."

"Pick up your money." The rasping command came from one of the foursome.

Undisturbed, Bullard spoke to the hypnotized bartender. "I want him."

"Pick it up and leave while you're able." Anger spiked the renewed demand.

The bartender came to life, flashing an agonized look at the group. "Goddamn, George, it's a thousand! I never *seen* one!"

"I don't give a rat's ass. Nobody ever heard of this Curtin."

Bullard rose, tossed a business card next to the money. "I'm at the Sunburst. There's my room number. I'll give the other half of the bill to Curtin. No one else. Clear?"

Rising, George said, "Maybe you need hearing lessons, chump." He was short and thick, a stump of a man, the marks of many battles on his broken nose and thickened brow. He stepped toward Bullard.

"George," Bullard repeated thoughtfully. He moved clear of the bar stool. "Probably George Bayonne. You worked for Curtin before he went belly up. Okay, if you need a brawl, I'll accommodate you, but think about two things. One, I'm offering Buck Curtin a chance at fifty thousand dollars. Second, even if I whip your ass, and I probably can, I'll still see you go to jail for assault and battery."

The shorter man stopped, uncertainty twisting the battered features.

Bullard backed toward the door, obviously aware of the general arrangement of the furniture between himself and the way out. That level of preparedness brought a grudging respect to George's belligerence.

Brief quiet followed the glaring burst of daylight accompanying Bullard's leaving.

"What makes Buck Curtin all of a sudden worth fifty clicks?" asked a voice from the seated trio.

George whirled. "Forget that shit. What's important is who the hell is Bullard?"

"Who knows?" The lanky owner of the voice walked over and looked at the torn bill.

The short man slammed a protective fist on top of it. "He's too anxious. It stinks."

The bartender said, "I'll put it in the register. You guys

find Buck. You know he'll share it. Like a finder's fee, like."

"And you'll split with him, right?"

Wounded innocence, the bartender shook his head at the rawboned man. "Jesus, John, what a suspicious fucker. When Buck gets the other half of this," he gently rocked George's hand to the side and slid the bill free, "we'll split it even, two hundred apiece. That's fair, ain't it?"

George clamped down on the hand clutching the money. The bartender's mouth formed a tight "o" of apprehension. "You are not to be believed," George said, retrieving the note. "You divide Buck's money without even counting him in for a share. There'd be six of us, asshole."

"So I'm bad at math." He massaged his freed hand. "Anybody can make a mistake."

John laughed, then spoke seriously to George. "Dude's laying out some heavy bait. What do you think?"

"I don't know. I wouldn't trust him."

"For a thousand bucks, a man can overlook distrust. And if the fifty's legit—" He let the sentence die, the prospect too dreamlike to pursue.

George grunted. "Bullard must think we're stupid. For that kind of money, you know something crooked's going down."

"Well, he's sure not stupid." John rubbed a bony jaw. Stubble rasped under the calloused hand. "He knows a lot about ol' Buck. Knows he needs money, where he hangs out. Even knows some of Buck's dumber friends by name."

"Anyone could do those things. All you'd have to do is ask around."

John flashed a bleak smile. "Heard anyone asking? Until now?"

For a few seconds George stared at the butts and burns on the wooden floor, then muttered deep in his chest and turned on his heel. Stuffing the torn bill in his pocket; he stormed out into the sunshine, his dark anger like a threatening cloud on a formerly calm horizon.

Chapter 2

Buck Curtin parked his camper on the hill overlooking the Oro de Mar Beach and Tennis Club. Pulling binoculars from a worn case, he scanned past the gleaming complex of tennis courts, swimming pool, massive clubhouse, and shining cars baking on the asphalt parking lot. Beyond all that, a line of wavering palm trees marked the beginning of the beach that sloped to crashing surf.

Curtin noticed those things, but his attention was fixed on a man in the nearest tennis court. Watching his style, Curtin gave an almost imperceptible nod of approval. Bullard played his opponent, not merely the ball. He discovered a weak backhand and hammered it, stretching his own game to the limit to concentrate on the flaw. It was like a boxer working over a cut.

Curtin watched the second man's face go from enjoyment through determination to sagging acknowledgment of defeat. Bullard's expression was hidden, but there was no need to see it. As his opponent's spirit shriveled, his own service grew even stronger, his shot placement more challenging.

"Like to rub it in, don't you?" Curtin muttered. "I wish he'd burn one up your nose." He leaned forward, resting his elbows on the dashboard. A drop of perspiration skidded through the hair on his forearm and he scratched at it irritably.

Fifty thousand dollars would repair a lot of broken air conditioners. With plenty left over to cool down an ex-wife whose alimony screeches were beginning to sound like fingernails on slate.

Fifty clicks could also get you dumped in the slammer. Or dead.

He decided Bullard was the sort of man who'd get every dime of his money's worth, in any event.

Curtin shrugged, leaning back against the seat. Nothing said he had to do anything. The thousand for showing up was easy money. Probably.

Bullard finished the destruction of the other player and dismissed him with a careless wave, walking toward the clubhouse. A woman on the other court turned Bullard's way and apparently spoke, because he gestured over his shoulder where the loser stood, bouncing a ball. The woman's white teeth flashed in silent laughter, the sun picking them out like snowflakes. The beaten player turned away quickly, his racket catching the ball off center. It skittered across the court and he left, ignoring it.

Bullard continued on into the clubhouse and, nothing better to do, Curtin amused himself watching the woman. Even at this distance, her easy grace pleased the eye. Her opponent was a man, and she was giving him all the competition he could handle. Overmatched in strength, she had a deceptive quickness that kept him constantly off balance. No matter where he placed a shot, she antici-pated it, crossing the court with almost languorous ease. Nor were her returns pitty-pat lobs. Speed blurred her racket through the heat waves, returning the ball as a streak.

Dressed in matching yellow top and shorts, she wore her hair in a braid, so black it reflected the sun in sharp points,

like glass. There was a small red bow at the bottom that
darted through the air behind her with every move. Distance made it difficult to judge her size accurately, but
Curtin noted appreciatively that everything seemed to be
distributed in fine order. Lastly, he realized the brilliant
whiteness of her amusement had been more than a trick of
the light. Her skin was darker than the bronze of California's
summer girls. This was a rich copper, rippling over smooth,
long muscles. He was sorry to pull his eyes away to check
Bullard's parked Ferrari.

It was moving.

He swore at himself as he gunned the camper engine to
life. Another ten seconds and Bullard would have been
gone, unobserved. Furious, he slammed through the gears,
the top-heavy machine swaying dangerously on the tight
curves leading to the intersection with Oro de Mar's private roadway. Before reaching the stop sign, he pulled to
the side of the road and slouched down until the Ferrari
swept past, then hurried to fall in behind.

He breathed a sigh of relief when another car pulled in
between them. Running a tail in a camper was about as
subtle as a cavalry charge, but it was either his vehicle or
George's broken-down beater. The picture of that heap
lurching along behind a Ferrari helped calm his angry
embarrassment.

They were on the freeway by then, where he wasn't so
noticeable. The Ferrari ignored the speed limit, but resisted the temptation to blast out of sight.

Even here, where it was easy work, Curtin fought the
uncomfortable sensation that he wasn't the only one on
Bullard. He had no explanation for the feeling, nor could
he shake it. For the entire two days he'd spent dogging
Bullard's activities, he'd felt other eyes were watching. It
was irritating.

So was having someone snoop your past, or throw
money on a bar and expect you to come running because
the sonofabitch knew you *needed* the money. And it was
especially irritating to run around behind some rich creep

while he enjoyed himself and you baked your ass in a frazzled pickup.

Worst of all was that constant little voice raising the hair on your neck with warnings of another watcher.

After a few miles on the freeway, Bullard turned at the exit for the Sunburst Hotel. Curtin let the Ferrari gain a few car lengths, pulling into a parking slot at a discreet distance. He waited a few minutes after the other man entered the rambling building, then went directly to Bullard's room and knocked.

The door opened quickly and Curtin was looking down at an Oriental man absolutely devoid of facial expression. Curtin said, "I'd like to talk to Mr. Bullard."

The dark eyes blinked. For a full two seconds it was the man's only sign of life. Then he said, "You have no appointment," in careful English. As if the statement ended Curtin's existence, the man moved to close the door.

"Hold it." Curtin put up a hand, and the smaller man was in the *hsu bu* fighting stance immediately, as graceful as the cat that gives the attitude its name. Curtin took a half-step back, poised for attack or defense.

"Who is it, Lu?" The voice came from inside the suite.

Lu's gaze never wavered. "Someone not invited."

Amusement colored Bullard's next question. "A tall man, wide-shouldered, light brown hair, very blue eyes, small scar on left cheekbone?"

"He is like that."

"Tell Mr. Curtin to come in. He's welcome."

"I understand." Lu stepped back, gesturing Curtin past.

Sprawled on the sofa in a maroon terrycloth robe, Bullard continued to dry his dark hair. He made no effort to shake hands, but gestured to the well-stocked bar. "Help yourself," he said. "Cold beer in the fridge."

Curtin said. "You've been looking for me. Why?"

"Fifty thousand reasons."

"Wrong. I had that many reasons to find you. Fifty plus one, actually. What do you want?"

"Remember Robert Chavez?"

"We were in Nam together. He got hit."

"Hit?" Bullard shook his head. "They blew the shit out of him. He still limps."

"I didn't know. We lost touch." Behind him, Lu's footsteps whispered on the carpet. A door opened and closed.

Bullard strode to the bar, where he splashed whiskey over jangling ice cubes. "You knew Robert had a wealthy father?"

"Yeah."

Coffee-dark eyes measured Curtin over the rim of the glass. "I'm the Old Man's oldest son, raised by my stepfather until I was eighteen. Robert's my half brother."

Curtin nodded.

"He's been kidnapped."

Angry color glowed from Curtin's cheeks and he pitched forward. "You've been screwing around with me. Why didn't you tell me?"

Bullard put on his challenging smile again, walked back to the sofa. "Sit down," he said. "This may take a while." He snapped his fingers, looked suddenly concerned. "Should Lu tell your two friends they can go home? The tall, skinny one and the gargoyle, George. They stand out like a pair of bonfires."

"Don't misjudge them."

Bullard sneered. "Clumsy oafs. I lost them every time I left the hotel."

For the first time, Curtin smiled back. "You were looking for them. You never saw me, sucker."

A knot of muscle welled in Bullard's jaw. Curtin remembered the tennis game. Bullard said, "That's one for you. Did Robert ever tell you what the Old Man does?"

Curtin shrugged. "Some kind of real-estate wheeler-dealer."

Oozing contempt, Bullard said, "I was told you were a reader, an intelligent soldier. I knew it was impossible, a contradiction in terms."

Curtin's expression changed to surprise, the insults of lesser importance than growing understanding. Almost to himself, he said, "Sonofabitch. *That* Chavez. It never crossed my mind."

"That's us," Bullard said. "Probably the greatest conglomerate operating in Central and South America. Land, manufacturing, shipping—all of it. And dear old Dad's the boss."

Something in the last sentence warned Curtin to remember the tone as well as the words.

George and John sat in George's car, hardly visible in the darkness. The radio's low volume smudged the words of a country-western lament about honky-tonk love. John tapped a foot in approximate time with the music. George jabbed the dial with a blunt finger. "Don't you know that shit'll rot your brains?"

"Only pinko commie faggots don't love country music," John said, continuing to tap.

George sighed. "Shitkickers."

John pretended to snore. He was quickly alert at the approach of a young man on George's side.

"You're with Mr. Curtin, aren't you? He's in with my boss, Harry Bullard. They're having drinks before the boss has dinner sent to the suite, and they'd like you to join them."

Opening the door, George said, "Great. I could eat a horse."

"Might as well," John said, unfolding onto the asphalt and stretching. "You already eat like one." Across the car roof, he asked, "Buck and this boss of yours getting along okay?"

Leading off, the man said, "Friends already. Sent out for a new fifth of Chivas."

"Oh, Lord," George breathed heavily. "I can't remember the last time I tasted Chivas Regal."

"Only the best for Mr. Bullard, man." Their guide led them between two vans.

Coming out of the tunnellike gap behind John, a movement to the right caught George's eye. As he turned to see what it might be, something like the flame from a small torch leaped at him from the night. There was a harsh, clattering sound. Instantly, his legs went numb, lifeless as ice. He felt himself falling, heard his warning shout at John, and then the pain hit.

He screamed, a mix of animal rage and agony.

A face appeared in front of him, a white mask, the eyes huge caverns of hate and terror.

George flung himself forward, ignoring another eruption of the flickering torch. Fingers spread, he speared at the eyes, saw them read his intent and flinch shut. They were soft, yielding to his strength like ripe fruit. Then he was on the ground, trying to move, confused by a welter of sound. Most penetrating was a thin, wailing cry that took him back to the smells of napalm and burnt, living flesh.

Someone cursed. The words were in another language, but he recognized the emotion. He expected to die then, so when the marvelously pain-relieving blow crashed into the base of his skull, he accepted it with almost as much resignation as regret.

Chapter 3

The howl of sirens came to Bullard's suite like a threat. Glancing around suspiciously, Curtin asked, "Did you send Lu after my friends?"

Bullard called, and Lu responded immediately, coming into the room. Bullard said, "Tell the two men who've been following me that Mr. Curtin wants them in here." As the Oriental left, Bullard shouted after him, "And find out what all the excitement's about."

With his servant gone, Bullard leaned forward on the sofa. His eyes burned at Curtin. "A few years ago, Robert convinced the Old Man we have to change our image in Central and South America. The idea is, we fight the communists by helping the peasants form co-ops, finance them so they can buy our corporation land as their own."

Curtin's grin held no humor. "You don't have to tell me what you think of that. It's all over your face."

Obviously straining, Bullard not only contained himself, he eliminated the telltale expression. "Rebels are for killing. But the Old Man decided to give it a run."

"Tell me what happened to Robert. The details—"

The door burst open and Lu rushed in, speaking rapidly to Bullard in a tonal language Curtin couldn't identify. Bullard answered with one harsh word. Lu shook his head, negative.

Bullard headed for the door, knotting the cord of his robe as he went. "Hurry," he said, "it's your friends. They've been wounded."

Curtin caught up in two steps. "How bad? Which way?"

"Shot in the legs. Both unconscious. On the side of the building where I'm parked."

Immediately, Curtin turned aside, moving down a perpendicular corridor. Bullard raced after him. "Where the hell are you going? The lobby's this way!"

"We can get there quicker straight through the building."

They forced their way through a crowd gathered at a side exit. Curtin stepped outside slowly, back against the wall. Ambulance attendants were closing the door of their vehicle. Rotating red and blue lights played across the avid faces of watchers while police set about roping off the scene. Contrasting with the swirling, carnivallike activity of the colored beacons, the hard white of headlights seemed drawn to the officers. Polished metal and leather, combined with their determined efficiency, separated them from everyone else. They looked untouchable, mechanical.

Bullard nudged Curtin. "Come on, let's find out what happened."

"No!" Curtin grabbed the robe, pulled him back.

Bullard sneered. "You're afraid! You think whoever shot them's waiting for you."

Unmoving, Curtin alternated his attention between the police and the crowd. It was minutes before he moved again, long after Bullard had lapsed into yawning boredom. Staring into his eyes, Curtin said, "The medics will patch up George and John. The only way I can help is to find whoever hit them. I'll get my turn."

Moving back into the building, Bullard scoffed openly. "Hard guy."

"Hard enough." Strain turned Curtin's normally angu-

lar features into sharp edges, made deep hollows of his eye
sockets. Lingering spectators hurried to step aside for him.

Once in the room again, Curtin switched on the radio,
then the television, minus sound. That done, he poured
himself a drink and settled into the chair by the telephone,
flipping through the Yellow Pages.

"Right at home, aren't you?" Bullard commented.

Curtin said, "Let me know if they interrupt the TV
program. I'm calling the ambulance company."

Bullard waited until he hung up, then demanded, "Well,
what did they say?"

"All they'd tell me is that the wounds aren't believed to
be life-threatening and which hospital they're in. That'll
do for now."

"Do?"

"I think I've been watched since you started asking
about me. It can't be someone working for you, or you'd
be bragging your ass off that you know every move I've
made and I never identified anyone. If you knew where to
find me, you wouldn't have stalled around waiting for me
to come to you, either." He raised his hands to massage
his temples, mouth drawn down in a bitter grimace.
"Someone else knows why you're looking for me, so they
have to know George and John have been following you
and meeting with me. If there's no connection between
Robert's kidnapping, your search for me, and what just
happened out there tonight, I have to believe my friends
were ambushed for spitting on the sidewalk. There's a
connection, all right, and the shooting got me involved.
That does it, no matter what else is true."

Bullard looked away. "I'm not as surprised, or impressed,
as you expect me to be. Robert tells everyone endless war
stories about your sterling qualities. He sets special store
by your loyalty. All my background reports on you empha-
sized it. I'm told it took days to convince you that your
partner'd screwed you out of your construction company."

A muscle in Curtin's neck twitched. "You like peeping
in windows?"

"Don't push. We don't need you that much."

"Sure you do." Curtin put his feet up on the coffee table, the worn jogging shoes an insult to brass and plate glass. "People like you don't come around people like me unless you need something. For Robert, I'd probably work with you. Now there's no choice." The simple inclination of his head toward the parking lot was eloquent.

"The money's not important, then?"

Curtin smiled. "I need it. You've got it. Or your daddy does, to be accurate."

Bullard refused to be angered. "You think being poor makes you morally superior. Balls! You're broke, that's all. A loser."

Suddenly Curtin spun to the radio, turned up the volume, getting "—terrorism at our very doorstep. An organization calling itself Force Red left a typed message at the scene of the brutal shooting, claiming responsibility and calling the victims, I'm quoting here, 'fascist mercenaries known to be in the employ of American big business interests supporting the dictatorship in Costa Verde. These men were involved in a criminal plot to discredit Force Red through a massive disinformation effort. To defend our honor and freedom we have administered justice. Americans cannot consider themselves above the law, and we warn them that future counterrevolutionary acts will meet with even harder blows.' That's the end of the quote. Our sources tell us the unidentified victims both suffered severe leg wounds, apparently a vicious form of 'kneecapping,' carried out with automatic weapons at close range. More details as they break."

Another voice cued in, unctuous. "Can you imagine that happening in this country? Is that incredible? Well, let's get our minds off this terrible tragedy. Here's that great new group, 'Silver Spider,' and—"

Curtin snapped the radio off. "Tell me what all that means."

Leaning back, Bullard tented his fingers, enjoying being in command. "Robert's arranging the land sales, plowing

the receipts into industrial developments, handicraft co-
ops—that sort of thing. He's even gotten other large
landowners to support him. Secretly, of course. The death
squads down there have only one answer to progress.
Costa Verde was his showpiece. He lived there. One
morning he went out and simply disappeared.''

"No ransom demands, nothing?'' Curtin was on the
edge of his seat, one fist wrapped in the other.

"We've gotten two ransom demands from Force Red.
They're genuine. Each includes a picture of Robert holding a newspaper. The date and headline are clear.''

"What do they want?''

"Two million dollars in gold. That's the easy part.''

Curtin rose. "Explain that one.''

"The official Force Red line is that they aren't kidnappers.
They claim they don't have Robert. Did you catch the
business about 'discrediting' them?''

Curtin nodded and Bullard went on. "In one hour the
Old Man will release the ransom notes and the photographs.
Only Force Red beat him to the punch. That's why your
friends were shot up.''

"I don't understand.''

"That's what I expected. Look, Force Red claims to be
a 'just' revolution. The world doesn't buy kidnapping as a
fund-raising technique. I talked myself blue in the face,
but the Old Man finally agreed to expose the bastards for
exactly what they are.'' He suddenly sat upright, snapped
his fingers. "Of course! Anyone who knows Robert knows
about your derring-do. When Force Red learned I was
looking for you, they undoubtedly had you, George, and
John investigated. With your histories in hand, they must
have suspected we were considering a rescue. By shooting
your friends Force Red gets international press coverage to
claim the kidnapping accusation is a capitalist lie before
my father even opens his mouth. They scream about
'mercenaries,' which tells him they're alert, and he'd better not be planning any raids. Lastly, they warn you to do
what you're told, although we mean to keep you on a tight

leash, anyhow. They thought the thing out very well. The Old Man must be furious.''

''It'll make George and John feel a whole lot better to know your daddy's upset because they got shot.'' Sarcasm blistered the words. Curtin paced, rubbing his knuckles. So deep in thought he might as well have been alone, he totally ignored Bullard's attempts to reopen conversation.

Muscles in his shoulders bunched, tendons in his neck strained. Impatient strength fought cold logic. It ached to lash out. Finally, he stopped in front of Bullard. ''You don't know where Robert's being kept, do you? You want me to go in blind and be your contact man.''

''Essentially, yes.''

''Give me a straight answer, if you know how. Why me? You people can buy the whole goddam Costa Verde army, but you go to a lot of trouble to find me. Why?''

''When Robert disappeared, the Old Man assumed he'd be taken into the jungle. He remembered Robert's stories about your skills. Now it looks like Robert's in the city, but the Old Man still wants you.'' A grin like warm grease spread across his face. ''He's almost eighty, remember.''

''Robert never told anyone I'm a bargainer. I already said I'd help, because of my friends. But what if they hadn't been hit? What then?''

''A long time ago Robert told our father you killed someone who meant to kill him. The Old Man thinks you're a soldier he can trust.''

''And you think he's senile.''

''What I think isn't your concern. I *know* he's the Old Man, and you'd better learn it.''

''Okay.'' Curtin nodded decisively. ''When can I see him?''

Bullard stood up. ''Be here at six in the morning. We'll fly to headquarters.''

''Headquarters?''

''There are two, actually. We keep an office in Denver and another in South Dakota. We'll be going to the latter.''

''Whatever. Now, where's the other half of that grand?''

"Oh, no." Bullard shook his head slowly. "We'll pay expenses now, but the fifty thousand comes when the operation's over. Whether you get Robert out or not."

"I want my money. We're talking a total of fifty-one, and I want the first one now."

"No."

They stared at each other. Curtin felt the adrenalin hit his blood. It gladdened him. He thought of George and John, wounded because he'd gotten them involved with this uncaring, cheating man. He wanted to strike someone, and sooner or later it would be Bullard's turn. Now would do. He shifted his weight, prepared to pivot away from a knee, braced to launch a retaliatory kick. The knock on the door and Lu's sudden appearance sent them both a step backward.

The woman from the tennis court stood beside the Oriental. Curtin worked to control the surprise pulling at his features. She stopped at the sight of the two men, instinctively aware of the forces in the room. It was an unconscious pose, and Curtin drank it in. She wore a green dress, the material so sleek it seemed liquid. A thin gold chain at her throat dangled a solitary emerald where enticing, shadowed cleavage plunged out of sight.

She dismissed his blunt interest, almond-shaped eyes sliding past him to Bullard. Full lips parted in the same sharp, white smile Curtin remembered. Bullard returned it, watching Curtin surreptitiously. Gesturing he said, "Flor, may I present Mr. Ralph Curtin? Mr. Curtin, this is my 'companion,' Miss Peralta. His friends all call him Buck, Flor."

Despite the almost insulting inflection of the description applied to her, the woman continued to smile coolly. She said, "Buck? What a queer name. Isn't that what one calls a male animal?"

Traces of accent colored the lilting voice. Curtin said, "It's Buck, like money. And when I get mine from your cheap friend, you're welcome to what's left over."

Bullard indicated Flor and spoke to Lu, who immediately set about mixing her a drink. Then he turned to Curtin. "I told you, you collect when you've done your work."

Slowly, Curtin said, "I could leave and let your old man know what a jerk you are when I see him. I could threaten to drop out. You'd come up with the money 'cause you really *are* afraid of him. But I'd rather just knock a thousand dollars worth of manners into your snotty head."

Bullard smiled and shrugged, turning away. Suddenly he was whirling, left arm extended in a vicious, spinning back-fist. Well-executed, it could kill. However, because the entire arm was extended, that side of Bullard's body was left unprotected. Curtin dropped, almost squatting before driving up with the strength of both legs as the blow shot by harmlessly overhead. He drove a hand like a spear into Bullard's side. The flaring maroon robe fluttered to a stop like a tired flag as Bullard's movement checked and his pained exclamation echoed through the room. His weak, off-balance swipe at Curtin's head failed to affect the knee Curtin drove into his crotch.

Bullard gasped and dropped like a stone. Curtin turned swiftly, knowing Lu would be there. A flash of approval touched the smaller man's eyes at Curtin's quick adjustment, anticipating a true test of skill.

Flor ran to Bullard, who had regained enough breath to commence a series of low, drawn-out moans. Curtin and Lu ignored them.

Curtin watched Lu's sure movements, achingly aware of his own rusted abilities. He faked a roundhouse kick, hoping to create an opening. Instead of blocking it, Lu moved inside, throwing explosive, short punches. One landed on the side of Curtin's neck. He fell, rolling, scrambling to his feet barely in time to avoid a finishing kick. Eyes watering, head ringing like the bells of hell, he backed away, gathering his senses.

Overanxious, Lu rushed.

In the instant between Lu's attacking shout and first movement, Curtin's mind retreated to a different time.

They'd trapped him again, the bully and his friends, ready for another afternoon's fun, beating up "the sissy." They never came at him fewer than two at a time, then called him names because he didn't want to fight. When he did, he lost, and they laughed at him. That was worse than the beating.

One day the largest reached for the sissy's shirt front, the way he'd seen a hundred Saturday-matinee heroes reach for a hundred villains.

Automatically, Curtin repeated now what he'd done that afternoon.

Peering between his forearms, he lowered his chin at the last possible moment, lunging forward, driving the top of his head between the pistonlike fists. One of Lu's blows struck his shoulder, and even that pain couldn't erase the savage pleasure of feeling Lu's face impact his skull like a bug squashing on a windshield.

Dimly, eyes wobbling in and out of focus, Curtin looked down at the slack features. Blood from the nostrils and mouth puddled the rug, gurgled in the Oriental's throat with each breath. Curtin rolled him onto his stomach and turned his head to the side so he wouldn't choke.

Straightening, he watched the woman help Bullard to the sofa. She aimed a venomous glare at Curtin as he walked to the bar with exaggerated dignity. Ice water on his face cleared his vision and reduced the clanging in his ears to distant chimes. His shoulder and neck throbbed insistently.

Flor said, "I guess you're very proud of yourself."

Curtin helped himself to a good pull on the Scotch bottle. "Put a lid on it, Flor. I want what he owes me."

A toss of her head sent the luxurious fall of long black hair tumbling across her back. "The police can settle it."

"No, no police!" Bullard struggled to his feet. "I'll get your money, Curtin." Slowly, bent over, he made his way from the room.

The woman got the ice bucket and a towel and ministered to Lu. Swabbing the bloodied face, she asked Curtin, "Do you mean to take Mr. Chavez's offer?"

"I'll do what I can."

Angrily, she asked, "Why? What happens in Costa Verde is our business, not yours."

"I need the money. That's enough, right there. But the men your rebels shot up tonight are my friends, and I want a chance to get even. Beyond all that's Robert Chavez, a man—" He stopped, clamping his jaw. A few moments later he continued. "I've said enough. You'd never understand anyway, but try to understand, you people made it my business."

He was satisfied. *It was enough. She mustn't learn. No one must know.*

Cheeks glowing, she leaned toward him tensely. "Do not dare call them *my* rebels, and do not ever call us 'you people' in that superior tone." She twisted back to Lu as he stirred. Quieting him, she went on, "You are not what Robert led me to expect. You are just another gringo, meddling in matters that are not your affair, things you can never understand."

Bullard reentered, still walking gingerly, extending the torn half of the thousand-dollar note. Curtin stuffed it in his shirt pocket and headed for the door.

Bullard's voice followed him. "That's going to be expensive money. Before this game's over, you'll wish you'd never heard of it. Or me. I promise you that."

Closing the door behind him, Curtin leaned against the wall. Pain and exhaustion brought on by tension whispered seductively how well he'd earned a rest. He closed his eyes, gathered strength.

Now it was time to go to the hospital to see his friends. Again. Always. No matter how often you thought you'd walked away from that kind of life, it caught up to you. It was like a curse, a mark of Cain that fell on the people around you.

Men in hospitals. You looked down at them and made

jokes and talked about how soon they'd be back at the job. And hoped they had enough class to go along without telling you what a lying bastard you were.

Was there no end to it?

There was, of course. It ended with a friend looking down at you, feeling as you'd felt so often.

He pushed himself away from the wall, walked the passage telling himself he'd heard threats like Bullard's before. They were always words, just empty words.

He wished he could shake the awful feeling that this time might be different.

okay? There's no change, is there? I mean, neither of
them'll lose a leg, right? Thank God. Thank you too—
everyone there. Listen, I mailed them something this
morning. They'll need things, and I'd be grateful if you'd
help them get them, you know? And tell them I said they
better get you something nice too. Gotta run, Molly. You're
a sweetheart.''

Squawking noises poured out of the phone until he hung
up, grinning. He was still looking pleased with himself
when Bullard came out. It seemed to irritate him.

The sun was bright in a cloudless sky as Bullard lifted
the Cessna jet into whistling flight. He handled the plane
with professional skill, as comfortable in the air as he
was driving his Ferrari down the highway. Curtin thought
of the money he'd spent on his own flying lessons and the
tremendous sense of ownership that came with his tiny
prop job and wondered why Bullard, with so many
advantages, had to be so thoroughly detestable.

Money had been poured into making the interior luxurious,
from the compact bar to the plush leather recliner seats.
They made Curtin think of barber chairs, and he wished
he'd had time to get a haircut. Stretching, leaning back, he
waited for a sense of well-being that failed to appear.
Something out of place plucked at his thoughts.

He closed his eyes and concentrated, tracing through his
senses to single out the disturbance. The sound of the
engine receded, became muted background. The faint vibration of movement was firm, reassuring. Then he caught
it, a rich, suggestive wisp of scent. Sitting up, he searched
until he found the bright, filmy scarf tucked in a pocket of
the seat closest to him. The initials FP were embroidered
in one corner.

Flor Peralta, obviously.

He twisted in the seat, uncomfortable in mind, if not in
body.

She was drawn to power. Well, why not? Everybody
had to be attracted to something, and rich beat hell out of
poor. But the power she moved with was brutal. People

lived and died in misery so she could enjoy custom jets and afternoons of tennis. Any woman teamed up with Bullard came with a strong stomach and a brain capable of blocking out a world of unpleasant truths.

He wondered if it might be easier to forgive her if she were ugly and not so damned gorgeous. Instead of making a decision, he ended up admitting he could envy Bullard a great deal.

The conflicts and uncertainties brought on an unexpected tiredness that pushed him deeper into the chair's softness. He closed his eyes, picturing the land racing past below. He saw himself moving toward a dreamlike Western showdown.

Exactly why would Chavez search out a busted contractor to negotiate with his son's kidnappers, old friend or not?

One thing was certain—Bullard, at least, wasn't aware that Robert had only to call and Buck Curtin would come running.

Did the Old Man know that? Could he know why?

A screech brought him bolt upright, clawing hands grabbing the chair. Sheepishly, he realized he'd dozed off and been wakened by their landing.

Bullard stopped on his way to the door. "We'll be here for a few minutes."

"Where's 'here'? And why'd we stop?"

"Not far from Denver. I have to call our local office. There's a restaurant across the road. Bring me your check when you're finished."

"I think I can afford my own."

"Suit yourself." Bullard dismissed him without another glance.

Fuming, Curtin sat alone at the counter and ordered two steak lunches, with a shrimp salad. He walked to where Bullard ate alone and dropped the bill on his table on the way back to the plane. The fluttering fall of the paper gave him a terrible premonition.

The prairie thermals between Denver and South Dakota

battered the plane in a roller-coaster ride of swoops and lurches. Curtin suffered every inch of it, teeth clenched against a stomach in open rebellion. He took turns cursing Bullard, pride, steak, shrimp, and the Wright brothers.

The most cheerful thought he could muster was that he was too busy holding down his lunch to worry further about what he'd gotten into.

Chapter 5

The plane landed on a controlled approach, Bullard obviously responding to instructions. Even Curtin's limited experience recognized the constant minor corrections and Bullard's tense concentration. Curtin wondered what the penalty might be for wandering out of the approved flight path and smiled. He was becoming paranoid, he told himself.

That was when he noticed the pit dug in the crown of the small butte off to the west. There was a net draped over it, and if the gap between the material and the earth hadn't caught his eye he'd have missed it. It was visible for only an instant, but there was no doubt that he was looking at something camouflaged.

Radar? Why hide it?

Antiaircraft guns? Here? That was ridiculous.

His stomach gave one last lurch as the wheels touched. He argued with himself he'd seen nothing more than some sort of ground-control hardware, shielded against the fierce sun.

The engines were still whining to a stop outside a small

hangar when Bullard hopped to the ground. Curtin paused in the exit, absorbing the prairie spring.

The light was thinner than the brassy glare of California, the air not so heavily burdened as the Coast's thick sage and saltwater tang. Here was a rich earth aroma of a thousand sources.

California's sun and smell suggested motion. This was different. It, too, spoke of change, but slow and circular, where seasons became part of man as surely as they were part of the grass. Curtin had never seen it, yet he felt he had lived here.

In the distance, flush against a range of bluffs, something huge and mirrorlike returned the sun's light defiantly. Shading his eyes, Curtin determined it was the front of a building. The construction blended with the earth so well that, except for the glass, he had no idea exactly where one ended and the other started.

Two men drove out of the hangar to meet them, one in a jeep and the other in a van. They loaded the luggage into the larger vehicle and left without speaking. Curtin had the impression they deliberately avoided eye contact.

Bullard drove, proceeding along a gravel road that snaked between numerous small hills. In a short while they were on an extensive prairie, where the grass rippled in receding waves until shimmering heat dissolved it against towering clouds. Then they descended an eroded slope, the road torturous. There were trees on the valley floor, and Curtin was surprised to realize he hadn't missed them until they suddenly reappeared. For the entire trip, the shining building was screened from view.

Turning to Curtin, Bullard said, "Welcome to the Chavez Institute."

"I never heard of it."

"It's not exactly well-known." Bullard smiled his pleasure at insider's knowledge. "It's mainly a conference site. What you'd call a think-tank."

Curtin gestured at the empty countryside. "For roaming buffalo and playing antelope?"

"A place where thinkers and developers from all over the world can meet. The only distractions are the luxuries we provide. It's very safe, confidential. You'd be surprised to hear the names of some of the Old Man's guests."

"It's not a government outfit?"

Bullard laughed. "Politicians are a commodity we buy and sell. We get minds here, the advisors who decide what can be done, what should be done."

The road doglegged around a hill and the reflective glass appeared before them, rising at least forty vertical feet up a facing slope. Curtin assumed the mirrored surface could be removed to take full advantage of the winter sun. The stone paving of the huge courtyard was a heat trap as well, he decided. His mind raced, trying to calculate the potential for heat storage, methods for keeping the glass free of snow in winter, techniques for cooling in summer.

"We go in over there," Bullard said. The van was stopped at the edge of the courtyard. "Your suitcase will be taken to your room. This is the main building. It's connected to the maintenance and agriculture complexes by tunnels. We're almost completely self-contained. We generate most of our own power, raise much of our own food."

Rippling heat waves distorted Curtin's vision. Sweat marked Bullard's collar by the time they reached the small entryway. Curtin wished he were back at the Command Post with a cold beer.

Where he belonged.

The wonderful bad jokes. Broken-down cars and friends who made hard times good times. And who understood the lonely times when life looked like one long losing streak.

Robert Chavez. So rich he could afford to worry about everyone else in the world.

And they expect you to risk your life for him.

The rush of cool air when they entered the building jarred him out of his daydreams.

At the distant center of the stone-walled room a fountain

splashed and sparkled. Its base was surrounded by a miniature garden. A shaft of light dropped on it from a square
hole above. Spattering water was the only sound in the
vast expanse, but Curtin had the eerie sensation of a breeze
blowing across his face. He turned his head back and
forth, searching for a source.

Beside him, Bullard pointed at a series of floor-level
ducts. "Pipes buried outside remain at the constant underground temperature of fifty-five degrees. Windmill-powered
pumps circulate air through them to balance it at a steady
sixty-eight."

Curtin nodded. "I've read about it. I didn't know it was
being done on such a huge scale."

"Everything—everyone—here is a little larger than life."

An unvoiced retort burned Curtin's tongue. Then they
were entering an elevator. Bullard pushed the button for
the third floor. Curtin noted two additional floors beneath
ground level. At the same time, he realized he hadn't seen
another human being since they'd left the landing field.

Bullard went on, "The first floor's a reception area.
There's an auditorium behind it, and a few administrative
offices. Two and three are labs, library, meeting rooms,
and offices. My father lives on the top floor."

The door sighed open onto a narrow hall. A man in a
casual white shirt and black slacks stood beside a plain
steel desk directly opposite the elevator. A communications unit and a stubby submachine gun sat on the otherwise bare desktop. The guard's hand rested lightly beside
the weapon. The embroidered patch on his shirt pocket
read "Security" in red letters. He nodded. "Afternoon,
Mr. Bullard. If you and the gentleman will step to your
left?"

Looking in that direction, Curtin saw the hall only
extended a few feet before ending in a wall. There was a
door in the wall, with a peephole at eye level and a slightly
larger, covered port at waist height. The door opened, and
they passed through into a small room. The opposite wall

featured the same fortresslike construction, and the solid
thud of the door closing behind them told Curtin it was
designed to stop explosives, not to mention small arms.

Another guard sat at another plain desk and watched
while his partner ran a thorough body search on Bullard,
then Curtin. The seated man's hands remained out of
sight, and Curtin never doubted there was a weapon aimed
at him throughout the entire process. When they were
finished, they exited into a bustling office.

Passing a dozen or so desk workers, Bullard pointed
back at the guard station. "Searching is mandatory. We've
learned that the terrorrists can force practically anyone to
do practically anything. No one'll smuggle any weapons
into our buildings."

They reached another door, this one of highly polished
wood with an ornate handle. A receptionist threw a chill
smile at Bullard, and he pushed through.

The inner office was spacious, richly furnished, carefully organized to direct attention to the farthest end. It
was a long walk to the massive oak desk and the man
seated behind it. Despite determined reclusiveness, Chavez
had been pictured on the pages and covers of numerous
periodicals. Still, Curtin was unprepared for the man's
commanding presence. Simply by fixing his almost-black
eyes on his guest, Chavez excluded his son.

Curtin felt no threat in the examination, but underlying
power and determination were abundantly clear. The mind
behind such an intense gaze would recognize failure, but
never accept it as final.

During the brief moment, Curtin was aware of that mind
searching his own, trying to establish a contact beyond
words.

Chavez came around to the front of the desk. He was
shorter than average, heavy through the shoulders. At
close range his skin showed the myriad small wrinkles of
age, but his thatch of still-black hair carried a vigorous shine.
His clothes managed simple elegance: a cool-looking off-

white shirt and trousers of an unusual material Curtin
guessed might be linen. They complemented his dark
complexion.

As they shook hands, Chavez spoke first. "I'm glad you
came. We need you." There was the faintest accent and a
peculiar rhythm that said the thoughts were formed in a
different language.

Curtin said, "I won't stall with you, Mr. Chavez. Why
me? Robert and I haven't had anything to do with each
other for years. I don't speak Spanish. You've got access
to hundreds of people who're better qualified. So what's
going on?"

Poker-faced, Chavez said, "You think something is
wrong?"

"Hell, yes." Curtin waved an arm. "You didn't build
all this playing hunches. You hire experts. I'm not an
expert, but you want me. Goddam right something's
wrong."

Nervous shuffling sounds from Bullard eddied around
them, ignored, as a rock ignores the stream. After a
moment, Chavez nodded. "You are what I expected. But
no explanations now. First you must allow me to extend
you the hospitality of my home. Rooms have been arranged,
I have planned a special dinner. Then, when we know a
little more about each other—"

Curtin broke in. "You lean back and set the hook."

Chavez smiled. "Exactly. You are perceptive."

"Sure. If I'm so perceptive, why don't I know what's
going on? For that matter, why am I even sticking around
to find out?"

Chavez took Curtin's elbow, who found himself smiling
back, allowing himself to be led out. Chavez bade them
goodbye from his entry, one hand on the frame and the
other on the door. The body bridging the space between
the timbers suggested to Curtin that both would be equally
unyielding. The black eyes probed him again. "I dislike
saying this, but I must, Mr. Curtin. Although you are a

welcome guest, you realize I could make it impossible for you to leave. Think about that, about my son, imprisoned by men who enjoy his suffering, men who kill without mercy for any measurable or imagined gain. Think. Then we talk.''

The massive door swung closed past his solemn, watching eyes. Bullard's eyes widened at the sudden naked pain in Curtin's face.

Chapter 6

At the ground-floor door, another security man introduced himself to Curtin, smiling easily. "Hi. My name's Ben Bradley. I'll show you to your room."

The waiting jeep was tan, with the Chavez logo. The word "Security" on the side was in a dark brown. The colors blended perfectly with the terrain. The nagging suggestion in Curtin's mind that he'd actually flown past an antiaircraft position refused to be shoved aside quite so easily this time.

Once they were moving, Curtin said, "Listen, all I've seen here are security people, some clerks, and the boss. What's going on?"

"Sometimes we have twenty, twenty-five people here. Conferences, discussions, or whatever. Right now you're our only guest. A lot of staff are on vacation 'cause we're in sort of a slack time, you know?"

"I see. What sort of conferences?"

"You'd have to speak to Research or Communications about that." The friendliness went cold, and driving demanded more attention.

"Who's Research? What's Communications do?"

Ben visibly relaxed. "We have computer and communications hookups with just about any source you can name. If a conference member needs information, Research or Comm gets it *more skosh*."

Curtin laughed at the pidgin. "I haven't heard anyone say 'quickly' that way for a long time. You were stationed in Japan?"

"There, and Okinawa. Almost all of us here were in the service."

"Most of my people, too." Curtin grinned crookedly. "My operation's a little smaller than this."

"Colonel Duffy said you had a construction company."

Curtin snapped around. "Who the hell—" The sentence stranded on surprise.

Ben was apologetic. "I thought Mr. Bullard would have told you. He's the Security boss. Colonel Duffy runs it, really. The Colonel briefs us on everybody who comes here." He chanced taking his eyes off the road to throw Curtin a worried look. "You upset?"

"I guess not. I already knew Bullard had me checked out."

"Somebody ought to kick his ass regular." The comment ended abruptly, bitten off. When Curtin turned, Ben was grimacing. "Boy, I'm having a lot of mouth trouble today. I hope you'll forget you heard that."

Curtin said, "So you heard about our fight?"

Slowing the jeep almost to a walk, Ben fidgeted uncomfortably. "I like this job. Good pay, they treat a man right. I hope you know how far I'm sticking my neck out." He inhaled like a man leaping into cold water. "Everyone in Security, from the Colonel down to us snuffies, believes Bullard set Robert up." He faced front and picked up speed, tried to sound casual. "You really waxed him and that little shit, Lu?"

"Not exactly."

Ben grinned broadly. "If either of them'd won, you wouldn't be walking around."

They entered a canyon, paralleled a small creek. Trees and brush crowded the banks, greedy for the steady source of water. Rounding a bend, Ben pointed. "The guest quarters."

The front of the building extended from the living rock of a hillside like a prehistoric cliff house. A series of individual balconies, five high and six across, indicated room locations. The glass doors glowed in the lowering sun, suggesting internal, as well as external, heat. It was uphill about twenty-five yards from the parking area to the entrance, from where he glimpsed the swimming pool and tennis courts at the other end of the building.

The guard station inside was unmanned, and his and Ben's echoing footsteps on the tiled lobby floor had an ominous hollowness. Curtin's second-floor suite consisted of a sitting room, adjacent bedroom, and a bathroom featuring a multinozzled shower stall. Until he saw the latter, he hadn't realized how weary he was.

Ben caught his expression. "There's a robe in here," he said, opening the door to a walk-in closet. "Over there's your refrigerator and bar. Mr. Chavez eats late, so if you want to take a nap, I can come back in a couple hours, okay?"

"Perfect, Ben. Two hours."

"Leave it to me. Oh, your clothes are in the closet, but I'll bring a sport coat and a shirt and tie for dinner, Mr. Bullard should have told you. Mr. Chavez says ties for dinner, always."

"And you know my size."

Ben smiled and winked. "We do our homework," he said, closing the door on his way out.

Curtin was already undressing, eyeing the shower like a camel on the edge of a waterhole.

Jetting water massaged aching muscles and livid bruises. Gradually, pain oozed away, leaving him limp. He toweled slowly, then fell on the bed. He expected to fall asleep immediately. Instead, his mind leaped wildly, with no logical progression.

Bullard. Had he betrayed his stepbrother? Could Chavez guarantee to keep him out of the way until Robert was free?

Chavez. The picture of sincerity, but controlling a wealth and power that assured cunning, hard dealing, possibly even treachery.

Flor. Did she fit into any part of the problem or was she simply Bullard's woman?

Robert. Had he changed over the years? Had the man of ideals turned into a foolish do-gooder? For that matter, did any of these people give an honest damn if he was ever freed?

Curtin. What good could he do? Was there one person he could trust? *What did Chavez really know about him?*

The knock on the door jerked him to his feet. Only when the surprise-induced bolt of energy dissipated and he had to lean against the wall to steady himself did he realize he'd been sleeping.

Ben's voice filtered through the heavy door. "Time to get up, Mr. Curtin."

Curtin mumbled.

It satisfied Ben. "I'll wait for you in the lobby, sir."

In the bathroom, Curtin examined his mirrored reflection. "Sir, my ass. I'm not that old yet." He sucked in his stomach. "Not too bad." Rubbing the bruised shoulder, he added, "Especially in living color." Making a face at himself, he left to dress.

Driving to the main building, Ben said, "Mr. Chavez lives on the top floor, you know? His own gallery and everything."

"You like him?"

"He's a leader."

There was enthusiasm in the answer, but a hesitation, like a man palming his chips, showing less than his original impulse suggested. Curtin changed the direction of his questioning.

"They must pay a bundle to keep you here in nowhere land."

"The company has jobs in plenty of places. We get paid extra here. The guys who do well can just about pick where they want to go next." His grin gleamed in the dark. "Just like the Corps, only more money and less horseshit."

"What's this Peralta woman like?"

"Stand clear. Bullard and Robert already fight over her." Harshly, he added, "With Robert gone, she hangs around Bullard like a T-town hooker. Family's money-up-the-ass rich. I think I know how they got it."

"She seemed a little nicer than that."

"Oh, she's polite to us enlisted swine. Everybody here calls her 'The Frozen Banana.' "

Curtin chuckled. "I'd like to see her face if she ever heard that."

"Christ, don't even think it." The jeep eased to a stop. Above the subdued entry lights, the fourth floor blazed like a suspended slash in the night. Ben said, "I'll be waiting here," his tone a hint Curtin was nearly late.

The guards examined Curtin with the same professionalism as previously before escorting him to Chavez's living area.

It was a wonderland. From the raised entry, the living room swept away to the front, while an open door on the right exposed part of the dining room. The predominant color was white—white walls, white carpet, heavy white furniture grouped in front of a massive white-marble fireplace. However, wherever the eye traveled, artworks vied for attention. Curtin recognized ancient pottery and stone carvings, wild impressionist paintings, sinuous modern metal sculpture. Each piece, completely individual, complemented the whole.

Moments passed before he realized he wasn't alone. Chavez, Bullard, and Flor stood off to his right, watching him. His first reaction was embarrassment, but then he was taken by their differing expressions. Chavez clearly enjoyed his guest's response. Bullard sneered. Flor's smile was a riddle. Did his surprised appreciation please her or did she imagine him stunned by such luxury? Ben's assessment of her rang in his memory.

Chavez said, "You know something of Central and South American art, Mr. Curtin?"

Curtin laughed and shook his head. "I don't know anything about any art. But I know this place and these things are beautiful."

Bullard opened his mouth, but his father's glance shut it. He turned on his heel and studied the bookshelves behind him. Flor moved to his side, whispering. Shoulders moved in shared laughter.

Chavez's welcoming smile twitched with annoyance. He joined Curtin, describing pieces in detail, identifying favorites. A waiter entered, carrying drinks on a tray. Chavez handed one to Curtin. "Old Bushmill's, neat, one ice cube," he said. "Unless my information's wrong?"

Curtin tasted it and smiled. "God help the poor devil who tries to take it away from me."

Chavez laughed. "A man's answer, a drinking man's compliment!" He indicated the dining room. "Dinner's in a few minutes. At least if you decide not to help me, you won't be able to say it's because I wouldn't feed you."

The meal rivaled the surroundings. The chef wheeled in a massive roast on a cart, carving it himself. Curtin lost count of the wines.

Through it all, Chavez talked of everything but his son. He seemed to be acquainted with every major political figure mentioned in the news. At each new subject, he asked Curtin's opinion, and he listened with careful interest.

At one point, when Curtin pleaded a lack of background, Chavez grew critical. "We drown in information in this country! And what good does it do? None! Zero! We must use it to grow stronger! People must be educated, given direction. We must create proper values. Look at how I must deal with criminals, as if they were normal humans. Next our government will tell me these kidnappers are a civilized ruling body. *Qué verguenza!*" He stopped abruptly, exploding into rough laughter. "Your first Spanish lesson in my house, Mr. Curtin. It means 'such a shame!' "

The waiter rolled in another cart, stocked with fruit, cheese, and liqueurs. Chavez rose. "That'll be all, Carl. See that we're not disturbed."

He watched the door close before filling the glasses. "A toast." He stared at the amber liquid. "To the end of the insanity in Costa Verde—in all of Central America—and may it never involve this country!"

From the corner of his eye, Curtin caught Bullard's pause and fleeting frown. Flor brushed his arm, lifted her glass almost gaily. Bullard touched his to his lips. Chavez savored his as though nothing else mattered.

Bullard said, "You did that to irritate me," and the older man's eyebrows rose.

"We have to get involved," Bullard went on doggedly. "You said yourself they're criminals. They'll destroy everything we've built."

"It's their country," Chavez said. His mildness surprised Curtin until he saw the almost malicious smile aimed at Flor.

Coloring, she rose to the bait. "Not 'theirs.' Mine. Ours. The rebels are traitors, murderers. This country must help us or we go as Cuba went. What of all the fine talk about liberty and democracy then?"

"The American government opposed a communist dictatorship in Indochina. When our soldiers died in the effort to prevent that dictatorship, our own liberals said they deserved to die. So. If the people of Costa Verde can't withstand the march of communism, then obviously they deserve communism."

Bullard got to his feet, ignoring his coffee cup's jangling tumble and the spreading stain on the linen. "You're growing weak. They've kidnapped your son and you prattle about what people deserve. If we don't destroy those bastards, they'll destroy everything the name Chavez stands for. I don't intend to just watch it happen."

Chavez stood up. Curtin caught himself wanting to lean

away from an almost physical aura of menace. Bullard's eyes widened and his lips paled, but he stood firm. Chavez's voice rasped. "I am what that name stands for. Show me the man who'll destroy *me*, take what's mine." He faced Curtin, steeled features quivering at the limits of control. "My son has the peculiar notion that governments have power, that borders are important. I ignore governments. I spit on borders." To Bullard, he said, "This man will free Robert. Then you will see how I deal with people who get in my way."

"Him! He's a killer!"

A blunt gesture held Curtin in place while cutting off the argument. "That was in combat, a man trying to kill your own brother! It only proves he is the one for us. You should praise him."

"You can't trust a man like him. Not with the amount of money involved."

Curtin gestured with both hands. "Hold it. I've got something to say."

Chavez ignored him, eyes boring into his son. "I know everything you and your spies have uncovered. He may read the reports, if he wishes. He must decide if he trusts *me*."

Hammering his fist on the table, Curtin shocked them into silence. He told Chavez, "Sit down." At the older man's furious scowl, he rose himself, repeating the words as an almost whispered command. Slowly, grudgingly, the thick body settled into the chair.

Curtin said, "You two may know a lot about me, but you don't understand much. You poke around in my life, throw money at me like bones at a dog, and now, goddam you, you argue my merits like I'm a piece of property. Let me save you some trouble. I'm not going." He waited a second for the announcement to sink in. "If it was a question of trying to bust Robert out, I might have a chance. But you want me to deal with politicians, haggle with terrorists, play your stupid social games. I was a pretty good soldier, but that's over. I'm a civilian. I feel bad about Robert, but I can't help you." To Bullard, he added, "Even if I thought I could, I wouldn't turn my back on you for a second."

Bullard's eyes narrowed. "At least you're smart enough to recognize your own incompetence."

"Be quiet," Chavez said, not taking his eyes off Curtin. Then, "You were a raider, a man addicted to excitement. You still take risks, always measuring yourself. You must always strive to be the man your heart wants you to be. You aren't saying you can't help Robert. You're saying you don't trust your skills in this different form of combat. You want vengeance. And more, right? More even than the uninformed approval of others?" A faint smile moved his lips. "You see how well I know you, how I understand? Why not? In the culture of my ancestry macho is not a dirty word."

He stopped to light a cigar. Curtin felt frozen, unable to breathe. An electric tingling shivered on his skin.

Flor broke, giving a small, almost-inaudible cry. She flung her chair back, stepped away from the table. "He insults you, your sons! He calls one untrustworthy! He refuses to give help to the other when you humble yourself to ask!"

After a sharp glance her way, Chavez continued to speak to Curtin. "I can find thousands with your qualifications. But you are loyal. You draw that quality from others, and two men proved it with their blood just last night. You won't rest until your honor and their wounds are avenged. You will give me that same dedication."

Flor laughed, a sharp, brittle noise.

Chavez turned to her lazily, almost contemptuously. "I think perhaps you live too much in my son's world. You think these things are matters of economics."

Bullard scoffed. "You think not? Ask him to help Robert for free."

Chavez's eyes, impenetrable as night, returned to Curtin. "He probably would do it, but what I'm asking of him deserves a great deal of money. I offer him that and more. I offer him my complete confidence.''

Flor gasped. "How can you? You have no reason!"

"I have. The best. I give him the chance to rescue something far more important to him than his friends or my son."

Bullard demanded explanation. Flor continued her vehement protests. Curtin watched them with the dead stare of sleepwalking, heard their agitated voices as muffled babble.

After so many years, the past was coiling around him, cold, damp.

The thing he feared—and desired—most in the world was here.

Robert talked.

Someone else knew.

Chapter 7

Harsh triumph burned in Chavez's eyes.

Curtin turned from it, focusing his attention on Bullard's angry departure with a snarling, almost-drunk Flor hanging from his arm.

With their departure, his mind rejected the present, raced across years into a past half a world away. Luxurious surroundings faded, the flavor of fine wines turned to a sticky paste that tasted of tropical decay and fear.

Fear.

A spear of ice that destroyed the will, left nothing but the whining desire to live.

Cowering in the grass, Robert beside him, he watched the advancing NVA troops, so close the sound of their passing was like a steady breeze. The darkness was rancid with the smell of them. Against a faint horizon, their heads bobbed past in what seemed an infinite stream. He eased the night-vision device to his eye and scanned the column. The green images in the scope flickered, mocking his shaking hand.

Robert nudged him impatiently. Dimly, Curtin realized

it wasn't the first time. He gestured Robert to wait, and received another sharp elbow in his ribs, hard enough to make him wince.

Robert whispered hoarsely. "What the hell are you waiting for? They're setting up!"

Curtin gripped the stock of the grenade launcher, wishing it would fire of itself. The sick knowledge that he couldn't squeeze the trigger shamed him, but it was powerless against the dread conviction that if he did, he died. In balance were the lives of the unwarned Marines who would be completely surprised if Curtin's team didn't take the advancing NVA under fire.

It was his duty. And he was too frightened to care.

He wanted only to hide.

To live.

Terror burst over him so violently he screamed aloud as Robert raked the troops with his M16. Then the grenade launcher fired, its fat, mushy sound innocent compared to the ear-burning crack of the M16. The rest of the team opened up. Cries erupted from the startled men torn by the lashing fire.

The ordeal that followed lasted for almost an hour. The column, its chance of surprise gone, reacted with the vicious reflex of a wounded snake. The ends coiled on the damaged center. Disregarding losses, cutting Curtin's men off from retreat toward their own forces, the NVA unit single-mindedly moved to destroy them.

Curtin heard himself talking on the radio, calling in the prearranged fires with a calmness that made him think of movie surgeons discussing life or death in an operating room.

He was surprised to realize thoughts of his own life had come second. The awareness that he had panicked, failed those who trusted him, made him want to vomit.

Chavez snapped him out of his memories.

"Robert told me of his amazement when you refused to fire. At first he thought you were merely waiting for the best target. When he realized your responsibility had fallen from your frightened shoulders to his, he did what the situation demanded without thinking.''

Curtin glared at the reference to his fear, but Chavez continued easily. ''Robert always felt it was a momentary thing, but Robert is a fool. Oh, I don't doubt your courage, Mr. Curtin. However, I believe—I *know*—you doubt it. The memory of that moment drives you to this day. You've spent your life since that night proving yourself in one way or another. I'm giving you the opportunity to make the final payment, by rescuing the man who saved you.''

''I don't have to prove myself to you or anyone else. Your psychology's as full of holes as your logic. I don't have any hang-ups about guts and I have no idea how to rescue a man from kidnappers. That's that.''

''You know what he's going through. The actual execution will probably come as a relief. He needs you. Perhaps as much as you need him.''

Jerking himself out of the chair, Curtin leaned on the table, face thrust at Chavez's. ''Goddam it, you know I'd help if I could! What you're talking about is an organization!''

''You have friends, connections. Men with expertise and experience. Men who don't know Robert, but who have the interests of their country to consider.''

''What's that mean?''

''That part of the world is ready to collapse. We could be drawn into the hole. Robert's work helped the people resist the tyrants of both left and right.''

Curtin grinned lopsidedly. ''That leaves maybe one percent of the population as his friends.''

Chavez's calm expression darkened. ''You joke about something you don't understand. Those people, and Robert, are fighting for a decent life.''

''I'm all for it.''

''Wait. Listen to me. The people of Costa Verde will support the communists because they promise and deliver education, medical treatment, jobs. When the people discover those are the privileges of prisoners in a huge jail, the controls will be too tight to be dislodged. Revolution in the Third World is a struggle for greater socialization. The rulers of this country can only prattle about democracy, as their fathers and grandfathers raved of Christ and your civilization to us ignorant niggers and Indians. The difference is the present group won't fight for what they claim to believe.''

"Don't preach at me. You're not in a good position for moralizing. Anyhow, let the people Robert's working for get him out. I don't even know the language, man.''

"All action incorporates a view of what's moral or immoral. It's true in Robert's case. Someone betrayed him. I need a man we can both trust.''

"And you trust me because I broke once? That's not too logical.''

Chavez smiled. "You won't break again. You *can't*. Not on this mission.''

Curtin ignored the smile, caught by the intensity of the almost-black eyes boring into him. He settled back into his chair and broke off the staring match, pushing wearily at the chinaware. "I can't argue anymore. What you say about me has enough truth in it to hurt. But what you want—'' He gestured.

"You can do it.'' Chavez came around to pat his shoulder, then paced. "Still, there are complications.'' Curtin's head came up, and Chavez continued. "Flor Peralta is from one of the oldest, most powerful families in Costa Verde. They are famous for resisting reforms. You must be careful of her and those she knows. As for my son, Harry Bullard is tough, a battler.''

"We've met.''

"That's just it. You've only met. I wish you knew him, really knew him. He's the only competition that's ever tested Robert. They fight constantly over who should control this organization when I'm ready to step aside.''

"Bullard's not just tough, he's mean. You could end up watching them destroy each other.''

"I see that they don't. For all their young strength, I'm still the man in charge. They understand that."

"You know that, but do they know it? Look, I want a straight answer to something that's bothering hell out of me. I don't like Bullard, and I don't trust him. Do you have any knowledge, or suspicion, that Bullard knows anything about Robert's kidnapping? And how can I be sure he won't interfere with me if I try to get Robert out?"

A deep glow spread from Chavez's cheekbones, coloring his face, working down to his throat. When he spoke, the words came through straining muscles. "My sons are rivals, but they are my sons. There is no chance—" He paused, walked to the bar cart and helped himself to a stiff drink. "I challenge your fears. If you prove any sort of interference or involvement by my son, I will double your pay. Further, because my sons and my work have been endangered, I challenge your skills. If you can rescue Robert without paying the ransom, I will give it to you."

Curtin stared. It took a determined effort to speak. "You're crazy." Chavez smiled patiently and Curtin repeated himself. "Crazy. Jesus. Two *million?*"

Suddenly he was furious. "I could buy everyone in Costa Verde! I could frame Bullard eight ways, take any wild chance to break Robert out. You're gambling with his life! What the hell are you doing to me?"

"There's no gamble. You'll take no chances with Robert. And if you free him, I'll be delighted to see Force Red's criminals embarrassed. Or killed. Whichever is easiest for you."

"You're as sure of me as he is."

"Yes."

"Funny. I can only hope you're right. But your money's no good to me if I'm dead. I want your promise to keep Bullard out of this. He's not allowed near our communications link. Second, I need a bank account to draw on for men, equipment. I want nothing traceable to your organization."

Frowning, Chavez rubbed blunt fingers along his jaw.

"My son can't be completely excluded, but I promise he'll have no details of your activities. Decide how much money you need and let me know."

They shook hands on it, the contact firm and assured, but both men regarding each other warily. Curtin thought to himself they must look like two strange dogs, unsure if territorial rights demanded a fight. Chavez stepped to the side, gesturing Curtin toward the door. Without speaking, they moved out of the dining room, where they parted with formal goodnights.

When Curtin stepped out of the elevator into the lobby, Ben looked up from his conversation with the Security guard and headed for his jeep. The engine was running when Curtin slid in beside him. "Back to the barracks, Mr. Curtin?"

Curtin tried to sound pleasant. "Yeah, that's it for tonight."

Ben tried again. "He knows how to live, doesn't he? Lot of class up there." He indicated the glowing windows behind them, using the movement to turn toward Curtin. "How was dinner?"

"What?" Curtin blinked, then. "Oh. Very nice."

"I saw Miss Peralta come out with Mr. Bullard. They didn't look too happy."

Curtin continued to stare dead ahead. Ben said, "There wasn't any real trouble, was there? I mean, are you okay?"

"Stop this thing."

"What?"

"I said stop. Pull over."

"Oh, shit. You gonna be sick?"

"No. I want to talk to you."

"No way, Mr. Curtin. I have to call in when I drop you off, so they know how long I'm driving around. And we don't answer questions. You know that."

Curtin grabbed the wheel. "Pull over, or I do it."

Indecision twisted Ben's face, then, abruptly, he jammed on the brake. Curtin's head hit the top bar of the windshield, not hard enough to do damage, but hard enough to illustrate Ben's opinion of the way things were going. His voice left no doubt. "Okay, we're stopped. Get done with your talk, so I can get going again."

"I'm sorry I growled at you." Curtin rubbed his head. "Look, I'm going to work for Chavez, trying to help Robert. I don't know much about the Old Man, and what I know about Bullard I don't like. I need someone who knows the ins and outs of things, knows who's pissed off at who, and why, and all that. Chavez will assign you to help me. You'd be helping Robert. Chavez is going to remember that."

Ben's hostility faded slowly. "I think Robert ought to be helped, but if I ask for the deal, Bullard'll be on my case forever. I have to think about that."

"Well, you think about it. Just don't blow it around, okay?"

The jeep leaped forward. "The first thing you learn with this outfit is to be careful. Don't worry about me."

"Thanks, Ben. Incidentally, when I asked you, I meant it as a compliment."

"I know. And thanks. I'll let you know."

They chatted lightly the rest of the way, Ben driving a bit faster than normal, making up for lost time. When they parked in front of the living quarters, he glanced at his watch and gave Curtin a quick thumbs-up before reporting in on his radio.

The pathway to the building was a glowing trail in the darkness, studded at intervals by knee-high lamps. In the distance, the illuminated front doorway of the building stood out against the brooding ebony of the mountain's mass. Darkened windows reflected the cold flicker of stars.

"Not the most welcoming place," Curtin said, laughing, and Ben joined him.

"I'll walk along with you," he said. "I'll have to show you how the elevator works. It's a little tricky."

"Tricky? How?"

"It's a code lock, so unauthorized people can't just ride up to the apartments."

The light bulb next to them expired with a loud pop, spraying the pathway with tinkling bits of glass, throwing that section of the way into blackness. Both men made sharp, startled noises. When they realized what had happened, they laughed at each other.

"A couple of red-hot daredevils, that's us," Curtin said. "A broken light bulb, and we're up in the air like goosed monkeys."

Ben continued to chuckle. "I heard that thing go and every single time I skipped Sunday school flashed through my mind."

They were describing each other's reaction, exaggerating, enjoying themselves, when the wood of the door directly between them suddenly resounded with a loud "Thump!" and splinters sprayed outward. For less than a heartbeat, they stared at the raw white lumber exposed.

Curtin grabbed Ben's shoulder with one hand and slammed open the door with the other, then bodily heaved the younger man ahead of him. As Ben fell, he looked back, startled, angered. Curtin shouted, diving inside, "Sniper! Get out of the doorway!" He landed rolling, seeing Ben squirming in the opposite direction.

Another round snapped angrily at the carpet, ripping a long gouge in it before ricocheting off the cement underlayer. The whining complaint stopped with a crack against the wall beyond the elevator entry. Ben was on his feet and running before the echoes died, slapping at the light switch just inside the front door. The lobby blacked out. The silence from outside pressed in on them, grew thick with the stink of burned plastic from the scorched carpet.

After a few seconds, Ben said, "You okay, Mr. Curtin?"

"Yeah. You?"

"I guess so. What the hell was it?"

"Probably a .22. Silencer. You hear anything more out there?"

"More? Shit, I haven't heard anything yet! I'm gonna make it for the phone at the desk. Holler, if anything comes up, will you?"

"Depend on it."

Ben chuckled nervously at the dry answer, then raced across the lobby, rolling over the desk counter, falling heavily behind it. When he spoke on the phone, it was with an urgent breathlessness that had an immediate effect. In less than a minute, sirens howled in the distance. The glow of headlights sped toward them, silhouetting the hilltops.

For the next half-hour, Curtin and Ben answered questions while teams of men searched for their assailant and any evidence of his presence. The slugs were found, each creating its own moment of excitement. A triumphant shout marked the discovery of the ejected cartridge cases. Curtin managed a smug smile at Ben at the sight of the .22-caliber brass. The torn part of the carpet was removed by cutting out a large surrounding square. The operation left an ugly scar on the cement like something obscene. After receiving a new bulb, the punctured lamp on the path glittered proudly through the entry and exit bullet holes.

The matter took an unpleasant turn when Colonel Duffy arrived. A trim, spare man, he favored Ben with a look of harsh disapproval that struck Curtin as approaching suspicion. All emotion quickly disappeared behind masking professionalism, however. He extended a hand for a brisk greeting.

"I apologize about this. I'm Colonel Duffy, Chief of Security for Mr. Chavez. Nothing like this ever happened before." Accusation was a soft undercurrent.

Curtin said, "I'm more concerned it doesn't happen again."

A muscle jerked in Duffy's jaw. "It won't. Could I have a list of those who know you're here, sir?"

"Anyone who knows I'm here *is* here."

"Perhaps." Duffy smiled indulgently. "We'll have to check for outsiders to learn who fired the shots."

"Be serious. This was inside stuff."

Ben flinched when Duffy's hard blue eyes touched him for an instant, and then the lean figure drew straighter. "You're wrong. Someone else knows you're here. You better face that." He turned to Ben. "I'll see you in my office at oh-eight-hundred."

"Yes, sir."

Duffy began snapping orders and questions at his men.

Over an hour later, with the last of the security people leaving, Curtin stepped into the elevator and leaned against the wall. "Show me how this damned thing works, so I can get up to five and get some sleep," he said. "I'm finished."

"Right." Ben lifted the cover on a device that looked like a touch-tone telephone number display. "The code now is four-four-seven-three. Punch that, and then punch your floor number."

"What if I punch the wrong number?"

"It sets off a light in Security HQ. There'll be a couple of men here to help you in just a few minutes."

Curtin smiled wryly. " 'To help me.' I'll bet. I hope they catch the sonofabitch who shot at us, so I can show them what real help is."

"I've been thinking about that." Ben's voice was thoughtful. "This has something to do with Robert's kidnapping. It can't be anything else." He stopped, looked away, his jaw set. "It'd be a good idea if I stuck close to you, I think. I'll tell them tomorrow I want to work with you on this. If you still want me."

"You bet." They shook hands, and it occurred to Curtin he'd gone through the same ceremony less than an hour ago. This time it felt different, as if the confidence involved was deeper, plainer.

Chapter 8

Arriving at his room, Curtin waited for Ben to open the door, then grabbed him by the shoulder before he could enter. "Wait," he said. First he examined the lock, then the door frame. Stepping in, he inspected the apartment and its furnishings like an animal seeking prey. Ben took the silence as long as he could.

"You think someone could have gotten in here? No way."

"An hour ago you'd have told me there was no way a sniper could drop a man on Chavez's property." Curtin gathered up his belongings. "I'm moving to a different room." He dared argument.

"I don't have a key to any other room."

"Too bad." Curtin stormed past him. "I'm not staying in any room that's probably bugged and maybe booby-trapped." In the hall, he paused before deciding to go to his right. He stopped at the third door down. "You don't have a key?" At the negative shake of the head, Curtin shrugged. Even as a horrified Ben managed to murmur

63

"No!" Curtin rocked back and let go a round kick. The jamb splintered.

"Oh, boy," Ben said, sighing. "Maintenance is going to have a rag-doll baby. I heard Colonel Duffy assign some guys as building guards for the rest of the night downstairs. I believe I'll let them report your room change in the morning, and I think I'll leave now, Mr. Curtin."

Throwing his gear on one of the easy chairs and whirling in the same motion, Curtin snarled. "Stop calling me mister, goddam it! I thought we were friends!"

Ben stared openmouthed for a moment, then spun and left. Curtin listened to wild laughter recede down the hall, puzzlement adding to his frown. As he turned away, he caught his reflection in the mirror. "You sure as hell don't look like anybody's friend," he said, breaking into a rueful grin.

Businesslike again, he moved the dresser to hold the broken door shut, then crossed the still-darkened room to peer out past the edge of the drapes. Distant flashlights of security personnel marked the widening search. A helicopter swept over from behind the building, the unexpected roar startling. Glare from its searchlight blasted the valley, and what had been pretty in the daylight or soft and secretive in the night turned stark and ugly. Searchers bent away, as if the power of the shaft would crush a man to the ground.

Curtin decided there was no need to concern himself about another attack while all that activity continued. Still, he double-checked his arrangements before turning in. He lay awake for a while, listening to the far-off ruffle of the helicopter.

He woke instantly when the noise disturbed him, completely aware of his surroundings, certain something was out of place. Despite a twisting force in his guts that made him want to roll out of the bed and scramble for cover, he remained absolutely still. All that came to him was a noise, as of a branch rustling on the rough outside wall.

He was five stories up, and there were no trees near the building.

Certain he was alone in the room, he rose swiftly, padding silently to the balcony sliding doors. Cautiously he peeled back the drape until he could see onto the small landing. The night was untroubled by searchers now. A pale moon gave him just enough light to spot the snakelike action of a dangling thin line. Every few seconds it dragged against the wall, making the dry scrape that had wakened him. A figure, a black mass blending into the night, rappelled into view and stepped silently onto the opposite end of the balcony. The person crouched, unmoving, until satisfied it was safe to scuttle to the bottom of the door.

Puzzled, unable to see clearly, Curtin watched. Suddenly he caught a familiar smell. Panic screamed for control of his body at the thought of gasoline being poured into his room, but then he realized his mistake. It was oil, not gasoline. The intruder didn't mean to incinerate him, but to attack from close range, and needed a silent entry.

After lubricating the track, the figure slid the door back. Shadowlike, it entered the room and advanced on the bed, one hand poised at shoulder level. Curtin held his breath, hoping the mussed sheet and blanket would appear like a body long enough to cover his own move.

The figure paused, reached. Curtin pushed off from the wall, forgoing stealth. The momentum of his charge tumbled both of them onto the bed. Forearm across the other's throat, he wedged his shoulder against the attacker's head, forcing the face into the smothering softness of the pillow. In a matter of seconds, there was no further resistance. Curtin reached to switch on the night light. It was enough to see by, but not enough to alert any backup watching from outside.

Lying on the bed, the figure looked unimposing, dressed in a loose black running suit with a pulled-up hood. The decorative red striping was nonreflective, and Curtin admired the foresight of the costume. It was perfect for night work, but until seen under the present conditions, it was no more than expensive exercise clothing.

The figure inhaled deeply and shuddered, fighting to regain consciousness. He rolled it over.

Flor Peralta's eyes fluttered weakly, the arched brows drawn into a small frown, as if she'd just heard a slightly offensive remark. When the eyes opened, they were unfocused, uncomprehending. They snapped to full awareness much faster than Curtin believed possible, and still laboring under the surprise of recognizing her, he barely had time to protect against her next move.

Her forearm slammed against his, interrupting her blow with a short stick about eight inches long and two inches in diameter. She still managed to bang his temple. He grabbed at the weapon while his other hand went directly for her throat and he straddled her, using his weight to hold her to the bed. Even as they strained for the weapon, Curtin marveled that she fought without screaming or crying out. Her efforts were skillful as well, but his superior position and strength finished it quickly, and he ended up holding the club threateningly above her face.

"Relax." The word came on gusting breath. "Quit kicking around or I'll use this on you."

She sneered silently, but he felt muscles loosening. He said, "If I let you up, are you going to try anything?"

"What do you want?"

"What do *I* want? This is *my* room! I didn't sneak in here!"

"I came to help you. You're involved with things you'll never understand, and if you don't get out now, you may never have another chance." She flung back the hood, freeing the lustrous black hair to cascade down her back. "I risked my life because I want to help you, and you tried to—to—"

"I tried to what? You're working up to screaming rape, aren't you?"

"What would anyone call the position you're in right now?"

"Self-preservation, that's what!" Curtin stood clear of her, gesturing warily. "That's a Japanese *yawara* stick, and no simple society tootsie would know how to use it. Don't give me any more cocktail-party revolutionary stories. It insults my intelligence. You could have killed me."

"Don't be dramatic. I know what I'm doing. You only got the better of me because I was careless. Anyhow, what do you expect? What would you do, in my place?"

He touched his head where she'd struck. It responded with an extra throb. "We're not *in* your place, we're in *my* place. You attacked me. I remember."

"I told you I only want to help you. You're in danger."

"Just because someone shot at me? Or because you want to bust my head?"

"Now you're trying to be funny. May I sit up?"

"Forgive me. I'm being a poor host." He pulled up a chair and sat facing her. She dangled her feet off the edge of the bed, completely dismissing everything that had gone before. He went on, "This better be good, lady, or I'll enjoy watching what Chavez does to you."

Briefly, she blanched, then, "Whatever you think of me, you're wrong. You're being used." She glanced down, before meeting his eyes boldly. "Yes, like me. But you risk your life. Robert would never ask that, never accept it. The best way for Senor Chavez to save Robert is to ignore the ransom. Force Red is sure to release him. A man like you, a stranger, a soldier, can only make trouble for everyone."

At his smug disbelief, her eyes flashed warning. "I'm not one of the ruling class who wishes to continue the old ways in Costa Verde, and I hate the communists of Force Red. They're equal evils. When I met Robert in my country, he confided his hopes and fears to me, and I shared my feelings with him. We fell in love."

"But then that silver-tongued devil Bullard came along and sweet-talked you away. He's such a charmer."

"Will you listen? Robert *asked* me to pretend to like Harry. He had a premonition something terrible was going to happen, and he thought Harry might know something about it. He hated asking me to spy, but I was glad— proud—to do it for him.''

Curtin nodded. There was defensiveness in the last words, and it struck him as a good sign. He decided to test her.

''So you end up in bed with Bullard while Robert's being kidnapped. And tonight, just because I'm such a sweetheart, you sneak away from the new boyfriend and rope-walk your way into my bedroom to tell me the story of your life. You're a class act, Flor.''

''Bastard!'' She flew off the bed, standing over him, trembling with fury. ''I don't sleep with him! My rooms are in this building, in the penthouse. There's no guard on your door, but there is on mine. I'm not his mistress, I'm practically his prisoner! If Harry learns what I told you, he'll give my name to the death squads. You don't know him.''

''I don't know you, either, so I have to wonder why I'm getting all this trust and confidence.''

She looked away. ''Robert spoke of you so much I thought of you as an ally. It would destroy him if you were hurt trying to help him. I think you shouldn't try, but I can't stop you. If you persist, I want to help you. I think you're a good man in a treacherous place, without friends. It's different for me. Harry Bullard frightens me, but I can escape.''

Curtin moved to the edge of his chair, closer to her. ''You're certain of that?''

She looked down at her hands, where the fingers formed a writhing tangle.

''Do you believe Bullard's behind this?''

When she shook her head, her hair caught the night light's glow and threw it off in a soft shimmer. ''I don't know. He's part of the power structure in my country, and Robert opposed those people. Both brothers mean to command the Chavez empire. That's a war in itself. I don't want to think Harry would let Robert be kidnapped, or—'' She swallowed, then continued. ''Or killed.''

"Not many men are capable of killing. Not even for all this."

Her eyes were dark and deep, peering up at him through the lashes. "Harry's given men's names to the Costa Verde police. At least two of those men disappeared."

"I see." Curtin breathed deeply, unwittingly drawing in the smell of her perfume. He found himself gazing into her eyes, drifting away from the moment, remembering her soft, supple strength. There was so much more to her than plastic beauty. All wasted, caught in a world of brutality and corrupt power. He told himself he should move, lean away, but he didn't.

"I made a deal with Chavez," he said. "It'll take a few days to put something together, but I'm going in. I'll try to get Robert out."

Tensing, she reached to touch his hand. "You mean a rescue operation? That's insane! They'll kill him!"

"No rescue, unless it's a gift. I'll pay the money and run."

Her hand withdrew, and he damned himself for wishing it was reluctance that slowed it, because he knew it was only preoccupation. Still, for a moment, her eyes changed, seemed to hold a question.

He bolted to his feet, turned away. "So that's where we are. Can you get back to your room okay?"

"Easily. But if you insist on doing this thing, at least let us help you. I'll tell my friends in Costa Verde to make themselves known to you."

"No! I don't want a bunch of excited amateurs around. You tell me how to reach them. If I get desperate enough, I'll call them. They don't call me."

Haughtily, she said, "They'll know who you are an hour after you arrive."

Curtin took her elbow, helped her to her feet and turned off the light. Moving to the window, he spoke over his shoulder. "Maybe. Maybe not." After inspecting the valley for a full minute, he said, "If they want to be helpful, tell them to watch my back and keep out of the way. I'll take care of everything else.'' Then, "I spot two guards. There may be more. Be very quiet. And careful. Your death squads can't do any more harm than a five-story fall.''

So quietly he almost missed it, she slid the door open. Her face was a pale, featureless oval against the darkness. She said, "You shouldn't try so hard to appear the calculating professional, Buck. You say you do this for money, but I know your pay is pocket change to Harry Bullard. You're risking your life for a man you hardly know, might not even recognize today. You say you owe him something, but none of us live without the debts you seem to fear so much. You're trying to own yourself in a world that'll never let you be free.''

"If you say so.''

Ignoring the bored rejection, she went on. "In my country, we admire courage, but we adore mad courage. One of our national heroes is a matador. He always stroked the muzzle of an especially brave bull before the final thrust. A gesture of courage, of gratitude, of madness. It is us.''

"Fascinating. Whose side is your matador on now?''

"Oh, one of his braver bulls gored him to death years ago. That's why you mustn't repeat the story there. They'd never expect you to understand, and they'd think you were mocking them. Maybe one day you'll be that well accepted, but don't risk it.''

"Thanks. I really am grateful. You've taken a helluva chance, coming here. I won't forget it.''

Her laugh was soft, almost a sigh. "Another debt?'' She touched his cheek. "You're a refreshing man. And in spite of yourself, not unlikable.''

Before Curtin could respond, she was outside, climbing. When she disappeared into her room, the line snaked the wall.

Curtin opened his drapes wide and, pulling up a chair, stared into the night.

He wanted to believe her while, at the same time, part

of his mind rebelled at the thought. She'd shown two faces, each as convincing as the other. Was she Bullard's woman? Or Robert's? Was she capable of being any man's partner, or had a world of deceit and treachery so conditioned her mind that she would always be alone?

The last idea was out. A person might survive to her age in Costa Verde without friends, but it was highly unlikely. Even more, it was impossible that she could play tag with a man like Harry Bullard unless she had an edge.

Someone in Chavez's outfit had to be pumping information to her to warn her away from traps.

He jerked upright in the chair, feeling his stomach collapse like a punctured balloon.

Flor knew exactly where to find him. The only person who knew he'd changed rooms was Ben.

Chapter 9

The security men ushered Curtin into Chavez's quarters with routine silent presence. Curtin was no longer impressed.

Chavez, casual in jeans and Western-cut shirt, met him at the door. "Welcome. You slept well?" He indicated the dining room, leading the way.

Curtin said, "Fine, thanks."

Chavez chuckled, deep in his chest. "I think you always sleep lightly but wake rested. You have the look." Curtin searched the heavy features for a hint of double meaning. There was none, and Chavez pulled out a chair for his guest. A small TV, the sound barely audible, glowed from the buffet. Ignoring it, Chavez went on. "My messenger reported you changed rooms. Violently."

"After I'd been ambushed outside your hotel, it seemed like a good idea to avoid being ambushed inside it."

Chavez's smile stiffened. "You have my personal apology."

"I don't blame you for what happened."

"Interesting phrasing. And a more interesting tone of voice." He waited for the waiter to slide platters of ham

73

and eggs in front of them, commenting that he assumed Curtin would enjoy that sort of breakfast. Curtin demonstrated his approval by digging in. Chavez took a few bites, then, with studied unconcern, said, "You suspect my son arranged the shooting, don't you?"

"I think I've got good reason."

The thick shoulders slumped, but suddenly he had eyes for nothing but the television set. Muscles bunched in his jaws as he leaped to raise the volume.

The commentator's cool professionalism riveted them. "Force Red, the revolutionary group claiming to hold Robert Chavez prisoner, issued a communique this morning saying they would delay Chavez's execution three weeks, while the Chavez Corporation collects the gold ransom."

Swiftly, Chavez snapped off the rest of the report. For several seconds he stared at the dead screen, breathing hard, regaining control. "Lying bastards. *They* tried to kill you, not my son. They see you as a threat, an intermediary who may work with an eye toward rescuing Robert. They don't question your courage either, Mr. Curtin. That's why they shoot at your back, from the night."

Curtin shrugged noncommittally, and a taut smile slid across Chavez's face. He said, "Don't worry about the ultimatum. They'll give me all the time I want. The press is giving them superb publicity. They don't call them 'terrorists' now, but 'revolutionaries,' who issue communiques, not demands. Next, Force Red will require the press to identify them as 'government opposition,' and the press will do so, or Force Red will deny them access. Meanwhile, I toy with all of them. The gold is already in hand, thirty-six ingots, each weighing ten pounds."

"It's Robert's life you're playing with!"

"Nonsense. I need time and they need publicity. We understand each other."

Pushing the empty plate away, Curtin said, "I believe that. What's the Costa Verde government going to say about me bringing their enemies three hundred and sixty pounds of gold? That's one helluva payday.''

''At this morning's London price, two million, two hundred forty six thousand, four hundred dollars. If the government learns your identity, it will expel you from the country. If it learns of the existence of the gold, it will confiscate it. Someday, perhaps, I would get it back.''

''I thought so. The government won't allow negotiations with Force Red.''

''Exactly, which is why I've created a cover for you. If you have objections, we'll change it to your specifications.'' He pushed a button on the wall by the television set. A man came in and cleared away the breakfast dishes. As soon as they were alone again, Chavez drew a briefcase from under the table. Opening it, he produced a display of well-traveled documents.

''Everything's in your real name. The government knows no better, and Force Red knows you too well to be fooled by a simple name change or disguise. We need only trick the government for a few days and it'll be over.'' He flipped Curtin a Canadian passport, making a joke of it. ''The new you.''

The picture was his own, the signature a perfect replica. He swallowed a question about the acquisition of the photograph. The papers showed he was self-employed, a dealer in used construction equipment. His offices were in Toronto, and a backlog of correspondence from satisfied customers, dating back almost two years, indicated he'd done business on every continent. It was a thorough job.

When Curtin looked up, Chavez was unfolding a small-scale map showing Costa Verde's border with a neighboring country. He spread it on the table and pointed to an area within a few miles of Costa Verde. ''This land belongs to one of our subsidiary companies. Notice the landing strip. If it's necessary for you to escape by air, this field can be of great importance. As part of your cover, I am positioning crates and material there. Most of the crates are empty, the machinery useless, but it's an easy fly-over for any Costa Verde government official who wants to see proof of this material you claim to be selling. To create some traffic and make it all look real, I've had items staged there and shipped elsewhere."

"What if they run a check on who owns this place?"

"Nothing can be linked to Chavez."

"I should have known."

Chavez's quick smile turned grim. "Until last night, I would have agreed. In fact, I would have bragged."

At the sudden knock on the door, he glanced up with mild surprise before calling for the party to come in. As Bullard stepped into the room, Curtin scooped up the papers and dumped them in the briefcase. Bullard favored him with a sneer before turning to his father.

"The driver we assigned Curtin is missing. His name's Ben Bradley. It looks like he left in the jeep right after the shooting."

Chavez froze, holding himself in check. "Your security precautions are an embarrassment. The man was an agent."

Bullard flushed. "We're checking, but I'm telling you, that's impossible."

"Then why did he run? No, we'll find your man was paid to maneuver Mr. Curtin into position for a Force Red murderer. Where's Duffy?"

"In his office."

"I will go there. You are scheduled to brief Mr. Curtin. Do so." Chavez spun on his heel and left the room, fists bunched at his sides, legs stiff, as if his knees hurt. Curtin made a note to remember the performance. The man was being hit at the heart of his empire, and it was burning him alive. Still, he attacked problems with disciplined control.

Bullard led Curtin through the desks outside the living area and into a luxuriously furnished briefing room. A dozen bulky leather chairs faced a screen wall. Each location featured a table with notepad, pen, and personal controls. A listener could stop film, hold a selected slide, or control an electric pointer to highlight an issue. It was a typical Chavez creation, Curtin decided. It suggested equality by providing everyone with the same set of controls as enjoyed by Chavez himself, while the very richness of the place made it clear exactly who commanded.

As soon as Curtin was seated, the lights died. A colored map of Costa Verde appeared on the screen. Bullard went into a smooth presentation.

"Oriente is the capital of Costa Verde. It's essentially a new city, the country's administrative hub. The old colonial cities are charming; Oriente is overcrowded, hectic, and what little is left of the older part of town is now slums. There's runaway poverty. Unrest breeds faster than the rats. Costa Verde used to have a tourist industry, but the political situation killed it off years ago. There's some spectacular scenery and ancient ruins, but people who wander off looking for those things often turn up dead."

"You think Robert's being held in Oriente?"

"Hard to guess." An electric arrow flitted across the picture. "The country has a Caribbean and a Pacific coast. The borders with neighboring countries run through mountains and jungles with very sparse population. It's perfect guerrilla country. Robert could be out of the country by sea, in one of their upcountry base areas, or he might be in the city."

"The government's looking for him?"

Bullard sped through several intervening photographs, stopping at one of a man in uniform. Curtin's first impression was of a series of edges, a face made of hard angles. He said, "Who the hell is that?"

"Hell, for sure." Bullard spoke with quiet venom. "That's Colonel Sandoval, Minister of Interior Affairs. He dates back to Castro's revolution. He was on the way up, but he got greedy and lost a power struggle. He ran to Costa Verde, where he hired on as a police informant, blowing the whistle on his former leftist buddies. Pretty soon he was an Army officer. Now he controls the national police, the military police, and the national intelligence organization. No one has his power or his pleasure in using it. It can't be proven, but he bosses the death squads. He's in charge of the search for Robert, and he's the man you've got to convince you're a salesman.''

"What can he do to me? Even if I'm negotiating with Force Red, I'm not trying to hurt his government.''

"He won't see it that way.'' Bullard moved into the colored light from the projector. It gave his face an angry, burnt look.

"That doesn't answer my question. What happens if he catches me?''

"We go to full power to get you out as fast as possible.''

" 'We'?''

Bullard smiled thinly. "Even me, Curtin. I don't like you. If Sandoval sets a couple of his zombies to kick the shit out of you, I won't care at all. But I don't want to think of anyone caught in his cellars. Not even you.''

"Heartwarming.''

Bullard rose. "You think I'm kidding?''

Curtin said, "I'm thinking if you scare me off, whoever goes after Robert will be one of your people. If he gets Robert out, Robert's in your debt. And if he fails, there's no Robert to deal with.''

For a long time, Bullard looked as if unsure what to say. Then he said, "I don't need you to succeed or fail at anything. I'm giving you the best briefing I can give you because the Old Man said to. Sit back and learn. If you can.'' He ran back through the pictures to the map of the city.

When Curtin stepped out of the room hours later, he thought of it as escape. His mind reeled with names and faces, hammered into his memory by a demanding, pressing Bullard. It was time to get off alone and review.

A guard directed him to the gym, where Curtin drew running shoes and shorts. The attendant pointed out a trail. "Don't go off cross-country,'' he warned. "First place, you'll get lost, and second place, they're combing the area to find that sniper and the guy who ran off this morning. All hell's broke loose.''

Curtin thanked him and trotted off, exulting in the simplicity of physical effort. He climbed a steep grade to a plateau. On the flat, featureless top, the trail led straight-away to another huge, yawning valley, then paralleled the edge of the near-vertical cliffs. The ground was marked by some folds, and Curtin crested one of them just as a helicopter rattled into sight. It cruised the valley wall, obviously searching, and when the lone pilot glanced up and saw Curtin, he sped toward him. The machine inched closer and closer until Curtin felt forced to stop and wave him away. The pilot, masked by yellow sunglasses, spoke into his microphone, impassive, holding his position, bom-barding Curtin with wind, sand, and dust. A moment later he spoke again, in apparent response, then heeled over into the valley.

Fuming, Curtin continued his run, trying to calm his mind and resume reviewing what Bullard had taught him.

The helicopter streaked for the far side of the valley. It stopped, hovering in the distance at the mouth of a smaller canyon. A figure sprinted from behind some rocks for the greater shelter of a brush-lined creek. Gouts of dirt and dust erupted behind the racing, dodging man. Seconds later the sound of a machine gun reached Curtin. Distance transformed it into a muffled growl. He watched, incredu-lous, as the fugitive ran for his life, narrowly escaping one burst after another, finally reaching the concealing brush.

Like a frustrated wasp, the helicopter prowled the area, slashing at the growth with intermittent fire.

Curtin thought of Ben, pictured him as the man in the valley, and cursed the inhuman determination of the hunt. Then he remembered the bullet from the darkness that so narrowly passed between them and hoped it was the sniper huddled in the scrub.

Curtin sped along the trail, unsure which direction was the quickest way back to the gym. He was delighted to see two camouflage-garbed men, and he waved furiously. They watched patiently until he stopped in front of them.

"Helicopter." Curtin gestured across the valley, sucking gulps of air. "Buzzed me, then crossed the valley. Flushed a man. *Shot* at him! Machine gun!"

One of the men drew the radio from his hip. "The runner was armed?"

"No, for Christ's sake! Your fucking helicopter!"

The men exchanged glances before the first spoke into the microphone. "Base, Patrol Two Bravo, checking in. We have Mr. Curtin on the jogging trail. He reports a helicopter firing at a man in Cotton Valley."

Crackling, the radio said, "Roger. Wait." The two men stepped away, spoke quietly. Curtin chafed for what seemed like minutes until the radio rapped back to life. "Two Bravo, Base. Tell Curtin what he said is being checked and get him out of there. Out."

Embarrassed by the curt orders, the men indicated they would return the way Curtin had come. He offered no argument, partially to avoid a confrontation but primarily because he was anxious to get back and confront Bullard or Chavez—both of whom were waiting.

Both of them waited with Flor when he hurried off the trail.

The two trail-walkers peeled off. Chavez said, "I heard of your report and asked Harry to explain. You saw a training exercise. I'm sorry it seemed like more than that."

"Training? I saw a man running and a chopper shooting at him! What the hell kind of training is that?"

Bullard said, "It may have looked like that, but it was simply target practice. I've got a helicopter standing by to take us out to the gunnery range."

"Let's go."

The aircraft sat on the nearby tennis court. At Bullard's signal, the pilot whisked them to the level of the plateau, then into the valley. Pointing, Curtin directed the flight.

From more than a mile away he saw he was being made a fool of. Cardboard targets littered the ground, white torsos with black bull's-eye centers like outsized belly buttons. No evidence would exist to contradict Bullard's story. Still, Curtin stubbornly insisted the pilot land far enough from the actual site to avoid obscuring bullet damage with prop wash.

Walking to the targets, he listened to Bullard's glib explanations. At the same time, he saw Flor standing alone beside the helicopter. She had started the trip wearing a scarlet head scarf, but now she gripped it in both hands, worrying it into knots while she scanned the nearby hills.

Curtin lifted a target with his toe. The earth was freshly raw under it, although no holes marred the paper. Looking closer, he saw what might have been blood speckling the rocks. Hopelessly, he acknowledged that even if he could establish that it was human blood, there was no one to tell, much less anyone who'd believe him in the face of so much contradictory testimony. And in that case, he decided, he might as well play along and hope someone would relax and make a mistake.

He said to Bullard, "I hate to admit it, but it looks like you were right. Even so, I think it wasn't too bright to pull one of your helicopters for gunnery practice when you've got a dangerous intruder running loose, plus one of your security people missing. That's a waste of valuable search equipment."

Bullard smiled. "The same chopper's shooting somewhere else right now. He'll cover the whole ranch. I want that young thief and whoever shot at you to think about an armed chopper. I want them to know we play for keeps."

The tone tugged at Curtin's understanding. "Do the police know you're running a shoot-on-sight operation here?"

Chavez said, "They know nothing of it."

"Nothing?"

"They've been told one of our men stole a jeep and left with it. No one has spoken of the sniper, and if the thief mentions him, we'll all deny it."

"Like hell we will. He tried to kill me."

"And he'll pay for it. Nevertheless, once that story breaks, you'll be identified. Then the mission to release Robert will go to someone else, perhaps less competent than yourself.'' As he spoke, Chavez sidestepped, a seemingly innocent movement, but as he finished, he was able to cut his eyes at Bullard without being seen by anyone but Curtin. The message was all too clear. Curtin headed for the helicopter.

Flor stood between him and the machine, and she fell in beside him. After making sure they couldn't be overheard, he fastened a hard look on her and said, ''I've been watching you. You're really spooked about all this.''

Eyes hot, she said, ''You're walking into a trap. Someone tried to kill you only hours ago. You must protect yourself.''

''Like, I should tell your friends every move I make? You know what occurred to me while we were looking over this little show of Bullard's? It dawned on me that Ben was as close to those rounds as I was. That's something to think about, isn't it?''

They were at the helicopter, and as he reached for her elbow to help her in, she jerked it free, turning away with a wounded look. She had difficulty eliminating it before Chavez and Bullard arrived. During the ride back to the base she avoided any contact. Once they landed and were clear of the helicopter's racket, she excused herself and left quickly.

Bullard laughed quietly, a possessive pride in his expression. ''She's a fire-eater,'' he explained for Curtin's benefit, ''but it's all theory. When she comes up against reality, she can't take the pressure.''

They walked toward the gym, and Curtin was wondering if Bullard might not be right. The night before, Flor had indeed failed in her attack, as harmless as she claimed it to be, and the latest developments obviously had her rattled.

Another, more sinister, possibility existed. Was Ben the helicopter's quarry? Did Bullard suspect he was working for Flor, as Curtin himself did? If so, Bullard would never have him killed unless he already knew everything Ben could tell him.

Flor would already have come to the same conclusion. "Mr. Curtin?"

He forced a smile. "Sorry, Mr. Chavez. Thinking. What was it?"

"I said I have to speak to you alone."

"*I* heard you," Bullard said. He was livid, torso thrust forward, hands half-raised. "Why don't you tell me to my face you don't trust me? You've let him convince you I don't want Robert free. Nobody wants him out of there more than I do, can't you understand that? I want him where I can beat him into the goddam ground! I don't want help from anyone! I'll take over this company with my own two hands!" He pushed his fists forward threateningly, and Curtin was impressed by Chavez's unblinking composure.

Bullard went on. "I'm going in with Curtin. I want to guarantee he doesn't do something stupid and risk Robert or the gold."

Curtin opened his mouth to speak, and Chavez cut him off with a swift look. Then, turning from one to the other, he said, "The responsibility for Robert, your lives, the gold—all is mine. This is what will be done. The gold will be placed on a ship in New Orleans. Harry, you will stay with it. The safety and delivery of our gold is your responsibility. Mr. Curtin will make arrangements with Force Red. Each of you has your task. You will execute it according to my instructions. Is that clear?"

Curtin wanted to cheer. Bullard was out, saddled with a job that would keep him far from Costa Verde until the last possible moment.

So why did he grin as soon as Chavez turned his back?

Chapter 10

The hostility hovering over Chavez's dinner table reminded Curtin of a thicket of interwoven secrets, not only ready to hold a stranger out, but equally capable of trapping him. In keeping with the image, Chavez was the only one trying to make conversation, the deep voice ominously heavy.

Oddly, it was Flor who contributed most to the tension. After two powder-dry martinis, she practically assumed control of the wine at the table, frowning impatience until empty bottles were replaced. She picked at her food. While the others ate, she stared into space, shifting in her chair, rapping irritable rhythms on the table.

When Curtin and Bullard weren't watching her with nervous anticipation, they were measuring each other. Even Chavez was affected, eventually falling silent.

With clear relief, he raised the last of his wine. "To the end of our final meal together before Robert is free." The men raised their glasses. Flor stifled a yawn before joining them.

Replacing her glass, she said, "None of you can understand how desperate I am to see Robert released. Still, I think you are all fools.'' She paused for the murmur to stop, then added, ''I am constantly assured that 'the people' are the power in my country. If that is so, and if Robert is so popular with 'the people,' why do they support this Force Red that kidnapped him? They're fools. Ignorant peasants. If they gave half as much support to the legitimate leaders in my country as they do the criminals of Force Red, we would have peace within a month. Isn't that right, Mr. Curtin, Mr. Voice of America?'' She squinted in her effort to focus.

''Not me. I won't argue about your country's politics.''

''In other words, if you said anything, it would be an argument, right? Why, I believe you're another people-lover under all the macho posturing. Will you ask those 'people' to help you? How, gringo? You don't even speak our language! What good can you do?''

''I can do what I'm supposed to do, which is wait to be contacted and exchange the gold for Robert. That's it.''

''I asked you—how? In English?''

''I know enough about your customs to get by.''

A minute tightening at the corner of her eyes revealed he'd struck home. ''The government can't let you succeed. They must never allow negotiations with terrorists, so they must watch all foreigners constantly. It's Force Red's fault. The only way we can protect ourselves is with strict controls. You will fail, and Robert will be the one who pays. My country will be shamed.''

Curtin felt his neck and throat heating, a sure sign he was getting too angry to be cautious. He overrode the warning. ''If your government gave a damn about Robert's life, they'd deal with anyone to save him. And if they gave a damn about their own people, they'd put an end to the death squads.''

Before Flor could respond, Bullard joined in. ''No legitimate government invites kidnappers to the conference table. Everyone seems to forget, Force Red does some death-squad work of its own, and the worst man they can point to in the government uses techniques he learned in Cuba.''

Feeling the last shreds of temper fraying under the weight of useless argument, Curtin reached inside himself for control. He shook his head. "I said I wouldn't argue politics. I'll do my job as best I can. That's it.''

"God, how blue collar." Flor's contempt was monumental. "Just when you were approaching genuine thought, you got frightened and backed away. Depressing.'' She rose, swaying despite bracing herself with both hands. "Mr. Chavez, Robert's only hope is the legal government of Costa Verde. This gringo mercenary is endangering your son and your wealth.''

Chavez remained unmoved. He said, "I understand your feelings, Miss Peralta. We will discuss the matter tomorrow. When you feel better.'' He paused before speaking the last word, an almost imperceptible hesitation. Flor reacted instantly.

"I want to return to my room," she told Bullard with frosty dignity. "I'm very tired and the wine is making me unwell.''

"Have some coffee. You'll feel better in a minute.'' Bullard glared at Curtin, who returned a pleasant smile.

"I want to go *now*, Harry." It was a plea and a demand. Bullard could only get to his feet. In a last effort to eliminate private discussion between Curtin and Chavez, he said, "Curtin, you ought to come with us. My father's more worn out than he'll admit.''

Chavez said, "You two go along. I have some things I want to tell Mr. Curtin. We'll only be a few minutes.'' The last was conciliatory, aimed at Bullard, who took Flor's arm and almost pulled her along with him.

"A taste of brandy?" Chavez moved to the bar cart. "Perhaps some B and B?''

"I don't think so," Curtin said. "I've got some things to iron out with you.''

"You should have that drink, then. At least you can handle it.''

"We shouldn't be too hard on Flor. She's under a lot of strain."

"My son was right about her. She doesn't stand up to tension." He waved at the ranked bottles. "Your pleasure?"

"The B and B."

Chavez nodded and poured, handing over the glass with a flourish. "Enjoy it. You won't find much in Costa Verde. What are these requirements you want to discuss?"

"No discussion. We don't discuss my requirements, any more than we discuss yours."

Eyebrows rising, Chavez waited. Curtin continued. "I want you to pull whatever strings it takes for me to get a new refrigerator into Costa Verde. I'll plant my own radio in it. That'll be my communications link direct to you. I'll transmit at ultra-high speed—burst transmissions—varying the schedule and frequencies. You'll get a master sheet and instructions, registered mail, and I'll express you a duplicate of my comm gear before I leave."

"How will you reach me in an emergency?"

"If I don't call according to schedule, you'll know I've got a problem. If I miss two days in a row, you'll know it's a serious problem. And what will you do about it?"

Chavez moved in his chair, sipped his drink. "We have friends in Costa Verde. And I'll go to D.C., to the State Department, personally."

"Wonderful. About the same thing Bullard said." When Chavez made blustering noises, Curtin waved him to silence. "Don't bother. We both know it's a crapshoot. I'm being paid to take the chance."

"You're determined to confine any definition of yourself to money, aren't you?"

"That's my next point. I need a bank account in Toronto, one I can use for expenses. Fifty thousand will be about right."

"Only fifty thousand? Am I buying the economy rescue mission?" Chavez grinned at his own sarcasm, but before Curtin could answer, he said, "It'll be in place this time tomorrow. I'll check it daily to keep it at that level.

Anything else? How will you get this marvelous refrigerator to Costa Verde?"

"I need someone who'll pick it up for me and a furnished house to move it into. If I'm going to look like a businessman, I have to look permanent. I'll air-ship it to New Orleans and check to see Bullard forwards it while I'm there."

"You're going to New Orleans? Why?"

"I want to see that gold before I go in."

For a long breath, Chavez was stone-faced, Indian-black eyes alight. Curtin met the gaze, absorbed it. In the end, Chavez laughed. First, a smile. Then a light chuckle. Laughter built up in him like dammed water before exploding into the room and subsiding. He got to his feet. "Good for you, Buck. Goddam it, that's what I'd do, in your shoes. I knew I picked the right man. I'll start arranging your requirements."

He was humming under his breath as Curtin let himself out.

When Curtin stepped into the huge lobby on the ground floor, rain sluiced across the flagstone courtyard, turning it into a frothing lake. The wind moaned at the corners of the building. A jeep waited in the storm, topless, the floorboards awash. The driver lounged against the wall, waiting for him. At his approach, the man drew his rain gear tight and stepped outside, leaving Curtin with no choice but to follow.

He was soaked before he could sit down, wind-chilled to the bone. At one point on the trip a brilliant flash of lightning caught the driver facing Curtin, and he was sure he saw a malicious smile suddenly disappear. Gritting his teeth, Curtin drew his body into the tightest possible knot and waited out the ride.

At the living quarters, he eased stiff joints into movement, stepping behind the driver to jump to the ground next to him. Too wet to care further about the rain, he leaned into the man's face, enjoying the change of expression from sly satisfaction to studied unconcern. Water sprayed off Curtin's lips as he spoke. "You got rain gear. I didn't get any. There's no top on the jeep. You think that's funny?"

The man half-smiled, reaching for the gearshift. Curtin grabbed a handful of his jacket, yanking his torso sideways so he dangled helplessly. The man's right hand fumbled at his holstered pistol.

Curtin jabbed a thumb under the man's eye. "You touch that .45 and you won't be able to see to shoot it." The hand crept up to the steering wheel.

"Whose idea was this?"

"Ours." The man sneered.

"Everybody agreed to shit on Mr. Chavez's personal guest? How about I give him your name?"

"Give it. We figured you'd go whining to the Old Man, so I took the detail. I'm leaving the company anyhow."

"Why? What'd I do to you people?"

"It's you and your buddy, Ben Bradley. He's a spy."

"For who? How d'you know?"

Uncertainty twisted the man's face. "We know. And we know how to handle finks. The ride was just to let you know what we think of you."

"Then you haven't found Ben."

"We will, don't worry. And even if he gets past us, he'll get busted for stealing the jeep as soon as the cops catch him."

Curtin let go. The driver hoisted himself back upright and shrugged his jacket into place. Curtin said, "What bothers me is that Ben probably thought of you all as his friends. Now, when he may be in real trouble, you're calling him names. What a bunch of assholes."

Once more the driver moved to shift gears. Curtin reached past him and pulled the keys out of the ignition. As the man watched in wide-eyed disbelief, Curtin threw them as far as he could. Jittering with indecision, the man tried to make up his mind if he should take on Curtin or hunt for the keys. With a muttered curse, he elected the latter, scrambling out the passenger side of the jeep. While he raced off into the darkness, Curtin jerked the microphone

from the radio and dropped it on the ground. Walking
away, he stopped, returning to pick it up. He bounced it in
his hand then strolled to the front of the vehicle and used
it to smash the headlights. Satisfied, he whistled cheerfully
on his way into the building, the tune distorted to unrecogniz-
ability by the rain.

Two guards at the elevator took in his sopping clothes
and squishing shoes and tried unsuccessfully to hide amusement that was already fading to puzzlement as the elevator
doors closed on the still-whistling Curtin. In his room,
Curtin looked out the window and was rewarded with the
sight of three flashlights, instead of one, probing the brush
for the lost keys.

A hot shower warmed him quickly, and putting on the
robe supplied by his host, he poured himself a light drink
and settled in to relax before going to bed. The TV set
provided an all-sports channel, and almost as an afterthought,
he turned the easy chair so he could watch the still-broken
door and see the football game at the same time.

Even so, he almost missed the stealthy movement of the
door's opening. When he did notice, he assumed it was the
guards, ready to escalate the evening's unpleasantness. He
jerked the door open, fist cocked.

Flor gasped and staggered back, hand to mouth.

Sagging against the jamb, he sighed. "You have a
problem with entrances, lady. Can't you just knock, just
once?"

She hurried past him, beckoning to have the door closed.
When he was too slow, she stamped her foot at his delay.

"What's it this time, Flor? More lectures on Costa
Verde's politics?"

"I was acting! I told you about my relationship with
Harry. I have to make him believe I'm completely on his
side. Can't you make sure no one can just walk in?"

While he maneuvered the bureau into place against the
door, he said wearily, "You knocked out your guard and
crept down here to tell me you and Harry aren't this year's
Magic Couple?"

"There are two guards, so they can cover each other.

They're in the lobby, watching the stairwell and the elevator.'' She made a face. "None of this is important. I came to tell you that things are worse. There's been a terrible argument. Harry and his father. They shouted at each other, dreadful things! Harry says he's going to Costa Verde before you get there, and Chavez tried to stop him.''

" 'Tried'? Bullard's setting me up!''

"It's possible.'' There was genuine concern in her face. "What you are doing for Robert is wonderful, an act of brotherhood, but now, with Harry going to Costa Verde ahead of you, there's a new dimension. You must refuse.''

"If he sets a trap for me, he risks getting Robert killed. Other people might be exposed to either Force Red or Sandoval. Is he capable of that sort of ruthlessness?''

Flor looked at her feet. Her words came in a pained voice. "I don't know. He is very determined.'' Suddenly she stiffened, faced him with her chin up. "You're not like us. Something inside is eating your heart. Chavez says you're brave. Harry thinks you're an opportunist. I think Chavez understands you better than Harry. I think he fears you a little bit. You want to trust other people, and that mystifies us. It's why I trust you.''

"I don't want anyone's trust. I've said I'll do my job. Leave me alone!''

"And if you persist, you will probably be killed. For a friendship all but forgotten over ten years? No. There's something more.''

"Leave it at that. Leave me alone.''

She cocked her head to one side, examining him. She spoke softly, almost to herself. "Maybe I understand you better than them, after all.'' Pacing, hands flying in quick, hard gestures, she said, "Ben was my ally, my source of information about this organization. He was my only hope of knowing if Harry was involved in Robert's kidnapping or meant to interfere with his release.''

"What did Ben tell you? Where is he now?''

"I don't know where he is. He never reported any

evidence involving Harry with the kidnapping. If he learned anything before he left, we had a place to leave messages. There was nothing.''

''What did he *believe?*''

''He suspected Harry. Very much.''

''And you?''

''Harry is ruthless. In a fight, he might kill a man, even Robert. I can't believe he'd try to kill a man from the dark.''

''But you think he'd arrange something for me.''

Once again, she faced him, erect. ''Or me, Buck Curtin. Believe that. If he discovers what I'm doing—'' She broke off, her unseeing gaze fastened on the frantic action of the television picture.

A chill clenched the muscles of Curtin's back. ''That sounded almost like you're anticipating more risk.''

She refused to look at him. ''When he goes to Costa Verde, I will go with him.''

''You've traveled with him before.'' He remembered the scented scarf in Bullard's plane. The image lent impetus to his hand as he twisted the television set off.

''Yes. This time will be different. You see, Colonel Sandoval already distrusts me. The only way I can feel safe in Costa Verde is under someone's protection, and the only way I can guard against possible treachery from Harry is to be with him. It's all very convenient, isn't it?''

''Flor, that's crazy. I mean, you think I'm taking a chance, but it's a fighting chance. You lose, no matter what. You can't let yourself be used like that. You'll never forgive yourself.''

When she turned, her face was sad and shy at the same time. ''In the real world one learns to forgive one's self before all others. All my life I have watched the compromises, the betrayals. Many of my friends—and enemies—have 'disappeared.' I have seen their bodies on the trash heaps, garbage fought over by the *zopilotes*, the buzzards. From that world, we must create freedom and justice. I can forgive myself for sleeping with a man I despise if it brings us one step closer to that end." She was trembling as she finished, her face flushed, arms rigid at her sides.

Curtin raised a hand as though to reach out to her. It was a slow, tentative gesture, and he stopped it. His pose was almost as awkward as hers. He said, "God, Flor, I'm sorry."

Her first tears welled through an unchanging expression, as if denying them would make them go away. The attempt failed, and the flow increased. Then, as silently as the weeping started, the sobs came. There was no denial at that, and her will deserted her. She swayed, drawing her fists to her chin, and sagged, was falling as Curtin caught her. He held her, making comforting sounds. In a while the racking crying stopped. She looked up at him. "Thank you."

"Hush. A bad moment finished. Don't think about it."

Her smile was wan. "Can we ever stop thinking?"

He looked down at her uptilted face. "No. Not really." Without meaning to, he bent to her, kissed her. She recoiled at first, and the muscles of his arms tightened in reflex, imprisoning her. He lifted his head almost immediately. "That wasn't right," he said. "I didn't plan it."

She stopped him with a finger to his lips. "I know. And for a moment, I stopped thinking. So you were wrong. We can stop."

He laughed, and when he realized he still held her in his arms, he told himself it was necessary, for her sake. And then he realized her weight against him was subtly different than a need for support. He ran his hand across the graceful curve of her neck, continued the movement forward to cup her chin. When he kissed her, it was with intent. More than physical intimacy, it was a message, one that soon became a demand.

Once more she resisted initially, then returned his passion with her own. He scooped her off the floor and she lay back against him, searching his face as they moved to the bed. She smiled, an enigmatic expression that somehow mingled joy and sorrow. One hand reached to stroke his cheek. "Poor *gringo*," she said. "Poor dreamer."

As he lay down with her, she caught his wrists in a fierce grip. Her eyes pleaded. "Don't tell me you love me, Buck, please. For now, no dreams. We must be honest, be what we are. Help me. Help me be alive."

He kissed her eyes closed, and turned out the light.

Chapter 11

Flor woke abruptly. She smiled, pulling the bedclothes up under her chin, then stretched slowly, languorously. Turning on her side, she discovered the coffee service with its candle-warmed carafe on the night table. She filled a cup and sat up to drink it. The open drapes revealed a day so bright the hills glowed with life. Leaves sparkled in the breeze.

"Oh." Curtin stopped in the doorway. For a moment they stared at each other uncertainly. Clutching at the towel around his middle with one hand, he gestured awkwardly with the other, burdened by his leather shaving kit. "I didn't think I was loud enough to wake you." He hurried to sit on the edge of the bed, dropping the kit to frame her face in his hands. "Don't go to Costa Verde," he said, his expression as bluntly concerned as his words.

"No." Shaking her head free, she made a sweeping gesture that included both of them and where they were. "What we had was beautiful, but it was wrong. Now we—what is it you say?—'do the job,' right? Yes, now we

97

do the job. We go back to being alone, to all the things we must be.''

He kissed her, a lingering contact that spoke of parting rather than union. ''I hoped you'd say something like that. Was afraid you would, too. Crazy.'' He rose, looking down at her like a man memorizing something he means to remember under any circumstances. Suddenly he grinned. ''I wish you could see yourself, that beautiful body scrunched up under rumpled blankets.''

Smiling back, she said. ''That's me. What you see is what you *think* you see.''

Each winced as the intended witticism missed. Flor recovered first. She laughed, but strain discolored the sound. ''I can never tell a joke correctly before my second cup of coffee. Sorry. Turn around so I can get something on.''

He obliged without comment, gathering up his clothes and retreating to the bathroom. Shortly, he knocked. At her ''Come in!'' he did, then, noting she was completely dressed, he said, ''You don't have to run away. You've got time to shower, if you want. I won't bother you.''

Quick discomfort twisted her studied calmness, and Curtin grimaced. ''That sounded mean. Everything's coming out wrong.''

''You're trying too hard, trying to pretend we can go back to where we were, that we can behave exactly as we have in the past.''

''I'd like to turn that into something wonderfully erotic, but even jokes are out of bounds for us, aren't they? You go on. I'll see you upstairs.''

''No! If I'm alone in the hall and someone sees me, I'll claim I came down to see if you wanted to go to breakfast. You *are* eating with Chavez again this morning?''

''Yes. And I may not see you before I leave. Good luck.''

She hurried to the door. Halfway out, she stopped, as if remembering something. She turned to face him, emotion crossing her features in waves. *"Y tu. Mil gracias, amigo. Bueno suerte siempre."*

He shrugged, and she translated. "And you. A thousand thanks, friend. Good luck always. But we must both never forget—the two people who spent the night here no longer exist." Then she was gone.

Curtin stared at the empty doorway for a long time before launching himself at the closet, where he threw clothes into his bag as if burying something.

A different driver took him to the headquarters building. They rode in an envelope of cold politeness.

On entering Chavez's quarters, Curtin said, "This is our last chance to talk until I wrap things up. I don't want anyone calling me, not for any reason. Is there anything you want to tell me before I shove off?"

Chavez took his arm, led him to the breakfast. "We'll eat. Then we'll talk."

Curtin kept pace with Chavez's small talk, noting the older man's nervousness, wondering how to bring up the matter of Bullard's proposed trip without compromising Flor. Chavez saved him the trouble.

"Harry is determined to go to Costa Verde before arranging the ship to transport the gold. There are people working for us he thinks have been selling off our land to the peasants at too fast a rate. In addition, he wants his own people in place, because he expects to have to conduct our operations even after Robert's release. He's right. Robert will need recuperation time."

"That's bullshit." Curtin drained the last of his coffee. "Your boy Harry's making a move to take over. What a sweetheart."

"Perhaps. They play hard. But Robert won't let Harry get away with anything. He won't be *that* exhausted when he's freed." He chuckled, the indulgent father.

"Bullard going to Costa Verde is dangerous, for Robert and for me. I know damned well he'd set me up in a minute, and I don't think he'd mind if Force Red punched Robert's ticket, either."

"Absurd. Force Red won't kill Robert unless they're convinced they won't be paid. Then, of course, they may kill him to retain their image with the population. As for killing you, why should they?"

"Thanks for the ego pop. I needed that."

"Nothing personal. You must see the entire board, not just your own pieces. Harry is helpless. If the government suspects him of even contacting Force Red, they'll deport him. If Robert's friends suspect him of obstructing the ransom effort, they'll destroy him."

"You say he's boxed out, but he's still going. Something smells." Curtin got to his feet. "We'll see what happens. Remember what he said when that chopper was shooting up the place—about playing for keeps? You tell Harry the new boy understands. I'm going way out on a limb on this one, and I'm nervous. If I think Harry's screwing me over, I'll blow him up."

"Blow—" The cold plainness stunned Chavez. He recovered quickly, signaling his willingness to understand by tenting his fingers in front of him and lowering his voice. "I've seen tension like this before in men of action. You don't have the mentality that examines and reexamines forevermore. No, you make your plan and proceed." He approached to plant his hands on the younger man's shoulders. "I know you. You've agreed to work for me, and now your loyalty is tied up with me as well as with Robert. We're much alike, you and I. Primitives, with a code that's as harsh with us as it is with our enemies. Given a few different turns of the dice, we could be living reversed roles."

Stepping back, Curtin smiled crookedly. "Maybe something in what you say. See you in a couple of weeks."

Chavez saluted gravely as Curtin walked away.

Curtin's departure, the lone passenger in the corporate jet, was uneventful, although this time he was sure he saw at least two antiaircraft positions. He decided they were antiterrorist equipment, a reaction to the threat of small aircraft as suicide bombers. It was only another example of Chavez's skill at anticipating the moves of his opposition.

But even Chavez could screw up. The sniper proved that. So did Ben Bradley.

Thinking of the sniper and terrorism wakened him to the fact that he could be considered at least a terrorist supporter by the government of Costa Verde. It jolted him upright. Not only that, they'd see any attempt to free Robert by force as an armed raid. They wouldn't waste much time on legal arrest formalities, not if half of what Bullard said about Sandoval was true. And the prospect of what might happen to him if he was captured alive didn't want thinking about.

Nevertheless, it was something that interfered with his attempted planning during the remainder of the trip.

As soon as he landed in San Diego and reclaimed his camper, he drove to the hospital. George and John lay in adjoining beds, firing insults at each other and the two fighters they were watching on television. It was obvious they each favored a different one, with the result that every punch generated vehement positive and negative comments. Before they saw him, Curtin said, "Whoever shot you missed your lungs, I can tell that," and George instantly flicked the set off.

John said, "Hey, welcome home, Buck. How'd the trip go?"

"Forget the trip. How are you two?"

"No sweat." George pointed at his legs. "I'm probably gonna have a limp. I'll get me a cane, look distinguished."

"Bullshit," John said. "You'll look like a punchy old bum."

George made a face for Curtin. "Bird-legged bastard. Never thought I'd envy him them pipe-stem legs, but they only nicked him."

John grinned satisfaction.

"How long before you get out?"

"Not soon enough." Both men were suddenly serious,

and Curtin felt a prickling sensation on the back of his neck. He waited, and George retrieved a letter from the bedside table. He extended it silently, and Curtin read.

When he finished, he crumpled it. "So they mean to kill you if you mess around in their sleazy politics, do they?"

Gesturing sharply, John said, "That's just to get our attention. All those outfits talk like that, Buck. But what bothers us is they know who you are, and they know you're coming to bail this Robert out. We think they mean it when they say they'll burn you and him both if things don't go just their way. Get out of this shit, will you?"

"What about the guys who shot you up?"

George raised his torso. "We don't know who they are. Your going down there only puts you out on a limb. If we can let it go, so can you." His laugh was unusual, piercing. "Look at us. What choice do we have."

Curtin shook his head. "It's a go. Maybe we get lucky, square everything."

Something moved in George's eyes. He sagged back on his bed, staring at the ceiling. John tilted his head toward his partner, then looked at Curtin. The long, hard face was troubled.

"You guys can help, if you want," Curtin said, and George looked at him suspiciously, as if anticipating a crumb of sympathy. Curtin hurried on. "I'll need the best electronics man you can find. I need to have a couple of radios built. They've got to get past customs. Trick stuff."

"What's the scoop?" George was even more suspicious now.

"You know better than that. Can you find me someone?"

"Jesus Christ, Buck, we're not magicians!"

"I don't want magic, I want an e-tech. I thought you knew people." He made a move toward the door.

George snorted. "We'll find someone."

"Tomorrow. Day after, at the latest. And get me Rochambeau."

"Aww, Buck." John's face was a map of disapproval. "The Roach? What d'you want with that maniac?"

"He knows weapons better than anyone I ever saw, he speaks perfect Spanish, and he's crazy. This operation's going to need lots of crazy before it's over."

They were arguing over first use of the phone as Curtin left.

He enjoyed the drive home, anticipating his arrival. Right after the divorce he'd let the place slide. It paralleled his personal skid into disrepair. The very rural environment that gave it a sense of sanctuary lent itself to not caring. It took a while before he realized that not having neighbors to offend was a crutch he leaned on too heavily. And the parties got a little out of hand sometimes, too. They featured another set of acquaintances, bad company, part of a behavior pattern that was a mixture of self-indulgence, self-pity, and not a little self-destruction.

That was all over now. True, the lawn fronting the rich brown of the A frame looked more like a grazed meadow than a putting green, but the vegetable garden was neat, and the flowers were healthy and colorful.

Nevertheless, he frowned as he swung off the road. His expression was positively forbidding by the time he parked. The red sports car in his driveway was a symbol of those bad times, and the woman who owned it was the very essence of the type who helped men kill themselves. It was his recognition of his headlong, unreasoning lust for her, and her voracious appetite for his blind need, that started him back to life.

He walked to the house with the hesitance of a man confronting something potentially too strong for him.

"Deb!" he called. No answer came immediately, and he raised his voice to a louder pitch. "Deb! Quit clowning around! Where the hell are you?"

An indistinguishable cry came from the back of the place, and he hurried through the house to the glass door leading from the kitchen to the large deck. Before he got there, he knew what he'd find, alerted by wisps of steam outside drifting past the window.

The blonde woman lounging in the spa was wearing a

bright smile and a gold chain bracelet. Lush, pink-tipped breasts bobbed just below the surface of swirling water that clothed her nakedness in enticing patterns of shifting light and shadow. Curtin concentrated on her eyes, blue and sparkling, like ice chips mired in cotton candy.

"It'll take ten minutes to unpack, Deb. I want you out of here before I'm done."

She patted the surface of the water beside her. "Come in with me. It'll relax you, and you look like you need it. You're home early. Something go wrong?"

"How long have you been here? How'd you know I was coming back today?"

"Coming back? From where?"

"I was out of town. I just got back."

She shrugged extravagantly, lifting the breasts to the surface for a tantalizing exposure. "I didn't even know you were on a trip. I thought it was just another workday. I want to talk about us, so I came over. Figured I'd be here when you got home."

"We don't have anything to talk about."

She smirked up at him through her eyelashes. "So we don't talk. Not right away, anyhow. Like I said, you look strung. Come on in and we'll take care of that."

He turned to leave and she stood up, held out her hands to him. "It doesn't have to be like that. We can make things the way they were at first, the good times."

"We provided a service for each other." He walked toward the kitchen. Her voice followed him, rising to a screech. "You still don't give an inch, you hardass! Living with you must have been a nightmare for your wife, man. I can really relate, you know? Like why she dumped you."

Curtin whirled. Deb raised her arms to cover herself and slipped back into the protective water. "I didn't mean it that way, Buck. I mean, your eyes get all squinched up and you lean at a person like you were accusing them of something. It's scary. I never know what to tell you when you're like that."

"The truth."

Curtin hurt inwardly at the contradiction. A man who slept with a prisoner's woman had no right to speak of truth.

No! That was an honest thing, a sharing!

Was it so few hours ago?

He went back to the camper.

When he reentered with his gear, she waited in T-shirt and shorts. He stifled a grin at her fake innocence, as transparent as the wet clothing plastered to her body. Producing two tall glasses of beer from the cabinet behind her, she held one out to him. "Truce," she said, smiling. Curtin sighed and took it.

After her first sip, she said, "You're right. It's over. We'd hate each other again in no time. To happy endings, okay?"

"Good." After draining his glass, Curtin put it on the coffee table. Deb finished hers. "See you, Buck."

He waited until he heard the small car squeal out of the driveway before starting to unpack. It was only minutes before he was done, and he wandered out to the kitchen to fix a snack.

He pulled out a slab of Swiss and the butter, took a loaf of bread from the freezer and dropped a couple of slices in the toaster. He smiled to himself while he sliced the cheese. Deb was the one who taught him to freeze the bread, because a person living alone has a problem with the stuff going stale before it gets used. When the toast popped up, he was ready with the butter already on the knife.

When he bent over to look into the refrigerator for the mustard, the smell of the food struck him like a club, and he wobbled on his heels when he straightened. He steadied himself with a hand on the door, wondering what was wrong. His stomach heaved, his knees buckled out of control. The counter slammed his chin on his way to the kitchen floor.

Rough hands grabbed him under his arms, flipped him

over on his back. Something metallic cracked against his teeth, pried his jaws apart. He tried to clear his vision, to see who was doing this to him, but the world was a smear of shifting, boiling colors. His nose was pinched shut, and a burning, choking liquid was poured into his mouth. Reflexively, he swallowed, and when his stomach tried to reject the stuff, his mouth was held shut until it was accepted. Twice more he went through the same process, and by then even his drugged brain identified the whiskey for what it was.

Then he was being dragged by the heels, head bumping over the juncture between the back door and the deck. The chlorine smell of the water and Deb's lingering perfume were overwhelming. Whoever pulled him to the deck undressed him. He tried to shout for help as he felt himself being rolled into the spa. He heard a faint, sickly noise and wondered if it was himself.

The water provided some relief, and for a moment he was thinking with some clarity.

He was too weak to fight. He had to look like a man drowning.

A push on the back of his head sent him under and provided his one chance at survival. A quick flutter of his hands aimed him at the drain. He held his breath until he felt the outlet under his nose. There was a space there. If he was very careful, he could take in sufficient air to live. Pushing his forehead against the edge of the tub, he strained to focus his reeling mind on the tiny actions suddenly so vastly important.

One breath. Out slowly. Slowly! Mix it with the bubbles from the water jets. Breath in. Don't hurry!

Again. Careful! Don't vomit! Oh, God, don't vomit! Breathe out.

Too fast, you inhaled too fast! You're going to choke!

Footsteps. Over the growl of the pump, vibrating through the plastic walls and the water, the thud of running feet.

Leaving!

But how many of them had there been?

Were they really footsteps?

No.

How could he be so stupid? Must have fallen asleep, been dreaming. Mortar rounds, it was. Incoming, and he hears footsteps. At least it was over. Safe to get out of the hole, go check on the troops.

How'd he get so tired?

Slick damned foxhole. Got the top half hanging out, anyhow. Take a break, haul the old legs up later.

Mortars. Footsteps. The guys'd laugh their ass off at that one.

Now what noise? Roaring, pounding. Head. Heart. Can't breathe.

Can't breathe!

Chapter 12

Darkness.

Fear blasted energy through Curtin's veins, and he managed to lift his head.

Only blackness touched his eyes. His mind, trapped in throbbing pain, fought to identify something, anything, to reassure itself that it lived, that the enveloping void was not death.

The drumming rush of water triggered memory, told him where he was, but he had no idea how he came to be there, or why. He turned his head once more, and this time tearing spasms rolled through his stomach and he was violently ill. Helpless, he shuddered through each wave of nausea, hoping for the release of unconsciousness.

The attack was over, leaving him gasping for breath, when the slow-speaking male voice said, "That's disgusting."

Even in his exhausted state, Curtin's face moved in an attempted smile.

The speaker went on. "You didn't used to start barfing

so early in the evening. You must be getting old. Mind if I turn on a light?''

Not waiting for an answer, the man hit the switch. Curtin winced at the sudden brightness.

The newcomer, as tall as Curtin but of a lighter build, and younger, looked at the still figure, and his amusement turned to worry. Kneeling, he moved Curtin a few feet from the spa, heavy black mustache and dark features twitching with distaste and exertion. Next he clamped a hand on Curtin's wrist, checking the pulse, while the other lifted an eyelid and inspected the pupil.

Weakly, Curtin pulled back from the hand on his face. The other eye opened. ''Roach.''

The dark man's reassuring smile failed to hide his concern. ''Yeah, it's me.'' He got a firm grip on both wrists. Pulling, his speech turned heavy with effort. ''You really got into some heavy-duty shit this time, my friend.''

Curtin tried to agree, but then Rochambeau was rolling him over, preparatory to moving him off the deck. The movement was the last straw for Curtin's drugged, confused mind.

When he woke the next time, he was on his bed. A pounding headache punctuated his recollection of everything that had happened. It took him an extra minute to screw up the courage to sit up, and a crashing roar in his skull rewarded the accuracy of his anticipation. He groaned aloud.

''Welcome back among us.'' Rochambeau's voice floated up to the sleeping loft. ''Coffee's ready. Hurry up, and you can watch the morning aerobic program on TV with me. They got this little brunette who's healthy beyond belief. I'm in love.''

Glancing at the bouncing, twisting figures as he passed on his way to the bathroom, Curtin groaned again.

Rochambeau was beside him in two quick steps. ''You sure you're okay?''

''I'm dying.''

''Oh, that.'' The dark man returned to his chair. ''Damn,

Buck, now look what you did. She's gone. They're show-ing the blonde, instead. You made me miss the best part.''

"My heart bleeds."

"Don't see how it could. Looks like all your blood's settled in your eyes. What happened last night? You don't do dope, so how come I find you stoned and about drowned?''

"Not right now." Curtin continued on to the sink, avoiding looking at himself until several splashes of cold water started his face tingling. He swallowed a couple of aspirin, and by the time he finished shaving, decided his body was becoming habitable once again.

Rochambeau snapped off the television as Curtin re-entered. "So?"

"You remember a woman named Deb? We stayed to-gether for a while.''

"I remember her. You two broke up. She did this?"

"She laced my beer, but then she left. I don't think she'd go for murder, but whoever put her up to it dumped me in the spa to drown. I was lucky as hell they left before the job was finished.''

Uncertain, Rochambeau paused while he considered if Curtin's story might not be a bizarre joke. Thoughtfully, he said, "You're serious? Somebody actually tried to kill you?''

"Damned right I'm serious."

"You said 'they.' Who?"

"I was afraid you'd ask me that. There's a list. It's embarrassing. Makes a man wonder if he shouldn't reevalu-ate his personality.''

"*A list*? Now I'm really glad I didn't call the cops. What the hell are you in, man?"

"Come on, I'll fix breakfast. You can listen while I do show-and-tell.''

Cracking eggs, grating cheese, Curtin made omelets, glad to be able to talk because the sight of food did unpleasant things to his stomach. As the preparations went along, however, hunger overtook the queasiness, and by the time everything was ready for the table, he was famished and Rochambeau was up to date.

Sardonically, his partner watched him eat a few bites. "Way to recover, buddy," he said, grinning at Curtin's mock growl. Then, "So it could have been this Oriental who works for Bullard who plopped you in the tub, or it could have been Force Red. What if Bullard's tipped off this Colonel What's-his-face—Sandoval—and the government's out to stop the ransom operation before it starts?"

"The government doesn't know I'm coming, and Force Red wants the money. It was Bullard's man, all right, the same one who shot at me and that kid, Ben. Who else could get on and off that ranch without attracting attention?"

"How would I know? All I know is, there's too many loose ends in this deal. Everybody knows everything except you, and you don't even know who's trying to kill you. Get out of it."

For a long time they sat without speaking. Rochambeau tapped on his juice glass with a fingernail, filling the room with a steady, gentle chiming. In a tree outside, a small bird took it as a challenge and answered with his own song.

"So you're taking in the ransom for this old friend. Where do I fit?"

"You're in?"

"What else? What's the pay?"

"Five thousand a week, or any part thereof, guaranteed three weeks."

Rochambeau whistled softly. "Good scale."

"You're the pickup-team leader. You get seventy-five hundred, same terms. When it's over, we'll cut up the melon Chavez is paying me." Curtin busied himself with a slice of toast.

"That's your money. You found the deal."

"It's a team show."

"We'll argue later. What does the pickup team do?"

"Hole card. If I can swing it, I'll stiff these Force Red bastards and save the gold."

"Forget it. Why mess around?"

"Because if we screw them out of it, we keep it."

Rochambeau choked on his coffee, sputtering and wheezing into a hastily produced handkerchief. When he was able, he said, "Two *million?*"

Curtin nodded.

"We could put the construction company back in business!"

"If we can get away with this thing. Everything has to be secure before I'll risk anyone's life, especially Robert's. That's why I don't want you mentioning Robert's kidnapping to your crew, but when you go recruiting, keep it in mind. We'll need hard dudes, but ones we can trust. Anyhow, to get back to the original point, I may need you even if Force Red isn't too tricky. The biggest crook in Costa Verde is this Colonel Sandoval, and he doesn't want anyone dealing with Force Red. I figure he'll grease me and scarf up the gold as quick as he finds out about it or me."

"You want me and some people to stake out this Sandoval and cover you while you work things out with Force Red?"

Getting up, Curtin started clearing off the table. "Absolutely not. I go in alone." As his friend began to protest, Curtin gestured him to silence. "We can't put enough people ashore to cover all the hot spots, but we can sure as hell put in enough to draw attention. And when the folks in Costa Verde take you down in the cellar for 'Twenty Questions,' buddy, you answer up. So you stay out of sight. Period."

"Then what are we there for?"

Dishes and silverware clattered in the sink. Curtin poured more coffee. "You charter a big sport-fishing boat, with skipper, for you and four men, all scuba-trained. You'll be hanging out off the coast. If I need cover coming out, you'll provide it."

"Scuba. You plan a beach extraction?"

"Too obvious. I've got an idea, but I won't know if it'll

work until later. Anyhow, the gold'll be on board a ship. I'll get an ID for you, and you're going to have to find it and shadow it while it waits for me to come make my pickup.''

''Communications?''

''I'll have a radio to reach you while you're at sea.''

''Any other special gear?''

''I already ordered another ultralight. I used your name. It's being remodeled the way mine was, so it'll seat two. You teach one of your team to fly it. Carry both of them on your fishing boat, disassembled, under wraps.''

''What the hell? You taught me to fly! You want me to teach someone?''

''No time for anything else. You can do it.''

Rochambeau looked glum. ''Look, it's an amphib type, and we've had fun hopping on lakes and all, but you're talking ocean. What if we hit a storm?''

''Hope we don't. Meanwhile, equip your team for a small war.''

''Goddam, Buck, this is going to cost.''

Curtin extended him a checkbook from his pocket. ''Pay cash. Give no names, destinations, addresses. Spread your purchases. Never spend more than forty thou in one day, okay?''

Rochambeau accepted the offer with a rapt expression that suggested a religious experience. ''No more than forty—'' The rest wouldn't come. He continued to stare at the papers.

Curtin waved a hand under his nose. ''Can you hear me?''

''Yeah. Yeah, sure.'' Rochambeau answered with growing conviction, acting like a man waking into a reality better than his favorite dream. ''You mean I just go out and spend—''

''You *can* spend it. Nobody said you *have* to. Use your connections. We'll need the best hardware you can find.''

Laying a finger against the side of his nose, Rochambeau looked solemn. ''The world is full of wonderful things, if one knows where to look. And Roach knows. Leave it to me.''

"This is no drill, buddy. You saw what happened to me last night. We're stepping into a revolution. Remember that. I want the people you hire to be aware of it. The planning and the blank check and so forth are great fun. But this could get into serious badness, you know?''

Smiling, the slim figure eased upright. "Why else holler for the Roach, man? Tell me how long I got and what else we need.''

Curtin considered thanking him for his understanding but rejected the notion as quickly as it had come. Instead, he said, "Two weeks. Let's go outside.''

"What do you figure to do about Deb and the setup?''

Curtin rubbed his chin. "I'll get John and George to track her down. Maybe she knows whoever paid her.''

"And she can't wait to tell you. Sure.''

They stepped out on the deck into sunshine as rich as cream. Glancing down, Curtin grimaced distaste, then hosed off the place where he'd been ill. Both men sat at the small picnic table. In minutes they were deep in conversation.

Rochambeau left the following morning, simply disappearing for a week. When he returned, he announced his purchases were stored in New Orleans and that he'd now train the other man to fly the ultralights and check everyone out on their equipment. "We're making it," he said, and from then on, Curtin saw him only fitfully. The dark, slim figure would appear without warning, smiling to himself, answering Curtin's questions briefly before falling into bed for sleep that might last one hour or six. Twice Curtin woke to find his friend had come and gone without disturbing him. It was an eerie sensation, but Curtin reminded himself The Roach had many eerie qualities.

He was amused by the new spring in the man's step, and the tightened features. There was a purposefulness about him that made him appear wolflike. One morning, shaving, Curtin stared at his own reflection and discovered he looked a shade leaner, as well.

The electronics technician John and George had found half-staggered into the breakfast area that same morning. His face was gaunt with exhaustion, his clothes musty with the smell of having been slept in. Leaning against the wall, he snarled at a seated Curtin.

"The goddamn job's done. All three radios tested out perfect. I packed one long-range set for shipment, like you said. Anything you do from now on, I'm not responsible for it. I'm going to sleep, and when I wake up, I take my money and bag ass for home." Without waiting for an acknowledgment, he picked his way to the sofa and collapsed. In less than a minute, he was snoring softly.

Rochambeau came in a bit later. Indicating the technician, he said, "If you're letting him sleep, the radios must be done."

"A few minutes ago."

"Any word on Deb?"

"George and John say she split. So far they can't find anyone who knows where. They can't find that guy Lu, either."

"Maybe he was never here. They uncover anyone suspicious?"

"No. We don't have time to fool with it now. Everything underway on your end?"

"Number one. I'll ship your boxed-up radio to Chavez and be in New Orleans tonight, so you can ID the gold ship for me. The charter boat picks me up tomorrow in Cozumel. We'll head for a fishing resort about forty miles north of Costa Verde. We'll replenish and base there. My skipper's an immigrant Cuban. Used to be a professional fisherman, has all the necessary papers to run anything short of a battleship. The other guys are ex-Navy SEALs, except one Vietnamese. Everyone scuba-trained and current, like you said. We'll be on station when the ship arrives."

"Everything's aboard?"

"M-elevens with four spares, all with sound suppressors. Five hundred rounds each. Individual night-vision devices, four spares. Twenty stun grenades, ten frags. The two

Zodiacs you wanted, with sixty-five-horse engines and electrics for silent running. The ultralights, painted gray. Scuba gear, with backup parts. Our air compressor. We're ready, Buck.''

"Great. How about giving me a hand crating and loading the refrigerator?"

Rochambeau shot him a challenging look. "On one condition."

"Maybe. What?"

"You've been pretty cute about that damn thing. I saw you messing with the two-by-fours of the box. What're you up to?"

Walking toward the garage, Curtin continued to frown heavily, then he laughed. "What the hell, I'm sort of proud of the rig. Come look."

Inside, he pointed out an almost invisible hairline mark running the length of a long frame member. "I split this, hollowed it out, and it's epoxied back together. The radio I'll reach you with is in there." Grinning at Rochambeau's disbelief, he went on, "Snap-together parts, like a kid's toy. Hook 'em together, reach out and touch someone. But wait! There's more!"

With a flourish, he produced a brochure from his pocket, laying it on the workbench. Rochambeau bent over it. Curtin said, "This is my jewel," flipping to an illustration of an odd-looking pistol. "Five-inch, stainless-steel smoothbore," he went on, proceeding to another illustration, this one showing a cutaway view of the ammunition. Externally the rounds looked quite conventional. The actual bullet, however, had a normal front and a closed, s-curved rear, as if it had been pinched and twisted with pliers.

"That's a rocket," Curtin said. "The weapon fires electrically, with no moving parts. The exhaust gas forces out the ends of that bent rear, giving it rotation, and the only noise it makes is like running water. Unless the round gets up enough speed to break the sound barrier. That's no problem, though."

"Why not?"

'' 'Cause you shouldn't be shooting at that range. The accuracy stinks by the time it goes that far. This thing's for ending close, unpleasant conversations.''

Rochambeau looked unconvinced. "Let me get you a nice old-fashioned piece with a sound suppressor.''

Curtin ignored him, stepping to the refrigerator. "The set for contacting Chavez is in the door of this thing. Pretty nifty stuff, huh?''

Shrugging, Rochambeau picked up a hammer. "You better show me where it's safe to put nails in this.''

It took little time to crate and load the machine, then dolly it to the pickup, which was now minus its camper, and load it aboard. Next, Curtin pitched his luggage in. On the last trip from inside the house, they returned with the radioman, who was still so sleepy he was more carried along than anything else. Curtin stuffed an envelope in his pocket. The man patted it, smiled groggily. As soon as he was on the cab's bench seat and the door was closed, he slumped against it.

Curtin stopped with a foot inside the truck. He turned to Rochambeau. "I'll be in touch. Hope you get in some good fishing while you're waiting around.''

"Be careful. Don't do anything until we can come in after you, Buck.''

"Don't worry about it. I'll be so low-profile they'll have to dig to find me.''

"Good." Rochambeau's concern remained. "See you.'' They shook hands, and Curtin settled into the seat. He waved briefly as he left.

He watched Rochambeau retreat to invisibility in the rearview mirror. When he couldn't see him any longer, the sensation of being completely alone swept through him like a chill, despite the sleeping figure next to him. For an instant, an unreasoning hatred for his passenger twisted in his guts. It faded rapidly, and Curtin admitted it was the product of simple envy. The other man would go home. When he woke, refreshed, he would return to a normal existence that supported and sustained him.

Curtin thought of his purpose, of how freeing Robert released him as well, freed him to pursue a reasonable, rational life.

He wished he could live without agonizing over a mistake on a night so long ago. He damned himself for a vain fool and pushed down on the accelerator, afraid that if he slowed down, he'd stop, knowing if he stopped, he could never finish the journey.

Chapter 13

Curtin parked in the lot of a suburban branch bank and reviewed the Canadian papers one last time. The radioman slept. Inside, a courteous assistant manager helped him buy traveler's checks and arrange a letter of credit for the remainder of the bogus company account in Canada. When Curtin stepped back out of the building, he was a fully financed Canadian businessman.

His companion opened his eyes momentarily as the pickup lurched across speed bumps, but he was sound asleep again by the time they were back on the freeway.

At the airport, however, Curtin roused him. "Time to go back to work." He shook the man's shoulder.

Grumbling, the man slid behind the wheel, blinking red-rimmed eyes. "Where am I going?"

"Look, the air-freight offices are over there." The man squinted uncertainly, then, "Got it."

"Okay. It'll save time if you'll ship the refrigerator for me. When you're done, come let me know it's taken care of, then leave the truck at George's and get home."

"See you in a while."

Bags in hand, Curtin entered the terminal, looked at the line snaking away from his ticket counter and grimaced. "My luck," he muttered and searched out a coffee machine, then sat down to watch the approach road. In a while he saw his truck in the distance, the bed empty.

A van immediately behind the pickup swung out to pass it, cutting off a rapidly closing car. Curtin tensed, anticipating the possible accident, but the car backed off. As the three vehicles approached a turnoff, the van switched lanes, getting directly in front of the pickup. The car made a move to pass them both.

When the back door of the van swung open, Curtin's mouth went dry. Instinctively, he was on his feet, racing outside. He stopped abruptly at the sight of his truck windshield disintegrating. The hot sunshine leaped from the glass splinters like something evil bursting free. It was underscored by the sullen roar of a shotgun. The truck drifted to the right, ignoring a second shotgun blast that ripped a huge hole in the top of the hood. The car passing on the left braked violently, skidding into the guard rail, only to bank off, tumbling onto its side. The van raced away on the turnoff as the pickup shuddered to a stop against the barrier, like an old horse leaning on a stout fence.

The first flames to erupt through the hole in the hood were almost invisible in the heat and glare. Smoke followed quickly. A jarring shock rattled terminal windows as the entire front end exploded. Traffic screamed to a stop. People ran toward the scene from all directions.

Curtin watched with a curious detachment, as if it were orchestrated excitement from a film. He remembered the comic anger of the radioman as he announced his job was done. The man never gave a name. Wise beyond his technical skills, he insisted only George know how to reach him, demanded payment in cash and no further contact. Now the money was ashes. Soon he would be.

Another debt.

Did the incinerated man think of obligations as the

buckshot tore his life apart? Whether he did or not, he died anyway. Not for justice. Not honor. For nothing. For being around.

It's different in my case, Curtin told himself. The other guy's number came up, that's all.

He turned from the still-growing crowd, hearing the first faint sirens in the distance. A feeling of eyes following his every move threatened to overwhelm him.

He passed ticket counters, scanning departure times. The first plane he could possible catch left for Sacramento in ten minutes. The agent barely got him aboard.

From Sacramento he booked himself to Denver, then on to Houston, then Baton Rouge. He rented a car to complete the trip. Later, tired, certain no one could have followed him, he stood on a deserted wharf in New Orleans looking at a small, aging freighter.

Bullard watched from the deck as he hiked closer.

Curtin enjoyed the heat, the minor nuisance of prickling sweat. He savored the pungent waterfront, wondering how many smells were combined in that mixture. Carrying all was the unifying river, a whispering mass that stroked the pilings with a soft chuckle to mark its passing. The mooring lines groaned in complaint at the unceasing current.

Bullard greeted him almost joyously. "The Old Man tells me the police in San Diego are anxious to hear you explain why a man was murdered driving around in your car, especially since one of the airline ticket clerks remembers a man of your description buying a last-minute seat out of there. And the cops in Vegas wonder what you can tell them about a woman named Deb Something-or-other who showed up dead in their jurisdiction with your house key, address, and phone number in her little black book."

"You have to have been there," Curtin said. "Where are we on shipping that refrigerator?"

"Don't worry about anything I'm supposed to take care of. It's leaving this evening. Is that all you've got to say about two murdered friends?"

"It's as much as I'm saying to you. I want to see the gold."

"You act like a really cold bastard, Curtin, but I think it's a scam. I think you're scared shitless."

"I want to see the gold."

Bullard made a harsh, sibilant sound, then turned abruptly. Inside, away from the noise of the outside world, their clanging footsteps vibrated in the metal around them, made them part of the ship. The security arrangements were clear. A series of steel doors were welded in the passageway, with two men for each position, one on each side. The doors were locked on both sides. Bullard led them past two such doors on the way to the hold.

Curtin also noticed the gun ports. Small holes, they seemed innocent enough, unless one recognized them for what they were. They commanded each sector from above as well as from the adjacent bulkheads.

At the final door, Bullard said, "This is the only way into this hold. Everything else is sealed off, welded shut. To get to this place, you run that gauntlet past my men."

With that he gestured the guard away and swung open the door. The ransom sat in a small, empty cubby in three nondescript boxes. Curtin opened one. The gold gleamed buttery welcome in the subdued light. Bullard laughed harshly. "I wish you could see your face. I thought you were only interested in your proper salary for this job."

"I am. I was just thinking how much this stuff is worth. And what it's already cost."

Bullard slammed the door home and locked it again, gesturing to the guard to return to his position. He said, "I suppose that's very deep and wise."

Curtain headed back the way they'd come. Bullard had to move smartly to keep up. Curtin asked, "Is Peralta here in New Orleans with you?" The quality of the silence impressed him, and he turned to catch Bullard with an expression that was too complex, too quickly controlled, for Curtin to define what he'd seen.

Bullard said, "She decided to stay in Costa Verde," and Curtin stopped so suddenly they almost collided.

"She did what?"

"Decided to stay. It's her home, for Christ's sake, so why shouldn't she?"

"Because it's too dangerous. And because she's a target."

"What makes you think so?" Bullard's eyes were round, striving for innocence. Too much shrewdness danced in them. Curtin knew he'd said too much, but the only way out was forward.

"I heard her blast Force Red. She won't control her mouth at home any better than she did here." Curtin watched Bullard closely for signs of disbelief. There were none. He decided to turn the screw once more. "A woman like Flor Peralta is going to have enemies on both sides of the political fence. She's smart and she's outspoken."

Instead of answering, Bullard pushed past Curtin, leading the way to the main deck. He stopped at the gangplank, and as Curtin reached him, one hand moved in what appeared to be an aborted try for contact.

Bullard looked down into the swirling, chocolate current. "Look for her, Curtin. Sandoval said she's been seen with antigovernment people. He impounded her passport while it's all checked out. She doesn't deserve anything like him, you understand?"

"I'll see what I can do." The urgency of his need to see her, to know she was safe, clawed at him. He barely heard Bullard.

"Don't forget."

"No. No, I won't." Curtin hurried down to the dock.

He bought his ticket to Costa Verde at the airport. There were no night landings at Oriente, or anywhere else in the country, he was told. The clerk hinted it was because the government identified anything that flew in the dark as unfriendly.

After he turned in his rental car, he phoned Rochambeau and, in clipped phrases, described the ship and gave her name. Then he caught a taxi to a nearby motel. A hot shower and ten minutes of television numbed both mind and body. When his wake-up call came the following morning, he was genuinely refreshed.

The flight to Oriente was completely uneventful, a time to be endured. He read. He dozed. He drank coffee and looked out the window. It was excruciatingly boring, and from the boredom grew apprehension.

In the customs line, Curtin's concerns were realized. As a rumpled immigration officer opened his luggage and stirred around in his clothes, another man approached with a bully's stiff strut. The unkempt immigration officer stammered when he addressed him. Following a brief exchange, the newcomer spoke to Curtin. "You will come with me."

Curtin waved a hand over his belongings. "What about my things?"

The heavily accented voice acquired an immediate edge. "Your baggage will be safe. Come."

Shrugging, Curtin followed, reminding himself to look puzzled. A few people watched his progress with passing curiosity. Most interpreted the relationship between himself and his solemn guide instantly. They looked away, found something else to interest them.

"Passport," the man said, extending his hand. Curtin handed it over. He was led through a doorway and down a dim hall. Stopping short, the escort pushed open a door and stood aside. The room held a formica-topped table with three unmatching chrome-and-vinyl chairs that seemed to have strayed there from different cheap dinette sets. A wall mirror was an obvious one-way observation port.

What caught his attention, however, was the utilitarianism. The windowless walls were covered with hard, yellow enamel that glared under the light of a single bulb recessed in the ceiling. The floor was glazed tile.

Enamel and tile—as well as formica, vinyl and chrome—wipe clean easily without staining. The decor said a lot about interrogation technique in Costa Verde.

Two chairs were placed at one side of the table. Curtin sat

opposite them in the single chair. When they came, there would be a pair.

For an hour he waited, glancing at his watch, wishing there was at least a fan to move some air, a bug to watch on the wall. Occasionally, faint laughter slid through the fake mirror. At one point he deliberately used it to comb his hair and straighten his travel-wrinkled clothing. Muffled laughter let him know the hidden watchers were convinced of his ignorance.

Suddenly, without warning, the door burst open. Two uniformed men rushed into the room, each grabbing a shoulder, practically throwing him into the hall. He protested, offering only enough resistance to appear frightened, and they hustled him away, never saying a word. Within a few yards, they were at another door. One guard flung it open, and Curtin barely glimpsed the concrete walls of the cul-de-sac and its waiting van before he was bodily heaved into the vehicle. It was as dark as the room was bright, and even hotter. He gripped the fore-and-aft seat to avoid being pitched to the floor as it sped away.

The van stopped, and for a moment he considered escape, even feeling for a handle on the rear door. There was none, of course, and he consoled himself with the thought that he had no chance if he ran. He stared into the blackness and reminded himself his documentation was excellent, his cover impeccable. He must *be* an innocent businessman, a victim of some bureaucratic bungle.

The van stank. He avoided analyzing the odor.

When the machine stopped again, the door swung open and his two guards yelled at him, gesticulating wildly. He came out tentatively, using the time to observe his surroundings. For added effect, he yelled back. "My government's going to hear about this! You can't manhandle people this way!"

He was obviously in an underground parking area. It stretched away in all directions, full of cars and several vans similar to the one that brought him.

Again, each guard grabbed a shoulder and an elbow and

shoved. Curtin had felt similar strength before—the brute muscle of stupid men to whom more brutality answered every new question. He took it, chewing the inside of his lip, playing his role with furious determination.

They went directly to an elevator, and in moments Curtin was in a bleak, austere waiting room. The ceiling loomed high above, and a tall, narrow window directly opposite the door had the lower part of its expanse plugged by sandbags, while the higher reaches featured woven wire. Stark, straight-backed chairs lined the two side walls. The place was cold. Logic told him the temperature was probably no lower than sixty-five degrees. Nevertheless, he shivered.

A door opened on his right. Colonel Sandoval himself stepped through.

Bullard's pictures had caught the man's high cheekbones, the slim, straight nose, and the crisp uniform. What the pictures had failed to capture was the cold curiosity in the eyes or the tiny downward curve of the right side of the mouth that made the whole face seem to barely cling to the polite side of contempt. His stride almost entirely disguised a limp in his right leg. The strength of his formal handshake surprised Curtin.

"It is unfortunate we had to detain you"—he paused, glancing at the documents before handing them over —"Mr. Curtin. We have many undesirables coming to Costa Verde now, and your visa application and travel plans seemed to be rather hastily put together. My man became suspicious." He pushed a button beside the door, and a uniformed man opened it as if the device were attached to him directly. Sandoval spoke in rapid Spanish, and the man backed out. When Sandoval smiled for Curtin, he refused to return it. Undisturbed, Sandoval continued the one-sided conversation. "We are a mild people, victimized by the insanity of a few hard-core terrorists."

The man returned carrying a tray with a steaming cup on it. The smell was wonderful, and Curtin's trembling increased. He steadied his hand by jamming his elbow against his side as he reached for the offered drink.

Sandoval said. "Hot coffee and rum. Two of our better products. I offer it to visitors, as I prefer a rather cool work place."

The liquid eased down Curtin's throat and settled in his stomach like a benevolent lava flow. His hand steadied. He said, "I can excuse being pulled out of the customs line, but I object to being manhandled."

The limp was more pronounced when Sandoval turned his back and walked to the far window. The incongruous sandbags reached almost to his chin. "We are at war." He spun around, advancing on Curtin. "When my men leave their families to go to work, they don't know if they'll live long enough to come home for dinner. And they don't know if they'll have a family if they do return. You think about that, Mr. Curtin." When he stopped, he was only a foot or so away. He reached inside his jacket and produced a sheaf of photographs. "These were taken this morning. I was examining them when I heard of your detention. Look."

Mutilated bodies lay in bloody, awkward poses. One picture featured a severed, burned skull, leering horribly. Curtin handed the photos back. Sandoval said, "Some Force Red victims, some death-squad victims. Suspicion can be a terminal disease here. So can political interference."

"I'm not interested in politics. I'm a businessman, here to sell used heavy equipment."

"Excellent. We will go to any length to cooperate with those who wish to see a prosperous, calm country. Unfortunately, some businessmen thought so little of us they imagined they could deal with Force Red. It is not that free a market, you understand?"

"Completely."

Sandoval reached past him to open the door to the hall. "You are most welcome in my country. I will see you to the parking garage. Your baggage is there. I have called a taxi. Have you changed your money to ours?"

When Curtin shook his head, Sandoval pressed a bill on him. "That will cover the taxi fare," he said, waving away protest. "It's the least we can do for the inconvenience."

In the elevator to the garage, Sandoval asked if Curtin had a place to live. Curtin explained. "I have a hotel room for tonight, but a friend of a friend has found me a house."

Sandoval frowned. "Our refugees have created a crime problem. You should hire a guard for the house."

Thanking Sandoval for the advice, and bending to get into the taxi, Curtin's attention was drawn to the rumble of a speeding truck entering the garage. It stopped with shrilling brakes. A soldier leaped to the ground from the cab. Others poured out of a side doorway. They flung open the canvas back-flap, and several scrambled up into the truck bed. Civilian-clad bodies flew out across the tailgate. Lucky ones landed running, only to be jerked—or clubbed—to a standstill by the waiting troops. Less fortunate ones tripped on the tailgate, or came out off-balance. They landed heavily and were hurried to their feet with a barrage of kicks and blows. One skinny boy sailed out higher than any of the others, wide-eyed, limbs windmilling. Arms extended to break his face-down fall, he was silent until the brisk crack of a breaking bone wrenched a scream out of him.

The noise stopped abruptly, and Curtin silently damned the man who turned it off. And cursed himself because he was glad the boy was quieted.

The taxi driver was underway as soon as he felt the weight of his passenger, not even pausing for the door to close. As Curtin tugged on it, Sandoval crossed his line of vision for one last time. He wore a smile Curtin could only think of as contemplative.

The hotel was three blocks away, and the driver covered the ground with no concern for speed limits or safety, then collected his fare as if afraid of the money. In his room,

Curtin sprawled on the bed and stared at the ceiling. Images grew and faded there.

The interrogation room, with its lying mirror that snickered and giggled.

Sandoval.

The way the boy's arm bulged just before the bone snapped.

The potent rum and coffee stirred in his stomach, and he concentrated on it. Within minutes he slept, unaware of hands clenching the bedspread, eyelids that jerked spasmodically.

A gentle knock on the door roused him.

"Who is it?"

The knock was repeated, and a thin, complaining voice said, "Rudy Kooseman. I was asked to find you a house."

Curtin opened the door, and Kooseman hurried inside without waiting for an invitation. A sidelong, sharp look expressed disapproval of Curtin's untidiness.

Kooseman's voice might be thin, but nothing else about him was. Rotund, almost round, of barely average height, his clothes strained to cover his bulk. He said, "I picked up your refrigerator, too. I don't know why I'm all of a sudden freight manager and real-estate agent for you. Me and my company don't owe you damned Canucks a thing—no offense—and I've got enough to do."

"I imagine they just looked for somebody who could get things done around here. I'm sorry for the trouble, but I'm grateful, too."

Kooseman continued pouting. It gave him the ridiculous look of an irritable baby in need of a shave. He said, "I guess I ought to show you your house."

Curtin excused himself to freshen up, and then they were on their way. The desk clerk looked up and smiled when they got off the elevator. At the door, Curtin glanced at a picture on the wall. Reflected in the glass of the frame, he caught the clerk indicating himself and Kooseman with a nod. A loitering man rose and ambled their way.

Bubbling fake indignation, Curtin grabbed Kooseman's

arm. "That clerk just pointed us out! We're being followed!"

Kooseman jerked his arm away. "Not we, buddy. You. All newcomers get a tail at first. If you see it, it convinces you to keep your nose clean. If you don't see it and you *don't* keep your nose clean, you learn what trouble really is."

"I think I may have a good idea. They pulled me out of the customs line today just because they thought my travel plans were 'too hurried.' "

By now they were on the sidewalk, walking toward a grimy Toyota. Kooseman said, "I hope you didn't mouth off at anybody. This place is murderous, Curtin. I mean exactly that. I hate it."

"Really? Why do you stay here?"

"I get paid a helluva lot more than I can make anywhere else." He unlocked Curtin's door. "Take your time. We have to leave time for the foot tail to signal the car tail. They get pissed if you lose them." He rolled his eyes on his way to his own side of the car. "Every day I look up at the sky and expect to see a huge scalpel coming at me."

"Scalpel?"

The sweaty features split in a suddenly infectious grin. "Costa Verde's the asshole of the world, and the fair city of Oriente is one huge hemorrhoid. I can't believe God's not going to cut it out one day."

"Some interesting theology. You must break 'em up at Sunday school."

Suddenly nervous again, Kooseman shoved the car into gear. "Just don't ever tell any of the locals you heard me say anything like that, okay?"

"No worry." Curtin sat back to observe. None of his reading had prepared him for the truth of Oriente. Women dressed in high fashion exited sleek automobiles to enter shops full of luxurious clothing and jewelry. They shared sidewalks teeming with young urban professionals, peasants carrying produce in woven sacks, and occasional children with the drawn, tired faces that mark the hungry.

Each street seemed to have its quota of begging cripples. Gleaming, modern buildings looked down on the teeming humanity, and a few blocks farther, they passed a magnificent colonial church. A little beyond that, the gray-brown ruins of an ancient temple glowered from the distance, content to be away from the smoke-blanketed traffic.

The house Kooseman indicated was pleasant, set in a quiet suburb. As nonchalantly as possible, Curtin sought out his refrigerator and then let Kooseman know he was tired from his trip and needed rest. With the man gone, Curtin immediately stripped off the wooden crating, hurrying to stow it in the garage, checking his watch anxiously. Back in the house, with much pushing and hauling, he got the machine in place and plugged it in. A faint, welcoming hum greeted his ears.

A few screws held the inner door panel, and Curtin had them undone quickly. Lifting it off, he examined the exposed radio and the miniaturized tape recorder nestled beside it. He spoke into the device's attached microphone. *"I'm in place. No difficulties. No contacts. Out."*

He turned the machine off, rewound the tape, plugged the recorder into the radio. When he hit the "Play" switch and the radio's "Transmit" switch simultaneously, the tape reel whirred almost too rapidly to see, its faint insect-screech lasting brief seconds.

Curtin looked at his watch. If everything was right, Chavez's radio would catch the signal, record it, and replay it as normal speech.

If not—

Minutes dragged by. He fidgeted, worried about the equipment. Could Chavez have the wrong time, the wrong frequency? He reinspected his own setup, laboriously examining connections.

A winking red light and a sudden whir from his own tape recorder forced a muted cry of relief from him. A moment later he listened to Chavez's voice. *"Glad you're safely arrived. The program is moving well. Good luck. Out."*

Feeling good, mumbling "Jabber, jabber," Curtin replaced everything.

The sound of the knock on the door was like an electric shock. He stared toward the living room, unbelieving. Feet scuffed on the porch. Jerking erect, he flung one last look at the refrigerator. The knock was repeated, louder. He ran to answer it.

It took a double take for Curtin to realize there was someone on the porch. The woman was child-sized. He looked down at her, dumb.

"I am here," she said, her piping voice biting off the unfamiliar English.

"That's very nice. Why?"

"I am Lucia. I am your—" She stopped and put a thumb to brilliant teeth, worrying at it. Then she brightened. "Maid! Maid for you!"

"I never hired any maid. You've got the wrong house."

"No." She shook her head. "Man point this house."

"What man?"

"Man what say you need maid, *por supuesto*." She held out a handful of crumpled bills. "Give me money, say I work your house, say he friend's friend. Understand?"

"No."

Her face fell. "No work?"

Curtin studied the tough, hopeful face, found himself wondering what kind of life created that network of wrinkles. He told himself he was going to end up with someone in the house, watching him, so it might as well be someone who at least looked like she needed the money. "Sure, work. Why not?"

"You no speak Spanish. I teach. Free."

"Never mind."

She walked inside, vastly at home. "Everything crazy this country, I think. You think?"

"Yes, I do.' He watched the small figure peering into corners, running her hand along bookshelves and windowsills. A spider ran for cover and she had a shoe off and eliminated it before it went a foot. She grimaced. "What name you?"

"Curtin. Buck Curtin."

She fastened a bird's-eye gaze on him. "No marry? No child?"

He shook his head.

"No okay." Unexpectedly, she broke into pealing laughter. "Don't worry. Plenty girls Costa Verde. Pretty." She held up two fingers. "Me, two husband marry. Die. Five sons. Big. *Grande*. I know men. Take good care you." She waved both arms, a miniature whirlwind. "You boss, my house. No trouble, you, hah? I watch!"

Curtin laughed, unable to resist the sparkling, peppery woman. All the same, her "I watch!" stung, and he wondered exactly what the hell *that* might mean.

The aura of her good humor lasted quite a while after she was gone, but with nightfall the silence of the empty house crept inside him. Lucia was forgotten.

Robert. What must his world be like right now?

George and John.

The radioman without a name.

Deb. Poor, greedy idiot.

Ben. And the unknown man racing death under the helicopter.

Why? Why any of it? And if he found out, what then?

The last face etched on his mind's eye was Flor's.

Chapter 14

The following morning, fortified by Lucia's hearty breakfast, Curtin called a taxi and set about acquiring the permits and papers necessary to do business in Costa Verde. Like most entrenched bureaucracies, the paperwork tyrants created as many obstacles to constructive action as possible. Then they charged a fee to bypass each one.

Bored clerks issued forms to be completed, took them back, dumped them on piles of other forms already high enough to totter dangerously. In one office Curtin idly examined a worker's typewriter while he waited. It was thick with dust.

Throughout the day, his overriding impression was of frightened apathy, as though these people knew something was happening to their country, knew it was terrible, and were too imprisoned in their routine to do anything about it.

A similar sensation dogged him when he walked from building to building. People in the streets were visibly uncomfortable near him. The first time he stood at a street corner and a man unobtrusively edged away from him,

Curtin was embarrassed, assuming he was sweating more than he realized. When he noticed the heavily armed troops eyeing him from a distance, however, he understood.

He was foreign, a target of opportunity for either faction in a political war. To stand close to him tempted the storm.

By the time he finished his errands, it was dusk and he was psychologically drained. Recognizing that made him want to dismiss the feeling he was being followed. Nevertheless, he aimlessly strolled the next couple of blocks, identifying no one. As in San Diego, however, the feeling persisted. At the next corner he came to a street market. Pretending interest, he dawdled, inspecting papayas, varieties of bananas, peppers—an array of colors and smells he wished he had time to enjoy. When he reached the end of the block, he crossed an open park.

Nothing looked suspicious.

But he believed someone was there.

Taking a direct route, he made his way to the lounge of his previous hotel and settled on a bar stool, luxuriating in the cooled air. He ordered a gin and tonic to savor the needling bite of the carbonation and the aromatic lime. The drink was more than half gone when the seats next to him were taken. A man spoke to his male companion in Spanish. Curtin lost interest. When his arm was jostled, he reacted with minor annoyance.

Courteously, the man made what Curtin took to be apologies. The spurt of English words was startling, coming almost unaccented in a harsh whisper. "Before any discussions, you must first be sure the police are not following you."

"I don't understand." Curtin affected wide-eyed innocence. "Police? I haven't done anything. They already looked at my papers."

The man smiled politely. "*Con permiso. No hablo inglés.* No English." Their eyes met. Curtin was pleased to see indecision and anger, knowing he'd either established a reputation for caution with Force Red or thwarted an at-

tempted entrapment by the police. In either case, he'd
scored a few points.

He drained the drink. Points weren't going to count for
much before this was all over, but it was the best he could
manage.

Making his way into the dining room, he ordered and
was comfortably awaiting his salad when Rudy Kooseman
wobbled to the center of the entryway and planted his feet.
With the fuddled concentration of drunkenness, he surveyed
the room, passing over Curtin once, then homing in on
him. His pace was stately, marred by a couple of jousts
with uncooperative chairs. Uninvited, he plopped himself
down across from Curtin.

"Might as well eat together," he said. The words were
only slightly thickened. "At least we both talk English.
How's your Spanish?"

"Nonexistent."

Kooseman nodded solemnly. "Good thinking. Let 'em
learn to talk to us. I got me an interpreter. That's how I do
business." He grinned slyly. "And he makes all the
payments, you know? I don't make any 'contributions,' or
any of that. If somebody says 'Pay off!' I just say, 'Not
me, buddy. Talk to Paco about it.' "

The first half of the meal passed with Kooseman explaining how to deal with "these people" and Curtin responding appropriately.

He lost all track of his dinner partner when Flor Peralta
entered the room.

She was with a group of young upper-class types. They
moved with self-assurance in their stylish clothes, every
gesture carried out with a measured flamboyance that guaranteed attention. Curtin thought of brilliant tropical birds
flocking to roost. When they were seated, they allowed
themselves surreptitious glances to measure their impact on
others in the room.

Flor restricted her attention to her handsome escort,
who talked to her animatedly. Not until Curtin rose to
leave did her attention drift away from her companions.

He was thinking he hadn't really heard a word of Kooseman's babble since she entered, and she picked that moment to lift her head, staring directly at him. The contact lasted but for a moment, and when she returned her still-calm gaze to the man beside her, only a sudden flurry of nervous hand gestures revealed her tension.

Curtin surveyed the disinterested crowd, amazed and gratified that no one seemed aware of what had happened between two people in their midst. Flor's secretiveness made it clear they could not speak. It hurt far more than it should have.

Kooseman broke through his thoughts. "I'll give you a ride home. Taxi drivers'll gouge you blind until you learn how to deal with them." Words of refusal started automatically. Curtin swallowed them. It would be worth listening to more foolish chatter to avoid argument.

Dodging through traffic, Kooseman cursed the other drivers. "See how these bastards behave? Jesus Christ, there's not a whole brain in this country! They're still in the seventeenth century!" He pointed, not looking where he was going, barely missing a bus. "See that church wall, right there? See the white spots? That's where they shot up a bunch of women demanding to know where their husbands and sons were. And that corner over there?" He swerved around a man on a bicycle. "The best hope this country had, a moderate, possibly honest politician, cashed in his chips right there. Force Red decided he was getting too important."

"I can see why you're depressed."

"You think so?" For an instant, Kooseman didn't look drunk anymore. Rather, there was a deep, pained sadness in his face, but then they were out from under the streetlight, and Curtin had no way to verify the impression.

A few minutes later the car turned sharply in the middle of a block, and before Curtin could ask what was going on, Kooseman stopped in a courtyard. A fountain splashed into a small decorative pool against the wall isolating them from the street. Kooseman grinned at his passenger.

"Thought you ought to see this place. Local landmark."
Then he was out of the car and headed for the door,
leaving Curtin no choice but to follow.

The thick wooden door sighed open at Kooseman's
push, revealing a spacious living room to the right. Soft
light gleamed on leather and polished wood furniture.
Trailing Kooseman inside, Curtin glanced to his left through
an arched entry and was startled to see what looked like a
restaurant, complete with intimate tables for two and a
discreet bar. Another step expanded his angle of view, and
he saw the women seated on sofas along the wall.

"Come on," Kooseman said. "Don't be shy."

The six women, attractive in revealing evening gowns,
flocked to him, giggling and caressing. They measured
Curtin as they did. Kooseman said, "Angelina. We haven't
been together for a long time. Tonight we make special,
okay?"

Angelina giggled harder, setting plump, half-exposed
breasts surging in creamy waves. Kooseman watched them
happily, half-turned to Curtin. "You're on your own, pal.
See you later." He swatted Angelina's comfortable behind,
drawing a squeal, and headed for the stairs to the right of
the bar.

Alone, Curtin stared at the women, all clearly amused at
his discomfort. They shouted to someone behind him, and
he turned to find a woman approaching from the living
room. She offered a hand. "My name is Evita," she said,
and at Curtin's raised eyebrows, laughed throatily. She
broke off the firm handshake with a lingering touch. "Of
course, I took the name. If it was lucky for one ambitious
woman, it may be lucky for another, right?"

Her English was very good, with an intriguing accent.
She looked at Curtin with a bold sexuality that challenged
without demanding. She was a striking, handsome woman,
not beautiful in the pale, dainty sense, but a hearty female.
She called herself ambitious. He was certain she could add
"intelligent."

He said, "Evita, I'm not a customer. Sorry."

She tilted her head. "You don't like my girls? You don't need a companion while you're here in Costa Verde?"

"No." Not wanting to offend, he added, "My name's Buck Curtin. Rudy Kooseman brought me here, and I have to wait for him. Will you have a drink and wait with me?"

She paused, considering, and he smiled. "I'll pick up a round for the girls too, if you think it'll make them feel better. Real stuff or tea, you choose."

She laughed out loud before turning to the bartender. She spoke in Spanish, but the delighted chatter and shouts of "*Gracias!*" from the girls translated adequately. Evita moved to the bar with him, making herself comfortable on a stool. Before the drinks arrived, two men entered. Curtin felt their hostility before he saw them clearly, some instinctive awareness triggered by stride or posture. They advanced steadily, ignoring the welcoming cries from the girls that died quickly under the strangers' cold disinterest.

Stopping in front of Curtin and Evita, they waited until Evita spoke. The taller one held up a commanding hand. "We will speak English, for the gringo. You—go away."

"You are in my house," Evita said calmly. "If you can't be gentlemen, I have friends who will make you understand."

Hardly glancing at her, the taller one reached in his pocket and pulled out bills. Wadding them, he stuffed them down the front of her dress. "For you and your friends, whore. We will talk to this one. No one—" He frowned, trying to remember words, then, "No one is to bother us. *Comprende?*"

"Of course. Talk as long as you want." She swiveled on the stool, stood up to leave. Curtin was surprised and disappointed at how quickly she surrendered until he looked around the room. A man carrying a shotgun came down the stairs. The bartender stood at the doorway to the kitchen, similarly armed, while a third man covered the entrance to the living room. He carried a pistol. Evita joined her girls against the wall.

The speaker continued in a hoarse whisper. "We are Force Red. Is the ransom ready?"

Curtin said, "I understood we had another day before starting to talk."

Sneering, the man said, "We have friends also. Even in Chavez's organization. He waits, hopes his son will escape. We kill him if he tries. Tell his father."

"If I was here to do business with Force Red, I'd have to see Robert. Myself. Talk to him."

The shorter one understood. He grabbed the spokesman's arm, whispering fierce argument. His one word Curtin caught was a clear "No!" They snarled at each other like dogs, until the taller one faced Curtin, seething. "You see Robert, talk. We tell you when, how."

He left so quickly his partner was momentarily caught standing alone in front of Curtin. Still, they didn't reach the door before Evita was in front of them, blocking their way.

"Never come here again," she said, arms folded across her chest. "Go. Never come back."

The spokesman stiffened. "*Puta!*" He slapped her, hard enough to spin her almost off her feet. The guard in the doorway leveled his weapon at the two men with the metallic clatter of a round being chambered. Curtin checked his own rush toward the pair to avoid being caught in the shot pattern.

Evita straightened, not deigning to raise a hand to the ugly red welt growing on her cheek. She looked at her guards and at Curtin, smiling thinly. "Leave them alone. I will not forget this one who likes to hurt women. Someday I will make him remember me." To the strangers, she repeated, "Never come back."

Their bravado punctured, the two of them swiveled to check the armed men. The short one broke first, almost running, with his companion following right after. Evita's crackling laughter spurred them. She walked to the bar again, gesturing Curtin to her side. The bartender took his normal place. The other two men went back to wherever they'd come from. Curtin wondered how large Evita's army actually was.

She said, "Curtin, I don't know who you are or why those men want to talk to you, but if they come here after you and make trouble again, I will have to tell you to stay away. Too bad."

"I doubt if I'll be back. You've never seen them before?"

"Never." He lit the cigarette she produced, and she shook her head, exhaling a cloud of smoke. "I have had the 'tax collectors' from Force Red, and always the '*mordida*,' the 'little bite' from the police."

Leaning forward confidentially, she said, "I know it must be business. Big. Listen to me, Curtin. Make the best deal you can, but let them think they win. People who are stubborn about principles die quickly in my country. It would be sad to lose a man who is *muy bravo*. You understand?"

"Close enough. And thanks for the advice. Now, how about that drink?"

"With pleasure." She called to the bartender, who set up two fresh ones, favoring Curtin with a friendly smile.

Curtin responded, but his thoughts were elsewhere. So far, he thought wryly, his stay in-country had produced an unwelcome visit to the brutal power behind the government, a maid he didn't really want but didn't dare fire, a drunken bigot of a guide, and the friendship of a cathouse madam and her bartender.

It wasn't a quality start.

Evita said, "You smile. You think of something funny?"

"Not especially. Tell me, how'd this guy Sandoval get so powerful? In a country full of generals, how's a colonel get to be the big gun?"

The strong features froze, and Evita looked at him from the corner of her eye. "We don't talk about Colonel Sandoval. Not to anyone. Especially strangers."

"Sorry." Curtin returned to his drink as Kooseman came down the stairs. He was considerably sobered up, but very convivial. He threw an arm across Curtin's shoulders, talking to Evita. "Good man, Evita. Too tired to party tonight, that's all." He winked broadly. "Wasted first night in Costa Verde, right?"

"Wasted. Right, Rudy." She rose with Curtin, taking an arm between the two of them, chattering of Kooseman's returning soon, how they enjoyed his visits, and so forth. Not until they were at the door did she speak to Curtin. Releasing Kooseman, she faced Curtin squarely, looking up into his eyes, reading them. She said, "I am grateful for the way you acted earlier. I am in your debt."

Kooseman frowned. "Debt? Who acted how? What's going on?"

"Nothing," Evita said. "A small argument, and Curtin took my side." She laughed. "In fact, he behaved like one of our local heroes, a famous, foolish matador." With that she guided them outside. The thudding closure of the heavy door echoed in the courtyard.

Kooseman shook his head as he drove onto the street. "What's with this matador stuff?" he demanded peevishly.

Curtin said, "A local legend. I'm surprised she mentioned it. Some bullfighter from here had a reputation for more guts than brains. They admire that, I guess. She was kidding about its applying to me. Nothing happened."

"Something happened. Evita's a hooker, and hookers don't forget who owes who or how much. If she said she's in your debt, it's for a good reason." He shook his head again, looked at Curtin oddly. "I really don't get this. I've been here seven years, and I miss the bullfights a lot—I'm a fan, an *aficionado*. What I'm saying is, they haven't had a bullfight in Costa Verde for a hundred years, and I never heard of any matador from these parts either. I don't know what the hell you two are talking about."

Chapter 15

Sunlight poured into the room, creating a flood of color. Curtin stood at the window, watching cloud shadows flow across the mountains, wishing there were time to explore the beckoning distance. Then he thought of the pictures Sandoval had shown him, the butchered victims who happened to be in the wrong place at the wrong time.

The land was brutalized. In those forests, men preyed on others, not in order to live, but in pursuit of power. The slopes of the mountains were deceitful with mines to shred the legs of whoever or whatever touched them.

Beautiful Costa Verde was no place to be distracted by beauty.

He wondered if it would end as Vietnam had, a permanent battlefield full of hatred and fear, her people no more than tyrannized survivors, discarded by their self-appointed foreign saviors once their political luster lost the polish of immediacy.

Showering, he restricted his thinking to a perplexing aspect of his own situation. His only contacts so far were well-arranged, but poorly conducted. Contradiction com-

ing from Force Red made him suspicious. They weren't
fools, nor were they clumsy.

The whole developing picture was off-center.

He went down to the kitchen where Lucia was rearrang-
ing things to her own liking. After learning he wanted
scrambled eggs and toast, she set her mouth as well as her
skills in action. "I come work little after sun come today.
See gringo."

"Here? Where?"

"By front. He walk slow, slow—see me look—he go."

"What'd he look like? Have you ever seen him before?"

"Too much dark." She slid the eggs in front of him,
buttering toast with swift dabs.

Curtin decided he could be cool, too. "The government
watches most foreigners."

Laughing, she tugged his arm, led him to the window,
holding him well back from the glass. She pointed at the
gardener crouched next door, then to an Indian woman
pushing a stroller while she held the hand of a second
child. "Government people," she said, sneering openly.
"Everybody knows but the *ricos*, the rich ones. Come,
come." Unable to reach his upper arm without an uncomfortable stretch, she grabbed his belt. She cracked the front
door open with infinite slowness, gesturing. A car down
the street pointed its front end at them like the muzzle of
an animal. Closing the door, Lucia patted his hand, glowing with pride. "Real *policia* watch you. Very good. But
no one so important they use other gringos to watch. Too
much money."

Getting back to his eggs, Curtin was sure she was right.
Which made the unidentified man more dangerous than
ever. If he wasn't government, he certainly couldn't be
Force Red. The only other possibility was someone working for Bullard.

He ate slowly, thinking it through. All he had going for
him was deception and speed. If he could keep the game
moving so fast that no one got him bore-sighted, he might
swing it.

The ring of the doorbell pulled him straight up in his chair. Lucia waved him back and hurried to answer. He heard her staccato Spanish and a brisk, quieter answer. Thinking he should investigate, he got to his feet in time to see Colonel Sandoval enter. Neither man offered to shake hands. Keeping his eyes on Curtin, Sandoval spoke sharply to Lucia. She made a face behind his back, but scurried away.

"Mr. Curtin," Sandoval drawled. "Here less than forty-eight hours and I have a second complaint about you. How do you explain that?"

"Explain what? I haven't done anything, Colonel."

"Oh, but you have. An argument—almost a fight—and in a brothel, of all places."

"It was a mistake. Nothing happened, anyhow."

"You don't understand." Sandoval helped himself to a cup of coffee, tasted it, raised it in an appreciative toast. "We deport people who cause disturbances. Quickly. If we think the disturbance is aimed at discrediting the government, we send you to jail, even more quickly. On the other hand, the death squads may consider you a threat to our national defense. Where they send you is in the hands of God."

"I'm not interfering with your national defense, not even in a whorehouse."

"You? Of course not. But Evita is a source of information for Force Red. Her girls report everything the customers say and Evita passes it to the terrorists."

"Shut her down." Curtin got some of his own coffee.

"The whore has many friends." Sandoval's taunting smile grew to an unpleasant grin. "You, on the other hand, do not. But a man can make friends. I can be a friend. Many think I am harsh, even cruel. Not so. I have friends, people I can share confidences with. That's the best part of friendship, I think—sharing the little secrets. Don't you?"

"I hadn't thought about it."

"Of course you have, Mr. Curtin. Not hard enough

perhaps. You know you need friends to conduct business in my country.'' He put down his cup, rubbed the rim in opposite directions with two fingers. It made Curtin think of forcing open the edges of a wound. Sandoval went on. ''I think we will be good friends. But if we are to exchange knowledge, it must be a fair exchange. You tell me who else was in Evita's last night.''

There was no way out. Did he know about Kooseman? Almost certainly. But if he didn't—

''Rudy Kooseman. He took me there. And the two who tried to pick a fight. They just don't like foreigners. It was over in a few seconds.''

Sandoval beamed, eyes glittering. ''There, you see? You have told me what I must know. Now I am obliged to return the favor.'' He patted Curtin's bicep. ''But, please, no more disturbances. Agreed?''

''I certainly won't start any.''

''Excellent. And now, to work. Goodbye.''

The crack of his heels on the tile flooring hadn't reached the front door before Lucia eased into the room through the back door. Peeking around the corner, she assured herself Sandoval was gone before speaking. She pointed at the door and her ear. ''I hear,'' she said, smiling happily.

''You listened?''

''Must know what you say. Be careful Evita. Maybe right, what he say. And *mas* careful Colonel Sandoval.'' Her face darkened, as if something foul shadowed it. ''He like what he do, Curtin. He like hurt.''

He stepped back and inspected her, top to bottom. Lucia shifted uncomfortably. ''What you look? What do?''

''I'm trying to decide who you work for.''

Doubling over, the tiny woman hooted laughter. She leaned against the door jamb and wiped tears from her eyes, then contemplated Curtin with amused pity. ''Who knows?'' she said. ''Last night a man come my house, say, 'What Curtin do all day, old woman?' I make him give me money, then tell him.''

''Damn, Lucia, that's spying!''

"No bad words. Bad say bad words. You no want people know what you do? Okay. Tell me what say. You nice. No yell, no say names, no many bad words. I lie other man, he never know, okay? What you do today?"

He massaged his temples. "I need some time to make sense of this. Of anything. Call me a taxi, please. I've got to go to town for one last permit."

Riding downtown, Curtin decided Lucia could be trusted. There was a firmness to her, a sense of *someone* under the visible exterior. Everyone else came at you from an angle, said one thing and meant another. Figuring them out was like trying to measure air with a yardstick.

Immediately inside the huge old structure housing the Ministry of Finance rose a looming dome. Circular balconies marked ascending floor levels. Hallways disappeared off the ground floor like rabbit burrows. The complex surface of the ribbed ceiling caught the bedlam of bureaucracy and reflected it in rich echoes, as if it remembered the courtly language of its centuries-old construction and refused to be corrupted by the gum-popping, machine-clacking, phone-ringing jangle of the present.

Curtin explained his business to four people in a huge office before one pointed at a man who would take his money and, hopefully, produce the required document. As Curtin neared, the man sensed the approaching necessity for a decision and fled, pretending not to hear the shouts that followed him out of sight. Furious, Curtin could only glare and mutter.

A young woman strolled over, smiling. She leaned on the counter and let him wait for a few seconds before asking, "Can I help you?"

For the fifth, tooth-gnashing, time, Curtin told his string of lies about his purpose for being in Costa Verde. This time he was wishing it were true so he could at least be angry for a legitimate reason. The girl listened absently, her eyes wandering to the greater importance of watching her co-workers.

When he was finished, she strolled away, returning with

a pages-long form, a stamp pad, several stamps, and a pen. The sheets of the document were meticulously arranged, side by side, on the counter. Curtin was gently pushed back to accommodate this display. The stamp pad was placed on the right of the ordered paper, carefully adjusted to a precise location. Next, the stamps were inspected before being aligned directly beneath the pad. They were double-checked for proper order. The pen was tested for working condition.

Without warning, she erupted with the frenzy of a flamenco dancer. Stamps were snatched up, hammered into the ink pad, slammed down with thunderous report. Pages flew. In a grand finale, she grasped the pen, daggerlike, scrawling a signature that zagged like blue horizontal lightning. A bead of sweat glistened at her temple. Curtin wanted to applaud.

"Your permit, senor."

The girl even helped him gather up the pages. As they folded them, she said, "We expected you today. Go home, and then go to the Oriente Country Club at eighteen hundred. Understand?"

"Yes." When he looked up to meet her eyes, there was nothing there but the disinterested bureaucratic glaze.

"Good. Now give me the money."

He blinked. "Do what?"

"My bribe, you fool! Do you want to expose us? Hurry! This must look perfect!"

Quickly, he fumbled a wadded mess of bills into her hand. She stuffed them in a pocket as he walked away, shaking his head.

In the cab, he marveled at the girl's chameleon existence. No matter which faction she worked for, she risked her life by becoming involved. She survived by hiding from everything, everyone. It was another example of the difference between them and himself. He understood camouflage. They understood deception. He attacked. They stalked.

It was confirmation of his earlier thoughts. He had nothing like their expertise at their rules. If he allowed himself to be caught up in their system, they'd destroy him.

On reaching his house, he told the cab to wait and went inside only long enough to drop off his briefcase before continuing on to the country club.

The building was another relic, a remembrance of banana-republic exploitation. Gleaming white, sprawled across manicured grounds, it leered across a valley that once stretched for miles with nothing but company cotton. Now the valley was divided among those who had been strong enough to depose the corporate kings. As the new barons, it was their turn to fatten. The houses of the peasants who worked on land they couldn't own still perched on the hillsides, waiting.

Parking in the shade of towering palms, Curtin walked up the long flight of stairs to be coolly greeted in unaccented English by a man standing behind what appeared to be a speaker's podium. He asked, "You are the guest of a member, sir?" as if there was a quiet joke involved.

Curtin said, "No, I'm just here to cruise the bar. I'll check with you later." He winked broadly.

The man winced. "If you'll sign the guest register, sir, we extend member privileges for one visit."

Curtin signed in. There were American names he recognized, politicians and media personalities. Inside, the harsh sun was defeated, strained through tall, jalousied windows. Polished wood and metal gleamed in the subdued glow.

A screened veranda stretched across the back of the building, overlooking an array of tennis courts. Curtin paused, hoping, remembering a yellow costume flashing across a similar place, the bright red hair-bow pursuing erratically.

Flor was not there.

"Senor Curtin?" The voice at his side jarred him back to the present. He turned to face the speaker, a man of about his own age, pleasantly earnest. "My name is Luis Perez. Seeing you here is a pleasant coincidence. A mutual friend in America asked me to introduce myself to you, help you get to know more about Costa Verde.''

It took only a glance at the benign innocence of the man's expression to make Curtin sure there was no coincidence involved.

He almost laughed. The place was getting to him. A few weeks ago, if approached by so pleasant and plausible a man, he'd have racked his brain to identify the mysterious ''mutual friend.'' Now his alarm signals jangled insistent warning. Nevertheless, he'd been told to be here.

''Thanks, Luis. I appreciate it. I have a lot to learn.''

''Will you join us? I am at a table in the other room with some friends. They will enjoy hearing the latest views from your country.''

Following him, Curtin said, ''I can't tell them anything they haven't seen on TV. I'm hoping they can tell me what *they* think.''

Luis's smile was confiding. ''If you live with us for another twenty years, someone someday *may* tell you what he really thinks of our situation. On the other hand, maybe no one will.''

Curtin laughed. ''Thanks a lot.''

He felt his smile freeze as they entered the main dining room and Flor's presence leaped at him. He had to force himself to return his attention to Luis.

Taking his guest's elbow, Luis spoke quietly, picking his way between tables, acknowledging waves and smiles from others. ''Look relaxed,'' he said. ''There is no way we can have contact with you and keep it secret, so we have decided to be bold. The spies will see only what is obvious and lose interest.'' Suiting action to his words, he became the stereotypic Latin, with flashing smile, immaculate grooming, graceful moves. Following him between the tables, Curtin felt his own bulk stood out like a barge being drawn by a speedboat.

They went to the table where Flor sat with another couple. Curtin managed to be a polite stranger, struggling through small talk. He learned that Luis was Flor's cousin and worked for the Ministry of Culture as an anthropologist. The other couple was married and ran a photography studio.

He was congratulating himself on hiding his inner turmoil when the photographers said they must be going. Luis excused himself as well, and they made a show of animated discussion on their way out. Curtin's newfound confidence in his skills fell apart. He stammered like a schoolboy.

She rebuked him through placid features with a voice that ripped like a saw. "Be careful! Never look at me that way!"

"Are you all right? Why was your passport taken away?"

"Of course I'm all right. Am I in jail? They're holding my passport because they suspect me. They suspect everyone. It was my turn, that's all."

"I don't believe you. Are you in danger?"

"You *must* believe me. Trust me and Luis."

"I trust you. I don't know him. I don't want to."

Forgetting her own warning, she glared with an anger that couldn't be mistaken. "That is fantasy. You are a stranger, someone I just met. Perhaps I will know you better someday, after the man I intend to marry is safely ransomed."

"I'm not proud of what's happened to us. I can still care that you're not in danger. Is that so unimaginable?"

"It's unforgivable. *We* are unforgivable."

Curtin shepherded drops of condensation on the beer bottle in front of him. Pushing with a fingertip, he created a larger and larger accumulation that trembled and shimmered until, succumbing to gravity, it sped to the tablecloth. A large gray area marked where many others had arrived first.

Luis's return broke their silence, gave them the opportunity to put on sociable masks once again. To Curtin, he said, "It would be foolish to stay here much longer, and you have a dinner engagement, Flor. And speaking of dinner, Buck, will you join us tomorrow at Flor's? We're having some friends for the evening, and you'd be quite welcome.''

"Thanks, I'd like that."

"Good. I'll pick you up myself, about six-thirty, okay?" Quietly, he added, "Wait a while before leaving here."

Curtin nodded slowly.

Luis got to his feet, pulling back Flor's chair. Curtin rose, touching hands with her. Her fingers were stiff, brushing his as if denying feeling. Luis's handshake was firm. He smiled his goodbye, and Curtin returned to his drink without watching them leave.

About twenty minutes later he paid his bill and walked outside. Night had fallen, and the waiting taxi drivers stood in a dim huddle beyond the edge of the hard light from the club building, their gossip and soft laughter cloaked in shadow. The next man due for a fare broke away on Curtin's approach, hurrying to open the door.

A well-marked police jeep fell in behind them as they left, and the driver turned to Curtin with a quizzical frown. Curtin tapped himself on the chest. "Gringo," he said, and the driver smiled halfheartedly. After the ride proceeded uneventfully for a couple of miles, he visibly relaxed. He was trying to make conversation with Curtin when they entered the small town. Headlights split the night behind them as an army truck lurched out of the alley. The police jeep had no opportunity to stop. It jerked hard to the left and ricocheted off the truck in a shower of sparks before collapsing its front end against a brick wall.

Curtin knew it was no accident and reached for the car door to bail out. Before he could open it, another sedan was beside them, a shotgun poked out the rear side window in his direction. At a shouted command, the cab driver slammed on the brakes.

The troublemakers from Evita's place leaped out of their car, gesturing Curtin inside. He considered a break, but the shotgun was less than six feet away, probably loaded with double-ought buckshot. If it went off, they'd bury what was left of him in a coffee can.

Interpreting the slight hesitation, the driver ran to get behind Curtin, pushing him forward and down onto the floor of the back seat. They tied his hands behind his back with several quick loops before draping a blanket over him. Then they were racing down the road.

In a few minutes they left the bumpy main road and veered onto an even bumpier secondary route. That lasted a little while, and then things really got rough. Curtin complained loudly and earned a heel driven into his kidney.

He shut up.

When the car stopped, he concentrated on anything his senses could bring him. There were pigs around somewhere, and a horse or mule. A cow lowed softly, and disturbed chickens muttered and clucked nearby.

They blindfolded him and changed the position of his hands to the front, binding them again before half-pushing, half-lifting him to his feet. Cramped legs bent, threatening to drop him, but the energizing pain of a jab from the shotgun helped him get himself together.

The taller of the two pulled Curtin's hand to his shoulder, then set out walking. Just as Curtin wondered how far they were going, he tripped over a threshold. A few steps across an earthen floor, and he was forced to his knees. His hand was pulled forward, then down, and he determined he was holding what had to be the top of a ladder. He got to the bottom without mishap. The blindfold was torn away.

The light of a kerosene lantern on a squat table the size of a checkerboard revealed an earth-walled room no more than four feet across and seven feet long. Its only other furniture was a filthy ragbag mattress on the ground.

Curtin gestured with the tied hands. "Okay, you know I'm not wired and I'm not armed. Untie me and let me see Robert."

The men looked at each other with sly, smug expressions, and when the taller one laughed out loud, the smaller followed suit a beat later. In his strange English, the tall one said, "We don't know nothing, Robert. Don't give no shit."

Curtin's hands were suddenly ice-cold. Of all the things that could go wrong, only one offered no hope. If these men were neither Force Red nor government, the party was probably over.

The man said, "Don't need Chavez. Got you. You got money."

Chapter 16

With nothing to sell and absolutely nothing to lose, these people wanted only the ransom money. They looked like men who'd kill for pocket change.

He said, "It's not just money. It's Force Red money. They'll find you and—"

The shorter man stepped forward and whipped a back-handed blow across Curtin's cheek. "Shut up," he said.

Exploring the torn flesh inside his jaw with his tongue, Curtin reflected that it was the first time he'd heard the little one use English. He obviously saved it for significant moments. The tall one grinned.

Curtin directed his argument at him. "You know Chavez won't show the money until he knows his son is safe."

The smaller asked, "How much is?"

Something sparked in the back of Curtin's mind. Without hesitation, he shook his head in a strong negative. "I make the arrangements. I meet Force Red, see Robert, send for the money. Chavez and Force Red talk about how much. I don't know."

"You know." Hatred rasped in the small man's voice.

"No, I don't. I really don't."

"Where is?"

"In the states. America."

The small one wound up, hit him again. Rolling away, Curtin dissipated most of the force by falling. When he straightened, they were in hot discussion. The tall one shrugged, obviously conceding a point, and suddenly reached out to turn Curtin completely around. He looked down to see a length of rope being wrapped around his ankles. Without warning, the line was yanked. Curtin fell heavily.

Easing through his scattered thinking, the comforting coolness of the dirt floor was deliciously welcome. Part of his mind urged him to let it soothe him completely, absorb all his pain and worry. The ladder creaked. He thought they were leaving. After a moment, however, hands grabbed him at shoulder and waist and flipped him over on his back.

The small man was coming down the ladder, trailing more line behind him. Curtin wondered what else they expected to tie up.

Then he noticed the line was actually wires.

The man carried one in each hand, carefully.

Metal rods glinted at the end of each.

At the bottom of the ladder, the man laughed. His teeth were brown, broken. He waved the rods, gripping their tape-insulated handles. A gasoline engine rumbled to life somewhere above as the sharpened tips swung close to each other. A vicious blue spark snapped between them and he yelled before rattling off angered Spanish.

When the tall one knee-dropped onto Curtin's midsection to hold him motionless while he pulled his shoes off, Curtin understood the intent, if not the meaning, of the words.

The tall man stripped off Curtin's watch before stepping away.

The rod points bit into Curtin's insteps.

It was like being hit with a bat. His heels dug into the

earthen floor and kicked him backward so hard his head thudded against the wall. The shock came again. He pulled his knees up to his chest, tried to roll away.

The engine roared faster.

The rods stabbed his side. Joints cracked under the stress of muscles convulsing so violently he thought they must tear free of his bones.

Torrents of sweat drenched him, blurred his vision, and he only partially saw the rods descending toward his groin. He yelled, a hoarse cry that escalated to a mindless scream as pain beyond anything he'd ever known exploded through his testicles.

When it stopped, he couldn't believe he was still conscious. Breathing hurt, each inhalation generating a shuddering, groaning exhalation. The stench of urine burned his nostrils. He worked himself away from that wetness, wedged his body to a sitting position against the wall at his back.

The tall man squatted beside him. The smaller one sat on the bottom step of the ladder and grinned around his broken teeth.

"Now tell how much money," the tall one said.

"Gold." Curtin had to force the word out. "Not money. U.S. dollars, maybe two million."

Excitedly, the two jabbered at each other. The small one laughed. The tall one said, "Where gold?" and Curtin couldn't keep his eyes off the metal rods.

He said, "You know how a deal like this is arranged. You know I don't have the money."

The man sobered, flattered to be considered knowledgeable. "I know money not here. You get." He sneered when he answered, but Curtin saw beyond it, caught the irresistible desire to be allowed inside such a momentous event.

"I can't, man. It's in the states—America. I have to send for it."

The tall man followed Curtin's glance to the rods, and he smiled. He spoke to his partner, and the small man rose. Curtin shook his head violently. The rods hovered over him. "It's the truth!" He wanted them to believe him, yet hated the genuine terror in his voice that made it believable. "Chavez has to know I've seen Robert and everything's okay!"

Again the two men argued. Curtin held his breath, but the rods didn't plunge down at him.

The tall man rose. "We go. Morning, come back. You tell then how make Chavez send gold, or we kill." He pulled Curtin away from the wall and untied his hands, leaving him to take care of his feet. He preceded the smaller man out, who frowned disappointment at Curtin before he picked up the lantern and followed. The ladder disappeared upward, and a large, heavy object scraped across the floor above, eventually sealing off the exit.

Curtin stretched out in the darkness, willing himself to relax. When he opened his eyes, he couldn't be sure if he'd slept or not. He was forced to feel for the walls in order to orient himself. As a result, he almost exclaimed out loud when the wire-thin line of illumination suddenly appeared on the ceiling. It added nothing to his vision, but it was definitely light.

He pulled the table under the hole and stood on it. The line marked the edge of the exit barrier. Excited, Curtin stepped down. He sat with eyes fixed on the slit, thinking each following minute would be the one that would see darkness return.

The light went out.

The darkness was total, impenetrable.

He counted to a thousand. Then two thousand. Then one more thousand. Then another thousand.

Crawling up onto the table, wobbling in the blackness, he felt for the thin crack. Steadily, carefully, he pushed upward. Under him, the table shifted. The object above remained firm. Then, scraping, something shifted. Little by little he forced it aside until there was a hole large enough to fit through.

Grabbing the edge, he chinned himself, then lunged

upward so he rested on his palms. For a few long seconds he rested, listening.

The silence remained unbroken. He hauled himself out, keeping in a crouch. His touch told him he was against a rough wooden wall, between it and a large packing crate. Peering over it, he saw through the hut's open door to brilliant stars. Their faint light revealed a clear path to freedom, but the rest of the single room flanked it with sinister darkness. Placing each foot with catlike caution, Curtin moved ahead.

Like a splash of scalding water, the harsh beam of a flashlight burned his eyes from a point immediately beside the door. Gasping, hands thrown up to ward off the dazzle, he charged.

His feet were swept out from under him. For an instant he hung sickeningly in midair before crashing to the floor. Bounding upward, his shocked vision still registering cannonbursts of color, he ran under something hard and heavy coming down across the back of his neck. Nearly paralyzed, he struggled weakly as calloused hands clamped around his wrists. Every bump in the floor echoed in his brain as he was dragged back to the hole. His feet were kicked into the empty space. Whoever was holding him lowered him part way, then simply let go.

Much later, Curtin stirred. Too battered to rise, he crawled around his underground cell, trying to get his bearings. The table was gone, the stinking mattress with it. He had only the featureless dirt walls. He slept.

When they moved the packing case away in the morning, he was already awake. The kidnappers laughed as they came down the ladder, the tall one pointing upward and out with broad gestures.

"You try go? Damn crazy. Him, he maybe kill you. He not smart."

Curtin nodded. "Listen, I'll tell you how to get the gold, but no more electricity. You have to promise."

The man cocked his head, birdlike, bright-eyed. "Pro-mise?"

"Your word, man." Curtin gestured, as if holding the rods. "No more. You say—no more."

"*Si*, sure—no more. You tell how get gold. No more *pak!*" The sound was much like the crack of the electricity, and Curtin's skin crawled.

He had his plan in order. Flor's tale of a cherished matador had been mentioned by Evita, but Kooseman claimed no such person ever existed. In the darkness, waiting, Curtin had decided the story was a signal, a way of letting him know the two women were connected.

It had to be.

If Evita could call on help, even another gang of crooks, she might get him out of this. The important thing was to outlive the present.

He said, "It is very complicated. Difficult. You understand." The tall one wrinkled his brow, leaned forward. Curtin continued, "The woman, Evita, is the only one who knows the message for Chavez. When I see Robert, see everything is okay, I tell her, 'The new matador has touched the bull.' When she hears that message, she will speak to Chavez. He will send a plane to the coast—the Pacific coast—with the gold. You understand?"

"Yes. 'The new matador has touched the bull.' " He glanced at his partner, then, "This place for the airplane. Where is that?"

"I don't know."

Without warning, the man drove a fist into Curtin's stomach. "Tell now, no more hurt. You say."

Sucking in air, Curtin said, "I can't remember the damned name! I've got a map at home. It's marked on there. Anyhow, the pilot doesn't land until I signal everything is right. He comes with many men, and they guard the gold until they see Evita, Robert, and me. Chavez doesn't trust me, and he doesn't trust Force Red."

The shorter man reacted to his companion's irritated indecision. They had another sharp exchange before the spokesman faced Curtin. "Okay. We keep you here." As they made their way up the ladder Curtin's stomach growled an accompaniment to the creaking wood, and the force of his hunger struck him.

"Hey, I need food! And water!"

The ladder scraped up through the hole, but the packing case didn't slide back over it. A minute later a basket came down on a string. It held a pop bottle full of water and an assortment of fruit. Curtin emptied the basket, and as wordlessly as it had come, it ascended out of sight. Then the case grated into place. He ate in darkness.

When one of her employees told Evita the two trouble-makers from the previous evening were asking to see her, her first reaction was to have them thrown out. Then she heard the strange sentence about the matador and changed her mind. After positioning men to watch the proceedings, she showed the newcomers to a table. Without Curtin to consider, they spoke in Spanish.

The tall one said, "We are from Force Red." One of Evita's eyebrows moved upward, the gentlest hint of disbelief. He paused, but went on. "We have decided Curtin must be hidden, or Sandoval's people will discover why he is in Costa Verde and deport him. We are ready to exchange Robert Chavez. You will make the arrangements Curtin told us about."

"Exactly what did he tell you?"

The man's suspicion flared like a torch. "You should know."

She quickly feigned scorn to cover the mistake. "Of course I know the plan, but I don't know you. You expect to come in here and tell me anything and be greeted like a brother? I trust no one like you, and no gringos. If you are truly from Curtin, you will know more."

Still wary, the man repeated Curtin's story. Evita said, "I must make a telephone call."

"We listen."

"Impossible."

"Then there will be no telephone call."

"Don't be a fool! You have Chavez. Now you have Curtin. Do you think I want their deaths on my hands?"

The smaller man sucked on a tooth. "She understands. One mistake, and those two die."

Not waiting for agreement, she hurried to the phone at the bar. In guarded language, almost code, she told the party on the other end that their friend was staying with other friends, but was in good spirits. As proof, she repeated Curtin's message. There was a long pause as she listened, her frown growing darker as the time extended. Finally she said, "You believe that's the only chance?" and then, "Very well. What must be, must be." She nodded, hanging up.

Raising her eyes, she saw herself reflected in the bar mirror and turned away. When she looked back, her face was professionally hard, calculating. She rejoined the men.

"It is arranged," she said. "The gold will be ready two nights from now. You must bring our friends to a meeting place at eleven o'clock."

The tall man tapped his fingers on the tabletop, eyes boring into hers. "How will the gold arrive?"

Evita felt a tickling at her temples, knew the perspiration was beading there. She said, "That is not my concern. My job is to send the message telling Chavez to send the ransom. Then I meet the gringo to give him a car and a driver to take him to the delivery place."

The two looked at each other. The tall one said, "If there is a trap, the young Chavez dies instantly. You too, only slowly and painfully. Why doesn't the gringo drive himself?"

Evita sighed fake exasperation, hoping against hope there would be no more questions, that her lies would hold up. "Would you let a gringo messenger know about so much gold without arranging for someone to stand behind him the whole time?"

Still drumming, the man continued to stare. The smaller one smiled. Evita's gaze drifted to him once, and the sweat at her hairline seemed to chill. She concentrated on the open hostility of the larger man, finding it less disturbing than that smile.

"Where do we meet you?"

As casually as possible, Evita sketched a map on the back of her business card. The man put it in his shirt pocket. The two of them rose as one and left.

Evita gestured toward the door with a quick nod, and one of her employees moved to a window. Turning, he indicated they were gone. She sat quietly for a moment, then furiously smashed a fist down on the tabletop.

"Interfering bastards! They'll get *everyone* killed!"

Chapter 17

The familiar grating sound overhead preceded pale light brightening the underground cell. Without his watch, Curtin had no idea of the time. He watched the basket descend, knowing only that someone had decided he should have something to eat.

Memories of other places, other times, struck him with the clarity of observed reality. Faces he thought long-forgotten filled his eyes. A voice rang in his ears, an interrogator he'd learned to despise. All those things underlined one fact—the first step in breaking a man was to disorient him. They were doing a good job, his keepers. The pain had been bad. Solitary darkness was worse. He called up through the hole.

"How about some light down here? I can't see a god-damn thing!"

The basket settled to the floor, tilting. The smell of hot food ended Curtin's immediate concern with light. He grabbed as the basket started to rise. Inside was a plastic bowl half-full of soup. The tilting had spilled the other half onto a tin plate, where two slabs of thick bread blotted the

169

liquid. Curtin wolfed down the meal before shouting upward again.

"I need more water! And I have to come out!"

He recognized the tall one's voice. "No!" Some Spanish followed.

Curtin tried again. "I've got to piss! You understand? Take a leak. Urinate. Come on, put the ladder down."

"No. Tomorrow morning, go west. Piss in morning." A moment later the water bottle was lowered again. Curtin winced at the contradiction of his thirst and the problem with its inevitable by-product. He tried thinking of something else.

At least Evita seemed to have grasped the significance of his message and was smart enough to stall for time. But what good would it do? While he was imprisoned, there was no chance to make contact with the genuine kidnappers or to arrange the ransom. If these men killed him, no one would believe his disappearance was the result of foul play. The message to Evita would be discounted. If he escaped or was freed too late to save Robert, everyone would be forever convinced he'd simply hidden out, a man who'd broken once more.

It was a debt that wouldn't be paid by dying. And one he was beginning to think he might die for.

Sounds filtered through to him from above, the hum of voices, footsteps. Something heavy scuffed and he leaped to his feet, thinking it was the box over his exit. No light seeped into his cell, and he finally admitted to himself it was just someone moving a chair.

Sleep was a long time coming, held off by persistent fantasies about getting his hands on the people up there.

When they came after him, they took no chances, ordering him to lie flat on his face with his hands behind him before they even lowered the ladder. After lashing his wrists together, they pushed and pulled him outside, where a battered truck waited in the thin light of dawn. Leaning to one side, its wooden slats and uprights stood out like the bones of starvation. Grabbed from behind, Curtin felt the familiar pressure of line around his ankles. An evil-tasting strip of material gagged him. Then he was lifted and flung face-down onto the splintered lumber of the truck bed.

They piled full sacks around him, rich with the smell of shelled corn. Steadily, grunting with effort, they enclosed him in walls of the stuff, then roofed over the cubicle with boards. More sacks went on top of that. In a few minutes he was completely enclosed, already stifling. Twisting onto his back brought his eyes inches from the boards overhead. They sagged alarmingly, and when the truck moved out, a distinct crack opened in one of them at the first bump.

Every jolt in the rough road was a direct blow. One nailhead in particular dug into his hip. He knew it wouldn't take long for it to work its way through his clothes and then through his flesh. He squirmed to avoid it.

Frustrating him further, the rope binding his wrists hooked on the projection. All his fury boiled out in a tearing lunge, and he felt something give. Unable to look, he felt for the nail. It was still there. Blood and sweat made his hands greasy, but he was certain he hadn't torn the flesh enough to account for the feeling of something breaking. Almost afraid to hope, he bent his fingers as far as they'd reach, feeling the cord. Frayed strands hung from the body of the line.

It took about twenty minutes to snap enough strands before he could pull the whole thing apart. The gag was easy. Getting the binding off his ankles demanded almost acrobatic contortions. Between that, the aftereffects of the torture, and the bouncing ride, he was mumbling a hymn of pain and hatred by the time he finished.

It was a while before he even considered lifting against the sacks overhead. It was fruitless. The boards rose no more than an inch, and the cracked one gaped dangerously when he let it drop back down.

There were gaps between the boards. The sacks peeked through, mocking him. Nothing but rough cloth and kernels of corn, they were enough to defeat him.

He managed to work a large sliver of wood free from the decking beneath him. It slipped between the overhead planks where his fingers couldn't go. Poking, sawing, tearing, he opened a sack. Corn cascaded down on him. He twisted to his side, exposing the holes in the truck bed, watching the grain spill out onto the dirt road flashing by below. He attacked another of the bags, and then another.

Soon he lifted off the remainder of the roof and stood.

His captors wasted no time wondering about his surprising reappearance. The smaller one stopped with a loud shout, and they both boiled out after him. When the tall one threw open his door, Curtin was waiting. He leaned over the retaining boards and drove a fist into his temple. The man tumbled back into the cab. The smaller one scrambled onto the truck's cargo, swinging a long knife. Curtin dodged, fell on his back. When the man lunged again, Curtin grabbed the knife hand at the wrist. Simultaneously, he bent his legs and got his feet into the other's midsection. When he pulled on the wrist and straightened his legs, his victim rose in a steady, rapid arc, disappearing over the side with a yell that ended in a satisfying thud.

On his feet again, Curtin vaulted to the ground as the tall one stepped out of the cab, left hand extended, jack handle in the right. Curtin heard the short one stirring and knew he couldn't afford to have both men able to fight at once. He attacked.

His enemy feinted a thrust and swung his weapon straight down. Warding off the blow with his left arm, Curtin stepped inside, driving his knee into the man's crotch as hard as he could. The man gasped, buckling, too hurt to cry out. Curtin stepped back, linking his hands behind the lowering head, pulling it down to meet the same knee, coming up.

With a sound almost like popcorn underfoot, nose and lips split and cartilage crushed. The man stumbled forward, spitting bloody teeth.

Curtin stepped back and let him fall.

Without warning, a massive weight struck him from behind, sending him sprawling, gasping for breath. Barely able to rise, he turned to see the shorter man climbing out of the truck bed, still carrying his knife. He stepped over the sack of corn he'd tossed at Curtin and kept coming. Curtin backed away on unsteady, rubbery legs, trying to get his breath. The man grinned. The knife jabbed busily.

A metallic clatter from the front of the truck froze them both in place. A sharp command in Spanish twisted the short man's smile, turned it desperate. He tensed, leaning almost imperceptibly toward Curtin. The voice snapped another command, and the man's eyes flickered, lost their fire. His smile melted, left him sullen with defeat.

Curtin straightened, allowing himself to relax as a uniformed soldier trotted forward to pick up the machete. Only when he had it in hand did he raise his head for Curtin to recognize him.

"Jesus Christ! Luis! Where'd you come from?"

Luis laughed. "Your friend can explain." He gestured at the rear of the truck.

"Friend?" Curtin looked as another soldier appeared. His eyes grew round and his mouth fell open.

"You just can't keep out of trouble, can you, Buck?" Ben holstered an automatic, walked to Curtin and shook his limp hand.

Finding his voice, Curtin said, "What the hell's going on? How'd either of you get *here*?"

Laughing, Ben put a hand on his shoulder, steered him to the front of the truck. A carryall was parked a few yards distant. "We came in that," Ben said. "Luis uses it in his work. He got us the uniforms, too. We were headed for the place where they were holding you when we saw the fighting."

Curtin shook his head. "Start at the beginning, will you? How come you're in Costa Verde in the first place?"

Ben sobered. "Flor says she told you about me. Those shots at Chavez's place were meant for me. No doubt about it. Flor asked if I'd help you and her try to get

Robert out of here, and I figured I'd be more use alive here than dead there, so I said I would."

"Who shot at you?"

"You know Bullard. Who else?"

The memory of the worried man on board the ship in New Orleans competed with Curtin's well-conditioned dislike of Bullard. Nothing was what it seemed. It wasn't even what it ought to be.

"How long have you been here?" he asked.

"I got in the day after Bullard and Flor. She got Evita to hide me out. I slipped out to your house once, real early. Your maid spotted me, and we didn't want her knowing about me. Evita's bartender hired her. She's not part of this." He grinned hugely. "How 'bout this—I'm a prisoner in a high-class cathouse."

"How'd you know where I was today?"

"Piece of cake. These goons never thought anyone'd follow them last night, but I did. Used Evita's old truck."

Luis said, "I suggest we take you to a safe place now, Buck. We must tie up these two first, and I will deliver them to some people who will hide them until everything is over."

Curtin looked confused, then his expression cleared. "Oh, I see. If the police get them, they tell Sandoval why I'm here. Once Robert's free, they can't talk because either Force Red or Sandoval will grease them for what they tried to do. But there's at least one other guy involved, someone who stayed at home while they went to Evita's."

"Then we must get that one, as well."

"Let's go. We can leave the three of them where they had me, until you can arrange for someone to pick them up."

Luis considered the suggestion, then laughed. "Perfect. We'll go in their truck."

Ordering the short man to load his semiconscious partner in the truck bed, Luis elected to drive. "Ride with me, Buck," he said. "Point out the house."

The old truck complained mightily under Luis's heavy

foot, groaning uphill, leaning sickeningly toward the yawning valley below as he pushed for the last bit of speed in the bellowing engine. Looking at the scant inches of road shoulder between the truck and eternity, Curtin wondered if the ride under the corn sacks hadn't been easier on him. Certainly he hadn't felt he was going to die momentarily.

When they broke out onto a plateau, it was a complete surprise. Forested mountains rose on all sides, the tallest of the ring wearing a crown of misty cloud. All of it had escaped Curtain before, and he saw it now at the same time he recognized the hut. He pointed. "That's it."

A figure squatting in front of the place, sharpening his farmer's ever-present machete, watched them approach until he saw the unfamiliar face at the wheel and Curtin's beside it. Wheeling, he sprinted into the field, headed for the closest hill and its protective growth. His feet dug into the soft, dry earth and a thin cloud of dust shimmered in the heat waves behind him.

Curtin yelled at Ben to watch the prisoners and leaped from the still-moving truck, giving chase. The field pitched upward toward the edge of the plowed land and the forest. The grade helped Curtin's longer legs eat away at the other's head start. Soon his quarry slowed, heard Curtin closing on him, and turned. He waved the machete, but he backed away, more interested in escape than attack. At Luis's distant shout, his glance flicked past Curtin and his expression turned desperate. He moved forward.

The plowed ground revealed many stones. The size of baseballs, or larger, they were capable of deadly damage. Backing away in his turn, Curtin hurled them at the farmer. One struck his chest, triggering a roaring charge.

Curtin fired his best pitch. The farmer's judgment was a fraction of an inch less than perfect when he threw up a shielding forearm. The rock glanced off, striking just above his eyebrow with the wet smack of a tomato splattering on a wall. He stopped dead in his tracks, swaying. The machete fell to the ground.

Luis pounded up beside Curtin, pistol in hand. "Twisted

my ankle.'' He was panting, squinting from exertion as well as excitement. The hand aiming the gun trembled. A quick movement from the farmer demanded Curtin's undivided attention. He was relieved to see the man was merely dropping to his knees, reaching out with one hand to steady himself.

The explosion of Luis's pistol was stunning. Only when the echo rolled back from the trees was Curtin able to speak, and then only to shout, ''What? Why'd you shoot him?''

Luis looked as unbelieving as the sprawled corpse. There was a major difference, however. Through his shock, something overwhelmed his amazement. His entire being cried out fascination with the death he'd created. Curtin had to shake his shoulder to break him out of his fixation. Even then, his gaze slipped back to the black-edged hole in the farmer's face before he answered. ''His hand—the machete. I thought he was picking it up.'' Without warning, he paled and gagged, doubled over.

When the ragged sounds of retching were over, Curtin said, ''What a goddam waste. I can't believe the poor bastard knew anything worth dying for, but we'll never know. Come on, we've got to hide the body.''

''Touch him?'' Luis grimaced.

''Goddam it, you shot the sonofabitch, you can help get rid of him! Grab his foot!'' Curtin lifted one of the limp legs and glared. Gingerly, Luis took the other, averting his eyes. They dragged the form to the edge of the forest. Luis looked skyward. ''They will come soon.'' He gestured. ''The black birds, the vultures.''

''Help me pile some of these damned rocks over him.''

In a few minutes it was done. From the protection of the trees and brush, they scanned the area. No other person was visible. They moved back to the truck as quickly as Luis's twisted ankle allowed. Once there, Luis was in better control. He asked, ''Where did they keep you?'' and Curtin led the way to the underground-cell entry. Luis nodded. "Excellent. We will leave these two to be picked up later."

Curtin looked thoughtful as Luis herded the pair down the ladder. "How long will they be here?" he asked.

Luis stopped yelling at the prisoners. "One day. Maybe as much as three. What difference?"

"None." Curtin rummaged through the place until he found the large jug full of water. He lowered it to the prisoners. As he retrieved the line, Luis said, "It was not necessary," and Ben added, "After what they did to you, I didn't think you'd do them any favors."

Quickly stacking everything available on top of the packing case to close off the cell's entry, they then hurried to the truck and squeezed into the cab.

It seemed to Curtin there was barely enough time to hear the brief tale of Ben's escape from the Chavez compound in South Dakota before Luis's carryall was in sight. The trip was much shorter the second time, now that he could see where he was going. As they abandoned the truck and Ben and Luis changed into civilian clothes, Ben expressed surprise at Curtin's account of the attack by the helicopter.

"Not me," he said. "I was way the hell and gone away from there by that time. No helicopter shot at me."

There was no time to pursue the matter. Luis bundled Curtin onto the floor in the back of the carryall. "Be careful," he said, hurriedly stretching a dirty tarpaulin over him. "I've got a lot of stuff from my archaeological dig under there."

From the driver's seat, he explained about the checkpoints. "Soldiers are patrolling everywhere. If you are discovered, we will have to explain how we found you. The kidnappers will be freed and tell Sandoval why you are in Costa Verde. We must keep you hidden until we can guarantee those criminals are safely in our control. After all, they may have friends who will look for them. Or worse, they may even know where you were held."

Grumbling, Curtin twisted in the darkness, trying to

rearrange the junk around him into a semblance of comfortable distribution. At least, he consoled himself, there was no need to try to escape from this ride.

"Uh-oh." The concern in Ben's voice was louder than his comment. "Troops ahead, Buck."

The vehicle slowed, stopped. A no-nonsense voice drifted back to Curtin, and he heard Luis's quick answer. A moment later, a shaft of daylight speared under Curtin's cover as Luis groped for something. Finally, under a fold, he found what he wanted. Curtin got the impression of a bulky, dirty, white object. The voice outside the truck rose sharply, almost cracked. Luis's hand appeared at the edge of the tarp again. This time Curtin saw what he was replacing. A skull grinned at him in the weird half-light.

When they were underway again, and Luis called his name, Curtin shoved the offending object away, throwing back the tarp before responding. "What's that thing doing here?" He pointed, backing up.

Luis chuckled. "It's from a dig. I told the soldier it was the head of an ancient priest, very evil. Until then, he wanted to search the truck. Whoever owned that head, he saved ours."

"Wonderful." Sarcasm twisted the word.

For the next few miles, Curtin recounted the story of his kidnapping. Luis was particularly scornful of the police surveillance, scoffing at how easily they had been eliminated. "Do you have any idea why they followed you?" he asked.

Curtin said, "None whatever. I sat around for a while, then left. That's it."

"Maybe they were just cruising," Ben said, "and took the same route you did. It's not like this country has a lot of roads to choose between."

Curtin rolled his eyes. "I expect Colonel Sandoval's anxious to tell me why his boys were on my tail. I don't look forward to that discussion."

The conversation lagged for a moment, and then Luis was turning off the main road, following a winding, well-maintained drive down the mountainside. Breaking clear of the forest, they were suddenly confronted by a large white home. Brick-red tiles crowned the roof, and the dark windows hinted of high-ceilinged coolness inside. The accumulated dirt on his clothes and body grew heavy on Curtin. He felt even worse when the vehicle stopped directly in front of the main entrance that centered the long porch and Flor stepped out.

"Welcome to my home," she said, but the formality of it rang hollowly. Before Curtin could return her greeting, she looked to Luis. "Mr. Curtin will call the police. He will say his kidnappers told him they mistakenly got the wrong man. He escaped, running off into the forest, where he remained hidden until he felt it was safe to return to the road. He walked here. No one can prove otherwise, and there's no time to create a better story. Come inside and rehearse the details. I'll arrange something to eat and drink." Turning on her heel, she disappeared through the doorway.

Curtin watched after her until the attention of the others pressed through his consciousness and forced him out of his trance. He turned quickly enough to see Ben's concern switch to embarrassment. The younger man looked away, pretending to have seen nothing.

Diplomatically, Luis said, "First I think we must get you to a hot bath and a razor, my friend. We must make you feel better."

Curtin wondered when that might happen.

Chapter 18

The tile of the bathroom floor was cool, a delicious contrast to the warm tub that had soaked away so much of the pain plaguing his body. A soft breeze filtered through the slats of the jalousied door leading to the balcony, and Curtin faced it, head thrown back, luxuriating in the physical and emotional sensations of freedom. He stretched, turning, but stopped abruptly at the sight in the medicine-cabinet mirror. Bruises new and old discolored his skin, and a swollen jaw gave him an unbalanced look. Ugly welts marked the places where the electrified prods had seared him. He made a face, remembering, then walked to the bedroom door. There had been hushed female chatter and giggling in there while he bathed, and he didn't know what to expect on his return.

His clothes lay spread out on the bed, warm as well as clean. They could only have been washed and ironed dry. He dressed, omitting shoes and socks, enjoying walking barefoot. From the balcony that stretched the length of the second floor he looked down onto the checkered brown and green of fields and the tiny figures of cattle in the pastures. Cooking-fire smoke rose from each of the small houses in the distance. The blue-white plumes played in the wind until absorbed. The calm beauty made the savagery loose in the land even more obscene.

A movement to his right caught his eye, and he looked to see a swaying hammock. He was sure the rich, dark hair tumbled over the side could belong to no one but Flor.

Silent on the polished tile, he moved to look down at her from behind. It was a full minute before she turned warily in his direction. On seeing him, she swept quickly upright. "I didn't hear you."

"I should've spoken. I didn't know what to say. I don't think I really wanted to say anything."

She looked away. Her features were controlled. "They say you were tortured."

He said nothing, and she faced him again. "Is it true?"

"Yes."

"That's all? 'Yes'?"

"It's not worth talking about."

"Did you tell them anything?"

"Certainly. I told them what they wanted to hear. I didn't tell them the truth, though."

Accusing, she leaned forward almost imperceptibly. "You involved Evita. Who else did you name?"

"No one. I named her because I had to try for help from someone. Should I have kept my mouth shut, died nobly?"

Color flamed across the copper-gold features, gave them a furnace glow. She looked away quickly. "I'm sorry. I should've known you wouldn't break."

"Don't kid yourself. I would have." She looked at him through lowered lashes, uncertain. He went on. "It's not the pain that breaks most people, it's the knowledge that it won't stop until the other guy's satisfied with the answers. Most people can stand up to a lot of hurt as long as they think there's an end to it."

"You lecture on suffering? After you've seen the way we live?"

"Why are you picking a fight with me? If it's because

of the two clowns knowing I'm connected with Evita, Luis already said he'll keep them under wraps until this is all over."

Carefully, as if each movement brought a new, harsher pain, she stood up and walked away. Curtin started after her, then stopped. He said, "Flor, stay, please. I have to talk to you."

Keeping her back to him, she put a hand to the wall as though bracing herself. "We have nothing to say to each other. Not alone."

"I know." Her shoulders slumped, and he hurried on. "Until this morning, I fought to forget you're in love with another man. If I lived, I was going to fight for you, make you mine any way I could. I had it all figured out. I'd spring Robert, and then do whatever I had to do to split you apart." He paused, shook his head. "A little while before they came for me, I knew I was wrong."

"I am glad to hear it. What you were thinking—it is very threatening."

"I wanted you to know how I feel about myself. Robert thinks of me as his friend."

"You must forget what happened. I have."

He leaned forward, clenched the line holding the hammock, hands turning white under the strain. "I can't! I want you! God help me, I never stop thinking of you. How do I forget what was, stop thinking about what might have been?"

She turned, but only to back away, not looking frightened so much as surprised by the force he projected. She nodded, a slow, almost preoccupied movement. Even her voice was more distant, softer. She said, "We must help each other. I said I have forgotten what happened to us. That was a stupid lie. But now we must protect him." Then she was almost running, turning into one of the many doors leading off the balcony.

Curtin remained motionless for a few minutes. As he moved to leave, he winced at the difficulty of releasing his grip on the hammock line. A knuckle popped. He exercised his hands on the way to his room, where he tied his shoes with only an occasional twinge.

He made his way into the hall, scarcely noticing the antiques lining the walls, although his professional interest was caught momentarily by the massive open beams of the ceiling and the intricate carving of the balustrade supporting the glossy banister of the stairway.

Luis waited in the dining room. He smiled, gesturing at the feast of fruit, vegetables, different cheeses, and sliced meats stacked on the table. Fresh bread filled the air with a rich yeast aroma.

Flor walked in while Curtin was putting together a salad and a huge sandwich. Luis said, "I was waiting for you, Flor. I wanted to tell you both I know someone who can contact Force Red and explain why Buck disappeared."

Curtin swallowed a mouthful of food. "What? They've never contacted me. Why do we tell them anything?"

"We must assume they have had you watched since your arrival in Costa Verde. They probably know as much about your disappearance as anyone." He laughed harshly. "They may even know more. But you see, having lost sight of you, even for this short while, they will be very suspicious of what happened during that time. We will have to reassure them, or we endanger Robert."

"I'm beginning to wonder if they'll ever make a move."

Flor said, "When they're ready, they will. They know how to wait for the right moment, give them that."

"Will they take your word for what's been going on, Luis?" Curtin asked.

"I think so."

Flor frowned. "Is there any possibility they were involved?"

"Buck says the men who held him said they knew nothing of Robert, but wanted only to steal the ransom. Without any other evidence, I have to believe they had no connection with Force Red."

Curtin said, "Fine. So where are we?"

Flor spoke first. "We must move the kidnappers. We can't allow them to fall into Sandoval's hands. They will expose you, and your mission will be a failure."

Luis looked dubious. "My first thought was to move them, but I was seen there once today, and I told the patrol I was *leaving*. Buck has to lead Sandoval to the crossroads nearest the hut and indicate he was freed at that point. If I'm seen in the vicinity for a second time, Sandoval will be very interested to know why I find the area so attractive."

"I don't like any of it. Does Buck have to talk to Sandoval?"

"After Sandoval's own surveillance team was ambushed? Of course! But the story should work. It's as close to the truth as possible."

Flor tossed her head, obviously unsatisfied. "We must assume Sandoval will investigate immediately. Buck must convince him it was all a mistake. For that to succeed, we can't have those men found. And if Force Red *does* know of them, and eliminates them, we have that on our conscience. There's been enough killing, Luis."

Luis walked to her and patted her shoulder. He said, "I know. Too well." Flor bit her lip, but Luis went on gently. "For your sake, I'll arrange to have them moved right away. Now, can you get Buck and Ben to town?"

"Yes. I'll have the car brought around." Her eyes sought Curtin's. He was waiting. Each turned away from the other as if burned. She left, and only as they were getting into the car did she appear on the rambling porch to wave goodbye.

Luis stepped to the side of the car. "Antonio will let Ben out near Evita's place, then take you directly to Colonel Sandoval. I'm going out to my dig and establish my own alibi. You're satisfied with what you must say?"

"As satisfied as I can be."

Luis nodded, then spoke to the driver. Curtin looked to see Flor again, but she was gone.

Ben said, "That's one helluva lady," and when Curtin

turned sharply, he was looking out the back window. He went on heedlessly. "It took a lot of guts to string Bullard the way she did. And she knew exactly what you were going to have to tell Sandoval. I don't know how she does it, man." He faced Curtin, who was carefully monitoring his reactions. "I hope this all works out for her."

"Yeah. So do I." Curtin leaned to the side and closed his eyes.

When the driver shook him, he responded irritably. "I'm just resting. What d'you want?"

Antonio pointed nervously. "Sandoval. Police. You here, please. Me go."

Curtin sat up, stifling a groan at the array of pains the quick movement generated. Ben was already gone. Sunlight blasting off the Ministry building assaulted his eyes. Shading them, he stared, collecting his wits.

"*Coronel* Sandoval," Antonio repeated. His fearful grin made Curtin think of the skull among Luis's artifacts.

The heat outside the air-conditioned car swatted like wet cloth. Antonio was moving with the click of the door latch.

Inside the building, the MP Sergeant at the desk stared at the gringo with undisguised boredom until he heard the name Curtin. Then he was on his feet in a flash, shouting and reaching across his desk. Doors Curtin hadn't even noticed flew open and troops stormed out, some with weapons, some empty-handed. They surrounded him. It should have been a Keystone Kops comedy, but raw menace eliminated any hint of entertainment. The Sergeant marched his prisoner to the elevator, selecting two armed troopers to accompany him. On the top floor he dismissed them and, in solitary glory, shoved Curtin into Sandoval's presence

The Colonel was angry. He stood beside his desk, leaning on it, a foot jerking irregularly in small arcs.

Curtin said, "Tell this goddam fool to get his hands off me! I come in here to report—"

"Shut up!" Sandoval's voice almost cracked, bringing a

rush of color to his face. The twitching foot cocked as if to
lash out. "Who arranged the truck? Do you think it will go
easier for you if you turn yourself in?"

Matching Sandoval's anger, Curtin leaned forward in
the Sergeant's grasp. "Turn myself in for what? I was
kidnapped! Where the hell were these apes of yours when I
was a goddam prisoner? You're pretty damned good at
pushing around innocent people, but you don't do much
with criminals, do you?"

"You lie." Sandoval poised. The Sergeant shifted, getting Curtin's body between himself and the enraged Colonel.

Curtin held out his wrists. "That's where they tied my
arms!"

Sandoval sneered. "Anyone can manage marks like
that. We will learn the truth from you, and then you will
truly have something to show."

"Like this?" Curtin raised his shirt, exposing the marks
from the electrical prods. With the impulsive gesture, the
chill of Sandoval's office struck through his control. He
gritted his teeth against a shiver.

Sandoval stopped short, then moved forward quickly,
reaching to touch the welts. "Electricity!" The sudden
change to cool professionalism, the almost scholarly appreciation of another's work, filled Curtin with a contempt
that reestablished his ability to ignore the cold.

The fingers on his flesh were another matter, however.
Quickly curious, they ranged his torso like small, preda-
tory animals. "The testicles as well? The head?"

"The testicles. Not the head. Other places."

"Amateurs, obviously. Varying current. Some sort of
generator." Sandoval barked an order at the Sergeant, who
scurried away, not letting the Colonel's radical change of
attitude slow him down. Sandoval headed back to his
desk, pointing at the chair in front of it. Without turning,
he said, "Sit."

From his own chair, he stared past tented fingers into
Curtin's eyes. "Something is very wrong here, Senor
Curtin. Very wrong." He tapped the tips of his fingers

together, waiting for a response. Curtin refused to take the bait and said nothing.

"Bluntly, you aren't worth kidnapping. You represent no major corporation. You haven't been here long enough to make enemies or establish a pattern kidnappers could use for planning. It would make no sense, except that four American senators arrived in Costa Verde this very morning. They say we are not police, only bullies and killers. How convenient that a Canadian businessman is kidnapped and tortured right under my nose! What a grand press conference you will all have! Is that the plan?"

"What plan? My kidnappers even told me they got the wrong man! It was a simple for-cash kidnapping. It's obvious. American senators! Christ, you think I'd let myself be fried for a press conference?"

"Nothing is obvious. As for your willingness to be fried, as you put it, I've seen stranger things." Sandoval rose, turned his back to stare across the top of the sandbags at puffy clouds in an incredibly blue sky. "Tell me exactly what happened."

"Suppose you tell me why I was being followed."

One of Sandoval's shoulders twitched. "Someone is always followed from the country club, usually a new arrival to Costa Verde. It lets people know we're watching. The men on duty didn't recognize you, so you were chosen. It was a coincidence. Believe me, it never will be again. Now, the details."

Curtin covered everything from the time he left the country club until his rescue, saying he walked cross-country after escaping until he came out of the forest at the crossroads where Luis and Ben actually rescued him. For Sandoval, he changed that part, claiming he walked on until he reached the Peralta home.

Sandoval made him repeat it. He remained motionless through both recitals.

After the second one, he picked up the phone and spoke quietly, but even without understanding the language, Curtin heard the threat in the tone. By the time they reached the first floor, three truckloads of troops sat in front of the building. A sedan waited in front of them. Sandoval touched Curtin's arm, pointing, and they climbed in. The interior was already cool.

As they moved out, Sandoval said, "Tell me again how it went." It was the only conversation during the ride.

Nearing the crossroads, he pointed and asked, "There?" Curtin appeared to study the place before affirming it.

The sedan stopped and a young Lieutenant ran from the lead truck to stand at a respectful distance, awaiting orders. Sandoval ignored him, pointing at the ground. "You said you leaped from the moving truck and ran into those woods. Why is a whole bag of corn here?"

"Maybe they saw me, stopped, and it fell off."

"You never said that before."

"I never thought about it before. I hit the ground, rolled a few times, got up, and ran like hell. It looks like they stopped, but if they did, i didn't see them. I never looked back."

Sandoval grunted, moving away. "They must have stopped, then returned to wherever they were keeping you. There's no trail of corn beyond here. We will trace it back. You saw nothing, you cannot remember how you came here?"

"No."

Muttering, Sandoval gestured the driver ahead. At each ramshackle farmer's hut, troops debarked, surrounding the building. They held submachine guns at the ready, and the expressions of the peasants left no doubt that they expected the troops to use them at the first excuse. The crying, frightened children bothered Curtin the most. It was bad enough to see the women cower and the men's helpless anger, but the children were the worst. Too young to deserve anything but sunshine and laughter, they watched the encircling men with wide-eyed understanding. More, they unfailingly dismissed everyone else to concentrate on Sandoval as soon as they saw him. Grimly, Curtin reflected on the possible sources of such wisdom.

He did his best to hide his feelings as the soldiers finally advanced on the hut where he'd been held. He felt better when he saw no buzzards wheeling over the cairn where the body of the farmer Luis shot was buried, and better still when no one answered the troopers' shouts. Made wary by the unusual silence, they advanced cautiously. Four men rushed the door and disappeared inside.

Curtin's heart banged at his ribs. His palms ran with sweat.

Had there been time to move the kidnappers? If they were captured, they'd expose him immediately. Would Sandoval throw him in jail, or could he be bought?

Responding to Sandoval's order, he stepped out of the car. Silently, he cursed Chavez, the kidnappers, the visiting senators, and sheer rotten luck.

One of the troops reappeared at the doorway. He spoke, laughing, and Sandoval turned a bleak gaze on Curtin. The man at the doorway went back inside. More laughter tumbled out of the building.

The packing case stood away from the hole. Curtin breathed deeply, aware of the awful smell of the place, surprised that it was worse than he remembered. Something different in it pulled at his memory. More immediate problems blunted the impulse to identify it.

Sandoval clamped a grip on his shoulder, guided him to the edge of the underground room. Two of the soldiers played flashlights into the hole.

The kidnappers lay on the floor like broken store-window dummies, their bodies ripped with gaping wounds. The short one's eyes were wide with terror and his mouth hung open in a scream that would last him through eternity.

Deep in Curtin's mind a connection clicked, and he recognized the elusive smell as the burned-steel stink of a hand grenade.

The kidnappers would tell no one anything.

Chapter 19

Steam coiled out of the aromatic rum-and-coffee mixture in Curtin's cup. He welcomed it. Anything that gave Sandoval's office a touch of warmth and humanity was good.

Sandoval was playing with his guest the way a chess master might torment a beginner. His questions had been innocuous. Still, each answer was followed by a drawn-out silence, as if he considered the answers weighted with significance. All the while, a smile ghosted the corners of his lips.

Curtin was undisturbed. He was sure Sandoval wouldn't waste time baiting a man he meant to break. It wasn't that he lacked the cruelty to do it; it was simply that he had too many other people demanding his attention. Whatever Sandoval was leading up to, it didn't involve jail for Curtin.

Sandoval sipped his drink. "You passed several houses before arriving at the Peralta farm. Why didn't you stop at one of them?"

"I was looking for a place that looked like it'd have a phone."

"But you never telephoned anyone? Why?"

"We tried, but couldn't get through. It was easier for them to have a man drive me to town."

"You take things like unfailing telephones for granted."

"I hope your country will too, one day. The sooner, the better."

Sandoval smiled, raised his cup in salute. "Thank you. Tell me, why did you come directly to me after your trouble? Why not go to your embassy?"

"The woman in the house—her name is Flor Peralta—insisted that I see you personally. She didn't know I knew you, but she said you were the man who would catch my kidnappers."

"That's a pleasant surprise." Sandoval chuckled, looking down at his desk. When he raised his face, the amusement was almost completely faded, as though the moment had a privacy that excluded Curtin. He added, "She is a close friend of a man named Bullard, who is the half brother of our celebrated kidnap victim, the Chavez heir. She's hardly Force Red material, because her family has too much to lose, but I had her passport impounded a while ago."

"Did she do something?"

"Not that I know of. I thought it would be interesting to keep her here to see who she talks to."

Curtin thought of the meeting in the country club, and his mouth went dry. If one of Sandoval's informants reported on that, the story of stumbling into the Peralta farm would collapse. He took a large swallow of his drink, then grinned confidentially. "A lot of people might object to that, but what choice do you have? You've got to uncover the people who're trying to destroy you."

"Exactly. You know, you are not like many of the foreigners who come here. They are uncooperative, looking for things to criticize instead of contributing to our progress."

"I try to see your problems from your point of view."

"That's it! Put yourself in my place. That kind of understanding is good to hear, especially from you. A man who knows how to get and move heavy equipment could be invaluable to us."

"That's my business."

"Yes. Tell me, is it true, the rumors I hear of much equipment stolen in Canada and Alaska and in the U.S.? I have also heard it reappears in other countries. Have you heard of this?"

"It's true."

"You know this?" Sandoval's earlier playful mood was gone. His eyes scoured Curtin's expression, searching for clues.

Curtin said. "Let's say I know enough not to talk about what I know, okay?"

"Excellent." Sandoval smiled openly. "I represent some investors who need equipment. I can arrange the necessary import papers and licensing for someone who can produce what we want at a discount. Some interesting profits would be divided. Are you the man?"

Leaning back, acting as though assessing the proposition, Curtin's mind raced through possibilities.

If he agreed, Sandoval would watch his every move and assume his every contact was involved in the deal. Flor, Luis, and possibly Evita would be in for constant scrutiny.

On the other hand, to refuse would anger the man, possibly drive him to investigate the false Canadian cover. If that were broken, everyone would be destroyed, and the mission as well.

And the mission was the important thing.

Or was it?

Was he thinking of anything except himself? Wasn't he merely using everyone else in an attempt to rebuild his own image in his own mind? Was that so different from running in the night to avoid death?

"You have no answer?" Sandoval's grating question pulled Curtin back to the present.

"There's some equipment positioned in a neighboring country. It'd be simple to ship it, declared for Mexico, then divert it to anywhere you choose."

Sandoval rose, leaning across the desk, beaming. "Set up a company to act as brokerage. I'll arrange government purchase orders." He interrupted himself with a wink. "The Americans send enough aid money to drown us. We might as well enjoy the swim, eh? The rates will be prime, the shipping costs of the very best. To make it look right, I want you to supply some items through proper channels, establish yourself as a legitimate businessman. Let me know whatever you need."

Curtin got to his feet. "I'll start right away. But what about the kidnappers?"

Sandoval blinked. "Kidnappers? What about them?"

"Don't you want a statement from me? Won't I have to testify, or something?"

"Piss on them! I'll find the rest of their gang, and they'll die, too. Forget it." He walked around the desk, moving to the door with Curtin. "Actually, they did you a favor. Before, you were only another informant. Now, you are my business associate. You will find life much different."

Curtin smiled, shaking the offered hand. He didn't trust himself to speak.

He was walking across the lobby, mentally composing his next message to Chavez, when he heard his name shouted. It echoed, challenging from every direction. On the other side of the room, Kooseman pointed with a hand that had trouble staying on target. When he called out again, drunken self-pity turned the words into syrupy organ notes.

"I know where you been!" He staggered toward Curtin. "You been suckin' up to Sandoval, cuttin' a deal, leavin' your old frien' in the friggin' cold." Stopping, he goggled like an owl. "Cold? Not friggin' likely, in this friggin' place." Serious again, he advanced. "Gonna get rich, leave ol' frien's inna dust, right? Bassard!"

Curtin hustled him toward the door. "Shut up!"

Kooseman looked around, suddenly sly. His voice dropped to a whisper. "Don' worry. I can keep a seecurt—seeget—Shit, I can keep quiet. All I want's a piece, buddy."

"You do, huh?" Curtin backed him against the wall. Passersby smirked at them. Curtin hoped none understood English.

"Sure. Sandoval an' his amigos use aid money to buy mil'tary stuff. Naughty-naughty." Almost crying, he pawed at Curtin. "Never thought my frien' get hooked on almighty dollar. Not even your dollar. Friggin' Canuck. *My* dollar, dammit. *My* friggin' taxes, and you don' let me in on it. Whatta bassard!"

Desperately, Curtin put on a friendly smile. "Hey, you got me all wrong! Sure, we talked, but nothing's definite yet. If I get a deal going, you're the first guy I'll come to. You know this place, man. I need you."

Kooseman swayed, hung his head. "Oh, geez, I'm sorry, buddy. I been drinkin', y'know? I shoulda known you'd never dump on a frien'. Rotten, what I said. I'm sorry, buddy, really sorry. I'm a bassard, you know?"

"Go on home. Sober up. I'll get back to you, okay?" Curtin signaled furiously for a cab, backing away. Kooseman continued to lean on the wall, looking at his feet, shaking his head. When he looked up, Curtin was fleeing in the taxi. Confusion washed across the fat little drunk's face until he located him, and then he waved sadly.

Despite Curtin's anger at having been exposed to so much attention, he couldn't get the last image out of his mind.

When he arrived at his house, however, Lucia gave him no time to dwell on Kooseman's loneliness. She flung open the door, obviously waiting for him. He was startled to see her trembling violently.

"What's wrong? What happened?" he asked.

"Why you made the *policia* mad with you? Sandoval came here! He tell me watch you all time, say you go

jailhouse. I no tell lie, no tell truth. Don't know nothing.
You make big trouble me.''

"Come on into the kitchen and sit down.'' The tiny
woman considered for a moment, then whirled and marched
away, leading. Curtin smothered a smile and followed.
Deliberately, she stood waiting for him to take a chair,
then poured them both coffee. Only then did she allow her
curiosity to force her to a seat. As Curtin detailed his
adventure, her determination to be hostile crumbled, and
she was first horrified, then sympathetic, punctuating the
tale with small cries and shocked gestures.

He stopped short of his final meeting with Sandoval. All
her previous emotions fled, crushed by the instant return of
fear.

"You think they mistake, get wrong man?''

"That's right.''

"*Loco*! You crazy man!''

"It's what I told Sandoval, and he believes it.''

Her hand flew to her breast. "Him? Believe? He believe
nothing! Nobody believe him! He talk, you think, 'Lies!
Lies!' Every time, you be right. Big trouble, even so—you
never know *why* he lie.''

Curtin studied his coffee cup. The little old woman had
said nothing he hadn't already told himself, but another
thought had come to him. When he spoke, he preceded
the words by patting her hand. She reacted with mild
surprise, but cocked her head to the side, anticipating.

He said, "Lucia, I think it's dangerous for you to keep
coming to my house. I'll pay you, but I don't want you
coming here anymore.''

She stiffened, insulted. "Pay me? Not work? No! I
work, you pay. Not work, no money. Honest woman!''

"All right, all right! But what if you come in the
morning, then leave and come back in the evening to fix
dinner? Would that be okay? I'll pay the same.''

"No talk money! Money okay! Anyhow, *el Coronel*, he
say I be here all day, tell him what you do. I like stay

here. I tell what you want me tell. I go, some other woman come. Tell truth.''

"What do I do with you? Look, no lies for Sandoval, you understand? I don't want you getting in trouble!''

She drew erect, jabbed a skinny finger at her chest. "Honest woman. Government always lie. Lie at government, not same like lie at people. You good man. Maybe not so honest, but okay. I like. I stay.''

Curtin sighed, then stood and bowed. "I am glad you are my friend, Lucia. I think you are probably the most honest liar in all Costa Verde.''

Lucia tried to hide her modest embarrassment behind both hands; but the delighted laughter rang too clear to be disguised.

Chapter 20

The radio remained stubbornly silent, no matter how hard Curtin stared at it. The tape recorder spun along happily, uselessly. Curtin reached inside the yawning refrigerator for another beer and yanked the cap off. Over ten minutes had passed and Chavez still hadn't responded to the last message.

Curtin tilted the bottle, drained a good third of it. He looked at his watch.

The brief squeal of the transmission pulled him to attention in his chair. He quickly separated the recorder and turned it on to listen to Chavez.

"Excellent work. The material you wish to sell is in place and can be moved at any time. Use it to reinforce your cover, but play for time until you have definite information about our mutual friend. The third party is on the way to the rendezvous point with the exchange material."

Returning the recorder to its place with the radio, Curtin replaced the refrigerator panel that concealed the equipment and stepped out into the afternoon sun. Alerted by Lucia's identification of the neighborhood snitches, he took some pleasure in their consternation at the sight of their pet gringo going somewhere alone, on foot. He hoped it was unusual enough to send them into spasms.

It was a short walk to the major boulevard, where he caught a cab quickly. The ride out of town was pleasant, the air clearing rapidly once they were away from the congested traffic. The ripe smell of turned earth and cut vegetation impressed itself on him, and he was surprised to realize the countryside always smelled like that. In this part of the world, planting knew no season, and fighting weeds was a continuous battle. Local hills stood back from the road, with distant mountains like mysterious challenges ranged behind them.

The scene drew him halfway around the world before he could control his mind, and he was thinking of similar views, and nights of fire and blood. It wasn't pure nostalgia that made him believe that way of life was preferable to this one, he decided. Things were direct then, fat with pure awareness and knowledge. If you lacked information, you used your skills to go out and get it. Winners survived. When it was over, maybe you were changed a little bit, but you knew who you were, and who your friends were.

Unless something went crazy.

Unless you broke.

"*Con permiso*, senor." The driver was turned around, smiling apology. "No *inglés*. No English."

"*Sí*." Curtin gestured weakly. The driver returned to his work, and Curtin silently damned himself for getting so engrossed in his thoughts he muttered to himself. For the remainder of the trip he rehearsed what he had to tell Flor.

She greeted him with reserve, rather than anger, and led him inside. At her gesture, he sank into a massive leather chair that exhaled a ripe aroma of cigar smoke and age as it enfolded him. It was obviously her father's favorite. For a moment he wondered if there was any significance in the fact. Quickly, though, he stated the reason for his return.

"I've got to know more about this Force Red lash-up, and I have to know the details of Robert's disappearance."

"Why?"

"Because I want to think about a rescue instead of depending entirely on the ransom. I need some idea of where to start looking for him."

"Impossible." She shook her head. "You'd be spotted in a minute, wherever you went. There's no chance of your learning anything. Not in this country."

"You have friends. Evita, Luis. It doesn't have to be me that looks for him."

"It won't work. Anyhow, Force Red needs the propaganda. They won't hurt him."

"*If* it's Force Red. What if it's someone using Force Red as a blind? Remember, that's what happened to me."

"That was different!" The firm thrust of her jaw collapsed as her teeth nervously worried at her lower lip.

Curtin refused to be put off. "Look, three people were at the shack where they kept me. There has to have been at least a fourth, the guy who drove the truck that cut off the surveillance jeep. If Sandoval had that one, I'd have heard about it. And the morons I saw couldn't have put together my kidnapping by themselves. Robert's in more danger than you're admitting, Flor."

"That's not true! You're trying to frighten me. You're cruel!"

"You're damned right I'm trying to frighten you. I need your help!"

She raised clenched fists. "You're as ruthless as the rest of them. You'll do anything to get your own way!"

"That's a damned lie! Robert can identify the people holding him! Those idiots we left in the hole are dead only because their partners couldn't get at me to shut me up. That meant they had to get rid of the other witnesses. It's their partners who may have Robert!"

Flor's hands fell slowly, as if the strength was draining from her body while Curtin watched. Her face paled, and as much as he hated seeing pain in her eyes, that was preferable to the sick surrender that filled them now. She half-turned, as though twisted by a blow. Tears slid down her cheeks. Her crying was silent, the supple body racked by sobs she was too brave to admit and too beaten to refuse.

Hesitantly, Curtin took her in his arms, telling himself he was comforting a hurt friend. At first she was rigid. He almost released her then, but it was too late. If he stepped away now, he reasoned, she'd only be convinced his reaction had more meaning than it actually did. Nevertheless, when she relaxed, leaning against him, he knew the first move had been a mistake.

Worse, it was self-delusion.

Of course he wanted to comfort her. But far more than that, he wanted to hold her in his arms, to feel her body pressed against his own.

And she was no longer resisting.

Gently, fearfully, she raised her head to meet his gaze. Her arms went around him. She tried to speak and failed. Full lips parted, she licked them in order to try again.

Curtin's mind threatened to explode, writhed with erotic imaginings. Unbidden, his grip tightened, drew her to him.

"It cannot happen," she said. She made no move to escape, choosing to make him aware that he must decide his own behavior. For several heartbeats they stood, locked in each other's arms, before Curtin found the strength to loosen his grasp. She withdrew her embrace simultaneously. She never blinked. Her eyes remained fixed on his as they stepped apart. He saw nothing in them now, when he needed it most. They were as unrevealing as stone.

He wished he'd never thought of the comparison.

She turned away from him. Before he could speak, they both heard the car on the gravel drive. Flor hurried to a wall mirror and exclaimed in dismay, "Look at me! How could I forget they were coming? It's Luis and Evita. Talk to them while I wash up." Rushing off, she left him to greet her guests. Evita glanced knowingly at Luis when she thought Curtin wasn't watching, but neither expressed surprise or disapproval.

They all carefully held the conversation to comments on the scenery and Luis's archaeology while waiting.

Curtin quickly understood their sympathetic acceptance of the situation they'd stumbled onto. Luis couldn't have been more attentive to Evita, and she basked in his presence. Instead of worrying about their opinion of his presence in Flor's house, Curtin found himself battling the urge to smile at their display of mutual affection. Then he thought of Luis, the product of an aristocratic family, and Evita, the madam of a brothel. Life found problems enough for everyone, he decided.

When Flor entered, Luis was all business. "I will be blunt, Flor. The elimination of Buck's kidnappers is very bad. We can't trust Force Red to free Robert. I am convinced they knew of Buck's kidnapping all along. They killed those two so they couldn't reveal Buck's true purpose in Costa Verde, and as a warning to others."

After a quick look at Curtin, Flor said, "We talked of the same thing, but Buck believes there were other kidnappers as well and they killed their partners to silence them."

Luis smiled. "Sounds like an American gangster movie. But it makes no difference. We must think more about rescue and less about paying ransom."

Flor said, "But how? What do we do?"

"Someone has seen or heard something," Evita said. "Until now, no one has asked. We have many friends—we must learn what they know. Or suspect."

"I agree. But there isn't much time," Curtin said.

"We know that." Flor's answer crackled. Then, more composed, "I know a woman whose cousin is involved with Force Red. The time has come to use some pressure on her."

"Exactly." Luis drove a fist into his palm.

Evita smiled at him before turning to Flor. "You could never come to my place, and it's equally dangerous for you when I come here." When Flor opened her mouth to object, Evita talked over her. "You must report to Luis, and he will report to me. It will give us something to talk about.'' Her smile turned wicked and her eyes sparkled. "For a change.''

Luis colored and laughed nervously. Evita moved to his side, patted his cheek. "Like a little boy," she said, then, "We will go now."

"I don't like your taking such a chance," Luis told her, struggling to remain firm. "You will know too much, and one can never be sure who is an informer. What if someone pretends to be helping us so we can be trapped? Have you thought of that?"

"Silly." She took his arm. "I already know enough secrets to end most of the marriages in the country. I am used to these things." Gently, she led him out, and they left flinging goodbyes over their shoulders.

Curtin watched him help her into the car, and, as soon as they were out of sight, permitted himself the laugh he'd kept bottled so long.

Flor understood perfectly, and she joined him. He wasn't surprised when she stopped abruptly and returned indoors, nor when she said it was time for him to leave, as well. "It's not wise for us to be alone, Buck. I have to go into the city myself, and I don't think it'll be too bad if I drive you, but I can't handle any more moments like what we just went through."

"I didn't expect any of that to happen, earlier."

"Neither did I. But it did."

He waited while she got her car keys, then followed her outside. The garage was a converted barn, some distance from the main house, and they moved slowly, the rasp of disturbed gravel the only sound. Halfway there, a movement behind one of the windows caught Curtin's eye, and he slowed perceptibly.

Flor looked at him curiously. "Is something wrong?"

"I don't know. A hunch. Is there anyone working in your garage?" He dropped to one knee, pretended to probe for a piece of gravel in his shoe.

"Maybe. I don't know. Why shouldn't there be?"

"I saw something move."

"You're paranoid."

"Only because everybody hates me and is trying to kill me." He straightened. "Humor me. When we get to the front door, you say you've forgotten your keys and go back to the house after them. I'm going to check the place out before we blunder in."

"This is stupid!" She bit the words off but, caught up in his taut mood, lowered her voice to the level of his. Standing at the door, she rolled her eyes dramatically and delivered her lines. Curtin winced at the disbelief in them.

When she stepped inside the house, he crouched and sprinted around the corner of the building. Easing up beside a window, he peered in.

A bearded man dressed in oversized fatigues sat on the hood of Flor's car, an Uzi submachine gun loosely cradled in his lap. Another man stood to his right, closer to Curtin. He was younger, dressed similarly, and much more tense. His weapon was carefully aimed at the door. Where the bearded man puffed easily on a cigar, his high-strung companion chewed gum as if it burned his mouth. Curtin ducked, coming up on the other side of the window, looking to the far end of the long building. A third man sat on a stack of cased oil cans, watching the first two.

Keeping low, Curtin hurried past the remaining windows to the back door. He pushed it open as delicately as he could, dreading the first squeak of a rusty hinge, assuring himself the man on guard was too interested in the potential action up front to be alert.

Curtin was silhouetted in the door when the man turned that way. His mouth fell open and his chest heaved with a sudden intake of air. Curtin gave him no time to use it to yell, driving rigid, spearing fingers into the man's throat. His other hand snatched the Uzi. For an instant the man's reflexes worked for him, and his grip remained locked on the weapon. Then, as his eyes glazed, he clawed at his damaged throat with his free hand, finally letting go of the Uzi. Curtin slid behind him, crooking a forearm across his windpipe, and dragged him into a stall. He squeezed until the body was totally limp, then lowered him to the floor and tied his hands with his own belt. A shirt sleeve provided a good gag.

The two men were still intent on the front door, but the bearded one was standing now, and his weapon was at a tighter angle. Curtin's neck tingled as he crept forward. The whiskered one was an old head, a survivor. He knew something was happening, and he didn't know what, and it bothered him a lot. He spoke to the younger man on his right, who answered shortly and then turned to look directly into Curtin's eyes. His own popped.

Curtin shook his head as the Uzi began to turn. The man continued to stare, as if the intruder standing in front of him might disappear as wondrously as he had appeared. The bearded man snapped a quick question, looking to his right. At the sight of his partner, he continued on around. Curtin waved the Uzi from one to the other. "Everybody be easy," he said. "Nobody gets brave, nobody gets dead. You speak English?"

"I speak it. How's your Spanish?"

"None. Tell the kid to put that thing down. He scares me."

Following instructions, the man provided an example by laying his own weapon on the hood of the car. The younger one struggled with his judgment.

Curtin said, "Tell him! Put it down, or go down with it!"

The Uzi sagged before the older man could speak. Rigid with hate and frustration, the youth bent to place it on the floor.

Raising a foot to the bumper, the older man said, "I am Comandante Noche, of Force Red—Commander Night in your language. The boy is named Hector. He understood you very well."

"He speaks English?"

"He speaks soldier, Mr. Curtin. We always understand that of each other, men like us. He also understands patience."

Curtin nodded. "Like you. Back away from that piece. Take him with you."

Noche snapped his fingers and gestured. Both men stepped away. Curtin collected the weapons.

Noche glanced at the back door. "You killed my other man?"

"Didn't have to."

"You were lucky to surprise us. You will need that much luck, and more, if you Yankees come here to fight us, though. If you get home, tell your people that."

The arrogance stung. Curtin laughed at him. "Luck is helpful when a man deals with back-shooters. And what can a back-shooter know of fighting?"

Biting on the cigar, Noche produced a hard smile. "You remember the man your helicopter pilot tried to kill, when you were visiting Chavez's palace? That man lived there for almost a month, hiding and watching. He is still alive, back with us. Someday we will attack the snake in its own nest. Luck, machines—nothing will help you against such men. They have character. You do not. But never mind. It would be foolish of us to make insults. You need our help."

"Stuff the hardass act. All I want from you people is my friend. If this fucking ambush is an example of your honor or your military skills, forget it."

"Be careful. You hold our guns, but we have others, and other days." Noche spoke calmly, but there was a quality in his voice that far outweighed the previous bluster. Curtin understood that what he was hearing was bedrock, and for the first time, he felt there was quality behind the bravado.

The bearded guerrilla went on. "For now, however, you need Force Red, whether you realize it or not. We are willing to help you ransom Robert Chavez."

Chapter 21

Curtin shuffled backward until he reached the wall. "Sit down," he said, using his weapon as a pointer to indicate the separation he wanted.

Noche assumed the position easily, watching the anger-induced awkwardness of his young partner with an indulgent smile that shifted to include Curtin. He said, "The young ones are so—how would you say?—direct. Yes. Hector has never learned anything but a straight line between two points."

"He's the only man in Costa Verde who hasn't, then."

Laughing, Noche nodded agreeably. Hector glared at him and was ignored. Noche said, "That is why I think you will believe me when I say we didn't kidnap Robert Chavez. He is not an evil man, like our Colonel Sandoval. In fact, some of his ideas are good, but the true revolution cannot accept competition. You understand. We must have complete authority."

"I've heard the song. What do you know about the men who kidnapped me?"

"Ordinary criminals. Nothing political. I suspect someone in our organization mentioned your name. I can only guess.''

"Great. If that's the best security you can manage, Sandoval's people must be even dumber than I thought.''

Noche's lips tightened, but he spoke slowly. "You have reason to be angry. However, we manage to survive our mistakes. You should think about that. Meanwhile, we have decided the situation with Robert Chavez has gone on long enough. We have enjoyed the media reaction, but if he dies, we will be blamed. We will help you find him.''

"Buck! Are you all right?" Flor's sharp anxiety interrupted them. Noche looked toward the sound, but Curtin watched Hector, whose burning gaze never left his captor's face. Matching that stare, Curtin called out. "I'm okay. Stay outside.''

Noche turned, smiling grimly. "Let her come in. Sandoval has dozens of pictures of the three of us here. We don't care if Miss Peralta can identify us.''

Without wasting time on argument, Flor pushed open the door, striding in with a submachine gun leveled. It was an M11 and she carried it with her weight forward, ready to resist the upward recoil if she had to fire. Curtin wondered where she'd gotten her lessons, not to mention the weapon itself.

There was no time to dwell on his curiosity. "You!" She jabbed the air in Noche's direction with the muzzle. Both guerrillas paled. "You dare to come on my land, spy on my house! Murderer!''

Curtin raised a hand. "He's here to help, Flor. Calm down.''

"Calm—" Her eyes widened in disbelief but remained fixed on the two seated men. "Do you know who this is? This is the famous Commander Night, a true hero of the revolution! Ask him about the bus they blew up just last week. Ask him how his brave soldiers killed a dozen ferocious women and children on their way to the market!''

Even Hector flinched from the boiling rage. Curtin put a

hand on the wavering barrel of the weapon, gently forcing it down. "We need their help, Flor. If anyone can find Robert, they can."

"They already have him!"

Noche shook his head. "No, we don't." He spoke quickly, ready to get away from talk of bombed buses. With Curtin controlling the M11, some of his dignity returned. The fists pressing against the floor opened up, and his lip curled as he spoke past the American at Flor. "We risked our lives to come here, woman. I have argued long against burning this capitalist monument to the ground, or you'd have no house for anyone to spy on, you understand? I tell my comrades that one day we will make it a school, or a hospital. Until then, you may live here. We will deal with you whenever we choose."

Curtin stiffened his arm against Flor's attempt to lift the submachine gun. "Cool it." He snapped the order at Noche. "I don't have time for this." To Flor, he said, "Give it up for a while. He came here to talk, and I'm going to talk." Again addressing Noche, he went on, "Whoever has Robert will probably burn him—and me—as soon as they see the gold. I don't need your help as much as I need protection. You find Robert and bring him to me, and I'll pay the ransom to you people and tell the media you rescued him as a humanitarian action. If that's too much work, then find him and let me know where he is. If I can get Sandoval to rescue Robert, I'll pay you half the ransom and when I get home where Sandoval can't get at me, I'll still tell the press you set it all up."

"We will risk none of our people to free Robert Chavez."

"Bullshit. You want that money. I'm giving you a shot at it. But only for a live, healthy man. No deals on damaged goods."

"Spoken like a true capitalist." Noche sneered openly.

"You're the one who came sneaking in here to bargain, *comrade*. And you'll gift-wrap your Hector's ass for Sandoval, if you decide it's a good idea. He's the way we used to be. Direct, you called him. Right. He thinks if he gets rid of Sandoval and his kind, everything's going to be peace and quiet. And when it's not, he'll be the new Sandoval. You and me, we lived long enough to learn the rules. I hope he does. You know why? 'Cause I'll bet he greases you and Sandoval the same day. Now, do we have a deal?''

The whirring of a single fly sawed against the silence in the barn. A rooster crowed suddenly in the distance. The windy, reedy sound jarred Noche out of a deep contemplation. He said, "It will be a pleasure to meet you sometime when I have no duty to leave you alive. I have my orders. You have your deal, on one condition. If we produce your friend, we are paid immediately." He paused, and a smile like a crack in ice creased his features. "What happens to both of you after that is your own concern."

"Fine." Curtin transferred his weapon to his left hand and extended the right to a startled Noche, who took it without thinking, eyes wide. Curtin said, "I don't like you either, but I believe you'll do what you have to do." To Flor, he said, "Dump their weapons in the car. Don't get between me and them while you do it."

She opened her mouth, thought better of her words, and clamped it shut with an almost audible force. Stalking behind Curtin, she retrieved the weapons and put them on the floor on the passenger's side. When the engine was running, Curtin opened the barn door, then climbed in beside her. Keeping his weapon trained on the seated men, he said, "We'll drop your stuff up by the main road. I know we're both on the same side now, and I really do trust you, but I'd feel bad about putting temptation in your way."

Noche threw back his head and laughed out loud.

Curtin continued to watch him until the curve of the drive took him out of sight.

Flor said, "Madness! He sounded like he wanted to kill you, but now he laughs at your joke like you were the best of friends. How can you laugh with him?"

"Look at me. Am I laughing? He's looking forward to putting me away."

"As another soldier, you mean." Flor tried to make it a statement of fact, but questioning eyes expressed her true feelings.

Curtin laughed, stopping abruptly when he heard how much the sound resembled Noche's. "As soon as Force Red has its gold, or as soon as they decide they can't get it, Noche and that pet scorpion, Hector, will be after me like a duck after a june bug."

"My God, doesn't it ever end? You bargained over a man's life like two market peasants, you shook hands, you laughed—and you know he wants to kill you? How could you?"

"We're honest men."

"Honest?" Scorn ripped the word, jerked her upright behind the wheel. "You plan to cheat Chavez, you talk of Robert like property—'damaged goods' you called him! —and you talk of killing and honesty as if they were the same word."

"They are, when things get to this point. When people like Noche and me bump into each other, we either both get the hell away or one eliminates the other. If we believe in the same things, we can be great friends. Otherwise—" He moved a hand, a tired, disinterested gesture.

"You should have let me do the talking."

"Couldn't. We established a dialogue. We know how to deal with each other, for money or terms. I had to get a handle on how he sees himself. Personally, he doesn't give a fiddler's whoop if Robert lives or dies, but Force Red wants him to live so they can collect the money, and Noche knows I respect his ability to find him. Those are powerful things, Flor."

She sighed. "I know. I don't understand, but I know. Sometimes I think women are born to learn about men, and that is their punishment. The more they learn, the more vulnerable they become."

They retreated into their own thoughts then, and Curtin gave a silent thanks. He watched the passage of towering trees, searched the thick, arched branches for clustered parasitic plants and orchids. The dominant aspect of the countryside was the number of shades of green fighting toward the light. Remnants of forest lingered at the edges of the fields, leaning toward the crops like hungry, frightened predators.

Flor asked the question he dreaded. "After talking to Noche, how do you see him?"

He considered begging off, contenting himself—and Flor—with a lying simplicity, such as calling Noche a monster. Not that it wasn't true as far as it went. What ate at him was the uncertainty that he'd be any different in the same situation.

"Noche and Hector know about losing. They've spent their lives as losers. They'll die to avoid losing again, and when a man thinks like that, killing comes easier all the time. All you can bet on is how he sees himself. It's the solitary human thing he believes in."

She was quiet for a while. Her fast, skillful driving had brought them to the outskirts of the city. Shacks crowded toward the roadway, the houses of the urbanized peasants. A great number of them boasted tin cans full of flowers nailed to the walls, sadly colorful attempts to draw the eye from squalor. Yelling, laughing children, their ragged clothes emphasizing their near-nakedness, chased each other between the battered dwellings. Curtin envied them their ability to get so lost in play they could forget the bleak present.

Flor said, "How very lonely men like Noche must be."

Curtin closed his eyes. "Yes," he said.

When he opened them again, they were much closer to his neighborhood. The huts and filth gave way to neater houses and paving. The children were almost as undressed as their poverty-stricken contemporaries, and they laughed as hard, but the clothes weren't mended remnants and the visible flesh jiggled more comfortably over its layer of baby fat.

He left the sedan a couple of blocks later with brief thanks. Flor looked straight ahead, avoiding his eyes. He said, "If Force Red contacts you, let me know right away. I'll do the same for you."

She nodded. He stepped back, and the car practically leaped away. Within a few yards, the pitch of the engine rose sharply as she gunned it toward the gear change. At the intersection, an MP jeep pulled directly across the street, blocking her. Flor's sedan braked, nosing down awkwardly, the streamlined grace of the machine suddenly transformed into a shining projectile. The rear end slued, and, as Curtin sprinted down the street, the car bounded over the curb and plowed to a stop on a front lawn.

Curtin arrived seconds after the MPs, who were already pulling Flor from behind the steering wheel. One of them leveled his M16 at Curtin and snapped an unmistakable command. Curtin stopped. "What the hell's going on?" he shouted. "You deliberately got in her way! Let her go!"

The M16 rose ominously.

"Stop it, Buck!" Flor was pleading. She pushed against the MP holding her, managed to get in front of the one training the weapon on Curtin. She spoke rapidly in Spanish, listening intently to the answer. When she faced Curtin again, her face was expressionless, her voice lifeless. It shocked Curtin. "I am under arrest. They say they don't know why. I'm to go with them."

Cautiously, Curtin moved forward as a thick-bodied Sergeant strolled up from the jeep. Standing beside Flor, Curtin waited until they were face-to-face. "Where are you taking her, Sergeant?" he asked, trying to sound calm.

The Sergeant shook his head, and when Flor spoke, obviously translating the question, he refused to acknowledge her. Curtin said, "Tell him Colonel Sandoval is my friend. I'm going with you, wherever, and Sandoval will hear about this as soon as I can get to him."

Flor spoke, but the Sergeant continued to ignore her. In fact, he moved his head, as if making some sort of signal. Flor's eyes widened as she followed his look, and Curtin ducked instantly, sliding off to his left, cursing himself for not keeping an eye on the trigger-happy MP. The butt stroke from behind missed cleanly, but the force of it threw the soldier forward into Curtin. Continuing his movement, Curtin spun completely around, laying a clubbing forearm across the exposed back of the soldier. The force of it launched the man full-tilt into the Sergeant. Both tumbled to the ground.

Before Curtin could regain his balance, the third MP struck, swinging his rifle like a club. It took Curtin in the kidney, lancing him with a paralyzing pain. He sagged to the ground. Unable to move, fully aware, he watched the Sergeant and his other MP get to their feet and unhurriedly walk toward him. The MP smiled. The Sergeant frowned slightly. He made Curtin think of a laborer faced with another time-consuming, but unchallenging, piece of work.

After the first couple of kicks, Flor's screams faded, and Curtin wondered if he were losing consciousness or if someone was moving her to the jeep. It was a terrible temptation to look and see, but just keeping his consciousness demanded all the energy he could find.

They stopped when they were tired. Curtin watched a pair of booted feet through slitted eyes, refusing to break the passive protection of his fetal ball. When a shadow fell across his vision, he tensed.

Unaffected by his weak resistance, the trio spread-eagled him on the grass. From the corner of his eye he saw Flor, handcuffed to the jeep's steering wheel. Her mouth was a red, flaming circle of fear, and her screaming had taken on an unbelieving sound. He looked for the Sergeant.

One of the MPs grabbed Curtin's left wrist, then sat on his chest, almost completely driving the wind out of him. The other held his feet. The Sergeant loomed into view. He gripped a .45 automatic. Stepping on the right wrist, he bent over to pull the fingers out flat, carefully stepping on the tips.

He still wore the faint frown. The lines across his forehead deepened a little as he concentrated his point of aim in the middle of Curtin's palm. After checking to see if Curtin was conscious enough to understand what was happening, he spoke to him briefly, then turned back to his work.

Curtin cried out, straining to pull free. The blast seemed to drive his hand deep into the earth. There was little pain.

It was a few seconds before he realized they were gone. He stared at the sky, afraid to look at what damage they'd done. Eventually, he rolled his eyes to his right, unable to make his head turn. Small black specks of burned powder tattooed the outer edge of his hand. There was no blood, no wound. The grass was scorched where the bullet had struck the earth, and not him.

Lucia appeared, panting, her wrinkled features drawn and pale. "I heard him say this to make warn you. That what they do. Make fear. Fat pig." She stroked Curtin's hand between her own, as if soothing a hurt animal.

He said, "Flor. The woman. Where will they take her?"

Lucia twisted her face away too slowly to hide the quick wince. When she turned back, there was a dark sadness in her eyes. She lifted thin shoulders, let them drop in a shrug Curtin knew was as old as the mountains of her people. She said, "*Quien sabe?* Who knows?"

Chapter 22

Lucia got her hands under his arms and lifted with a strength that surprised him. Half-falling, the two of them made it to Flor's car, where he steadied himself. Heat from the sunbaked metal flowed into throbbing muscles, drew off some of the pain. Over the top he stared at the small crowd of children and Indian servants. The combination of heat waves shimmering off the roof and his own dizzinesss gave them the appearance of a school of fish, all eyes and mouths. Past them, housewives stood in their front yards to observe the excitement.

Servants and the children edged close. Middle-class adults hung back, advancing to the ultimate edge of their property for a better view, but absolutely unwilling to step an inch beyond that illusion of safety. Curtin laughed in spite of himself. The Indians regarded him solemnly until one of them grasped the source of his amusement. She was a little woman, much like Lucia, and she pointed at the landholders and spoke in a soft, rolling language Curtin knew was not Spanish. Her companions looked around, as did Lucia, and then they were all laughing.

For Curtin, the incident capsulized the immense gap between the poor and the rest of Costa Verde. Poor was not a function of economics here. It was a matter of culture, of almost ethnic separation.

Worried mothers called from up and down the street. Children began to break off from the knot around Curtin as they responded. The servants followed.

Curtin said, "Help me get inside the car, Lucia."

Her jaw dropped. "You go? You no go! You hurt!"

"Damn' right. And I don't want to hang around and wait to see if they come back." He wrapped a hand around the door handle and leaned, relying on his weight to open it. When it popped, Lucia caught him to keep him upright. She muttered dismay as she helped him onto the seat. As soon as the engine caught, she marched at attention back to the house, refusing to be part of such foolishness. After bumping over the curb and into the street, Curtin looked in the rearview mirror and caught her peering out the window, her fist to her mouth.

He made his way to Evita's, the only place he could think of where he might find help. Pulling into the courtyard, he gave in to the complaints of his body and slumped against the steering wheel to pull himself together. He was just getting out of the car when Evita came to her door.

Recognizing trouble in his slow, difficult progress, she called over her shoulder to the inside of her house before hurrying to him. Two of the girls and the bartender ran out behind her.

"What happened to you?" she cried, getting one of his arms over her shoulder. "Carlos, quick, get his other arm. We'll put him in the suite. Lola, Anita—go get the bed ready. Hurry!"

"I'm okay," Curtin protested. "I can walk."

"Of course," Evita soothed him. "We're just being careful. Who did this to you?"

Curtin explained until they reached the stairs. He paused at the bottom, gritted his teeth, and let Carlos do most of the climbing. At the top he signaled another short rest, then let himself be guided to the bed. He barely heard Evita shooing the others out and offered no reaction while she stripped off his shirt until he heard her sharp intake of breath. Raising his head, he looked down at the raw flesh where the boots had dug in.

He smiled crookedly. "I've felt like forty miles of bad road before, but this is the first time I've ever looked like it."

Evita stared blankly, and he shook his head. "Old joke." He lay back on the pillow.

The next thing he knew, she was putting a pill between his lips. "Swallow," she ordered, handing him a glass of water. "For the pain."

"What is it?"

She grinned. "We use it at certain times. It helps with headache and cramps."

"Oh, Lord." He washed it down, closed his eyes. "If I wake up a soprano, you're in deep trouble, lady."

Evita sniffed. "With you in your condition? Most sopranos would be too strong for you."

"What a cheery darling you are. Look, I need to rest. Can you find out where Flor is? When I'm back in order, I'm going after her. Help me, Evita?"

"I'll see what I can do." He thought her hand trembled as it stroked his brow, but he was too exhausted to be sure. Her steps faded out of his hearing.

It seemed only moments had passed when he felt a sudden lift, as though he were perfectly awake. Comforting darkness, like black velvet, enclosed him. His mind acknowledged the continuing pain, but ignored it. He looked at himself from a great distance, scornful of the unnecessary, vulnerable body.

When he woke, it was with a violent start that wrung an involuntary curse out of him as his injuries asserted their presence. Slowly, drowsily, he came back to himself.

He felt much better. The body ached, but the mind was clear and refreshed. Still, something persistently nagged at him, and he felt that he'd dreamed and should remember the details because they were important.

He was buttoning his shirt, glowering in the mirror like a bear scenting hounds, when Evita came in. She put her hands on her hips in a pose of resigned exasperation. "What now, macho? Instead of resting, you kick and swear. Then you get up too soon."

"I have to see Sandoval."

"You're crazy."

"Probably. I've got to find out about Flor."

"This is not California. You do not ask the police questions. They ask you. You will go to jail yourself."

"I don't think so." He stepped past her into the hall.

"And Robert?" She pitched her voice low, but the intensity cut like a knife. He turned around.

"I've got to get him out of the country as fast as possible, once the arrangements have been made. Do you think he'll leave if she's still in jail?"

"He doesn't have to know."

Curtin laughed. "She'll be his first question. I can't lie to him." He continued on toward the stairs. "Not about that."

As he eased behind the wheel, she said, "I hoped you would be too weak to do this, so I wouldn't have to tell you. I was told one of the Peralta servants told Colonel Sandoval about Comandante Noche as soon as you left Flor's property. She was arrested on Sandoval's personal orders, Buck. You must be very careful. You can help no one from inside a jail, or—" She stopped abruptly and looked away. He nodded, driving off.

The first dream-memory struck him a few minutes later when he swung the car out to avoid a burro loaded with a veritable mountain of cane. One moment Curtin was looking at traffic, and then his vision was gone, a swirl of light and shadow. Through it he heard a word in a voice not his own. It said, "Gold."

Or "Go."

He couldn't be sure.

He would have sworn he thought about it for at least a minute, but when his eyes focused again, he was barely past the burro. The car had drifted to the right, and several angry horns let him know it. He swerved back into his own lane.

A little farther on, it happened again, while he waited for a khaki-clad traffic officer to let him pass. As before, everything dissolved. This time the voice said "sea."

Or "see."

The cop's whistle screeched impatiently. The confused fog disappeared and Curtin gunned the engine, almost stalling. People stared. Sweat poured down his neck. He lurched across the street and on his way.

He found a place to park near the Ministry building, selecting a skinny, tough-looking kid to keep an eye on the car. Drained, he wished the enervating heat would stop, hoped the chill of Sandoval's office would invigorate him, putting an end to the recurrent flashbacks.

He never thought Deb would drug him. Evita had given him a pill.

He shook his head violently, as if force could dislodge the cynical distrust growing inside him like a mold.

In Sandoval's waiting room, he stared at the rigid, precise arrangement of chairs and told himself Evita was in greater danger, at all times, than any of them.

The Colonel's smile was distant as he came in. "You have a preference for bad company, my friend." He made no offer to approach, keeping the length of the room between them.

Curtin marked off another piece of insight for the man. The hollow echo was intimidating, gave the impression of an irresistible presence. He said, "Why did your men arrest Miss Peralta?"

"You should ask why they did not arrest you. Interfering with the military police is no joke here."

"There aren't any jokes of any kind here, Colonel. But arresting Miss Peralta is a farce."

Sandoval's lecturer's facade broke in an outburst of

genuine emotion. "Comandante Noche and two other terrorists came to her and she said nothing. *Nothing!* That is
against our law! It is aiding the enemy!"

"What chance did she have? She insisted on dropping
me off, Colonel. She was on her way here to you. She told
me so."

Sandoval examined him for a full ten seconds, his eyes
dead, noncommittal. Curtin could only wait. And hope.

At last, Sandoval said, "So she says. I told you once,
she's not Force Red material. And I'm glad you're interested in her. She was linked with Robert Chavez, you
know. Having you around her will keep me informed if
there's still a connection."

"You're going to release her? When?"

"She can leave with you now." He opened the door to
his office. "Wait here. She'll be brought to you."

Curtin paced, too impatient to sit still. He hoped the
extra movement would help flush the drug out of his
system. The initial flood of relief at knowing Flor was free
disappeared quickly in a renewed concern over what had
happened at Evita's. Yet there was nothing he could do.

The high, narrow door swung open behind him. A bony
jail matron in a shapeless dress half-guided, half-pushed an
unresisting Flor into the room. The woman's eyes looked
through Curtin like light penetrating glass. Then she was
gone. Flor stood unmoving, shoulders slumped, hair mussed,
although not in wild disarray. Across the long space between them, her body spoke of fear.

Long strides had him to her in seconds. When he moved
to take her in his arms, she shrank away, murmuring.
"No. I don't dare. Don't touch me. I'll come apart. Talk
to me. Make me believe I'm out of there. Tell me you're
all right." Her eyes sought his hand.

"I'm fine, just fine." He gripped her shoulders clumsily.
She flinched, then steadied. He said, "The shot was a
warning. He never meant to hurt me. But are you sure
you're okay?"

She looked up at him. "They didn't do anything to me.

Some questions. They showed me things. Cattle prods. They had one—it was painted. It looked like a—a—'' Her eyes shimmered with unshed tears, and she bit her lower lip. Curtin squeezed her shoulders, and she went on. "They wanted to frighten me. And they did. My God, Buck, they're not human!"

He ushered her out the door and into the hall, an arm around her waist. "Yes, they are," he said. "Only humans do those things."

"People screamed. First one, then another. Sometimes two or three at once."

"Put it out of your mind. Think about it when you can do something about it. Right now I'm taking you to a hotel. You can't be alone at home tonight, not after this."

"The servants—"

"Forget it. I want you surrounded by people, lights, noise."

"You may be right. I don't think I'll sleep anyhow."

"Then it's agreed."

On the street outside the Ministry building, Curtin noticed how passersby took in Flor's appearance with a certain wary double take, looking once, then looking away, then finding a reason to check again. Once they were sure of what they'd seen, they never turned that way again. When he drove up in front of the hotel, only a few blocks away, people reacted in a completely different manner. They looked at her, then at him. The speculation and dislike in their faces was too clear to miss. Flor smiled at it, eventually.

"They think you're responsible for me being mussed up."

He nearly remarked how those outside Sandoval's headquarters knew better, but caught himself. Instead, he burlesqued a leer. "Dirty-minded creeps. I wish they were right."

Her brief laugh rewarded him as they entered the lobby. While Curtin made arrangements for a room for her, she busied herself in the small boutique. When he went to tell her the bellman was opening the room, she put her hand on his arm.

"Come up with me. I want to wash off the stink of that place, and I can't bear the thought of being alone while I do. Will you wait until I'm finished?"

"Certainly."

At the room, she vanished into the bathroom. He stood at the window, looking down at the bustling streets. By leaning forward and twisting, he could almost see Evita's.

The rap on the door spun him around, crouching, ready to defend or attack. Feeling foolish, he straightened and moved to answer it. The bellboy extended a large cardboard box. "The senorita's order," he said.

At the bathroom door, Curtin said, "Flor, did you order something sent to the room?"

"New clothes!" The water stopped running. She peeked around the edge of the door, extending a bundle of material. "Take this. Throw everything away. Leave the package on the bed and wait in the hall until I tell you you can come back in."

She watched until they were gone. In the corridor, the bellboy held back the major part of his grin until after Curtin tipped him.

A few minutes later she called, "Okay!" and he reentered to see a flash of brown leg as the bathroom door closed behind her. He made himself comfortable, searching across the radio dial until he found some music.

When she came out she was restored. A faint tightness of the skin at the corners of the mouth, a certain quickness in the eyes when they shifted, were the only visible reminders of her visit to Sandoval's cells. She wore bright clothes. A red blouse with yellow accents blazed above a skirt with just enough yellow to keep it from being stark white. Even the old shoes were gone, replaced by a white, summery pair. She spun in a circle, enjoying showing off, laughing easily at his approving applause. Then she struck a pose.

"And now—the biggest surprise." She reached into the cardboard box and produced an embroidered short-sleeved

shirt in a plastic bag. When she tossed it to him, he lunged
to catch it with awkward surprise. A pair of cotton trousers
followed and, as she feigned shy embarrassment, under-
wear in another plastic sack. She said, "I don't want to eat
alone, Buck, and I couldn't stand to call any of my friends
here tonight. They'd want to whisper about what happened
and scheme and plot and dream about a perfect world. I
just want to relax, talk about unimportant things. I want to
enjoy myself for a little while. Is that wrong?"

He rose with his bundle of clothes. "It's a great idea.
But you're a scheming wench."

She giggled, a childlike amusement that gave him his
first suggestion of what she must have been as a girl. He
forced answering laughter and hurried into the bathroom.

The image of that happy, spontaneous expression lingered in his mind through the shower and the following
meal. He deliberately led her to tell stories of her youth,
watching the nervousness fade from her eyes as better
times claimed her thoughts. The soft light and muted
laughter around them was a tonic for her, giving her the
strength to pull her mind away from the stresses waiting
outside. She insisted he have dessert, and they were enjoying a butter-smooth custard called *flan* when Luis appeared
beside the table.

"I heard what happened today." His face worked against
tight control. "Are you both all right?"

Curtin watched Flor, saw all the good work of the
evening fall apart in one blink. She said, "We're fine,
Luis. They didn't hurt us. Join us, have some coffee."

Pulling up a chair, he thanked her, then directed his
attention to Curtin. "We know the pig who shot at you. In
the past, he's always damaged his victims. You were very
lucky, I think."

Before Curtin could comment, a waiter said, "Senor
Curtin? There's a telephone call for you, sir." Frowning,
Curtin rose. As he did, Luis did the same. He said, "I'll
come with you, Buck. If it's someone speaking Spanish,
you'll need an interpreter."

Curtin continued to frown, following the waiter. "Who the hell could it be?" he asked, neither expecting nor receiving an answer. The cashier handed him the phone at her desk, and Curtin turned his back, shielding the conversation from her and the rest of the room. As soon as he spoke, a heavily accented feminine voice responded. "Listen closely, Curtin. Force Red is about to locate the goods you discussed earlier today. We will contact you again. The real purpose of this call is to make you understand we know where you are at all times. Is that clear?"

"What kind of B-movie silliness is this? When you've got something, let me know. I'm not interested in your goddam games."

"It's not a game, gringo. You'll see." The woman paused, then she laughed throatily and continued. "Tell me, did you and the little rich girl enjoy your shower this evening? Exactly how big is the bathroom where the wealthy people play?"

"Not big enough for you to wash your dirty little mind clean, sweetheart, but any time you want to try, you let me know, hear?"

The crack of the receiver hitting the handset on her end was whip-sharp. Curtin grinned tightly as he hung up. At Luis's raised eyebrow, Curtin shook his head. "Not now," he said, heading back to the table.

Flor looked away as soon as she saw them in the doorway. She sat stiffly, looking past the crowd of diners, past the confines of the dining room. Curtin asked, "Is something wrong?" and was surprised at her answer.

"I'm exhausted. I don't understand—I felt fine a few minutes ago." Her eyes pleaded for belief. "It must be a delayed reaction."

"It must be. Come on, we'll get you to your room." Her hand was cold as he helped her to her feet, and when he took her arm, it was limp in his grasp. Luis rose, made some concerned comments neither of them really heard, and sat back down. Curtin waved briefly, then concentrated on Flor.

Her expression was the same as when the matron shoved her into the Ministry's waiting room. No emotion, no hint of interest in her surroundings forced its way through.

She never asked about the telephone call.

As soon as she was safely in her room, Curtin went to the elevator and directly to the hotel garage. Checking out her car, he drove rapidly to a position where he could watch the front door from a distance. Less than an hour later, Flor appeared. The uniformed doorman approached, saluting, only to be rebuffed.

The doorman would have asked if she wanted a cab.

She had refused.

Minutes passed, a progression of winking lights on Curtin's digital watch that hammered at him with mocking, monotonous insistence.

A sedan slowed to a stop in front of the hotel, the driver an indistinct mass against the background light. Flor walked to the passenger side, leaning down to talk to him. The door opened, closed behind her.

Curtin pulled out to follow.

Chapter 23

The lights of the car ahead speared the rural darkness as the driver cruised easily, either unaware of, or unconcerned about, a hostile presence. Curtin decided it was the latter, and a tight grin moved his lips, his first change of expression since starting the engine.

Costa Verde's war wasn't up to the dimensions of an El Salvador, much less a Vietnam, where a late-night drive such as this was a ticket back to "the world" in an aluminum box. People killed here, but the tendency was still to do it at close range, with small arms or machetes. Murder waited offstage, selective butchery to deaden the social nervous system, blunt its ability to reject killing and tyranny as legitimate answers to problems.

They'd graduate to artillery and aircraft, he thought bitterly, but for now the politicians were happy to restrict the dying to small doses they could administer personally.

Curtin's philosphizing was interrupted by the appearance of headlights ahead of him. They blazed directly across the road as a car moved with ominous slowness into a barricading position. He considered forging past, but the spot was well-planned. Heavy trees denied use of the right side. The left provided too little shoulder between the block and the eight-foot drop to the cornfield below.

The rearview mirror confirmed another car moving to cut off his retreat.

He was neatly trapped.

Coasting to a stop, he shielded his eyes as a spotlight sought him out. A voice called something unintelligible. He extended his hands out the window, waving, showing he was unarmed. A moment later two men pounded up to the car. One pushed him aside to turn off the headlights while the other held a pistol to his neck. That done, they stepped back, each aiming a pistol.

Heels rapped on the hard road surface, a rhythm Curtin recognized immediately. Shielding his eyes, he said, "Sandoval? Colonel Sandoval?"

"Exactly right. I thought you'd be coming. My men will take care of Miss Peralta's machine."

Curtin got out, still ducking the spotlight. Sandoval led the way to his own car, where a driver and another soldier in the front seat impassively watched their approach. At Sandoval's order, they manuevered back onto the highway and continued after Flor.

"I guess you know what's going on?" Curtin said.

"Of course. It is my business to learn these things." He turned to look at Curtin, the soft light of the interior picking out his white smile. "You understand you have been betrayed. I leave it to you to determine by whom. You might even ask yourself how often." He gestured, his hand ghostlike. "When we make the next turn, you will see my country house."

The sight was enough to interrupt Curtin's wonderings. Perhaps a half-mile away, a huge house squatted behind a forbidding wall. The building itself gleamed with an almost pearlescent luster under the glare of craning light towers that stood like gawky sentries on the length of the wall. Most of their strength fell in or close to the compound, forcing the night back.

Turning off the road, the car followed a secondary trail to a side gate, where one guard inspected the car while another kept an M16 trained on it. Passed through, they proceeded under the harsh lights to a small door. Sandoval stepped out, indicating Curtin should follow. He moved briskly, the slight limp giving an odd rolling motion to his walk. After entering and passing through a dimly lit large kitchen, they moved into an even darker dining room, its only illumination the weak glow that managed to penetrate the drapes from the tower lights outside.

Sandoval reached for a large picture on the wall, pivoting it out on a hidden hinge, and Curtin was looking through a window at two people in a luxurious living room. The furniture was quite formal. The heavy blue drapes that were almost certainly of velvet picked up the major color of the upholstery and the deep Persian carpet. Occasional items such as vases and statuary spoke of unspared expense in the decor.

A couple embraced in there, oblivious to anything but each other. The images had the astigmatized texture created by one-way mirrors.

All those things registered with icy clarity while Curtin's mind strained to reject the reality of Flor in the arms of Robert Chavez.

He stepped back, turning away, and faced the muzzle of Sandoval's pistol. Smiling, signaling silence with finger to lips, Sandoval forced Curtin's head back around with the barrel. He reached to a switch beside the mirror, and Flor's voice blurted from speakers as she pulled away from Robert.

"You're safe! And here, of all places! Did Colonel Sandoval's men rescue you? Are you all right? Why haven't they told everyone? This is wonderful!" They kissed again, and Curtin told himself it was Robert pulling, not Flor advancing, that created the act.

Once again, Flor spoke, "What's happening, Robert? Tell me everything! I'm so excited, so happy!"

Robert whirled her in a dancing circle. "I've done it, Flor! I've got them all!"

Blankly, Flor stared up at him. "Got who? The kidnappers?"

He hugged her, then held her out at arm's length. "There was no kidnapping, Flor. I planned it all, made it all work. Listen to me! I have men at the very top of Force Red, men who owe their lives to me. I have men like them who run this government, who know if I speak, they're destroyed. They are *mine*."

"But—but why?"

"I need money. Just enough to control a few more men, buy some machinery. And I've done it! I even tricked my father into helping, and I'm going to push him aside, Flor! *I'm going to beat him!*"

"Beat him at what? Why are you doing this?"

Unaware of her increasing concern, Robert raced on. "The world thinks Force Red kidnapped me. Now the government is embarrassed, determined to crush the movement. Force Red will fight back. Between them, they'll eliminate those who might interfere with me. I'll protect my own people, move in on the greatest prize in the hemisphere."

"I still don't understand. You've lied to everyone, endangered everyone."

Closing her hand in his, he was too engrossed to note its unresponsiveness. He said, "You were never in any danger. Curtin's the only one, and he's being paid well. I worked hard to be sure my father would choose him to bring in the ransom, because I needed someone who wouldn't try to steal it and who'd take any risk to get it to me if things went wrong. There's an empire involved! Curtin would understand. He hasn't taken on more than he can handle."

Curtin grunted, remembering John and George in their hospital beds, imagining how Deb must have cried and begged to live. Sandoval tapped his shoulder. "Robert has a high opinion of your toughness." He smiled as he said it, a knife slit of more derision than humor. Curtin said,

"He's got to learn a man feels more than what happens to himself."

The retort puzzled Sandoval.

Flor pulled her hand away. "He's been beaten! Tortured! A man threatened to maim him today, Robert!" Suddenly, aware of growing irritation in his expression, she dropped the subject of Curtin. Her voice rose to a nervous treble as she added, "And your father—you lied to him, you're cheating him!"

"That's the best part." Robert's burgeoning jealousy evaporated. "He thinks Sandoval's his man. Actually, the Colonel's completely loyal to me. Together, we're going to create something that'll make the Somozas of Nicaragua look like beginners."

He moved to a large map, where he pointed, talking to Flor over his shoulder. "The oil field discovered off this coast is one of the largest in the world. It ends here, where the rock structure changes." He turned his back on the map, eyes blazing. "That change is nothing more than a huge spear thrust into the oil-bearing formation, splitting it into separate pieces. The second piece is here. *Here!* Right under us!" Abruptly, hands linked behind his back, he began pacing. "Unimaginable wealth, Flor! Power! For me, for a perfect society. A country where everyone has his place."

He stopped beside her, shedding harsh intensity for a soft persuasiveness with a blinding swiftness that made Curtin think of a glass image shattering. "And your place is with me."

He took her arm. Flor stared as if waking into a nightmare, letting him lead her toward a sofa. He said, "This is ridiculous. We've been apart so long, and now I'm wasting time talking about dreams. The dream is right here." His free hand reached for the top button of her blouse.

Curtin turned away. Sandoval raised the pistol again, but after matching stares with Curtin for a moment, he reached over to cut the speaker switch and swing the picture back into position. The weapon remained centered on Curtin's abdomen as he pointed to a door in the opposite wall.

When Sandoval turned on the light in the next room, it revealed masses of books gleaming in a spacious library. He sat behind a desk, indicating a leather chair for Curtin. He said, "I have been Robert Chavez's right hand from the start. I have always wanted to eliminate him. Would you care for a drink? You have much to learn, and it may help if you can relax a bit."

Curtin shook his head, and Sandoval gestured. "As you wish. The discovery of the oil has decided me. It is *our* oil. It will change us from a poor Third World nothing to a major source of energy for the world. Costa Verde has its own leaders. We will decide how to use this new wealth."

"And you're one of the leaders." Curtin delivered the line with a straight face, and Sandoval responded as soberly.

"Of course. I have proven that, as I have just proven that I am your friend and Robert Chavez is not. I need your help to get the ransom money, and I need your help to rid myself—us—of him." He leaned forward, fists balled on the desk top. "Now you understand why I want heavy equipment. You should also know something Robert does *not* know. His father is stockpiling military equipment near here. He thinks to put our Generals in his debt, that we will come to him and pay his robber's prices when we can get such supplies nowhere else. He expects me to enlist my associates in his plans. Both the Chavez bastards think they own me. *I* own me."

Curtin gave him a thumbs-up. "Okay. Now what?"

"You're very agreeable. If you think—"

"I'm going to double-cross you?" Curtin supplied, shaking his head. "I'll leave that to you experts. All I want is to finish this thing."

"Good." Sandoval leaned back. "You probably guessed Senor Chavez expected me to be the secret observer of the connection between his representative and what he believes to be Force Red kidnappers."

Curtin stared.

Sandoval went on. "This evening I received a message
from him telling me to watch a Canadian businessman
named Curtin, who would transfer the gold. Imagine my
surprise. I congratulate you. Anyhow, shortly after that,
Robert decided he needed his woman. I took the opportunity to kill several birds with my single stone."

"I noticed. You know where the gold is?"

"Chavez would never tell me. Or Robert. He keeps us
all in our little boxes, so when Robert says his father
knows nothing of the oil, nothing of the plot to twist the
gold away from him, I don't believe it. What Chavez
doesn't know, he suspects, which means we must destroy
Robert in such a way that if the old wolf ever doubts our
version, it'll be too late for him to strike back."

"Why bother with any of this? Just throw Robert out
and develop the oil field in your own way. Any bank will
lend you all the money you want."

Amused scorn twisted Sandoval's features. "I need that
gold to buy support from certain people. Only then can I
approach the bankers with assurance that the proper leaders will control the new wealth. And, should it occur to
you to simply kill him, I assure you that would mean
unending investigation until his death was solved. He must
be rendered harmless. You must help. He has cheated you,
risked your life for his own gain."

Raised voices interrupted him. Both men spun toward
the sound. Robert practically shouted his anger. Flor's
answer was quieter, taut with strain. The words were
indistinguishable. Suddenly they stopped, cut off by the
smack of flesh on flesh. Her sharp cry half-lifted Curtin
out of the chair. The noise subsided, and he lowered
himself, still tense.

When he looked to Sandoval, the lean face was split in
another humorless grin. "Here is my plan," he went on,
imperturbable. "Robert means for you to die, once I've
arranged the delivery of the gold to him. You already
suspected that, I'm sure. I will arrange a different outcome.
I will make it appear that the genuine Force Red raided the

payment site. You will make a heroic escape and report to Senor Chavez. That guarantees he will not send a counter-stroke against us.''

Throngs of ideas roared in Curtin's head. None offered any hope.

Misinterpreting the delay, Sandoval leaned forward once again. ''With the gold, I can take over everything Robert's prepared. I'll pay well for your trouble. You can even be my salaried liaison to Senor Chavez—offer him the opportunity to help us develop it. A fine irony. Those are generous terms. However, I can never be sure about men like you. Your motives confuse me. So, to keep Robert more manageable, and to assure me of your loyalty, Miss Peralta will stay here until I'm satisfied all is accomplished.''

''If you think you have to, okay, but I'm going along with you, no matter.''

Sandoval's eyes narrowed. He leaned back in his chair, arms folded across his chest. For several long moments he silently probed, his only movement an occasional blink and the rhythmic rise and fall of his breathing. He reminded Curtin of a snake, a constrictor, patient as the very branches it lived on. Always waiting in hiding for one mistake.

Flinging his arms wide, Curtin said, ''Quit looking at me like that! What'd you expect? So he was my friend! *Was*, man! If Robert Chavez can change, so can Buck Curtin. It's my turn. And for openers, I want three things. First, half that gold is mine. Second, I want the woman. Last, I want approval of every step of your plan.''

''You ask too much. I will pay you fifty thousand dollars—there will be no discussion. I will release the woman when she's served her purpose. As for the plan, you will learn as we go. You are too cooperative. It makes me nervous.''

Curtin shook his head. ''Two hundred thousand. And what makes you think I trust you any more than you trust me? I want some details. I have to cooperate. I'm stuck here. I've done a lot of work, taken a lot of punishment. I should get paid for it.''

"I've already said I'd release the woman. I meant to you.''

"Swell, but we're talking cash."

The bleak expression cracked in a short, hard laugh. "A man of flaming passions.'' At Curtin's quick frown, Sandoval waved a placating hand. "No, no—I didn't mean to offend you. I was merely commenting that you have your priorities in correct order.'' He paused, growing serious before continuing. "One hundred and fifty thousand, final. No more haggling.''

"U.S. dollars.''

"Done.''

"Not quite. If Chavez ever suspects I conned him, he'll snuff me. There has to be some cover.''

Sandoval drummed a finger on the desk. "I will tell you this much of my plan. There will be a raid on the transfer. It will be a fake, naturally. I have some Force Red prisoners I have kept segregated for such an event. They will be killed on the scene and left for the press to examine. My agents in Force Red will spread the rumor they were traitors. The organization will tear itself apart looking for others.''

"And Robert?''

"Some day, when my takeover is complete, I will expose his true nature to the world. After that, who cares what he says or does? Can you imagine his father's reaction?'' Sandoval clapped, the sound too much like the earlier slap between Robert and Flor, and Curtin winced. Drawing his own conclusion, Sandoval said, "Yes, an unpleasant prospect. For him. Not for us.''

Rising, he added, "Take the woman's car and go home. She'll be going nowhere, and you've been here too long. We will discuss details later.''

"One more thing,'' Curtin said. "The general location of the ransom payment has to be on the large lake to the north. I want all that water on one flank. It eliminates attack from that direction, anyhow.''

"And the lake has a short river exit to the sea. So the gold is coming by ship.''

Curtin failed to restrain a reaction at the incisive deduction. Sandoval accepted the unintentional compliment with grand superiority. "It had to be. No one would attempt to hide anything like that in our neighboring countries. You had no chance to keep the information from me. As it happens, I know a place I think will satisfy you. We'll visit it in the morning. Now, however, you must go.''

He paused at the door, ostentatiously listening. Turning a cruelly burlesque innocence to Curtin, he said, "It's very quiet in there. I wonder what they're doing.'' He winked. "No matter. I have other mirrors. In much more interesting locations.''

His laughter chased Curtin through the racket of the slammed door.

Chapter 24

Holding the small tape recorder in his hand had the perverse effect of making Curtin feel farther from, not closer to, home. That, combined with the deepening comprehension of the totality of Robert's deceit, made it even more difficult to think out exactly what message to send Chavez.

During Robert's speech-making with Flor, he'd made up his mind what to do.

The ransom gold was going to Buck Curtin and the pawns in the game.

All he had to do was make the decision stick.

Light leaking from the almost-closed refrigerator door cast long shadows around the kitchen as he stood, tapping a foot, checking his watch. Only a few minutes remained before he had to tell Chavez something.

"Speed and deception." He whispered the words, enjoying the sibilance of them in the silent gloom. Pushing the "Record" button, he composed his message. *"I have located what I came for. No definite arrangements for exchange have been made yet. If the ship is in position, monitor tomorrow's frequency continuously until my next message. If the ship is not in position, I must be informed now, in order to make alternate plans. I must be certain everything is ready. Over."*

Rewinding the tape, he attached it to the radio, then hunched over his watch. As the second hand swept to the correct minute, he hit the switch. The message squealed out, and he rewound again, sitting back to wait. The answer came quickly, the tape catching the excitement in Chavez's voice. *"The ship is in position. I'm in constant communication with the man in charge. Have you seen Robert? Is he well? Can we trust them to release him unharmed?"*

Cursing quietly, Curtin requested acknowledgment of his requirements, adding. *"He's perfectly all right."*

Chavez was contrite. *"Congratulations. Will monitor, as you request. Two questions for you. What is your emergency escape route, and can I be of help? Is your local contact still under control, still involved in the deal you proposed? It's our best assurance of his neutralization."*

Curtin chuckled, then spoke out loud. "Cunning bastard. You knew I'd have a rat hole to run to, didn't you? I think I've just been complimented."

He unconsciously avoided looking at the tape recorder as he spoke. *"The emergency plan is for a friend to fly in from the field you pointed out to me. He arrives there tomorrow night. He'll come here on my signal and knows where to look for us if things break down. The local man is satisfied our arrangement is legitimate. He wants the equipment you've stored at the field. I'll wait five minutes for anything you have to add, and then I'm shutting down. Over."*

The time dragged, and he peered at his watch with growing impatience. As soon as he could, he detached the recorder and stored the equipment. That done, he turned on the overhead light, raised the window blind, and opened the back door. The flow of cool night air surprised him. He hadn't realized how hot the kitchen had become. He wiped sweat from his forehead and, helping himself to a cold beer, stepped into the living room.

Kooseman sat in the overstuffed chair against the far wall. That alone would have been enough to stop Curtin in his tracks, but even more compelling was the large automatic with the businesslike silencer aimed at him. The chubby face was pulled into a weary frown, as if the mind behind it was puzzled beyond endurance. The weapon was solid as rock. Kooseman held it in both hands, elbows on his knees, and something new in the squinting eyes told Curtin the little man knew exactly how to use it.

Frozen in position, Curtin said, "Let's not get in a hurry, okay?"

Kooseman's smile flickered like a candle flame. "Sit on the floor. Hold the beer in your left hand." As Curtin moved, he went on, "So you're here to bail out old Chavez's kid. That means you're an American, too. I never guessed."

Curtin said, "Whose kid?" and Kooseman smiled. There was more strength to it. He said, "We'll play for a little bit, while I bring you up to speed. You've done well just to stay alive, you know it? And getting me to front for you while you smuggle in that tricky radio—that was cute. You prick."

Sipping the beer, Curtin waited. Kooseman said, "I know the field and the equipment you and Chavez talked about."

"Why the gun? I already said I'd cut you in on anything Sandoval throws my way."

The frown returned. "Enough already. You've never been near that field. If you had, I'd know it. It's huge, a supply dump, a staging depot. We're dealing with construction machinery, sure. And weapons. Enough for a small war." He lowered the pistol to the floor, held up empty hands, palms out. "Listen to me. You're a good man. You fooled me and Sandoval, but now I know. If he doesn't, he will soon. You've lasted longer than you've a right to ask. You're out of your league. This isn't one of your neat

little wars, but you can be useful. I can't do the things you
can do. I need help, so don't think I won't use what I
heard to squeeze cooperation out of you, because I sure as
hell will. I'm telling you straight, whatever you think,
you're being used at every goddamned turn.''

He waited patiently for Curtin to stop laughing. Then,
''So cards on the table. I've got some friends in Force
Red. Moderates. They know Comandante Noche and the
other wild dogs will eliminate them as soon as the
revolution's won. On the other hand, you know what
Sandoval has in mind for these poor people. But who am I?
What's it to me? You think I'm a fat, scared little
businessman, but now you're wondering if I'm maybe not
CIA. Right, both ways. I've been here long enough to
understand change is coming, and why. It's my job to see
if we can't salvage some kind of good relationship with our
own country. Now, Chavez's equipment dump has to tie in
somehow with two of my agents telling me something
very, very big is going down soon. Too many insiders in
this government, the sort of people who always know
what's happening a day or two before everyone else, are
suddenly charging everything in the world, spending money
they don't have. They're excited as hell, and I swear they
don't even know why themselves. They smell a big payday coming, and I can't figure what it is. I think you might
have an idea, and I need your help.''

''Why should I believe you, much less help you? What's
in it for me?''

''Don't screw around with me. We don't have the time.''
Kooseman shook his head like a horse getting rid of a fly.
''You'll help me because you know damned well you
ought to. Give me something to help the moderates and
ordinary people in this country have a chance. Freeze out
my friends, and Comandante Noche wins the whole pot.''

''Who says Force Red's going to win?''

For a moment Kooseman looked as if he hadn't understood the question, and then he laughed. Curtin drained his
beer in large, angry gulps while he waited for the peals to

end. Kooseman gestured weakly before continuing. "Because they know how. We saw it in Nam, for Christ's sake, and in Nicaragua. They identify legitimate grievances and fight to correct them. They understand control of the populace. The lower classes cooperate and get schools, medicine, land, and promises. The leaders live well. And punish hard. Fuck with them, and they destroy your entire family. We Americans tell ourselves communism is foreign repression, but it's Cubans who control the masses in Cuba, not Russians. The communists give the people the illusion of freedom and a sense of nationality even when they're taking away their churches and newspapers. We back assholes like this government here that gives them nothing but death squads to keep them in line."

"So what're you, a communist for the CIA?"

"Oh, Jesus." Kooseman rocked in the chair and closed his eyes. When he opened them, they were sad. "What I'm trying to tell you is, we can't graft our democracy onto these people like a damned tree limb. All we can do is help them establish some kind of representational government. Is that subversive?"

"I guess not."

"Thanks. Beyond measure. Now, will you help me?"

The temptation pulled at Curtin. The blue-black weapon lying untended on the floor beside Kooseman was a telling symbol, a matter of great psychological strength. Still, Curtin knew it was only a selling point. While it appeared forgotten, Kooseman's hand would be on it instantly at the first suspicious move.

The fat man sighed into the extended silence. "I don't blame you. You've got a deal going, and Chavez pays his bills. You can depend on your boss better than mine, sometimes. And you know why that bothers me? Because guys like you and me are willing to risk our butts for everything these poor, ignorant bastards believe in, and in a little while everyone here'll hate us and our country and some frigging Sandinista'll be writing their schoolbooks." He rose slowly, unscrewing the silencer with a preoccupied air. "Anyhow, think about whose side you're on. I hope you'll understand that I have to sort of keep an eye on you from now on. What you know would get me killed awful quick."

"Wait a minute." Curtin rose, careful to make no sudden moves, watching the pistol. "Come on in the kitchen. I'll get us a couple of beers and fill you in."

They sat at the table with the lights out, depending on the tail end of the light from the living-room lamp. Speaking slowly, diagraming his tale with a forefinger on the stained wood, Curtin picked his way through the facts. He omitted mentioning anyone except Sandoval. Kooseman listened stolidly, his only movements an almost metronomic hoisting of the beer bottle and an occasional nod of understanding. When it came time to describe Robert's treachery, Curtin failed. Without understanding why, he lied.

"Sandoval's holding Robert. I'm going to give him the ransom and we're taking off."

"He'll burn you both. You're meat already."

Curtin's try at a confident smile felt strained.

Kooseman's expression tightened, but he said nothing. Curtin provided one last alteration of fact by saying that Sandoval had revealed the oil discovery. Kooseman pursed his lips in a silent whistle while Curtin explained the geology of the find.

"That's it," Curtin finished, flattening his hands on the table. "All I ask is you let me run my operation, make my money, and evac this place. After that, it's yours. You save the free world. I gave up on it after Nam."

Kooseman cocked his head to the side. "Sure." When Curtin added nothing else, he rose, then said, "I'm not sure you've told it all the way it happened, or if you've told me everything you could, but you've helped me. I'll return the favor if I can."

"I want a favor now." As he said it, Curtin felt a bitterness slide up his throat from somewhere deep inside him, but he pressed ahead. "What can you tell me about Flor Peralta?"

"The Peraltas?" Kooseman was already into the living room, and when he turned, the light caught him from below, accentuating his nose and chin. His teeth gleamed in a twisted smile. "Old aristocrat family, too nice for a war. They're in Switzerland, except to come home when the smoke clears. They—" He stopped, examining Curtin, then went on lamely. " 'Course, she's not like the rest of them. She stayed on, sort of looking out for the farm and the locals. Not a bad gal at all, really." Clumsily, he stuffed the pistol under his belt and fitted the silencer into a holsterlike arrangement under his trousers leg. He left with a brief wave.

The following morning Curtin waited at the front window with Lucia. "Taxi you call," she said, pointing. "Why no drive? You have car."

"Curiosity." He sipped his coffee. When the driver headed for the door, he said, "Tell him I'll be a few minutes."

She looked at him questioningly, but hurried to do as bid. She was back to Curtin before the driver reached his seat. Curtin continued to enjoy his coffee. Lucia could stand it no longer. "What you do? No go. Why?"

Curtin pointed at the gardener across the street. "He never looked up, and that probably means he knew the taxi was coming. And the driver's not a real taxi driver."

Lucia waggled a tiny finger under his nose as she pulled him from the window by main force. "How you sure?"

"Boots. The damned fool's wearing army boots."

Lucia clapped her hands together and almost danced, cackling. *"Bueno!"* she said, then, puzzled. "Why do this? He tell where you go!"

"Because if the car is here, you'll watch it, let me know if anyone touches it. Yes?"

She laughed again. *"Muy bueno! I very happy!"* Then,

as suddenly as the laughter started, it stopped. "No good be too good. Be careful, all time, okay?"

Curtin squeezed her shoulder on his way past. "I'm learning sweetheart. Wish me luck."

Chapter 25

The driver revealed no awareness of Curtin's destination prior to hearing it. Curtin swallowed an urge to name someplace besides Sandoval's Ministry, knowing the soldier/driver had his orders and would spin like a top if his passenger failed to perform according to plan.

Through hundreds of darting cars, smoking, groaning buses and hurtling trucks, all pounding life into the early morning city, he swerved from lane to lane with confident abandon. Questions, phrased in mangled English, trailed out of the corner of his mouth like a tattered banner. How long Mister in Costa Verde? Where from? And on and on. Almost to the Ministry, passing a particularly pompous statue, he got down to business. "You try marijuana here? World super, I think."

"Never use the stuff."

Dark eyes flicked in the rearview mirror. "Buy here very cheap, sell Canada, U.S. Much money."

"Much jail." This time Curtin met the eyes in the mirror. The driver made a small face of disappointment.

At first Curtin was amused by Sandoval's persistence,

the effort to tempt an ally into an act that would compromise his bargaining position. Then he was offended. As if any genuine driver would pitch drugs to a man headed for the Ministry housing the national police. It insulted the intelligence.

Sandoval, on the other hand, was unusually affable. He greeted Curtin with a firm handshake, making steady conversation on the way to the sedan. As they rolled out of the city he pointed out landmarks and commented on local history.

Soon they sped down a pockmarked road slicing between lush crops and pasture. Once more, however, Curtin's attention was drawn to the ever-present hills beyond, the forest-clad giants that seemed somehow alive, sadly aware of their great strength and their eventual doom at the hands of the squalling humans ripping them apart.

Unbidden, the driver pulled off at a short driveway leading to a huge wooden gate in a cement wall Curtin estimated to be at least eight feet high. The driver trotted to open the gate as Sandoval gestured to both sides. "Open fields to both flanks. Very difficult to approach." They swept through, confronting a vista of luxury. A manicured lawn, spotted with fruit trees, edged with glowing flower beds, drew the eye down the gradual slope to the massive house and the unruffled blue-gray lake beyond.

Sandoval continued. "Only one road access. The lake to the back, as you specified. The wall will be guarded, of course, and the nearest house is a good thousand meters away." He finished as they reached the house.

It was, Curtin concluded, a beautified bunker, with its barred, narrow windows and a door almost as heavy as the one at the gate. They passed through a tiled entryway to the hollow interior where blossoms glowed in a lush garden between the exposed, pillared walkways down each side. Sandoval led the way across the garden and into the main room. Scrolls of vines and leaves executed in wrought iron formed the wall facing the lake. Wide-drawn drapes revealed the view. The center section of the protective ironwork was actually a pair of hinged gates that could be swung out of the way. Sandoval said, "This is the place to bring the gold."

Curtin said, "There are some things you have to know about this transfer," and Sandoval frowned darkly.

Now was the point of no return. To survive, Curtin had to create time for his escape. He'd had one night to think it out. He took a deep breath and started spinning the lies that would either save him or end the game on the spot. "I'm the only person they'll allow to approach the ship, and I've got to come alone. Also, the cases are booby-trapped."

"Que?" In his anger, Sandoval slipped into Spanish, then corrected himself. "What?"

"There's a radio receiver-transmitter under the gold bars. When the box is opened, a signal goes from that set to one on board Bullard's ship. I can keep the box open for fifteen seconds, long enough for you to satisfy yourself the gold's there. After fifteen seconds, if the box isn't closed, twenty-five pounds of plastic explosive packed under the ingots goes off automatically. The plastic stays armed until the ship sends a disarm signal to the radio here, and Bullard won't send one until I get back to the ship and tell him to."

Sandoval was growing angrier by the second, and Curtin hurried on. "There's also a pressure release fuse under the gold. It's activated and deactivated by the same system. Don't even think about emptying the boxes before the timer sets off the explosives. Anyone trying to get the gold without releasing Robert buys the most expensive hail-storm in history."

Sandoval moved stiffly to one of the easy chairs. The lame leg swung in a chopping arc at each step. When he sat down he unconsciously extended it to the side. "We will return to this problem. Now you will tell me how you expect to return to this ship with your money and without Robert." He forced a tight, false smile. "I could make arrangements for you to fly out of here. You might even choose to live with us. There are worse places."

Muscles moved in Curtin's back, a sensation of flies walking on exposed skin. The question was a test. If the answer didn't satisfy Sandoval, he'd know Curtin had given no proper thought to his announced escape plan. He'd realize all the elaborate precautions were Curtin's desperate lies.

"The only way I survive this deal is to go back and convince Chavez I did my best. If he thinks I ditched Robert, he'll have me hunted down if it takes him forever." Curtin paused and grinned. "Anyhow, staying here, you knowing what I know, might tempt you to do something unethical."

Sandoval's lip twitched. "All things are possible in this imperfect world," he said dryly, continuing, "Very well. What is your plan?"

Curtin wiped wet palms on his thighs. "First, I have to get out to the ship where Bullard has the gold. There's an inflatable boat aboard, and I'm to use that to bring the ransom in-country. The boat has a removable wooden deck, a plywood thing that folds out from the middle, like a book opens. I stash my money under that when I leave."

Sandoval interrupted. "And when you arrive at the ship, you simply walk on with your money in your hand?"

"I always had my doubts about this scam." Curtin raised his chin defiantly. "There's a guy in the deck crew who'll help me. We arranged it a long time ago. I always figured I might have to grab what I could and run, and I knew I'd have to run for the ship, 'cause there's no other way I can get away from here. So I protected myself. There's nothing wrong with that."

"And Robert?"

Blinking, Curtin said, "He was my friend. I don't want to talk about it. That's your end, man."

"Which I know how to take care of. But what of your return without him? And my puzzle with the explosive boxes?"

"Easy. You're staging a fake battle with Force Red, right? So when I get to Bullard, I tell him Robert bought it while we were running away during the fighting. You get in a helicopter and fly out to the ship, where you tell Bullard he only gets the gold back through official channels. That means he's got to disarm the booby-traps, which the Force Red survivors told you about, okay? That puts the gold in your personal control. You can keep it wrapped up in red tape down here for twenty years. Maybe even forever."

"For the first time, I am confident of this plan. There are still small details, however. For one, when you leave here after you have delivered the ransom, a picked group of my men will escort you to the sea."

"I can get away by myself."

"Probably. But if you do not, everything falls apart. They will protect you."

"I don't like it. How do I know they won't rob me?"

"Because they are my men." Sandoval bristled.

Curtin smiled, ingratiating. "If you think it's that important, sure. What other details are bothering you?"

"You must complete the operation as an outlaw. We are working for Costa Verde, of course, but there are powerful men here who would destroy our plan. You have been resourceful. You must be even more so, for just two more days. All depends on you." He approached to place his hands on Curtin's shoulders, looking into his eyes.

There was no depth to the stare, no more life than polished metal, brightness with no hint of thought or conscience behind it.

Still, that very fact revealed unmistakable twin truths.

Sandoval meant to kill Curtin at the first sign of a breakdown.

If he could figure out a way to get at the gold, he wouldn't wait for anything to go wrong.

Faced with inescapable momentum now, Curtin hardly acknowledged Sandoval's good fellowship on the way back to the car. He managed to respond politely on the trip until he realized they were taking a different route. Curious, he looked at the landscape, actually seeing it for the first time.

Sandoval's country house rose in the distance. A slow smile wrinkled the corners of his eyes at Curtin's reaction. "The Peralta woman is well," he said, correctly guessing Curtin's question. "I have not seen her, naturally, but Robert tells me. I have been forced to declare her detained for investigation in order to keep her friends from thinking she's missing. Her car is being delivered to your house. You will need transportation and Robert needs her." He heaved a dramatic sigh. "Affection. It's so useful to us in my work. A dangerous ailment. Robert risks everything to have her close, and I'm not sure she really wants to be with him any longer. I have seen signs that Robert may be suffering the same suspicions. That could be troublesome for me, but quite dangerous for her, you know? Another good reason for you to work hard for the success of our mission, I think."

Turning, Curtin bit off his words, and in that instant understood why the poor of Costa Verde reacted with such wild swings between mute acceptance and berserk violence. To reveal offense, even to argue, was ridiculous. The cost was certain to be unpleasant. It could be catastrophic.

A man pushed down to that level struck only to kill. He would count minutes until his opportunity came.

Curtin watched the small fields and rough homes pass by. Those people asked for little material wealth. Without the experience of food processors and unnecessary horse-power, they were satisfied with enough to eat, hope for the future, and the companionship of friends. If they picked up arms and went to war against their leaders, it was more to salvage pride than to acquire riches.

Sandoval said, "You find the peasants something to smile about?"

"I was thinking I have lot in common with them."

"With them?" Sandoval laughed heartily. "Americans! So romantic! One night in one of their huts, and you would be on the first airplane back to your canned food and air conditioners.''

''I spent a night in one of them. You're right — it made me understand a lot about my own life.''

Sandoval pursed his lips, became professorial. ''You should think about such things. Believe me, peasants are not like us.''

Not much later, the driver sped across the sidewalk, horn blaring, scattering pedestrians on his way down the ramp to the Ministery's underground garage. Curtin wasted little time on goodbyes, anxious to get his next move underway.

No surveillance fell in behind him, and a careful program of backtracking and complex passages through stores and a market convinced him none was in the area. Accepting the probability that Evita's place was constantly watched, he decided there was no choice but to go there for the help he needed.

The earlier suspicions about the pill she'd given him crawled through the darker corners of his mind, but he determined to ignore them. There had been no more of the dream flashes after all, and she herself had pointed out how restlessly he slept.

She greeted him from one of the tables. Ben sat beside her. Curtin took a chair, gesturing to the bartender to bring him a beer.

''Evita, I need help. First, I've got to get out to sea. Unseen.''

Unperturbed, she said, ''A boat and a guide. What else?''

''Trouble. Flor's in Sandoval's place, that fortress he calls a country house. I want to get inside. How do I do it?''

''Impossible!'' Her eyes were huge, unbelieving.

''I'm going. You can help me.''

Ben said, ''If Evita says it can't be done, give up.'' Curtin glared. The younger man met it without flinching.

Evita said, ''Sandoval does not use his home for prisoners.

If Flor is there, it is for another reason. Can you be so sure she does not *want* to be there?''

Curtin ached to tell her the full story, but he had to say, ''No, I can't be sure. I have to know. I do know she hasn't gone over to his side.''

''You have more faith than I.'' Evita looked away. One of the girls smiled at her, but when the concerned eyes continued to focus on a point far past her, she rose and left the room.

''She won't turn me over to Sandoval. I'm going in tonight, Evita. If you help, I've got a lot better chance.''

Continuing to look off into a private distance, Evita finally answered, her voice soft. ''In the middle of so much fighting for power, we still come back to the everyday reasons for dying, don't we? Perhaps there is a way. We will try.''

For the rest of the day Curtin sat in the living-room side of the building while the girls described the wonders of Sandoval's house. Little by little, Curtin sketched a floor plan of the entire establishment. Entering into the new game enthusiastically, the girls rummaged for snapshots of themselves with Sandoval's more favored guests. Rooms took shape in Curtin's mind; the approaches from inside the wall became workably familiar. When Angelina described the central control for activating the eavesdropping system throughout the house, Curtin promised her the largest steak in the country for dinner. Her retort was muttered Spanish through a sly grin, and from the following shrieks and giggles of the other girls, he was glad he didn't understand the language.

He remembered the excitement and shared anticipation later that night as the illumination from Sandoval's wall lights crept into the cramped space behind the seats of Angelina's sports car.

She said, ''You are ready?'' and Curtin grunted acknowledgment. Her voice trembled. ''Quick! I make slow when say three, like you say!'' Unconsciously, she counted in

Spanish, and was up to *"Dos!"* before Curtin realized what was happening. At *"Tres!"* the car was barely moving, and he flipped out into the darkness. Immediately, the engine roared, and the machine bucked wildly down the road. As Curtin rolled into the weeds, a searchlight already raked the fields toward the car. He watched until the vehicle conveniently "broke down" almost immediately in front of the gate. Silhouetted guards moved rapidly to investigate.

Curtin took off toward the side gate. In his dark clothes, with hands and face blackened, he moved swiftly and silently, crouched low. It felt good, and the old skills filled his muscles with purpose and intent. Senses primed, he realized how exhausted he'd become from constant lying and cheating. This was where he belonged. He paused, listening, vainly pleased at the regularity and ease of his breathing. Sharply, he reminded himself to concentrate, to be alert.

The lone guard remaining at the gate, a boy in his teens, stood atop the wall several yards away, craning his head toward the tight knot of men and the flirting women. Curtin couldn't restrain a nervous grin as he slipped through the small entry. The junior man caught the duty, as always.

The door was no problem, left unlocked out of faith in the now-distracted guards. Curtin crouched in the darkened kitchen and blessed his good luck. The men would never have been so lax if Sandoval himself were home, which meant the house should be empty except for Robert and Flor. Now he had to hope they weren't together.

He made his way to the library. Under a dictionary on an intricately carved cabinet-stand he found the control buttons for the microphone system, exactly as Angelina had described. He remembered her sly laughter as she spoke of the ones connected to the bedrooms.

The first try drew nothing. Nor did the second. Curtin wondered about his luck holding, dried his palms on his trousers, and tried again. Music drifted out of the small speaker. He raised the volume as high as he dared. Heavy breathing, almost liquid-sounding, blended into the music. Another sound insinuated itself, and Curtin's face twisted at the grating of bedsprings.

He slumped against the cabinet, depressed by his discovery, equally disgusted with his eavesdropping.

Another sound snapped him upright. For a moment his emotion-drugged mind refused to respond properly, and he instinctively sank into a tense crouch. He heard it again.

Snoring?

He pressed his ear to the speaker. The damp, labored breathing was gone. Whoever had the radio on, whoever made the springs complain, had been turning over. Now that person snored contentedly.

He punched the next button with renewed determination.

More silence. He was about to try another room when he thought he heard something. Raising the volume another notch, he waited. There was someone in that room. He was certain. And then she coughed. He hurried from the library, picturing the top-floor layout as he went.

Outside Robert's room, he listened. The snoring continued. Creeping down the hall, he arrived at Flor's room. He knocked, then stepped back into the darkness. It was best she identify a form, rather than see the raider's blackened features and be startled into a scream. As it happened, she barely controlled herself even when he whispered his name. Looking up and down the hall, she reached out and jerked him into the room, pushing the door closed with a speed she checked in time to avoid a slam. Finger to lips, she rushed him to the porch, reaching out to switch off the light on the way.

"What are you doing here? How did you get in? Be quiet! The whole place is bugged, and something has the guards very excited tonight!"

"I know about the disturbance. And the bugs. I came to tell you I know about Robert."

"The others will help you get away. You must all get out of the country. Sandoval will get you if you don't!"

"The others don't know about Robert."

"What? What do you mean?"

Curtin held out his hands, an unconscious plea. "As long as they think he's worth saving, they'll help me ransom him, but I mean to destroy Robert and Sandoval together, if I can. If I fail, Robert will eventually find out you knew me."

"That's not important. It's not even your concern."

"You're important. I won't endanger you. I have to be sure you won't be hurt, or he can have the damned gold."

She reacted as if slapped, her hand flying to her cheek, stepping back unsteadily. "You could think that of me? You have no right! This country is all I dare think about! Everything else, every other emotion in my life, has been cheapened by all this struggle for power. After what it has cost me, *is* costing me, you would throw it away!"

Roughly, he reached for her, framed her face in his hands. Her eyes burned and her nostrils flared with defiance. The need for stealth turned his whisper into a coarse growl. "What I'm telling you is that if he lives, you may die! I've got to know if you love him, Flor. I have to know. I love you, and I have to know!"

She stepped away from his grasp, put a hand on the wall. Her voice was hardly audible. "I hate that word. It brings pain, shame. I made Harry Bullard think I loved him. I thought I loved Robert. Now you say it to me. How do I answer? Do I tell you I love you?" Her body moved with laughter, silent gusts coming from a face that parodied amusement. "I only know I'm not in love with Robert. That's enough, I think."

Curtin took a step forward. "I'll get you out of here."

"I want out. God help me, I want away from here! But you must promise you won't help them, won't give them the gold."

"I'll do my best. I'll be back for you."

"You'll need help." Hope strengthened her words. "Contact Luis. And if you need anything unusual, the little businessman, Kooseman, may be helpful."

Shocked, Curtin pretended disbelief. "Him? That wimp?"

"I've heard hints from friends. I'm the one who told Harry Kooseman to find a house for you, because I knew he spent a lot of time at Evita's and he'd take you there, too. I think he knows people who may be able to help us escape."

"Are you sure Evita doesn't think he's more than a businessman?"

Flor made a cutting gesture. "She'd never let him in, if she did."

Relieved, Curtin said, "Forget him. Believe me, your friends are chasing butterflies. And one fat one, in particular."

"Perhaps. But now you must go. You've been here too long."

The words hung in the soft darkness, full of more meaning than either was willing to acknowledge. Curtin broke the pained silence with a grin, saying, "We look like two high-school freshmen from Tacoma trying to say good-night on our first date."

Again, surprise widened her eyes, and then with one hand she covered an edged, strained laugh. Reaching out with the other hand, she touched his. "I think you're mad, I really do. Maybe that's why I"—she stopped, then went on—"why I think you'll do what you mean to do. Go with God, gringo."

He had her check the hall. On his way past, he paused at Robert's room. The snoring was stopped, but no light came under the door. The house seemed to watch him from all angles as he stealthily made his way back down the stairs.

Everything was uneventful until he was a few feet outside, crouched between rows of corn in the small kitchen garden. Raucous laughter broke over him. Muscles in his arms and legs bunched, ready to strike. Heavy footsteps approached, heels striking the earth with assurance. Slowly, dreading the spear of light he was sure was coming, Curtin turned to face that direction.

A squat, thick body strode past, no more than ten feet away. A slighter figure moved beside it.

The guards. Profiled against the house, the heavy one performed gestures that left no doubt of the subject of his tale. Evita's girls were doing their job to perfection. The younger man groaned disappointment.

Curtin sprinted for the unguarded gate as the two rounded the corner. In the fields again, he retraced his steps to the road, then paralleled it past the first bend. Making himself comfortable at the base of a tree, he waited.

Clouds of invisible, whining insects descended on him, overjoyed at this unbelievably succulent meal. He brushed at the fiercer ones, settling down to wait.

Robert.

The old debt was gone.

Now there was another.

Angelina's slow approach jolted him out of his thoughts. He sprinted to the roadside, angling to catch up to the slowly moving vehicle. Getting a handhold on the luggage rack, he put a foot on the bumper and rolled into the hole behind the seats. The car immediately picked up speed. The other girl turned to look down at him, her features indistinct in the darkness. "You okay? Flor okay?"

"Okay. You?"

"No trouble." She sniffed. "*Soldados.* Boom-boom. Finish." Angelina laughed. The two of them lapsed into Spanish, Curtin worked to find a comfortable position.

When they pulled into Evita's garage, the girls helped out and showed him up the back stairs to Evita's room. She was waiting for them. "No trouble?"

"None." Curtin stopped on his way to the shower. "How about the boat for tomorrow night?"

"All taken care of. Flor is safe?"

"Yes. Listen, your girls—how can I thank them? They made the whole thing possible. I'd offer to pay, but I know they'd be insulted as hell. What can I do?"

Evita's pride showed. "I'll ask them." She spoke to the two, and they smiled appreciation at Curtin as they answered her. He was surprised at how innocently ordinary they could appear, and was embarrassed at being surprised. Their response surprised him even more.

Evita said, "They say, when you go home, tell everyone the truth about this country. We are only people who want to live in peace. We don't want your soldiers, your charity. Help us get rid of the ones who oppress us, the military you support and the guerrillas the communists support."

"It'll be a pleasure."

Evita rose. "Have your shower, then you must go. You need rest. There is much to do tomorrow."

Her words broke a dam of reserve in Curtin's mind, and he was suddenly exhausted. Numbly, he got to his feet and practically staggered into the perfume-thick confines of Evita's bathroom. The cloyed air did him no good, but the shower was bracing, and he felt a little better when he came out. Evita waited to escort him back downstairs.

No sooner had they stepped out, when down the hall, Kooseman abruptly half-fell out of one of the rooms closer to the stairs. He caught himself on the banister and studied the descent as if contemplating a sheer wall. Curtin hurried to his side, grabbing a swaying shoulder. Kooseman smiled owlishly at him.

Forcing the smaller man into a stumbling rush, Curtin spoke loudly. "Let me give you a hand. You're about to go on your butt."

Leaning close, he whispered. "Listen! Your cover's not as tight as you think. Hit the deck, you hear?"

Kooseman paled, and when he turned to Curtin, his eyes sparked briefly. Drunkenly dignified, he smirked. "I know what you're saying. Well, get lost, buddy. I'll take care of myself." He pulled free with comical majesty.

Curtin waited for Evita. She tapped her lips with a finger as she approached, eyes fixed on the door where Kooseman exited.

She said, "He asked about Flor. When I told him she

was arrested, he said no more. Later, he asks if I see you. He bothers me.''

''He's a harmless drunk.''

''He talks all the time and says nothing. He never tells his thoughts to my girls.''

''Maybe he just enjoys his privacy.''

''He never asked questions before. It makes me afraid.''

The conversation had gone too far. Curtin said, ''You worry too much. He's nothing.''

Her hand on his arm was an unthinking gesture as she looked after the departed man. She said, ''Don't try to teach me how men behave around women. There is trouble going on inside that one. The more I think, the more sure I am.''

Curtin watched her turn and walk to the stairs. Her head was down, and she was lost in her thoughts.

Chapter 26

Shrill screams tore the dawn, and Curtin came fully awake already in a prone position, flat against the juncture of wall and floor, knowing they came from Lucia.

What had seemed to be fear, at first, was clearly anger, and he raced downstairs to help.

He was unprepared for troops in his kitchen.

There were four men, three in camouflaged fatigues, armed with M16s. At Curtin's approach, they faced him with a sort of surly relief, weapons loosely held, unalarmed.

Lucia stood in the middle of the room, screened from view behind a grubby customs agent, whose shirt front she held bunched in her fists. Curtin peered past him and Lucia stretched to meet his gaze as he said, "What's going on? Who are these men?"

"Ladrones!" She spat the word. "Thieves! They come for *refrigerador*."

Curtin kept his voice steady. "Why? It came through customs. I have the papers."

The customs man disengaged himself, faced Curtin with wounded dignity. Greasy offended tones discolored his

Spanish explanation. Lucia translated. "The *refrigerador* is no registered. The city has not enough of electricity. Every new electric machine be registration. You not have."

"I'll pay it right now. How much? And how much for him?"

A lopsided smile lifted one corner of Lucia's mouth. "You no understand. They no give number when you bring machine to Costa Verde, okay? Now they take *refrigerador,* you pay fine ten times more bigger than license, then pay license."

Curtin's neck grew warm. The cheap little scam could get him shot. "Tell him I'll pay the fine and the fee. I don't want that refrigerator moved!"

Lucia hesitated, and Curtin erupted. "I'll pay twice the fine! Tell them!"

Lucia's anger disappeared. The small face transformed into a mass of nervous wrinkles. "Maybe not good. Later, you go pay fine. Go to warehouse, pay them. Make registration for government, pay them. Happy. *Refrigerador* here tomorrow. You say pay two times now, maybe too much they want know why so *especial*, no?"

Finding a smile, Curtin said, "You're right. Tell him."

Although Curtin understood not a word, the language smoked. The heretofore stolid troopers grinned among themselves as they watched the agent rush to get the machine on a dolly and into the waiting van.

When the house was theirs again, Curtin turned to his diminutive housekeeper. "I want some fresh fruit for breakfast. Go to the market and pick out something. Different kinds of bananas. Anything."

She looked up from under knitted brows. "You want me out of house." It was a challenge.

"Right."

She shrugged, and with no further ado, picked up her shopping bag and left. Curtin watched her go down the street. Then, still in pajamas, butcher knife in hand, he raced for the garage.

The stacked rectangles of the refrigerator's packing crate

were already home to several spiders. Curtin swept them
away, stripping the plywood from the two-by-fours. Locat-
ing the hairline crack in one of the long formers, he placed
the knife blade against it and tapped it with a rusty screw-
driver conveniently lying against the wall. Working fast,
he split the entire length of wood. It opened like a pea
pod, exposing the gleaming multicolored bits and pieces of
transistors, resistors, and other technical exotica of electronics. He hooked the numbered components together
until they formed one solid rectangle about the size of two
bricks.

That done, he repeated the splitting process with one of
the shorter pieces of lumber, exposing the stainless-steel
barrel and grip of the rocket gun. A dozen cartridges
nestled in a separate wooden pocket beside two batteries.
He unscrewed a cap from the breech end of the tube and
dropped the latter in the resulting receptacle. Following
that, he pushed a small side button. A recessed light
indicated proper connections and voltage. A spring com-
pressed inside the pistol grip to accept the ammunition,
which was then attached to the barrel. Sliding the barrel to
the rear jacked a round into the chamber against the electrical contact of the batteries. Another slide ejected the first
round and fed in a second. He replaced the round in the
grip.

Everything seemed to be in order.

In a few seconds the equipment was stowed under the
seat of Flor's car, and Curtin was pouring himself a cup of
coffee.

Less than an hour after that, he was in Sandoval's office,
trying not to think of that equipment down in the underground parking facility, available to the first inquisitive
policeman who wanted to feel under the seat. It was too
dangerous to leave it at the house and expose Lucia to the
possibility of a search.

And he had to see Sandoval. He said, "Flor has to be
part of the deal. You promised she'd learn the truth about
Robert, and that's how I want it done."

He was astounded when Sandoval raised his hands in surrender. "What good is a friend who won't help his friend? If it means so much to you, she'll be there to see the gold delivered."

Fawning thanks, Curtin practically bowed his way out of the office, then hurried to the car. He sped out Country Club Road, stopping when he found a place that offered some seclusion. Pulling out the miniature radio, he connected it into the car's cigarette lighter and began sending. *"Linkup, this is Beach Party. Do you read? Over."*

No one answered. A small bird came to watch and listen, flitting through the thick brush beside the car, one glittering eye always intent on the interloper. Occasionally it twittered a thin, high song, as if defining its boundaries. Curtin continued to send his message.

A peasant with a horse-drawn cart rounded a distant bend, plodded along until abreast of the parked car. Curtin hid the radio and smiled pleasantly. The dark, seamed face blinked once, then slowly turned away. It was not so much rejection as total refusal to acknowledge.

Curtin glared at the silent radio. He was getting a lot of refusal to acknowledge, he thought.

He tried again. *"Linkup, this is Beach Party. Over."*

"Beach Party, this is Linkup. Your signal weak but readable. How do you read me? Over."

The tinny crackle from the miniature speaker apparently challenged the small bird. It dashed to the topmost branch of a shrub and trilled argument.

Curtin gripped the steering wheel. *"Read you clear, Linkup. Is your target in sight?"*

"Affirmative. Is everything all right?"

"Close enough. Maintain your position. Expect me before daylight. Over."

"Roger, Beach Party. Out."

Unplugging the radio, sliding it back under the seat, Curtin cut a quick U turn, heading back to town. He went directly to Evita's. She needed only to look at him to send for Ben. Curtin asked if Ben could bring a good map of the country, and she instructed the waiter to get one as well as a beer for Curtin. She gestured him to a seat at the table where she was finishing lunch. When he was settled, she said, "It's starting, isn't it?"

He shook his head. "Don't tell me I'm that easy to read, Evita. I've got enough trouble without you telling me everything I think is written on my face."

She smiled, patted his cheek. "Pretty soon the hiding and lying will be over."

He drank his beer in silence, studying the mindless bubbles rushing to explode. The thought depressed him and he took another large swallow. Ben hurried down the stairs, map in hand, and sat between them. Curtin drained his glass and Evita waved for a refill.

Curtin spread out the map, pointing. "Ben, you have to be at this village on the north shore of this big lake, with a truck, by nightfall tomorrow. You'll have to pass for a local with a broken vehicle. I want you on the east side of the village, here where the map shows this church. Stay with the truck. Some friends of mine will find you and tell you where to take them."

Ben nodded, but Evita would have none of it. "His accent is terrible. He knows nothing about us. If one soldier asks what village he is from, he is finished. He can't go!"

"I have to." Ben's face was drawn. "It's a little risky, but it's no big deal."

"It is!" She stood, so obviously upset the bartender took a few steps in their direction. Leaning toward Curtin, she said, "I go in the truck with him. We will be brother and sister. He will be mute, unable to speak. I talk for both of us."

Cutting off Ben's objection, Curtin said, "I can't let you take that kind of chance, Evita. If we're caught, we may get some help from Chavez. You won't, and Sandoval would give his good leg to arrest you."

"You can do nothing without me."

Curtin accepted his second beer from the still-watchful

waiter. "If there's trouble, everyone who's ever spoken to me will be in danger. How would you feel about leaving here?"

"Never. This is my country. My friend—I mean, my friends—will hide me."

"To you." Curtin lifted his glass in a toast. "Costa Verde doesn't need matadors. She has you."

Evita's smile reached almost to her eyes. She sat down again, and in a businesslike voice that strained against trembling, she said, "Your boat and guide are arranged." She pulled the map around. "This place. The south side, as you asked. A fishing and resort village, Chiltejo. There is a small park on the shore, with three benches. A man named Manuel will wait for you on the middle one. His eye is bandaged from an accident, so he will be easy to know. Ben can drive you there in Flor's car any time."

Curtin said, "Before you two leave for that village on the north shore of the lake, can you get word to Lucia to go into hiding for a few weeks?"

For a moment Evita studied his expression. She half-smiled. "I can manage that. Thank you."

"For what?"

She moved her shoulders, part shrug, part wriggle. "For nothing, I guess. But thank you, anyhow."

Ben got to his feet. "You ready?"

Quickly, Curtin bent to kiss Evita's cheek. "Don't tell Luis," he said, laughing. Flustered, she waved them away.

Both Ben and Curtin remarked on the number of impressive cars on the road to Chiltejo. Practically all carried young people, some barely in their teens. Bathing suits streamed from radio antennae and flapped wildly out windows. There was little other conversation until they arrived. Ben parked in the lot of a hotel that was attractive enough in its design and setting, but without the bustle of a happy tourist crowd, it had a forlorn aura. The few cars present only underscored the irony. Guests appeared to be limited to more young people, interested only in swimming, eating, and each other.

Ben said, "Who are these guys I'm supposed to meet, Buck? And where are we going?"

"No." Curtin opened his door, stepped out, and continued his answer by leaning down to speak back into the car. "You can't tell anyone what you don't know, Ben. That's a hard thing to say, but there it is."

Reddening, Ben said, "You think I'd blow the whistle?"

"Oh, shit." Curtin sat back down, turned off the air conditoner. "I know you're not going to inform on anyone. Unless Sandoval goes to work on you. Don't tell me you won't break, because you don't know that. No man does. So that's what I'm saying. Okay?" He extended a hand. Ben took it almost shyly.

"I'm sorry. I wasn't thinking."

Curtin got out again. "Don't worry about it. And take care of Evita, hear?"

"I will. See you."

Ben backed out fast. Spraying gravel rattled like hail, the sound triggering in Curtin a wave of nostalgia, memories of pines and the crack of fresh apples. He looked up at palm trees as he walked south, the only person using the cement pathway across the hotel grounds, and smiled at such reminiscence. Someday, when he was freezing and unsure of what to expect around the next bend, he'd think back on heat, humidity, and the distant laughter he heard right now.

The man named Manuel waited on his bench, staring out at the lake. After his first glance at Curtin, he said, "I have other clothes for you. Come." He adjusted the bandage on his eye, and Curtin noticed the other one was inflamed and sore, as well. When Manuel saw the attention his injuries were getting, he turned away quickly, spitting on the hot sidewalk. Curtin half-expected it to sizzle. He said, "I'm glad you speak English."

Manuel gave him a stony look. "We are not so stupid we would supply a guide you can't talk to."

" 'We'? Who's we?"

"Your friends." Manuel smiled, and Curtin had the

unsettling feeling it was meant for himself, that he was pleased with the quick, clever answer.

He led the way to a disreputable-looking bar, where the customers said nothing, but watched Curtin pass with the look of men weighing out livestock. When they were in the small storage area in the back, Manuel indicated the clothes. Curtin wondered if such filthy authenticity was really necessary, but reminded himself it was for only a few hours and made the switch.

Manuel eyed the odd-looking pistol, but made no objection when Curtin tucked it under his belt.

Continuing out the back door, the guide pointed to a motorcycle. Riding out of town, Curtin kept his face down, hanging onto the hat that further obscured his features. The road degenerated rapidly, going from cement to dirt, to narrow track, and finally to a trail threading through forest. When that ran out, Manuel carefully locked up the machine and struck off on foot.

A fifteen-minute walk brought them to a small creek. Manuel traced it a few yards, where he parted some brush to reveal a canoe like those Curtin had seen fishermen using on the lake. As soon as they were in it and poling their way downstream, Curtin asked, "Why all the secrecy? The damned lake's full of boats just like this."

"My last catch was cocaine. I unloaded it where the police don't come. You understand."

"Completely."

The grimy engine started easily, moving them toward the fishing fleet in the center of the lake at a good rate. Its racket held Manuel's conversation to instructions. As they paid out a large fishnet, he directed Curtin's attention to the police boat cruising through the midst of the fishermen.

Finally the net was out. Both men sat back with a sigh. Curtin enjoyed the respite. The sails, brushed by the setting sun, were no longer merely soiled white cloth, but had a warm, heated glow. Some, angled just right, took the rose-hue of South Dakota gold.

He thought of that place. It seemed centuries removed.

The police boat veered off and came at them. It moved between other boats, changing course from side to side. Curtin thought of a dog quartering, seeking to verify a scent. Not a large cruiser, it still mounted a fifty-caliber machine gun on the bow, and it loomed over the slim canoe.

Bored official eyes swept the sparse gear exposed in the boat. Manuel stirred, tugged on the net line. The cruiser slid past.

Manuel again snapped instructions at Curtin, showing him how to pull in the net. When Curtin put his back into it, the guide snarled angrily. "Not so fast! We want to follow these stupid bastards back to shore, not beat them there! You don't have to show me how macho you are."

Several beautiful fish spilled out onto the deck, glossy in the day's final light. The luminous eyes seemed startled, unable to comprehend the cruelty of this empty environment that killed without touching. By the time the net was stowed, their excitement was reduced to twitches. The eyes dimmed.

The boats ran for shore under sail. Changing course frequently, Manuel managed to lose the wind twice, falling behind everyone. He watched the police boat. As soon as it increased speed, he dropped the sail. Plunging his paddle into the water, he turned the canoe sharply and ordered Curtin to keep as low as possible. "They watch for smugglers among us, but not very hard," he said. "Now they go to their barracks. We head for the outlet to the sea. Use the paddle in the bow."

Night breezes stirred the surface of the lake, raising small waves. They slapped at the hull, sometimes wetting the silent men. Curtin stroked mechanically, fastening his eyes on the distant lights of the combination military and customs facility, where the lake emptied into its sea-bound river. A sliver of moon and an immensity of stars touched the water with diamonds. Little by little the post grew closer until Curtin became nervous about the increasing light level around them.

A subtle change in the movement of the canoe turned him around quickly, one hand reaching for the pistol. Manuel was on his feet. A cold line like polished silver gleamed from the razor edge of the machete in his hand.

Curtin aimed the pistol at him in a smooth arc.

Manuel's expression didn't change. Whispering, he said, "They told me to kill you or be sure the border police catch you. The choice is yours."

Curtin remained silent, unmoving. Manuel went on. "The goal is to keep you from paying the ransom for Robert Chavez. Me, I want the police to have you."

"The police aren't going to get me. You're going to get me past."

Laughing quietly, Manuel said, "You shoot me and everyone will be after you. I don't think you want to spend the rest of your life in one of our jails for murder." He raised the machete perhaps six inches. "It pleases me to know you will spend some time there, however. Smugglers are unpopular. But I will let you save your life. Swim to the shore and tell the police any story you like. They will send you to prison. While I wonder if I will ever see properly, you can wonder when you will see your home again. Your mission will have failed, and we are even for this."

Using the hand holding the machete, he touched the bandaged eye. With the weapon raised, he slid first one foot, then the other, forward.

Curtin said, "This weapon is silent, Manuel."

The answering chuckle mimicked the small waves against the hull. "The police or me. Live or die, you sonofabitch." He repeated the shuffling move. It put him almost within striking distance.

"Hold it!" Curtin raised a hand. Manuel paused, wary. Curtin said, "Evita set this up, didn't she? Did she burn everyone?"

"Evita?" Even in the darkness, Curtin saw the surprise on Manuel's face. It faded to scorn. "That whore? You think I would work with a whore, trust her? Her business is lies.''

He lunged.

The pistol made a noise like hot soda water fizzing out of a bottle. What appeared to be a flaming child's marble leaped from the muzzle to Manuel's chest. It impacted with a hollow crunch, spinning him over the side. The machete dropped harmlessly into the water. He thrashed momentarily, an attempt to cry out drowned in a bubbling gasp.

A greasy stench lingered in the stillness that followed, and Curtin puzzled over it while he crouched, watching the guard post for action. When there was no sign of activity, his mind turned to the smell, and he realized the small rocket had continued to burn until it expended its fuel inside Manuel's body. He grimaced at the ugly little weapon and shoved it back under his belt.

Easing back to the stern of the canoe, Curtin pulled the body aboard. He said, "Adios, asshole. Hard way to go," and began the task of maneuvering downstream.

A searchlight beam traversed the river entry with mechanical regularity. The light didn't even cover the entire navigable area, and it was child's play to time his passage. His only moment of concern came when a hoarse shout boomed across the water, but the quick laughter that followed marked the incident as horseplay among the careless guards.

Once clear of the area, he started the engine, racing to beat the sinking moon. Without its help, the river would disappear, making the sinister logs drifting past even more dangerous. Worse, the forested banks would blend too well with the night, and he could find himself running headlong into an overhanging branch that could scrape him into the water.

He broke out of the forest into the marshy approach to the sea as the moon touched the horizon. Pouring sweat, batting at blankets of mosquitoes, Curtin pressed down the waterway between the reeds that screened off everything but sky and surface.

The canoe swirled past beckoning exits. He considered them, turned into some, ignored others. Each decision had to be right. If he hit a dead end, the insects would quickly turn him into a puffed-up, disoriented lump. In a few hours he would die.

He wiped his brow and his hand came away wet. When it stuck to the wooden handle of the rudder, he realized it was smeared with blood and crushed insects.

The flesh around his eyes was swelling, interfering with his sight.

Suddenly, miraculously, there were no reeds in front of him. The breeze was thick with salt, not cool, but rich with promise. He swatted at the mosquitoes for the last time, bending to his searching with renewed strength.

Within another half hour he sighted the lights of a stationary ship. He willed it to be Bullard, counting aloud as he continued toward it.

When he shouted up at the deck, Bullard himself answered. "What the hell are you doing out here? Why haven't you been on the radio?"

"Drop me a ladder!"

A minute later a Jacob's ladder clattered over the side. Securing the canoe to it, Curtin made his way up. Bullard winced at the sight of him, then plunged ahead. "What's gone wrong?"

Curtin swallowed laughter, knowing it could go out of control too easily. "Just about everything, but we're getting there. Look, there's a stiff in the canoe. I want him lost. I mean, *lost*. Seal him in a weighted drum and sink him, you understand?" He caught his breath, slowed himself down. "I had to come out because the bastards hijacked my radio." At Bullard's quick alarm, he waved him to silence. "They haven't found it, and they won't. Anyhow, I wanted to recon the route out here. I'll be back for the gold tomorrow night."

Grabbing Curtin's shirt, Bullard said, "I want to know

what's going on! Everything! Is Flor all right? Have you talked to Robert? What's the Old Man say?''

Disengaging the hand, Curtin answered, disappointed by the unerasable tremor in his voice. "We're getting there, I said. No one's hurt, and your father knows all he needs to know. Don't screw with me right now, Bullard. I had to kill a man tonight.''

Bullard looked at Curtin as if assessing a stranger, then turned on his heel, barking orders. Men scrambled to carry the body aboard. Curtin clambered back down the swaying ladder and was underway as soon as the engine coughed to life. Maneuvering away from the hull, he looked up at the ship.

Manuel's right arm hung over the side. Swells rocked the peeling hull. The dead man waved goodbye.

Chapter 27

The noise of the canoe's engine overruled the rumbling thunder from the heat lightning to the north, but Curtin felt the vibrations in his bones. The clouds were nearer, too. He could only hope the weather held fine locally.

The support boat was nowhere to be seen. For the tenth time is half that many minutes, he checked his watch and the small compass.

One of the stars on the horizon seemed to move. A few points off the bow, it appeared brighter. He wet a hand, wiping cool seawater across his swollen face, hoping his eyes weren't tricking him.

It had to be Rochambeau's masthead light. He altered course, leaning forward in his impatience.

The rest of the boat rose into view. They were playing the part to perfection, an obvious seagoing party. Lights blazed everywhere. Rock music blasted the night.

Nevertheless, when he was a few feet away a dark-clad figure detached itself from the darkness and leveled a weapon at him in a very businesslike manner. Curtin's thrown line lay unattended while the small man kept him

covered and spoke through the porthole behind him. The
music stopped. Lights went out. Another man with a
weapon edged into a firing position behind the live-bait
well.

"Good to see you, buddy!" Curtin heard him before he
saw him, and then Rochambeau was leaning over picking
up the line before it fell back into the water. "You made
good time."

Hauling on Curtin's extended arm, he pulled him aboard.
"Welcome to the Costa Verde Invasion Armada."

"Good to see you, Admiral. You were out of position.
How come you're wandering around the goddam ocean
when I'm looking for you?"

"Your buddy on the freighter's got a search radar working twenty-four hours a day. We've been dancing in and
out of range to show up at different locations."

"Good work. He didn't seem suspicious when I left
him."

Rochambeau's smile faded. "How's everything look?"

"Hairy. Let's get with it."

In the main cabin, Rochambeau exclaimed at Curtin's
mosquito-battered features and produced ice in a towel to
ease the swelling before introducing the four men of his
support element and the boat's captain. While they got
acquainted, he spread a map on the dining table.

The Americans and the Cuban dwarfed their Vietnamese
companion, both in size and exuberance. Where the larger
men joked about the operation, the Viet shook hands
formally and stared at Curtin with unrevealing passivity.
He still carried the M11 he'd pointed at Curtin on his
arrival.

Curtin indicated the north shore of the lake. "This is a
pretty isolated area. There are roads, but they're more like
tracks. After the switch, there's going to be a lot of
military movement, but those roads mean they'll play hell
getting close before we can get back out to sea." He
pointed to where Ben and Evita would wait. Rochambeau
noted the spot without marking the map. "I'll have two

people waiting here with a truck. Once you guys haul out of the lake, it's a short sprint for the coast and a good beach exit, here. The skipper will pick you up with the second Zodiac.''

Still bent over the map, Rochambeau twisted his head to look up at Curtin with a speculative eye. "What about the ultralights? Why the beach pickup? Why not swim?''

"I think you better all get a good look at this situation. Satisfy yourselves we can get in and get out.''

Rochambeau straightened. All the Caucasian faces turned as impassive as the Oriental's. Still the spokesman, Rochambeau said, "Something's gone nasty.''

Curtin looked directly into each man's eyes, working around the table. He said, "We're going for the pot. From day one, every sonofabitch connected with this deal's tried to screw me. Nobody knows about you people. You're the hidden numbers. I'm taking in a ransom for a man who was never kidnapped. They figure to get rid of me as soon as I deliver. *I* figure we take it and split the three hundred and sixty pounds of gold; equal shares for us, our two friends in the hospital, the truck team that picks you up, and the widow of the guy who put together our communications.''

In the ensuing dazed silence, Curtin matched the Vietnamese's stare, then said, "You ever smile?''

"If I'm amused. Or pleased.''

Curtin glowered and said, *"Sat cong!"*

The sober face split in a grin, and then pealed laughter. He slapped the weapon, making it rattle.

Rochambeau looked from one to the other. "What the hell was that all about?''

"It means 'Kill communists.' ''

"These guys are communists?''

"Maybe, maybe not. Same difference.'' He turned to the other men. "It's a lot of money, but if you're caught, you're common terrorists. They'll say you were helping Force Red, and they'll hang you, but not until they've had fun with you. In or out?''

After exchanging glances, all said "In" except the Vietnamese, who nodded, still smiling. Curtin was unsure if he was amused or pleased.

One of the Americans drove a fist into another's shoulder. "Payday in the swamp, partner!"

"They don't have enough army to keep me away from that kind of money!" someone else affirmed happily.

Curtin went on. "Understand this. Any man who's hit gets the best help the rest of us can manage, but no man takes another man down with him. You should also know I'm nervous about one of the people who's supposed to be there with the truck. I'll do something about that, if I can, but we go in trusting no one but each other. We kill anyone who tries to stop us. *Anyone*."

It was acknowledged without words.

"Sit down," he said. "This is how we're going to make it work."

For the next few hours they huddled over the map, tracing the course of the river, noting distances, calculating times to cover ground on foot, by Zodiac, or in the ultralights. Instead of taking a break after a few hours, they inspected the equipment, the night-vision devices, the luminous diving compasses and watches, and the silencer-equipped M11s that exuded viciousness simply lying on the table.

The last time Curtin checked his watch, he said, "That's it. I've got to make it back to the lakefront house before dawn. One more thing, Roach. Everyone leaves a name on board, for whoever gets the share if he goes down."

"Got it. Now I got one for you. All the stuff about me covering the Zodiac's withdrawal with the ultralight is okay, but you haven't said where you'll be with yours."

"They may launch choppers after us. I'll hang back and watch. If they do, I'll divert them and join up later."

Skepticism brushed Rochambeau's lean features, but he seemed to reconsider whatever he meant to say. Instead, he leered and dove into the forward cabin. He returned with a plastic bag. Tearing it open, he dropped two olive-drab tubes on the table. "Heat seekers," he said, fondling them. "Fire and forget. Didn't I tell you the Roach knows where to find wonderful things?"

"True. Which reminds me, I want a replacement for that." Curtin dropped the rocket pistol on the table. "And some bug repellent."

While one man went for the latter, Rochambeau toyed with the pistol. "Why you want a different piece?" he asked.

"They're going to shake me down when I get back to the house. I don't want to lose that thing."

Rochambeau took a .45 automatic from one of the Americans and handed it to Curtin. "I'm glad. Our leader shouldn't be caught carrying that weird-looking pea-pooper. Let 'em find a man's gun."

Slathering repellent on exposed flesh as he headed for the Zodiac, Curtin remembered Manuel splashing into the lake, a torch flaming in his guts. The .45 seemed innocuous by comparison.

As Rochambeau gave him a hand into the inflatable, Curtin said, "Break up that canoe and deep-six the engine before it gets light, okay?"

Rochambeau assured him it would be done, then added, "The skipper's been steering a course that has us just off the mouth of the river. What about the guards upstream?"

"Bums. See you tomorrow night."

The trip upriver was quicker, by far. When Curtin drew near the guard-post lights, he switched from the reasonably quiet outboard to the silent electric, whispering past in the dark with no trouble.

Pulling the boat up on shore at the lakefront house, he sprawled on his side to catch his breath. Dawn was breaking, brushing the tops of the mountains with a gentle, golden light that grew stronger so delicately the change was imperceptible. One moment the tip of a mountain was barely picked out of the darkness, and within a few seconds it was aglow, its shoulders becoming visible.

Exactly as he anticipated, soldiers advanced on him,

M16s ready. They were pleased to find the .45, searching him all over again with renewed enthusiasm.

"Beautiful," he said, speaking seriously to the uncomprehending faces. "If Costa Verde puts you clowns out to stud, they can make stupidity a major export."

One of the troops shook his head in a firm negative and shoved him toward the house.

Wearily, Curtin made his way inside. Sandoval waited at the huge, dark dining-room table. He sat in a formal, high-backed chair, with nothing on the wooden expanse before him but a single white porcelain cup and saucer. He lifted the cup in salute, drank, and replaced it so gently it made no sound.

Curtin said, "We're set."

"You're sure?"

"I'm here."

Sandoval bowed his head, acknowledging the all-encompassing commitment of the statement. He rapped his knuckles on the table and a soldier entered. "You'll be hungry," he said. "What would you like?"

"Steak. Eggs over easy. A couple of bottles of beer. Coffee." He defied them to produce it.

Sandoval didn't blink as he translated. The soldier listened intently, then half-trotted out of the room. Sandoval rose. "Good work. I see you discovered our mosquitoes. Eat now, then sleep. I will return later."

The food was perfect, the steak thick, seared on the surface, hot and red inside. Curtin couldn't finish the second beer, and only half a cup of coffee was enough.

Sated, falling asleep, questions snapped across his mind, flashes as random as the heat lightning.

Had Robert's charm changed Flor's mind?

Manuel's statement: *Her life is lies*. Could Evita inform on them, even see her own lover destroyed? Was Manuel simply speaking of a prostitute as his own standards required of him?

What if Bullard had a scheme of his own? Thousands—

hell, probably millions—of brothers had been greased for
a lot less than two million dollars' worth of gold.

What about Buck Curtin? Everything that had happened
so far was unexpected, off the wall.

*You can see this one coming, Buck, taking shape in
front of you just the way that NVA column broke out of the
tree line. No instinctive responses, no alternatives. Tomorrow night you go for broke, and you get to watch it come
to you.*

You came apart, before.

Remember?

He practically staggered to the bed the soldier indicated
was his. When he woke, most of the swelling was gone
from his face, and he managed to wash and shave without
too much difficulty.

A no-nonsense Sergeant made him understand that Colonel Sandoval was gone, would return later, and that Curtin
was to remain inside the house at all times. It was the most
exquisite torture the sadistic Colonel could have imagined,
and, ironically, he would never be aware of it. With
nothing to do, no place to go, Curtin was forced to think.

About himself. And Flor.

It was dusk when the car arrived. Hearing it, Curtin
shoved past the guards onto the small entryway steps.

The first person out of the car was Kooseman.

There was no sense of the fat comic in the man now.
The eyes darted, seeing everything with the hard certainty
of camera lenses.

The magnitude of the surprise dazed Curtin. It took a
moment for him to see Kooseman's handcuffs.

It took less time for him to recognize the next man out
of the sedan as Robert.

Curtin's first awareness of Sandoval's presence was a
series of commands in the Colonel's cutting voice. Two of
the soldiers stepped in front of Curtin and jammed their
weapons into his stomach, forcing him back inside. Shouting indecipherable instructions, they herded him into a

chair in the living room. They took position with one behind him, the other to the front and side.

Robert and Sandoval entered together, stopping far enough away that their conversation was a muted hum. Two more soldiers escorted Kooseman. One left, returning with a heavy dining chair. They lashed him to it, leaving the handcuffs on.

Kooseman made no sound. It was as though he were not in the room.

Or already dead.

The thought would not leave Curtin's mind. He stood up, defying the guards. "Somebody better tell me what the hell's going on here."

"Or else?" Sandoval laughed at the emptiness of the suggested threat.

"I said somebody. When I want to hear from you, I'll say some*thing*. What about it, Robert? Any scoop for your old buddy?"

Robert was unruffled. "Wish it didn't have to be this way, Buck. I figure we're about even, though. Colonel Sandoval confessed his momentary weakness, told me how you almost convinced him to help you steal the gold from my father and me. It was close. Strange, too, because you're the last man I'd have thought would dump me."

"*Dump* you?" Curtin took a step, and the guard beside him clubbed his weapon into his ribs. Reacting, Curtin flung out an arm, knocked the man sprawling. Sandoval had his pistol out, shouting orders.

For a long moment, no one moved. Curtin felt the presence of the soldier behind him, felt the weight of a submachine gun only inches from his back. The hiss of held breath being released told him how close things had gotten. The soldier on the floor retrieved his weapon and left, glaring poisonously at Curtin. The other soldier followed.

Sandoval holstered his automatic, leaving the flap open.

Curtin said, to Robert, "While this shitbird was telling

you what a rat I am, did he tell you about his wired rooms and the funny mirrors on the walls?''

Robert's features seemed to draw in on each other. "The Colonel and I will deal with that. It's useless to try to create friction between us.''

Sandoval said, "I knew you'd try something like this. You'll pay for every word, I promise you.''

Robert continued as if uninterrupted. "I always liked you, really, but guys like you never see the whole picture. You just do your job and figure that's it. That night in Nam, I knew if I started something, you'd get us out of it. And I knew I'd have you in my pocket forever. You can't live with the thought that somebody saw you break, that you let down your friends.''

"That was over a long time ago.''

"You're still doing penance.''

"No more.''

"I don't blame you for being pissed, but I'm building something here, something important.''

"You've been playing with lives, goddam you. Mine and other people's.''

"Lives?'' Robert was genuinely surprised. Suddenly he was wild-eyed, ablaze with emotion. "Lives? I'm creating a *nation!* You'd have died for a worthless fucking rice paddy, and been proud! Some politician got off on 'doing something for the rights of free men everywhere' and you *ran* to get your ass shot off. Well, listen. Fuck freedom.'' Calming almost as quickly as he'd exploded, Robert continued in a voice of rigid certainty. "People really want peace and order. That's what I'm going to give them. So I used you like the politicians used us. When the world recognizes what I've done, you'll be bragging how you helped me get started.''

Kooseman's whining interruption startled them all. "I don't understand any of this. Why am I here?''

"A filthy spy.'' Sandoval's words hammered Kooseman to silence. "We've known about you for a long time, and now you'll tell us who you work for, and all about Curtin's emergency escape plan.''

"Escape plan? Spy? Me?" The round chin trembled. There were tears in his eyes. Curtin watched, admiring. The man might actually get away with it.

"Try to show some character." Sandoval strode to Kooseman, slapped him. "My friend is convinced Curtin has a plan. He knows three people here, and his maid. You and your whore are the only two who could help him, and she has unfortunately disappeared. Unfortunately for you."

"I don't know anything!" Kooseman wailed.

Robert said, "You'll tell us if you know anything, or not." He glanced at his watch. "And quickly. We don't have all night."

Curtin half rose, subsiding when Sandoval leveled his pistol at him. "Leave him alone. He's a salesman, a harmless drunk. He doesn't know anything about me."

At Robert's shout the two soldiers who'd tied up Kooseman returned. One of them wore gloves.

Light flared in Robert's eyes. Bent fingers tapped at his thighs. "I'm a winner, Curtin. Only losers have to ask forgiveness. Watch. See how to win."

Sandoval bent to speak in Robert's ear, smirking. Robert shook his head, disagreeing. To Curtin, he said, "The Colonel reminded me you've become fond of Flor Peralta. He thinks you'll speak up if we hurt her, but I don't want to do that. We have an interesting relationship, and I'm not through with her yet. I'm telling you this so you'll understand I don't inflict pain insensibly."

Robert nodded at the soldiers. The one with the gloves stepped in front of Kooseman, aligning himself with the care of a golfer setting up a putt. The other soldier braced the chair from behind.

Curtin locked stares with Robert, rather than see the beating. He found some pleasure in the other man's inability to match him, but was sickened by the avid pleasure that suffused Robert's face when he looked to see what was happening. Sandoval stopped the action occasionally to ask a question.

Kooseman admitted his CIA identity quickly. Soon he was pleading with Curtin to tell them what his escape plan was, to prove that they were torturing him for nothing.

Curtin looked away. He pictured Rochambeau and his men. He thought of Luis and Ben.

Once more, he wondered about Evita.

He denied any plans.

The soldiers traded places.

Kooseman's denials grew fainter, dwindled to simple grunts. The thudding blows became the only sound answering Sandoval's crisp, persistent questions.

Robert cared nothing for Curtin's stare. His fingers bent in claws and beat a rapid, irregular tattoo that never paused.

The soldier stopped, his labored breathing loud in the silence. He felt Kooseman's neck, then lifted an eyelid and examined the pupil. To Sandoval, he said, "*Muerto.*"

Curtin looked. Kooseman hung in the ropes, a soaked mass that vaguely resembled a clothed man. A dazzled moth blundered onto a torn cheek. The thickening blood trapped it as effectively as ancient amber.

Sandoval spread his hands. "He must have been telling the truth."

Robert said, "Looks like it. Get him out of here." He faced Curtin. "That makes it a bit easier to deal with you. You bring me the gold without any screwing around. It's going directly into the swimming pool. Cotton bales will be floated on the surface. If my brother blows it up, we lose nothing."

Kooseman's heels scraped as the soldiers dragged his body across the tiled floor. Curtin had to swallow to speak. "The gold doesn't come in unless I bring it. I want a guarantee that I get my money, and nothing happens unless I take Flor out first."

Robert shook his head, amused and astonished. "It sounds like you love her. That's good. You do exactly as you're told and she'll live. I may even let her leave here

290 Conn Alan Charles

someday. You'll be allowed to leave without any trouble. But when you're tempted to get cute, think about Kooseman.''

A car engine grumbled outside. The beam from the headlights swept the section of wall visible through the window, and then it was gone. Curtin continued to look where it had been.

"Your father'll blame me. So will Bullard. You're not giving me a chance."

"Don't try to bullshit me, old buddy." Robert grinned. "You'll still have the phony raid to help you explain, but I don't think you need it. You still think you've got something up your sleeve, in spite of what that CIA jerk didn't know. I'm going back to Sandoval's to be with Flor. I promise you she'll die cursing your name if you try to fuck me over."

Sandoval said, "This is all taking too much time. Get on your way."

Curtin didn't bother to look at him, but moved to obey.

It had been a hard night. And it was just starting.

Chapter 28

The lights of the guard post beckoned upriver. The weight of the gold constituted no problem for the sturdy Zodiac, but its responses were clearly affected.

Not that agility was so important tonight. Now that the gold was aboard, everyone was properly bribed.

Twenty-four hours earlier if the guards had caught him, they'd have blown him out of the water. Tonight the searchlight would shepherd him to where Sandoval's patrol boat would escort him to the lake house.

All of which made his night-vision binoculars particularly damning, should they be discovered. With so much help tonight, Sandoval would wonder why they were necessary.

On top of everything else, Curtin didn't like them. They enabled a man to see, but they transformed the world. He found the flat, green-on-black images eerie. Worse, when they came off, the friendly night was strangely oppressive, as if resentful.

A light flared briefly in front of him. It was at water level, toward the right bank. Without the glasses, it would have been a speck. With them, it was a lingering, damning beacon.

It blinked the proper three-short, one-long signal, and he immediately pitched a small white buoy over the side, paying out a black nylon cord attached to it that disappeared in the night-dark water.

Two objects appeared astern, closing rapidly on the bobbing buoy. The searchlight chose that moment to sweep the river ahead. For a second Curtin saw the buoy as a torch glaring in the night, exposing himself and the scuba-equipped men retrieving it like burglars in a room.

The light passed harmlessly, and he realized they were too far away to be distinguished.

Magically, the buoy disappeared, replaced by a hand that waved once. Then it, too, was gone.

The last of the line payed out, drawing tight with a jerk that staggered the inflatable as the weight of the swimmers hit the end of the slack. Curtin increased the engine speed to offset the increased drag of the submerged bodies.

Within seconds the searchlight swept past again, this time halting to swing back. Once again it overshot, and then the harsh eye centered him and held fast. Driving into the glare, Curtin chanced one last look for the swimmers' line and, to his satisfaction, almost couldn't see it. He stripped off the binoculars and dropped them into the lake before facing forward again.

He wondered if the M11 so carefully taped to the hull was making the trip in good condition. Or if it already rested in the mud at the bottom of the river.

He heard the approaching police boat long before he could see it. He shielded his eyes, squinting into the searchlight glare, but it was several seconds before he made out the power cruiser approaching from his left front. It was a relief to have it block out most of the beam. He waved, but received no answering response.

Like a wolf circling a baited trap, the vessel checked the Zodiac from all sides before dropping back to assure no other vessels were behind. Curtin could only hope the swimmers were deep enough to avoid the props or that the boat would be too far aft to run over them.

He kept a hand on the line, dreading the moment it might suddenly go limp under his touch.

The boat came up quickly from its search, the vibration of its engines touching the hull of the inflatable, as if some prehistoric creature of the deep growled at the disturbance of its lake. They were clear of the guard post's searchlight by now, and as the boat took station astern and off to the left, it aimed its own small searchlight at him.

Curtin waited until the last moment to change course for the shore. The police boat followed for a short distance, then stopped. Curtin turned to look back, shielding his right arm from their observation as he released the nylon line.

Aiming for the twelve-man reception team on the beach, Curtin drove the bow ashore. Once again, he was searched. They looked inside the boat, neglecting the underside. He hoped no one noticed his pent-up exhalation. He brought up the rear as they carried the boxes inside the house.

Sandoval paced like a caged fox, the limp more pronounced than Curtin had ever seen it, waiting for the men to put down their burden. He ordered them out to join the perimeter guards before they could straighten up. Eyes fixed on the boxes, he said, "Open them," and his voice almost cracked.

There were no locks, and Curtin flipped the first clasp. "I haven't seen my money yet," he said, pitching his voice to a whine.

Twitching impatiently, Sandoval said, "When I'm ready. Hurry up!"

Curtin finished opening snaps on the first box. He lifted the lid perhaps a quarter of an inch, then turned to Sandoval, prepared to stall for a few more seconds. When he saw the sudden widening of Sandoval's eyes and the bloodless line of tension around his mouth, he changed his mind. A quick move, and the gold was revealed, sunshine bright, innocent of the madness it generated.

Sandoval crooned under his breath, a sound like a lullaby. One hand reached, of its own accord. He pulled it back reluctantly. Suddenly he stepped back, alarmed. He pointed. "The bomb! Close that one, quickly!"

As the lid dropped, he cursed Curtin. "You whore's son! You distracted me! You didn't give me time to count the bars!" He put his hand on his pistol.

Curtin moved to the next box. "It's all here, Colonel. I wouldn't cheat you. I'm satisfied with our deal."

Sandoval sent him a brittle smile.

Bending to the second box, Curtin opened it slowly, feigning difficulty with the catches. Sandoval urged him on.

They heard the soldier's weapon clatter to the floor, simultaneously. Sandoval whirled, clawing at his pistol. The man staggered into the doorway from the lake side of the house, eyes glazed in shock, blood trickling from both corners of his mouth. Silent, unbelieving, he wobbled drunkenly, then pitched forward on his face.

Sandoval was moving before the body hit the ground, turning the pistol on Curtin. He was a few inches too slow. Coming up from his crouch, Curtin pivoted, presenting his side, the slimmest possible target in case Sandoval did get a round off. As he turned, he pulled his right arm across his body, parallel to the ground, breast high. Once he was inside the extended hand holding the pistol, Sandoval was finished.

Curtin drove his elbow into the Colonel's chest, feeling the ribs break, hearing air gust from crushed lungs.

Sandoval literally flew backward, landing on his heels. He struck the wall hard enough to bounce forward. Curtin slid toward him, holding his arm in the same position as before. He struck exactly the same place in exactly the same way, combining his strength and momentum with that of the falling man. This time the force of the blow felt wasted, as tissue simply spread away from the thrusting spear of the elbow.

Snatching up the fallen pistol, Curtin found no pulse from the ruptured heart.

When he straightened, one of the scuba team stepped over the dead soldier. "We've got the police boat. I think I heard the ultralights on my way in. There's no guards left on this end of the building, but I seen a shithouse full up—"

He raised his arm to point and froze in that attitude as an immense explosion rocked the building. He said, "What the fuck was *that?*" and was answered by small-arms fire, screams, shouts, and cries of "*Fuerza Roja! Fuerza Roja!*" A tracer howled past a window, cherry red.

"That's the real thing!" Curtin wasted no time explaining. Each man grabbed a box, groaning at the weight. Clumsily, they stumbled out the back door, where Curtin literally threw his on the ground as the Vietnamese team member ran up. Wordlessly, he dragged the box toward the lake. Curtin ran inside for the third box. As he came out, both men met him. The Vietnamese crouched, providing cover as the larger men loaded the boat and retrieved the M11 from the hull bottom.

Panting from exertion, they still managed to grin and slap each other on the back as they sped to the police boat.

Clambering on board, Curtin dropped into the cockpit, relieved to see no fire aimed at them yet. Their luck was holding. He called to one man to start the engine, and the other hauled in the anchor.

Aiming the boat parallel to the shoreline, Curtin was lashing the wheel into position when the ultralights landed, one on each side of the boat.

The noise of their arrival alerted the men ashore. Bullets cracked overhead. One slapped the surface of the lake, screaming away in a dying ricochet.

The swimmers and one ultralight pilot scrambled into the Zodiac, adjusting their night-vision devices, and as Curtin revved the police boat engine, they raced away with the gold. Once the night covered their departure, he turned on the boat's lights and sent it on its way. Leaping overboard, he caught the low freeboard of the empty ultralight and hoisted himself in.

Rochambeau pointed at the headset he wore, and as soon as Curtin had his own on, he asked, "You okay?" Gunfire already beat the water around the decoy boat.

"No sweat."

"Great. Let's move it."

Taxiing away from the continuing gun flashes and grenade explosions, Curtin picked up the extra night-vision binoculars from the seat next to his. Before putting them on, he said, "There's something I've got to do, Roach. You join the others at the boat, get out of these waters. I'll catch up."

"No fucking way. What's up?"

"It'd take too long to explain. I won't kid with you, though—I could sure use some help."

"Figures." Curtin was surprised to realize he could actually see Rochambeau's grin without the night-vision binoculars, then realized the huge house behind them was burning fiercely.

And in its light, they were visible.

Tracers arced overhead, getting their range.

Feeding fuel to the roaring little engines, they sped farther into the darkness, the battering of the water on the hulls growing from a rhythm to a vibration, and then, with a lurch, they were free and flying. The tracers fell off behind them, vicious red blobs, searching blindly.

Rochambeau came back on the radio. "Like I was going to say, I'd probably get lost trying to fly this twinky plane back to the boat, anyhow."

"Thanks, Roach."

"Thanks, your ass. You'll get my bill."

"Bill? What bill? I let you come to my party and you want pay?"

They had their laugh. It broke the tension. Curtin pulled back on the control handle, climbing.

That was how it'd been with Robert once, the way

things were supposed to be. Nevertheless, he'd put Rochambeau at terrible risk.

The thought created myriad questions, and he decided the risk was the key. There had been a time when Robert understood that. Men took chances together, and it made them more than their individual strengths. For some men, that bond was a need.

For some, it became a weapon against other men.

Already far behind them, the house on the lake burned fiercely. Ahead, the first faint glow of Sandoval's fortress waited.

Chapter 29

Curtin spiraled upward, drawing Rochambeau with him, until he was sure they were too high to be heard from the ground before starting a pass over the fight below.

The adrenaline was in charge now. The exhilaration was on him. He recognized it, knew its rewards and perils, and welcomed it.

This was what it had been like. *Before*. When he was whole, before he came apart. There was fear, but it made the heart beat faster, not congeal into an icy lump. The senses threatened to overload the brain, tuned to an edge he'd forgotten. Best of all was the excitement. It filled him with a savage anticipation that bordered on joy but had nothing of routine happiness in it.

He aimed the boatlike nose directly at Sandoval's lights.

Once they were within easy range, he told Rochambeau, "We go down without engines. Hang back as far as you can and still keep me in sight. If there's trouble, head for the boat."

"Sure." The glib response was a lie, as Curtin expected. The next line proved it. "You think we can get in and get out without being spotted? These engines don't always start right off.''

"Peachy. You hang on to that good thought, 'cause we're cutting the power right now.''

Robbed of its strength, the sleek craft shuddered, as if unsure what was being asked of it. To the right, Rochambeau's engine was enormously loud, and then, with menacing suddenness, it was gone. New, softer sounds replaced the machine racket. Strut vibration cut through the more comforting laughter of air across smoother surfaces.

Lights pockmarked the earth below, farms, plantations, small open fires. In the distance, Oriente's sprawling glow smeared the horizon.

Curtin banked into his descent. Rochambeau trailed him.

Through the night-vision devices, the ground had a wild, other-world look. To the left the tower lights were an almost dazzling presence. For a moment Curtin's imagination transformed them into mantislike creatures, waiting, but then the field was suddenly there.

The landing sounded like a hurricane to him. Each bump convinced him the wheels had fallen off and he'd never again get airborne, but finally he stopped.

He sat, scanning the field, sweeping the M11 back and forth, until he was sure they were unheard. The only obvious damage to the plane was the broken fixture where the missile had been mounted. He dismissed the problem. Beckoning Rochambeau, he scrambled out of the seat, and together they raced across the field.

Tonight there was one guard. Curtin decided the others must be at the lakefront place. Leaving Roach to cover, he inched across the intervening ground. The eerie image in the night-vision equipment showed a bored figure stargazing, yawning. Curtin risked slithering closer.

Some faint sound or sense of another body present alerted the man. He raised his rifle and stared into the night, seeking.

Slowly, Curtin raised to one knee, lifting the silenced

weapon as part of the same movement. The man looked directly at him, tilted his head to the side, uncertain.

The bolt of the M11 clattered, and the sound of the rounds striking the man was like massive fists.

Curtin rushed to the gate, leaping over the guard's body. There was no sound of alarm. As soon as Roach was beside him, he whispered to him to watch the gate. Then he sprinted for the house

Moving silently and rapidly, Curtin went directly to the dining room and Sandoval's one-way mirror.

Flor sat facing to his left, looking toward the living-room door. Robert stood behind her, bent over her right shoulder, only half his face available to view. He appeared amused, although engaged in earnest argument. Flor shook her head. Curtin considered turning on the listening switch, then decided there was neither time nor need.

The dining-room door was closed. He launched a kick that blasted it open.

Bursting in, weapon ready, Curtin's heart sank even as he stumbled to a stop.

Robert's right hand held a gun jammed into Flor's throat just under her jaw. He grinned.

"I've been expecting you. I had an observer with a radio watching the house. You faked everybody out with the ultralights, and I still can't figure out how you got so many troops into the game. It'll give us something to talk about, before your execution. You're a terrorist now, old buddy. I warned you, remember? Guys like you don't belong in this league. You'll always win the fights and lose the war."

He used the gun to gesture, wordless, and Curtin bent to lay his weapon on the thick rug. At another gesture, he hooked a toe under it and flipped it the other way. Robert nodded approval, then reached with the other hand for the telephone on the table beside Flor.

She turned, grabbing him. "You said you'd let him go! You gave me your word!" She broke off, wounded eyes seeking Curtin's.

Robert's face tightened his grin into a vindictive snarl.
He said, "He's through. He belongs to whatever's left of
Sandoval's outfit. They'll be glad to get their hands on
him after tonight."

Flor dropped her head into her hands, shaking with
silent crying. Robert picked up the phone again, saying,
"Whatever you did with the gold, I'm going to have it,
you know. This time Flor *is* on the line."

An agonized scream froze the three of them. It stopped
abruptly, but a spatter of shots followed immediately.
Hoarse shouts erupted from the general direction of the
back gate.

Flor reached for Robert's gun hand, twisting it away
from herself. The action rotated his arm so the elbow
rested against the top of the easy chair. When she pulled
down, there was no way the joint could bend. Robert
yelled with pain, even as his body responded. Rather than
draw back against the pressure, he surrendered to it, vault-
ing over the chair before she could snap the arm. In spite
of everything, he managed to shoot. The round harmlessly
shattered a vase. Curtin grabbed at the gun as Robert
rolled to his feet, but the combined speed of their movements turned it into a clumsy swat, and the gun spun
across the room.

As if in response to the report, a submachine gun rattled
in the distance.

The two men charged each other, more animal than
human, neither trying for one of the guns on the floor.
They were beyond weapons, past rational thought. Pent-up
rage demanded physical contact.

There was no science in the struggle. Each swung, was
blocked, and fell against the other. They strained and pushed,
clutching, knees pumping, feet slashing. Suddenly Robert
went slack, dropped toward the floor. The failed resistance
trapped Curtin. He stumbled forward.

Robert drove his shoulder upward into Curtin's stomach,
lifting him to his toes. Simultaneously, he drove a fist at
Curtin's crotch. Wrenching sideways, Curtin avoided the

blow. His weight pulled them both off balance. Robert let go to save himself from falling. Curtin staggered back, arms flailing.

His vulnerability spurred Robert. He leaped after him. Curtin hit the wall with barely enough time to use it to bounce off. He threw a block at the running legs coming at him. There was a momentary resistance, and then a slick, crackling noise, followed by the thud of Robert's face driving into the wall. He collapsed in a groaning ball, hands clasped around a knee as if to strangle the pain.

Before Curtin could rise, Flor was pressing the M11 into his hands. "Take this! I can use the pistol if we have to shoot. Hurry! We have to escape!"

Curtin got to his feet. His lungs burned. His legs felt a hundred years old. "I'm taking him with us."

Flor's jaw sagged. "Taking him?"

"I owe his old man."

Robert looked up at him, trying to sneer through his injury. "The guards'll be here in seconds."

"Get up, you sonofabitch." Curtin bent forward, poking the gun into Robert's stomach. "Get up, or by God, I'll blow your guts out!"

Robert managed a barking laugh. "No way. Not you. Not her, either. You can't." He was laughing again when Rochambeau's harsh, muffled cry came from the hallway.

"Coming in!" He literally tumbled past them, coming up with his weapon ready. Blood stained his right side. Flor crouched, her pistol steady on him.

Rochambeau took in the scene. "I hope I'm not interrupting anything?" He jerked his chin at the door and spoke to Curtin. "About a dozen troops. We caught them at relief time, and when they couldn't find the guard we greased, they started searching. I had to off one, and I fucked it up. Sorry, buddy."

"You're hit."

"Jesus Christ, I know that! It's a scratch. Come on, man, we got to move! They think I took off down the road out front. They'll be along as soon as they know different."

From his position on the floor, still cradling his knee, Robert said, "Listen to me. Give up. Save your life. I'll make you rich!"

Curtin ignored him. "Get this bastard's arm," he said to his partner.

After a disbelieving stare, Rochambeau moved quickly. "Silliest shit I ever heard," he growled, helping Curtin hoist the reluctant Robert to his feet. He nudged the dangling limb with his own knee, eliciting a yip of pain, and said, "You make this easy for us or I'll twist that leg off. Honest."

Shouts accompanied the sound of running feet outside. Curtin slapped off the lights, and dragging Robert along, they crept across the darkened living room and into the kitchen.

The door flew open and men ran in, dark, bumbling shapes against the tower lights outside.

The escaping trio opened fire from behind the central counter. Caught completely unprepared, most of the men were driven against the wall dead, falling along with a cascade of canned goods from shattered cabinets.

Return fire roared from the survivors, sending cookware clanging. The electric stove began to spark furiously. Curtin was appalled to see Flor leap to her feet, aiming deliberately.

"No!" He screamed it. She fired calmly, almost leisurely. A soldier rose, turned, fell.

Curtin saw movement, fired a quick burst. The man squeezed his trigger in his death spasm, and the rounds howled off the floor.

Then it was over. The silence was leaden.

The stove crackled, unleashing sizzling blue arcs.

Flor sought Curtin's eyes, shaking like someone coming out of a deep sleep. He grabbed her arm. "Better kick off those heels." He looked to Rochambeau as she did. "She can't cook though," he said, and she looked stunned, then choked off a giggle that was pure nerves.

Each man grabbed one of Robert's shoulders, and they

picked their way through the bodies of the soldiers. Then they ran. They were through the gate and into the field when the first rounds cracked overhead. Curtin turned over the job of supporting Robert to Flor and dropped to a kneeling position as they continued on.

With the light behind the oncoming four troops and the night-vision binoculars, it was cruelly easy. The weapon spit out its silent death, and all four jerked and went down like puppets cut from their strings. One screamed, drawn-out wails of frightened hopelessness.

Two men stopped just outside the gate, listened, turned and ran back inside.

Rochambeau was starting the second plane's engine when Curtin arrived. Flor was standing over Robert where he lay on the ground, and Curtin went to them. Rochambeau joined them. "He says he won't get in the plane," he said.

Curtin had to work to draw a breath. His heart beat as though it would break his ribs. He aimed the M11. "Men died back there. They weren't much, but you're not worth them, or anything, except to me and your father, and we've got different reasons. Get up, or die. It's all one to me."

Robert's smile wavered, but Curtin saw something deeper than sham bravery. There was desperation behind the smile. There was also the resignation of a man capable of walking alone, capable of facing disaster with whatever dignity he could muster. He struggled upright. "Do it," he said.

"*Stop!*" Flor pushed the rising muzzle to the side. "Buck, you cheat yourself if you kill him!"

A flare popped, too far away to make trouble, but a disturbing development. Rochambeau said, "Leave the sonofabitch. Let his friends do him."

Breath came easier to Curtin now. His finger slipped off the trigger. He slammed the weapon into Robert's chin, who collapsed like wet cloth. Ripping off the fallen man's shirt, Curtin tore it into pieces. "Make strips of those," he said, dragging Robert to Rochambeau's ultralight.

By the time he had Robert in the seat, they were tying

his hands. That done, they lashed them to the frame, then ran a makeshift line from there to his bound feet.

They were in the air seconds later, unaffected by the sporadic fire from the demoralized guards. In the distance, headlights raced down the highway toward the house. This time Curtin kept close to the ground. He had no idea of what kind of radar existed in Costa Verde, but he knew anything that worked would be looking for them.

They reached the inland extremity of the lake without incident, the light of the burning house providing reference.

As they left the shore behind, Curtin saw the blinking lights of helicopters approaching. Beams of light leaped from them, sending coin-silver disks racing across the black water as they hunted for the ultralights.

"Company," Rochambeau said.

"Got 'em." Turning to Flor, Curtin pointed at the helicopters. She squeezed his hand before pointing her pistol in that direction.

One of the searchlight beams flashed across them, making Flor turn away, wincing. Instantly, it was after them, the sweeps drawing steadily closer despite Curtin's maneuvers. In moments the light spiked them like an insect on display. When the helicopter opened fire, the ultralight's engine drowned out the sound. Tracers floated toward them like harmless, glowing golf balls. Only when they shot past was their menace apparent.

Curtin put Flor's hands on the controls, yelling for her to keep everything exactly stable. Then he fired back with the M11. The helicopter banked away.

From the corner of his eye he saw the other chopper catch Rochambeau and start firing. A gout of flame erupted from the ultralight, and Curtin shouted a curse, thinking the fuel cell was hit. The flame seemed to fall away, however, hanging in the air. Then, stranger yet, it picked up speed, moving on the helicopter.

"The heat seekers!" Curtin cheered. "Oh, Roach, you goddam *marvel*. Way to go!"

The destruction was short, violent, and complete. A ball

of fire pulsed once, twice, and then, as rapidly as it had appeared, it was gone, falling in small, flickering bits that winked out in the lake as if eaten.

The second helicopter dropped after the pieces, turning broadside to Curtin. He raked it with the M11. It heeled over like a wounded animal before plummeting.

Rochambeau exulted. "Beautiful shooting, Buck! Beautiful!"

"He was going down to look for survivors."

"There weren't any. He'd have been on us again in a minute. You done good."

"I guess. Let's get out of here while we can."

Steering by the lights of the guard post, Curtin had them crossing the dense marsh sooner than he thought possible. The first light of daybreak picked out the mazed delta. Remembering it, with its mists of tormenting mosquitoes, he shuddered. Flor's hand sought his, pressed it between her own.

Deciding to chance altitude in order to enlarge the search area, Curtin guided the little plane upward. Shortly into the climb, Flor shook his arm, pointing to the south.

A smudge of black smoke marred the molten copper of the dawn clouds. Frowning, Curtin leaned closer to be heard. "Could be Bullard's ship." To Rochambeau, he said, "We're going to check out that smoke. I think I know what ship it is. We'll get high, cut the engines, and come in with sun behind us."

Together they lifted upward like hawks, drifting across the sky, watching their target, working into the sun. Swooping toward the ship's stern, Curtin recognized the vessel long before the small powerboat came into view. It suddenly appeared from under the bow, where the smoke billowed from a mass of crates on the main deck. Flashes and reports from the cockpit and cabin of the boat were unmistakably gunfire. Bullard and Lu fired back from a wing of the bridge. Only then did Curtin discover the others, also shooting up at Bullard and Lu from the main deck of the ship itself. He directed Rochambeau at the boat.

Striking with total surprise, they battered the attackers. Yanking the starting cord, Curtin got his engine back on, climbing for another pass. Flame boiled from the cabin windows of the small boat, and men leaped into the sea from it as Rochambeau also swung into a sharp turn.

The men on the ship, seeing their transportation destroyed, stormed the bridge desperately. Before Curtin could close on them, he saw explosions where Bullard and Lu hid. The smoke blew away, and they rose together, leaning on each other and on the steel bulkhead. Firing continuously, wildly, they were struck down within seconds.

It sickened Curtin. Bullard and Lu were more enemies than friends, but their deaths were needless casualties of greed. The raiders didn't care if Robert Chavez was a good man or a monster. They wanted the gold. And Marx. Or Hitler. Or Divine Right. Anything, as long as it put them in charge.

Chavez would understand.

Swearing, Curtin blasted at everything that moved. One man dashed onto the hatch cover to fire back and was bowled over. Another dove for a doorway, dying in midair.

When Curtin moved to turn back, Flor caught his hand. Without words, she demanded his eyes, forced him to see the concern in hers, made him understand there was nothing but senseless risk in further effort.

He inhaled, released the air in a long sigh. The pounding excitement ebbed. The anger that remained was rational. Rochambeau closed on his wing, and they headed north for their boat.

He was almost sorry to see it. The stout little ultralights settled to the water with sad grace, as if understanding they'd done their job perfectly but now must be abandoned. Two of the team jumped over the side to help Rochambeau with Robert. Curtin and Flor scrambled aboard unaided.

Evita rushed to them. Ben followed with a black scowl.

The Vietnamese, perched on the roof, watched them coldly, his weapon never leaving them.

"Tell them!" Evita cried. "Tell them! I didn't tell anyone your men were coming! Don't let them kill me, Flor! I didn't tell anyone!"

Ben caught up to her as she fell into Flor's arms. He reached for Curtin's shirt, wadding it tightly. The Vietnamese made a soft, warning sound. Ben ignored it.

"You better square away these thugs, Curtin," he said. The Vietnamese laughed, and Ben colored.

Curtin looked at the hand. "What the hell's going on?"

One of the men said, "We came up on the truck careful. Damned good thing. There must have been ten guys had them and that damned truck staked out. If we'd just walked into it, they'd have us now. We had to dust most of them to get away, and us lugging those frigging boxes. These two were making it for the woods, but we caught them."

"Hell, yes, we ran!" Ben dropped Curtin's shirt to advance on his accuser. "So would you, with people shooting all around you!"

"Forget it for now." Curtin's tone stopped the budding fight. "We'll straighten this out later." He spoke past them. "Roach, get us to that ship as fast as you can. Some of the answers may be there." To Robert, he said, "I hope your brother's alive." He said it sympathetically, but he remembered the way Bullard fell. The words left a bad taste.

"Not likely." Robert cut his eyes at Flor, and his cold bravado trembled for a moment but returned, stronger than ever. Curtin turned away. "Keep him tied up," he said, leaving to join Rochambeau.

Flor brought Evita with her to stand beside him. "You know Evita never betrayed us," she said.

Curtin nodded, eyes on the horizon where the ship was just coming into view. The smoke had dwindled. He said, "I don't believe she did. That's different than knowing."

Evita began to cry. He looked at her briefly. "I'm

sorry, Evita. I know that hurt. But it's honest, goddam it."

To his surprise, she managed a faint smile. "Maybe that's enough," she said, and then to Flor, "He wants it to be so. He'll learn I'm telling the truth. I don't know what happened, but I didn't inform on anyone. I swear it."

Men appeared at the railing of the ship as the fishing boat neared, and Curtin's group took up firing positions. A sheet fluttered and draped from the rail. Instead of shooting, the survivors hastily lowered a gangway and started down, hands in the air. Curtin told Ben to order them back to the main deck.

Then the skipper brought the fishing boat to the gangway, and Curtin's group boarded the ship cautiously, one group covering from the boat as the other climbed up. The last wisps of smoke from the burned crates mingled with the smell of expended ammunition, cloying the clean air of the sea.

On deck first, Curtin stopped in shock as Luis presented himself with a sharp salute. A half-dozen men stood in a ragged line behind him. Two were wounded, one of them badly.

"I am an officer of Force Red. I am willing to negotiate with you," Luis said formally. "Provide us with transportation to the coast and I will not demand your extradition to Costa Verde for piracy when we are in power."

Curtin said, "That can wait. I want—" A stir among the others interrupted him, and he turned to see Flor and Evita step onto the deck. Flor reacted much as Curtin had, but Evita almost fainted. Only Flor's quick outreach caught her. Luis looked at her briefly, then faced Curtin again, expressionless.

Unable to do more than frown about the women's unexpected presence, Curtin went on. "How'd you know about the ship?"

"When you asked the woman to arrange the canoe, it was obvious. We attacked as soon as we could, but you moved too quickly for us to intercept the gold and prevent

Robert's escape. We let you get away, and the bitch working for you, as well."

A small moan escaped Evita. From the corner of his eye, Curtin saw Flor lead her to the two wounded stretched out behind Luis. Evita watched woodenly as Flor tended them.

To Luis, Curtin said, "You knew about me all the time."

"Flor never suspected I was Force Red when she asked her bourgeois friends to shield you from the government and us. We had already tried to frighten you off. We wanted to force the govenment to confess the kidnapping was a lie. Once you were here, however, it was decided to get the gold for ourselves."

Heat welled in Curtin's head. Sweat covered him, ran across tightening muscles. "You hired Deb, back in San Diego, then murdered her. Shot my two closest friends. The three who kidnapped me—they were yours. You blew them up so Force Red wouldn't find out about you."

Luis frowned and licked his lips. His eyes rolled nervously toward the survivors from his group. "Lies! All lies. I am a patriot. The revolution is my life! The woman was not my fault. Others overruled me. Once she could identify me, I had to eliminate her. Your friends—" He shrugged. "Fear is a tool."

Curtin swallowed hard, and Flor's voice rushed into the delay. "You kill because you like it! You worship power and death! *That* is Force Red. Murderers!"

Luis colored but refused to turn and look at her. He said, "My only regret is that Robert Chavez and the pig, Sandoval, died in honest combat last night. How did you escape?"

"Robert's alive. I've got him."

Luis brightened. "*Bueno!* To find him and kill him will protect our honor, show the world our new society will not permit his sort of foreign interference."

Almost out of control, Curtin rammed his weapon into the soft flesh under Luis's chin, forcing his head up and back. "You miserable bastards. You and Robert talk about improving society and bettering mankind like farmers talk about better barns and better cows. In the end it comes out to the same thing for us—a trip to the slaughterhouse."

They stood bound together by the metal of the M11. Luis's throat worked spasmodically and a vein pumped at his temple. The only sounds were the creaks of the rocking ship.

Evita came up behind Luis and spoke with pained gentleness. "You said if I drugged him, you would ask him your questions for our protection, but in truth, it was for these plans. How could you do that?"

Reluctantly, Curtin pulled back the weapon so Luis could speak. "Well?" he said. "She deserves an answer."

A grimace of distaste clouded Luis's fear. "A soldier uses any weapon he must. Whores are supposed to be used."

Hands clasped at her waist, fumbling as if massaging pain, Evita said, "I believed you. So foolish. Of all people, a whore should know hope is always partly a lie, and love is the most dangerous of all hopes."

Luis finally whirled to face her. Weapons readied all around, but he made no other move. Instead, he shouted, "You *are* a whore, nothing else! There is no place for you in our society!" He spun on his heel, rigidly ignoring her again, confronting Curtin. "You will put us ashore."

With the soft tenacity of a child, Evita persisted, "I had to sell my body to live. Am I so evil, Luis? I lied for you. Never to you. I didn't destroy your dreams. You have dirtied me more than any man who threw his money at me. You hurt me more."

She leaned even closer behind Luis, as if to brush his neck with one last kiss. She never completed the caress. Nevertheless, Luis stepped forward abruptly, as if the impact of Evita's indictment was a physical thing. He blinked repeatedly, his eyes widening at the same time. Slowly, like a man experiencing great comprehension, he raised a hand toward Curtin. When there was no response, he turned to Evita.

Her hand drifted away from the knife in his back, uncovering the silver and ivory handle. The sun glossed the ornate design, keen brightness accenting a dull plum-red stain growing on the dark shirt. Even after he fell to the deck, his staring eyes continued to marvel at the burden of his new wisdom.

Chapter 30

Standing in front of Chavez's desk, Curtin suppressed a smile as he felt Flor's hand tremble in his. She still saw the Old Man. She would probably think of him that way for the rest of her life.

Curtin knew better. There was a flabbiness in the features now, a melted look that acknowledged defeat even if the spirit would never allow the words to be spoken.

Chavez said, "You're a foolhardly man, coming here."

"It's the only way to balance the books. The Feds have Robert. The oil find is common knowledge, and the people of Costa Verde intend to own it. Ben, the guy Bullard tried to have wasted because he was helping Flor, is talking to your Colonel Duffy, telling him and the rest of your troops exactly what you are and what you've done to them. All the bills are coming due."

"Where's my gold?"

"Divided up. We kept it."

Chavez's eyes narrowed. "I'll see you in hell."

"Later, maybe." Calm no longer, Curtin leaned across the desk. "You knew the kidnapping was a scam."

"That's a lie!"

"Give it up." Curtin straightened, scornful. "Sandoval was always your dog. The military-equipment dump was for him and his pals, to make people think it was covert aid from our government. When I told Kooseman's friends I cashed in Sandoval, they showed me the documents you forged with my name. Christ, you had me framed for selling armaments over a year ago! I was going broke as a contractor! My signature was the only one on anything. You never meant for me to leave there alive."

Flor pulled on his hand. "Please, Buck—the guards."

"Forget them. They won't do anything."

Chavez roused himself. "He's right. They won't do anything today. There will be many tomorrows. This time, Curtin, I concede you your cleverness. You were Robert's most glaring error. He really believed I couldn't see through his determination to make me 'choose' you as the messenger. Nor did he guess I knew about his oil. It was convenient to let him undermine the Force Red scum and other competitors. Poor Robert! Even if you hadn't been such a blunder, he'd have been second man in his own empire."

For a few seconds, he was the Old Man again, spinning out his web, watching the rest of the world entangle themselves in his schemes.

Knowing it was cruel, Curtin said, "And your other son?"

Wilting, Chavez said, "I never thought he'd be killed. I never meant—"

"You never meant!" Curtin was scathing. "He died because you were having so much fun playing God! This time you get to share in the hurt. Think about it, Chavez. Eat it. Dream about it!"

Dark, sunken eyes sought escape. They met Flor's eyes, saw the compassion in them, couldn't hold the contact.

Flor said, "I'm truly sorry for your sons, Mr. Chavez. For you I have only pity. Your great plan was nothing more than setting two desperate, confused men against each other for the entertainment of a lonely tyrant. All you have left are ruins.''

Stung, he sprang to his feet. ''You think I'm destroyed? Look around you. I started with nothing. I fought for this! My sons fought and I fought them! One died. We'll mourn him our way, avenge him our way.''

He paused to calm himself and pointed a blunt finger at Curtin. ''You're no different than I am.'' He whirled on Flor, his sudden laughter threatening. ''You pity me, do you? He'll teach you about pity, and for yourself. He's as driven as I am, but all he knows is foolishness! Causes written on water!'' Looking back to Curtin, he went on. ''Life has no meaning for you without risk. One day it'll kill you. When I hear about it, I'll laugh.''

Flor clutched Curtin's arm and hugged it to her. ''I don't want to listen to this,'' she said. ''Take me away from here.''

Smiling down at her, Curtin said, ''Don't let him frighten you. He's made another mistake, that's all. Come on.''

At the door, he assured himself Flor wasn't watching, then turned to look back at Chavez. He was seated again, shoulders slumped, the thick torso hanging forward over the desk as though caught in the act of falling onto the immaculate surface. His index finger traced a repetitious circle, around and around and around.

BESTSELLING BOOKS FROM TOR

☐ 58725-1 *Gardens of Stone* by Nicholas Proffitt $3.95
   58726-X   Canada $4.50

☐ 51650-8 *Incarnate* by Ramsey Campbell $3.95
   51651-6   Canada $4.50

☐ 51050-X *Kahawa* by Donald E. Westlake $3.95
   51051-8   Canada $4.50

☐ 52750-X *A Manhattan Ghost Story* by T.M. Wright
                                          $3.95
   52751-8   Canada $4.50

☐ 52191-9 *Ikon* by Graham Masterton $3.95
   52192-7   Canada $4.50

☐ 54550-8 *Prince Ombra* by Roderick MacLeish $3.50
   54551-6   Canada $3.95

☐ 50284-1 *The Vietnam Legacy* by Brian Freemantle
                                          $3.50
   50285-X   Canada $3.95

☐ 50487-9 *Siskiyou* by Richard Hoyt $3.50
   50488-7   Canada $3.95

Buy them at your local bookstore or use this handy coupon:
Clip and mail this page with your order

TOR BOOKS—Reader Service Dept.
P.O. Box 690, Rockville Centre, N.Y. 11571

Please send me the book(s) I have checked above. I am enclosing
$_____ (please add $1.00 to cover postage and handling).
Send check or money order only—no cash or C.O.D.'s.

Mr./Mrs./Miss _____
Address _____.
City _____ State/Zip _____
Please allow six weeks for delivery. Prices subject to change without
notice.

MORE BESTSELLERS FROM TOR